For Tom and Edna

Acknowledgements

'Hello. I'm writing a novel right now, and I wondered if you wouldn't mind . . .' Faced with the daunting reality of having 100,000 words of novel to write (and a deadline), quite the nicest diversion I know is to ring complete strangers and badger them for bits of information instead. That they offer their help so willingly and cheerfully is a source of constant joy. I am so pleased, therefore, to be able to thank Inspector Trevor Taylor, of the South Wales Police Motorway Department, Angie Coombs, from Cardiff University, Melissa Robertson at *Changing Rooms*, and the staff at Paramount Cars, Cardiff. Go on. Give us an XJR. Pleeease . . .

I'd also like to thank the artist, Kevin Sinnott, for creating the glorious *Running Away With the Hairdresser* (which hangs in the National Museum of Wales, in Cardiff, and is well worth a look if you're passing), my beloved husband, who inspires me daily, my children, who have graciously refrained from destroying my hard drive, my friend, Nigel Walker, for letting me take his name in vain . . . and, as ever, my incomparable friends and my fantastic family. And last but not least, thanks to my oldest friends, Debbie and Steve Scott; the girl I shared my first everything with, and the man who can make boilers sexy.

Lynne Barrett-Lee was born in London in 1959 and is married with three children. She has always written in her spare time, and her short stories and articles have been published in women's magazines for several years. Her previous novels were the acclaimed *Julia Gets a Life* and *Virtual Strangers*, and she now writes full-time. In 1994 she and her family moved to Cardiff, where the singing never stops, the sun always shines, and the Welsh rugby team always wins . . .

Also by Lynne Barrett-Lee

JULIA GETS A LIFE
VIRTUAL STRANGERS

ONE DAY, SOMEDAY

Lynne Barrett-Lee

BLACK SWAN

ONE DAY, SOMEDAY
A BLACK SWAN BOOK : 0 552 77136 8

First publication in Great Britain

PRINTING HISTORY
Black Swan edition published 2003

3 5 7 9 10 8 6 4

Copyright © Lynne Barrett-Lee 2002

The right of Lynne Barrett-Lee to be identified as the author of
this work has been asserted in accordance with sections 77 and
78 of the Copyright, Designs and Patents Act 1988

The extract from *The Poems* by Dylan Thomas, published by
J. M. Dent, is reproduced by kind permission of
David Higham Associates Ltd, 5–8 Lower John Street,
Golden Square, London W1F 9HA.

Set in 11/13pt Melior by
Kestrel Data, Exeter, Devon.

Black Swan Books are published by Transworld Publishers,
61–63 Uxbridge Road, London W5 5SA,
a division of The Random House Group Ltd,
in Australia by Random House Australia (Pty) Ltd,
20 Alfred Street, Milsons Point, Sydney, NSW 2061, Australia,
in New Zealand by Random House New Zealand Ltd,
18 Poland Road, Glenfield, Auckland 10, New Zealand
and in South Africa by Random House (Pty) Ltd,
Endulini, 5a Jubilee Road, Parktown 2193, South Africa.

Printed and bound in Great Britain by
Clays Ltd, St Ives plc.

I drive through the street, and I care not a damn;
The people they stare, and they ask why I am:
And if I should chance to run over a cad,
I can pay for the damage if ever so bad.

Arthur Hugh Clough, *Dipsychus* (1865) sc.5

It's amazing what you can do with an
E in A-level art, twisted imagination and
a chainsaw.

Damien Hirst

1

It's only a bloody car.

Only that. Only four wheels, a chassis, an engine, a gearstick, some seats, a few knobs, a bumper and boot. Only, in short, an inanimate object, that would waste not a second on grieving and tears. Which was all well and good, and quite a reasonable assertion to have, well, *asserted* at you, I suppose, given the grand plan, the rich tapestry of life's priorities and so on. But this wasn't a nugget of pocket philosophy. This statement wasn't meant as an encouraging noise. It was more along the lines of an exasperated roar.

More an IT'S ONLY A BLOODY CAR! type of thing. You know?

And thus it occurred: this pivotal moment, this end and beginning. Or so I now see.

It was also the end of that particular conversation. I may – I forget now – have suffixed it slightly; with a well-rounded 'Stuff you!' or 'But *my* car, you bastard!'. But then again, surely not. This was my boss, after all. More likely I would have said something more prissy, like 'Oh, *really*? It may be only a car to *you*,' etc., before dissolving, which was what I *actually* did, into a flurry of impotent fury and tears.

The morning had started well enough. As had the

9

week. The offices of JDL (Cardiff) Ltd, where I had recently started in temporary employment, were situated above a dancewear and lingerie shop in St Mary Street. They were bright, stylish offices, full of plant-life and chrome, and with a carpet that announced its attention to detail by means of a mono-grammed three-colour border that followed minutely each turn of the walls. Dead grand. Dead posh. Dead everything, basically, that your average urban comprehensive-school staff room was not.

I had opened the post, fielded two irate callers, replenished the Cona and tidied my desk. Iona, who did pretty much everything in the office apart from the translating and donkey-work, which was my depart-ment, slipped her head in and smiled. 'Is Joe due back any time soon, do you know?'

I nodded. 'He said half eleven,' I replied. 'But you know what the M4 is like weekday mornings. I doubt if he'll make it back much before one.'

'Well, if he calls, could you let him know I need a word? I've had the accountant on the phone about the Luxotel contract.' Iona rolled her eyes in benevolent stoicism and retreated to the back office.

It couldn't have been much after that – about ten thirty – when he did call. And thus the conversation began.

'Lu?'

'Is that you, Joe?' The line was appalling. I switched ears, and so missed the next thing he was saying, catching up with '– *and* a bloody hulking great artic, and, Christ!'

My boss wasn't noted for quiet, measured talking so I scaled down accordingly and took him to be merely in some sort of jam.

'Are you going to be late, then?' I asked, sucking my pencil.

'Late! LATE! What the hell are you on about? Lu, I'm lucky to be here *at all*!'

I mentally backtracked, was still none the wiser, then finally woke up. 'What do you mean? Is there some sort of problem?'

'*Problem?* Lu, I'm at the hospital in Swindon. I have broken my left arm, I have a cheek full of stitches, a query cracked rib and I'm probably in shock.'

'In shock? Good God!'

'Well, that's not actually been diagnosed as such. But, believe me, this is no Band-Aid job, I can assure you.'

'Oh, my Lord!' I squeaked, as the full implication of what he was saying dawned. 'You've had an accident! Oh, God! Are you all right? I mean apart from the broken arm and the rib and the stitches and everything. Oh, God! Are you all *right*?'

'Of course I'm not all right!' he barked. 'I'm in bloody Swindon! I have to wait here and make a statement for the police, and I've got that meeting with the bank at two thirty. There's no way I'm going to make it now, is there? Plus I can't drive, of course, so I've got to get a cab to Swindon station and get a train back to Cardiff, and then hike back up to the office, and—'

He *was* in shock, I decided. He was ranting.

'Joe!' I interrupted sternly. 'Can't they put you in an ambulance?'

His voice dropped an octave. 'Get real, Lu.'

'But you're hurt! That's outrageous! Look, let me speak to someone there. I'm sure I could—'

'Lu, I don't need an ambulance. But there's a thought. Perhaps it would be better if you – let me think – yes. What you need to do is ring Budget or Avis or whoever and see if they've got anything available now, then get yourself down there and drive here and get me. It'll only take an hour – so that's two for the round trip – and then I won't have to faff around with the train. Yes, that's the best plan. Do that and then call me back on my mobile. OK?'

And that was the end of the first bit of the conversation. I put down the phone, reached for the phone book, then got on to Wheels To Go to organize the car. That done, I went next door to see Iona and to tell her what had happened. To tell her, at least, what little I knew.

'An accident?'

'Yes. He's in Swindon.' I detailed the injuries.

She gasped. Just a little. She had worked there for aeons, apparently. Even then I deduced a touch of drama-fatigue. But she did look concerned. 'Oh, the poor lamb! How on earth did it happen?'

'I don't know yet. I have to ring him back. I'll go and do that now. Do you think I *should* ring the hospital? He sounded pretty agitated.'

She shook her head. Agitated, it seemed, was quite normal. 'Best you just get there, I think, lovely. Dear me. What a start to the day! And what about his Jag? Is it badly damaged, d'you know? If I know Joe, he'll be fretting more about that car of his than—'

And then she stopped speaking and her mouth opened wider. Not much, just enough so her fillings winked up at me. Just enough to confirm she'd remembered as well.

'Oh, my Lord! It was *your* car he drove there in, wasn't it? Oh, *cariad*, your new one.'

My car. Exactly. Poor lamb indeed.

By the time I got back through to Joe, he was sounding for all the world like he'd just stopped off at McArthur Glen for a spot of shopping. 'All sorted?' he trilled. 'You on your way or what?'

'I'm on my way,' I confirmed, just a tiny bit tetchily. 'But are you sure you're OK? Don't they want you to stay in for observation or anything?'

I could hear the sound of a siren in the distance.

'I'm fine,' he reassured me. 'They're interviewing the guy in the tanker at the moment, then it's me. I'll be clear by the time you get here, don't worry.'

'But aren't you in pain?' I persisted.

It was like pulling hairs from a nipple. But not before knowing Joe was OK could I consider the fate of my precious car. It wouldn't be seemly.

'Not a twinge.' Something rattled. 'Cocodamol,' he read. 'Though doubtless I'll pay for it later, of course.'

'But what *happened*? A tanker? You got hit by a *tanker*?'

He chortled.

'Christ, no. Not me, I'd be toast! No, the tanker had a blow-out, which meant he lost control and went into the back of the juggernaut, and the pair of them slewed all over the shop, and I just happened to be in the way, and made a bit of a cock-up of trying to get *out* of the way, and then I hit the Mondeo, and then the central reservation, and then the Mondeo again, and then rocketed off sideways – thank God there was nothing in the inside lane – took out an emergency phone and ended up on my side half-way up the embankment.'

'Oh dear!'

' "Oh dear" is right.'

'And is – and *are* the others all OK?'

'The tanker driver's fine, the guy in the artic has concussion and a broken ankle, I think, and the woman in the Mondeo – hrrrmph – is OK . . .'

'Hrrrmph?'

'No comment.'

13

Which meant *what*, precisely? I took a deep breath. 'And my car?'

My beautiful, much loved, *precious* little car.

He sighed, with some feeling. 'Hmm,' he said finally. 'Not good, I'm afraid.'

Which was some way distant from his later bald assertion, both in content and in tone. He was at this time, admittedly, completely contrite. So much so that as I drove fearfully down the strip of valley-of-death style horror-movie Devil's-Gulch speedway that the entire road network of Britain seemed suddenly to have become, it was with a reasonable quantity of compassionate concern, and only the tiniest smidgen of woe. My car was bashed up, but my boss was OK. My car could be mended, and I had to keep things in some sort of perspective: a human being, after all, was in pain. (He wasn't, I know, but then I was also reasonably intelligent and had myself been victim of that treacherous just-post-the-dentist euphoria; the one you enjoy while your mouth is still numb, that makes you go around saying, 'Wow, it's OK!') And, yes, it *was* the car my father had left me, and yes, I felt bereaved, and yes, I did love it and, yes, I was cross. But it *was* just a car and it wasn't his fault.

I had no way of knowing that for sure, of course. I had been acquainted with Joe Delaney for barely a month, and didn't really know the first thing about him. Only that he ran a successful business, and that he was divorced with one daughter – a pretty nine-year-old, called Angharad, whose picture was on his desk – and that he worked hard, played hard, and was hard to get on with. Unless you knew how to handle him. Or so Iona had said.

'Joe Delaney? Difficult? Oh, rubbish! He's a *doll*!' My sister, Del, had assured me before I met him. She knew him quite well. 'He's a sweetie and a dish,' she said. 'He has these green eyes, you know? Not emerald but, oh, I don't know, *luminous* – like greengages. Greengages, sectioned, and back-lit by spotlight. And his hair is sort of Rhett Butler meets Pierce Brosnan. And he's got the *loveliest* smile. He's a bit of a darling all round, in fact – though the ex-wife's a bitch, of course. Anyway, *I* wouldn't kick him out of bed.'

But, then, she would say that. My sister, much married and without economic factors to consider, was apt to wax rather lyrical where men were concerned. I was rather more discerning. Anyhow, none of her twaddle was in the least relevant to his status as the person with whom I had secured paid employment.

Though I had to concede she'd been right about the eyes.

But his being in possession of particularly arresting optical equipment was insufficient to quell my increasing annoyance that not only had I been rudely prised from my desk, but also that my car had been prised from *me*. When I pulled up at Swindon hospital just after one, Joe was sitting on a wall by the ambulance entrance, chatting up a nurse. He had a Marlboro Light in one hand and his mobile in the other. He'd wedged it against his thumb, in the crook of the plaster.

'Jesus, not a Micra!' he whined, as I climbed out. He launched the cigarette into a distant mahonia and smilingly watched the nurse shimmy back in.

'It was all they had left,' I said. 'Do you need help getting in?'

'I'll cope,' he grunted, though he clearly could not. His jacket sloughed off as he dipped his tall frame to sit down and I hurried to spare it an oily encounter with the Tarmac. Joe's face was pale and drawn and bisected

15

on the left side by a livid red weal that extended almost from temple to chin. A rank of tiny blue stitches had pulled it to attention, but it still oozed and dragged, and looked painful.

'That looks nasty,' I sympathized, as I closed the passenger door behind him. 'Shouldn't it be covered? Is it deep?'

'Haven't a clue,' he replied, with equanimity. 'Go on, then – get in. Get going. I've got a meeting to get to, remember?'

I drew a mental line through the appointment I'd anticipated with a coffee and loo stop, reasoning that we could do it *en route* at the services instead. But was soon disabused of such frivolous notions.

'Doesn't this crate go any faster?' Joe growled, as I coaxed it back on to the motorway.

I told him sniffily I had no intention of being the cause of any more road-traffic accidents today, and that there was no meeting on earth worth risking a life for. All a bit dreary and earnest, I know, but it seemed the right thing to be saying at the time. And I wasn't wrong.

'Yeah, yeah,' he said, flapping the plaster-free arm. The tone of his voice and the absence of a rejoinder reminded me that as yet we hadn't broached the subject of my car. We drove for some minutes in silence, while the radio burbled.

At length, I ventured, 'So, what did the police say?'

He shrugged. 'Not a lot. They never do, do they?'

I hadn't the faintest idea, so I said so. 'And what did you mean about the woman in the Mondeo? That "no comment" bit. What was all that about?'

'Oh, just that she's a tight-arsed crone with a problem,' he said mildly. 'Seemed to think I had something to do with it. Which is bollocks, of course.'

'Is it? So why'd she think so?'

'Because she obviously hates me. Probably a dyke.'

I ignored him for long enough to make my disapproval clear, then said, 'But why?'

'Because I overtook her. Well, *was* overtaking her. What I actually did was hit her, of course.'

'When the tanker hit the juggernaut.'

'When the tanker hit the juggernaut. The tanker was overtaking the juggernaut when the tyre blew and the Mondeo was behind the tanker – middle lane – and I was in the outside lane, about to overtake the Mondeo, and the tanker and the juggernaut skidded into the outside lane so I swerved back into the middle lane, bounced off the Mondeo, spun, veered left, hit the emergency phone, hit the barrier, ended up on my side.' He flipped his good hand over to illustrate. 'Can I smoke?'

'No, you can't. Anyway, I see, then.'

'No, you don't.'

'No, you're right. I don't.'

'And the bitch – well, I think the bitch has told them I was doing a ton.'

'A ton?'

'Yes, a ton. Which I wasn't, naturally, because the car wasn't up to it.'

Which it was.

'But you *were* going too fast.' It sounded horribly plausible. And was obviously true. He turned to face me and put on a petulant voice.

'*Yes. Probably.* I *was* going too fast.'

'Oh dear,' I said, easing my foot from the accelerator pedal. 'So the police think you might have made it worse than it would have been.'

He growled. '*Exactly*. But that's not the point. Well, it *is*, from a penalty-point situation, I suppose, but the main thing's the insurance.'

'Your insurance?'

He nodded. 'If the tanker's insurers get a sniff of contributory negligence they'll do everything they can to reduce the pay-out.'

'On my car?'

He nodded again. 'If they pay out at all.'

'So your insurers will have to pay, then.'

'Exactly. Which means my no-claims is up the bloody swanee.'

Tough, I thought. *Tough*. 'Oh,' I said. 'And what sort of damage is there? Is it likely to cost a lot? And where is it, for that matter?'

A lorry full of lambs thundered past us so I couldn't hear his answer. But obligingly he said it again anyway.

'It's a write-off. I told you.'

'A *write-off*? A complete *write-off*? My precious car?'

'Look, it's not your problem.'

'Not my problem? How do you work that out?'

'Because it's not. We'll have to get you a new one, won't we?'

'But it's irreplaceable! And, *God*! I just spent six hundred pounds having it serviced!'

'Jeez – they saw you coming, then.'

'And it was a special edition. A classic! It could be three months before I – *you* – find another one like it!'

'So? We'll rent this one!'

'*This* one? We certainly won't! Anyway, that's not even the point! It was my father's car! And you've just – just – ' it was beginning to sink in now. The toe-rag. '– just *demolished* it. Killed it! Just like that!'

I decided I must be having some sort of delayed psychosomatic response to Joe's accident because I was more furious than I had felt in a long time. I glared through the windscreen and grieved. Appropriately,

18

low cloud was massing ahead. How *dare* he do a ton in my car? How dare he? I could picture him doing it. I was *not* happy.

'I'm mad at you. *Mad.*'

'It wasn't my fault.'

'Yes, it was. If you hadn't been speeding—'

'I wasn't!'

'You were!'

'Eighty-five, tops.'

'*Eighty-five?* Eighty-five miles per hour – in *my* car?'

'God, listen to you – you sound like my granny. Lu, give it a rest, will you? I'll sort it, OK?'

'That's not the point. It's the principle of the thing. I lent you my car in all good faith and now I find you treated it like a – like a – like a bloody Maclaren!'

'Drove it.'

'Hammered it!'

'OK, hammered it, then. But it's a car, Lu, not a bloody kitten!'

'*Was* a car! And *my* car. Not *your* car. *My* car!'

'Er, *ex*-car,' he quipped.

His jauntiness, I supposed, was an attempt to lighten the atmosphere a little. But it certainly didn't.

'Exactly! Men! You're all so irresponsible! And how can you joke about it? Here you are with a hundred-weight of plaster up your arm, a face like bloody Bluebeard—'

'Blackbeard.'

'*And* query cracked ribs and—'

He swivelled in his seat and slapped his good hand on the dashboard. 'Exactly! *Exactly*, Lu! IT'S ONLY A BLOODY CAR!'

2

I have never been much of a planner.

I never planned to become a French teacher. I never planned to fall in love with a scumbag. I certainly never planned to get pregnant by one. Having done so, I will admit that I did, briefly, nurture a rather juvenile affection for the prospect of a wedding/babies/happy-ever-after/roses-round-the-door type arrangement. But not for long. Oh, no. Turned out he had other plans.

'I have a plan,' I had said to my sister.

We were now ten years on. And this had been six months earlier. A cheerless late November afternoon.

'A plan?' she'd asked, narrowing her eyes. 'What sort of plan?'

We were sitting in her kitchen. She, I remember, had been making mince pies at the time. With mincemeat she'd remembered to buy back in August, and puff pastry she had remembered to rest.

'A life plan,' I told her. 'I have decided upon a life plan. I am going to resign from my job.'

She stopped cutting pastry circles and peered at me over her glasses. 'Goodness. As plans go, that's a fairly radical one, Lu. Resign from your job and do what, exactly? Go to another school?'

'Nooo. I thought – well, I thought I might go back to college, actually.'

'*College?* Whatever for?'

20

'I haven't decided yet. But something creative. Something – oh, I don't know. I just don't feel I've ever really had time to explore that side of my personality, you know? So I thought I might do an art degree or something.'

'A *degree*?' She blinked at me before resuming her cutting. 'Uh-huh. Just a minor career shift, then. And what are you and Leo going to live on while all this artistic exploration is going on?'

I picked up a piece of raw pastry and nibbled at it. 'I know you think it's stupid, but I've been doing some sums and I think it's feasible. I really do. I've got to get *in*, of course, which will mean producing some sort of portfolio or something, so I thought the best thing would be if I got some sort of job in the meantime, something nine to five, for a change – something without a marking component, at any rate – and maybe do an access course or something in my spare time.'

She began popping her circles into a greased bun tin. 'Hmm. Sounds like an awful lot of somethings, Lu. Couldn't you just carry on as you are and do something at night school? See how it goes for a while?'

I shook my head emphatically. 'That's exactly what I *don't* want to do. That's exactly what I *can't* do. If I don't do this now, then I never will. I know I won't. I know what I'm like. I'll just keep bumbling along like I always do and then one day I'll look around and Leo will be grown-up – off to college himself, with any luck – and I'll still be teaching, and still hating it . . . And, well. I just *know*. It'll all be too late.'

'And it's what Dad would have wanted for you, by any chance?'

Del was right. It *had* been a mortality thing. My father had died, very suddenly, that summer. Died, without warning, one rainy June morning and left the

21

pair of us grief-stricken, rootless and bereft. But also with a little money. Not a huge amount, but still substantially more than I'd ever seen in my life before. Enough, at any rate, to make me feel restless. Enough that I'd begun to greet every school morning with the knowledge that I wanted to be somewhere else.

The thing about best-laid plans, of course, is that unless you are my sister and have sensibly planned something biddable and brick-based like an extension, what generally follows the mice and men bit is a long, long row of dots. Because, though I had indeed left my job and filled in all sorts of encouraging-sounding forms, it turned out that getting into university might prove a slightly more intractable problem than I had at first anticipated, mainly because just about everybody else in the entire world seemed to want to do an art degree as well. So I would just have to wait and see. In the meantime, I had an exciting temporary job at a company that installed boilers. And I had, at that moment, a written-off car.

But all was not lost. The one bright spot on my rather watered-down artistic horizon was the fact that I *had* enrolled at night school, as Del had suggested. On a course that, though rather unimaginatively entitled *Impressions of the Impressionists*, was actually proving to be very enjoyable. It ran for an hour every Tuesday evening, and though it was only a mere splodge on the vast landscape of my portfolio requirement, it was beginning to look like offering other interesting areas of development.

His name was Stefan Llewellyn, and he was the tutor. And I, for all my no-nonsense, sensible planning was – suddenly – in the grip of an intoxicating crush.

*   *   *

22

But, speaking of impressions, I am *not* very impressed with Joe Delaney. Only a bloody car, indeed! This one, this hateful old crate, is the colour of a custard slice and drives like a Sherman tank. And looks like it's been driven by a tank battalion. Of TAs, on some sort of weekend manoeuvre. And, quite possibly (given that we're talking Wales here), with a couple of recreational sheep in the back. It has ash in its ashtrays. It has Big Mac boxes in its glove compartment. It has the remains of a green wine-gum welded to the edge of the driver's seat. Mainly, however, and how ridiculously this rankles, it is a Micra – the best they could do at such short notice – which means that as I park opposite the museum entrance this evening, I have been deprived of that small glow of pleasure that being in my dear little car always brings.

Isn't that childish? Isn't that silly? But I can't help it. Much as I know that such preoccupations are juvenile, my little MG is – was – very dear to me. It had been my father's last car – his one small extravagance – the car he'd only just bought when he died. The car he had left me, the car that still *smelled* of him, the one piece of him I could still keep as my own. And here I am in a grubby old, smelly old, horrible old Micra. Grrrrr. *Horrible* car.

I turn my back on it and scan the front of the museum.

And there *is* Stefan. He is waiting on the steps. Sitting on one of them, shaggy golden hair corralled in a ponytail, face in the sunshine, clipboard in hand. I'm not sure quite why Stefan brings a clipboard to *Impressions of the Impressionists* because he never actually does anything much with it. I think Stefan carries his clipboard because it makes him feel important. Different from his eclectic bunch of mature students, at least. The tutor. The man to whom we all must pay homage. Which makes him seem vulnerable, somehow. And I love him for that.

Oh, I have *such* a thing for Stefan. Which is stupid, but nevertheless lovely. *He* is lovely. He is an artist, for one thing. A creator of beauty. And, were that not sufficient, he is beautifully packaged. In a glorious, breathtaking six feet three inches of sculpted and exquisite masculine flesh. Of course, Stefan doesn't know *quite* how I feel about him and as, until last month, he was still at the tail end of some sort of unsatisfactory relationship with another student (who has now, happily, abandoned her art-appreciation endeavours), I have no intention of telling him. There has been a definite *frisson* between us for some time – of that I am sure – but to date we have only skirted around the penumbra of the periphery of the possibility of the reality that we might just become some sort of serious item in the near future. But we have only been out together four times so our relationship is not sufficiently advanced to allow me to play fast and loose with delicate things like admitting I am completely besotted with him, or, indeed, interpreting feelings, and, as history will testify, I'm not much good at doing that anyway. For now, it is sufficient he knows that I like him. That I fancy him. That kind of fun, non-threatening stuff.

But he hasn't noticed the car anyway. Cars are not big on Stefan's personal agenda. Stefan cycles to college. Stefan likes bikes.

'You're early,' he remarks, without giving the statement any particular inflection. He smiles, though, and pats the space beside him on the step, so I judge that he's pleased to see me.

I'm early because I have had to deliver Joe to a pub in

Pontcanna, which for some reason he felt would be a more therapeutic activity than simply going straight home to bed. I put my keys in my bag and sit down on the still warmish stone.

'My boss had an accident,' I tell him. 'On the motorway. On his way back from London. He's broken his arm and he's written off my new car.'

Stefan nods at this. As if writing off cars were the only natural end product of being silly enough to drive them. Then asks me how such a thing came about. So I tell him, in the manner of a reluctant teenager. Which, bar the reluctant bit, is how he generally makes me feel.

'Well,' he says, rising and elbowing the sun out, 'I must say, I think you were very silly.'

I stand up again as well. And groan. 'I know.'

'I mean, couldn't the guy have simply hired a car in the first place? Why did he need to borrow yours?' Stefan smiles as he says this. A polite, enquiring, sensible smile. A smile without any undermining ulterior motives. A very, very *kissable* smile.

'Because his car was in the garage and he didn't know it wasn't going to be ready until seven and he had to get to London for a meeting, and—'

He waves to someone behind me. 'So why didn't he take the train?'

'Because he – well, I suppose because he—'

'It would have – hello, Cerys – been simpler, surely?'

I turn and wave a hello at my fellow student, an overweight twenty-something with a very pretty face and a penchant for violently coloured patchwork dungarees. Yes, I think. Of course it would have been simpler. But Joe obviously didn't see it like that. Taking a train involved sitting next to people, organizing tickets, adhering to someone else's timetable. Being generally trammelled. I shrug and nod.

'But instead he asked if he could borrow your car and you said yes. Yes?'

'Well, I wasn't using it, was I? Well, I was, but only to get home. And he said he'd pay for a cab, so it didn't seem – well, anyway, yes. I did.'

Stefan makes no response to this other than to nod his perfect, leonine head. He swings his eyes back towards the road, and stretches. Then squeezes my arm. Then strokes it a little. Woweee.

'You're too kind, you know that,' he tells me gently. He's *so* gorgeous. 'You should have said no. People take advantage, Lu.'

'Oh, bloody hell,' says Del, when, an hour or so later, I arrive at her house to pick Leo up. It's a little after seven, and the night has yet to draw its breezy tendrils around the ebullient spring light of the day. Through the window, I can see Leo and Simeon making some sort of den in the living room. They both wave a hello, then return to their game.

'Oh-bloody-hell what?'

'Oh-bloody-hell I just remembered it's Wednesday tomorrow and I haven't finished hemming Simeon's Harry Potter outfit.' Her eyes drift across their immaculate front garden and blink at the Micra. It looks hunched and insubstantial and faintly shame-faced in the gloom. 'Whose car is that?'

Sighing, I shrug my bag from my shoulder and step past her into the hall. 'It's a rental car. Mine is a write-off apparently.'

She gapes at me. '*What?*'

'Oh, Del,' I groan. 'I'm such a klutz. I let Joe borrow it yesterday. And—'

'*Why?*' She closes the front door behind me then shuffles me into the kitchen. 'Why would Joe need your car?' She feels the kettle for warmth and flicks the switch on.

So now I tell *her*. And she listens, then snorts.

'You are unbelievable, you are,' she decides. 'I mean, how crazy can you get!'

'I know. I *know*! Oh, God, Del. What on earth possessed me? But what else was I supposed to do? No, don't answer. But how could I say no? It was a reasonable enough request, and the accident wasn't his fault, after all. No, stuff it. I don't know why I'm even bothering to defend him. But he says he's going to get onto it tomorrow, and if he doesn't . . .'

Del pours hot water on a tea bag for me and snorts again. She has long since perfected the art of the big-sisterly snort.

'But, in the meantime, I've got that Micra.' I angle my face doorwards. 'Leo! Ten minutes!' Then I sigh. 'Trouble is, it could be for months.'

She shakes her head and plonks the tea down in front of me. 'Lu, what *are* we to do with you?' she says.

'*Aurora?* Lucienne *Aurora*? Is that for real?'

I couldn't see Joe, of course, because he said this down the telephone. Because he had, for some reason, telephoned me. I had returned from my sister's and had finally managed to get Leo to bed. No small feat when his activity of choice that evening would have been to drive straight to Swindon and track down what was left of my car. He had apparently left twenty-six Pokémon cards in the glove compartment. I was not very popular. And I was not in a good mood. I sat down wearily on the floor by the phone.

'Of course it's for real. My mother was French.'

'Well!' he exclaimed. 'I've never heard anyone called

27

that before. Luci*enne*, eh? And *Aurora*. With an A? Is it actually a name?'

'She was a goddess in Roman mythology, apparently.'

'Is that right?'

'And it means "light of the morning". "Dawn".'

'Ah! Yes, of course. As in aurora borealis.'

'Exactly. Joe, is there a point to your question?'

'Of course.' I could hear rustling. 'I'm sorting out your insurance.'

I looked at my watch. It was almost ten. 'At this time?'

'Of course. When else do I get a chance to deal with this crap?'

He sounded tired. 'But *why* sorting my insurance?' I asked him. 'Wheels To Go already have all my details.'

'Indeed they do, Lu. But I've decided I'm going to put you on *my* insurance.'

'Why?'

Had Joe been in possession of a small bugle I'm sure he would have blown down it at this point.

'Because I've had an idea.'

'An idea.' Oh dear.

'Yes. A very sensible one. Change of job spec. I've decided the best thing will be if you become my chauffeur for a while. You wouldn't mind that, would you? Sorry, chauff*euse*. Whatever. The main point being that your car problem's sorted.'

'Sorted? How so?'

'Today is your lucky day, Lucienne Aurora. Because I am going to let you drive *my* car.'

3

This is all my sister's fault.

My sister is a very sociable woman. My sister has a network of friends that could form the basis of a global dot-com conglomerate, as long as the market for tea bags holds up. My sister has, in particular, a friend called Julia, who has a friend called Lily, who is French, and used to be her au pair. Lily (for reasons I really can't fathom, given that she comes from balmy and beautiful Bordeaux) has lived in Cardiff ever since coming over for her nannying stint here, and is married to a man who teaches woodwork, called Malcolm. Their second child is due any day. Which is why she's on maternity leave from her job. Which is why JDL, her employers, one of whose biggest clients is a chain of thrusting French hoteliers, have need of a French-speaking PA until she comes back. Hence me. Hence *moi*. Because I speak French too.

And I can certainly swear in it.

'*Merde!*' I exclaimed. 'I can't drive your Jag!'

'Why ever not?' asked Joe.

'Because I can't. It's a ridiculous idea!'

'Ridiculous *why* precisely?'

'Because, well, because. Because I don't want to. Because it's way too big, for one thing. Because it would barely fit in my garage. Because I'd feel ridiculous sitting in it. Because it represents, oh, I don't

know. Because it's *your* sort of car. Not – *emphatically*
not – *my* sort of car. Because – because I'd feel, I don't
know – twitched.'

'*Twitched?*'

'Yes, twitched. It's—'

There was a titter. 'Only a bloody car, Lu.'

'We've been there,' I snapped.

'Exactly. And what a load of tosh you do talk. It's not
ridiculous at all. You're just scared of it.'

I could almost hear his patronizing smirk.

'*What?*'

'But you don't need to be.'

'I am *not*. I just don't happen to fancy—'

And then a snort. 'Yes, you are. But, like I said, you
don't need to be. It's a complete pussy. Drives itself
virtually.'

'So let *it* drive you, then.'

And a tut. 'Now you're being silly. Look, doesn't it at
least strike you as a sensible solution to our current
problem?'

'*Our* current problem? Oh, no. This is *your* current
problem. My arms are both fully functional, remember?'

'And currently in employment.' He left a long enough
pause here to make his point for him. 'Which is why it
makes sense for them to drive for me. And also means
I'll have you on hand, won't I?'

'On hand? On hand for what?'

'On hand to translate, of course. Should the need
arise. Anyway,' he finished, 'I'm going to get drunk
now then try to get some sleep, so goodnight.'

'Should you be drinking while you're on those pain-
killers?'

'You're right, actually. I'd better stop taking them.'

Tell me. Did I dream yesterday?

Brring! Brring!

Did I?

Brring! Brring! Brring!

'*Did* I?

Brrrrriiiinnnng!

Then I remember. No. I did not.

Or maybe, yes. Maybe I'm *still* dreaming. Maybe I'm having one of those fight-or-flight marathon nightmares, where car-eating gorgons take over the world. Maybe the *brriiiing* is the rasp of crushing-machine monster against chassis and the thump in my temple is the tyres blowing out. Or something like that. But, please, tell me I dreamt it. Please tell me my dear little car's still outside. I pluck the receiver from its rest and try to pull it to my ear. But because I am left-handed and therefore unable to manage a telephone cord without deforming it into a mulish and argumentative two-inch-long swizzle, the whole phone, plus the latest Joanna Trollope, plus a blister pack of Ibuprofen, plus (oh, *bugger*!) a half-glass of cranberry juice all come too.

'Right,' Joe says. 'You're up. Good. Tell you what we'll do. You go and take the Micra back to Wheels, then pick up a cab and come over to me. Then we'll go and pick the Jag up and then you can drive us to work.'

No. No. No. No. No. I am NOT BLOODY UP.

'Do you have *any* idea what time it is?' I bark at him.

'Yes,' he sings. 'Eight seventeen.'

Shit.

Eight forty-six.

I am going to wring bloody Pikachu's fat little neck.

'But, Mum, you *have* to.'

'But I already told you. I can't!'

'But if you don't someone will steal them.'

'I'm quite sure they won't.'

'They *will*. Mum, you just don't realize, do you? Dark Charmeleon is the rarest card in Britain! And I told Owen Davies that I'd swap my Fossil Dugtrio for his Charizard Shiny. Mum, you *have* to go and get them.'

'Leo, I cannot drive to Swindon this morning. OK?'

'But you must!'

'Put your coat on.'

'Mu-*um*!'

'And pick up your PE bag.'

'Mu-*um*!'

'And what on earth is that disgusting blob on your sweatshirt? Come here. Look. I told you. I will ring the police and find out. Here. Take your lunch-box. And if they've found them I will ask them to send them to us—'

'But that will take for ever!'

'No, it won't—'

'It *will*!'

'*No*, it *won't.*'

'OK. Then you'll have to buy me the Team Rocket Pack instead.'

'The *what*?'

'It's only seven pounds forty-nine. You can get it in Smith's. Or in that card shop in Llanishen. But you *have* to go in and get it this morning because Liam told me his mum is going in there today to get it for him and Richard said there was only one left. So you have to go as soon as you've taken me to school. *Straight* away. OK?'

'Seven forty-nine! Leo, do not imagine for an *instant*—'

32

'Hang on! Did you say the *police*, Mum? *Really?* Lush! Will they bring them back in a police car? *Lush!'*

Having collected Simeon from Del's, dropped both the boys at school, driven across Cardiff to take the cake-shop Micra back to the car-rental office, waited for a taxi to take me back to Joe's house, been driven to same (massive, mock-Tudor, burgeoning magnolia, etc.), waited outside for Joe to complete some sort of complicated manoeuvre involving a fax, an e-mail and a bacon sandwich, taken the taxi with him back to the other side of Cardiff, involved myself with the intricacies of a trouser pocket to which I had no right (or inclination) of egress for his wallet, we fetched up at Excelsior Cars (a showroom of some distinction with a lot of flagpoles outside), to pick up his Jaguar, at something approaching ten thirty. Sod this for a job.

The cut on Joe's face had congealed overnight into something that looked less medically alarming, though it now lent his face an aura of latent aggression. Which obviously hadn't gone unnoticed by the girl on the service desk when he queried two items on his terrifying bill.

Those sorted (expunged), we retraced our steps along the broad swathe of thick carpet that connected the showroom – all leathery hush and coffee-'n'-biscotti style opulence – to the real world that existed beyond the ten-foot glass doors. Joe's car, I saw immediately, had been brought round to meet us, and sat, quietly gleaming, in the watery sun.

We were wafted outside by the thick double doors. Joe aimed his key and it peeped at the pussy. The pussy peeped back at him. Peep peep! it went. We approached it (JDL 3 – *très* pretentious) then walked along the length of its muscular black flanks. It was so long. So *big*. He opened the passsenger door. Schlup! went the airlock. I grabbed my own handle. Plip! it went. He mouthed the word 'harder'. I yanked harder on it. Glunk! went the handle. 'No, *harder*,' he said. I pulled harder still. At which point it hissed in resentful defeat. I got in. Smelt buffalo. Sank. Then found my eyes to be on exactly the same plane as the dashboard. But with my trembling feet floundering a good eight or so inches from the business end of the footwell.

We then spent some minutes adjusting for my complete inability to make the situation any easier by having the good grace to be six foot two. This involved twiddling with the seat height, the cushion height, the angle of the seat back, the position of the steering-wheel and the location of the remote-control door mirrors. It might also have involved making an allowance for the conjunction of Saturn and Uranus and, quite possibly, the Great Bear being up Orion's Belt. What there should have been, and wasn't, was a gin-and-tonic option, and a handy wipe-dispenser with which to mop my brow. So many variables. So little time. And we hadn't even *started* on the driving bit yet.

But we did, soon after. I turned the key in the ignition and the beast came to life. A deep, purring life with a low, feline bass note. I released the handbrake, and pressed my foot on the accelerator. It growled momentarily. And nothing happened. Nothing whatso-ever.

'Jesus Christ! You really *can't* drive, can you?'

I couldn't hear the engine any more. But it was, I knew, impossible to stall an automatic. So if this one had stalled, it had done so itself. I said so.

'Nooooo,' Joe replied, Slush-Puppy sweetly. 'It hasn't stalled. But it generally doesn't go anywhere if you leave it in *Park*. There,' he said, pointing his uninjured hand at it. '*Drive.* By there. Surprising though it may seem, Lu, it's the one that says D.'

'I'm not completely stupid,' I snapped. 'And look, this really has to be the first and last time you make any comments about my driving. Any at all! OK? *OK?* I am *perfectly* competent. I have a *full* UK licence. So I think I can manage to *drive your bloody car!*'

'Fine,' he said, nodding benignly. 'Be my guest.'

By the time we were up and (to use the expression loosely) running, another big fat Jaguar had arrived on the forecourt. Its owner, a short man with a pink tie and sock-braces, had thoughtfully parked it right across the only bit of forecourt that was not already occupied by immaculate, close-coupled, fifty-thousand-pound cars. Thus I had two options. I could either reverse out on to the main road and die backwards now or do a three-point turn and die nose first later.

On the seventh of the turns in (what eventually would turn out to be) my fifteen-point epic exit, it occurred to me that there was, in fact, another option. I could, if I so wished, stop the car, get out, slam the door and simply walk away. There was little chance in the future that I would ever run into any of the people who were currently witnessing my disgrace. Just as teachers did not discover wealth until they were offered lucrative early-retirement packages and index-linked pensions, so artists, with a few hyped-up Brit Art exceptions, did not generally achieve anything like wealth until they died. And even if unimaginable wealth *did* ever come my way, I would not, I decided with conviction at that moment, ever, *ever* purchase a Jaguar car. And what would it matter if I lost my job? I could get another. I could supply-teach French to appallingly behaved teenagers. Or, less dangerously, become a collier in the last South Wales mine. And sue him for mental cruelty or something. Oh, yes. I could certainly do that.

Once I had chewed all this over (at about the eleventh turn, I think) another thought occurred to me: that if I chose that course of action I would have to endure the rest of my life knowing that in a pub somewhere, not a million miles from my home in Cefn Melin, I would, should the conversation turn to women and their many shortcomings, be the butt – the *sad* butt – of some low-life man's joke. The man beside me, perhaps. And then, in time, another. A real-life example. A misogynist's dream anecdote. Proof that women, when it comes to it, just can't do cars.

And I was *not* having that.

Thus (and ignoring Joe's increasingly anxious directives) I finally turned the car round and lurched out into the road. To his credit he uttered not a word for ten yards. And when he did, it was in the faintest of whispers. 'I have to tell you, Lu, that I am a *really* bad passenger. So if we go on like this you won't have to worry about me making any comments about your driving. I will probably be incapable of coherent speech.' And then he threw back his head – he was already sitting a good foot behind me, so it felt as if he was in the back anyway – and laughed. Laughed loudly and enthusiastically, with his plastered arm clutched to his chest. I would probably have chosen that moment to leave the vehicle entirely, were it not for the fact that he then gulped, gasped, said, 'Jesus! My rib!' went white and doubled over, breathing hard and fast, and with his jaws tightly clenched. Ho bloody ho. Ho bloody *ho*.

We drove on in silence for ten whole minutes.

Then he asked, 'Mind if I smoke?'

*　　*　　*

We have somehow arrived in the centre of Cardiff. I say somehow, because apart from my vibrating-legs contribution, I didn't seem to have a lot to do with it. I just sort of pointed and the car just, well, shot. That and the fact that we spent much of the journey rowing. Just because I wouldn't let him smoke. What a baby.

'Look,' he whined, 'the window's open, isn't it?'

'Doesn't make any difference.'

'Of course it does. The smoke goes out of it.'

'No, it doesn't. It just swirls around then comes back in.'

'So put the air con on, then.' He started rootling in his pocket.

'Look, I know you think I'm being unreasonable,' I said reasonably, 'but I've always had a real problem with people smoking in my car – '

'Ah! But this is *my* car.'

'– because it makes me feel sick.'

'Well, I feel sick as well.'

'Then smoking won't help you, surely?'

'Yes, it will.'

'I'm sure it won't. It'll make you feel worse.'

'Look, I'm feeling crappy enough. I certainly don't need you to tell me how it'll make me feel, thank you.'

'I'm not! I just think that if this whole driving-you-around thing is going to work, then I've got to be honest with you. I really couldn't do it if you smoked. That's all.'

'Hrrmmmmmph.'

'Pardon?'

'Nothing. OK? *Nothing*.'

As parking is at a premium in the centre of Cardiff, Joe has done a deal with a guy at his accountants'. The deal is that he can use his spare parking space in return for unspecified accounting-related favours. His accountants are based in a street of late-Victorian buildings that were once homes but are now offices. And the parking is round the back, in one of those horrible narrow cobbled lanes that obviously worked well in a cart-based domestic scenario but has nothing to offer the twenty-first-century motorist apart from pranged exhaust pipes and lateral scrapes. Not that it seems to put anyone off. Also in residence are a small independent car-repair garage, an upholsterer's, a purveyor of antique fireplaces, and a door in the wall that says 'Bilbo – knock twice'. Consequently, in this genteel little alley, there exists all manner of active commerce and about eight billion vans. I know all this, incidentally, because we are creeping along it at one and a half miles an hour. (Or whatever the speed is that automatics do when you don't have your foot on the brake or the accelerator.) And as if that were not enough to make the faint-hearted take up the cudgels for pedestrians, the car-parking space that Joe so obviously cherishes is at the very end, and is minuscule.

It has to be smaller than the car. *Has* to be. How the hell – how the *hell* – am I going to get into it? I do not need this stress. I do *not* need this stress.

I take a deep breath and smile confidently at him. 'Right. That one there, then.'

'That's it. That's the one. And you'll need to reverse in.'

Oh, my God. Oh, my God. 'Oh,' I say lightly. 'Can't I drive straight in there?'

He shakes his head. 'No, you can't. Because of that Fiat parked over there.'

He points.

'Oh.' I do *not* need this stress. 'Are you sure?'

'Yes, I'm quite sure, Lu. Because if you try to drive into it forwards your offside wing will hit the wall. Unless, of course, you back up and straighten up a bit, and if you *try* to back up and straighten up a bit then you will find you have hit the Fiat instead.'

He affects a superior expression and waits.

'Ri-ight,' I say, nodding. 'Ho-hum. So how *am* I supposed to reverse into it? How am I supposed to turn the car round?'

'Simple. You drive into that space first.'

He points again. Uurgh.

'That one opposite? But there's a car in there already.'

'Ye-es,' he agrees. 'But it's only a small one, and if you pull up hard behind it you will find you will then be able to reverse into *my* space without any problem at all.'

I do *not need* this *stress*. Deep breath. Deep breath. *Without any problem at all.* I grip the wheel hard so he can't see me trembling.

'In here, then?'

'That's right. In you go.'

So I ease down the pedal. The car starts to creep forward. 'Like this?'

'Almost. But – um, whoa – you need to get further over. No, no. Further than that. No. Left hand down now. That's it.'

I brake. 'That's it?'

'Hardly. Don't be such a wimp, Lu. You've got yards in front. *Yards*. That's it, that's it . . . Stop! *Jesus.*'

'There's no need to flap. I *was* stopping.'

He ploughs his hair with his hand. 'OK. Into reverse, then. Into *reverse*.' I get into reverse. 'Right. Hard round. Watch your wing. That's it. No. Noooo! No. No. No. You'll have to come out and straighten up a bit—'

'I can *see* that, thank you.'

'All right, all right – God! Watch your *wing*, will you? God! You've got—'

'I know what I've got, thank you very much.'

'OK. Right. In again, then. OK, now right hand down again. *Right* hand. Hard down. *Hard* down. That's it. Dustbins, remember – the dustbins behind you. Dustbins. *Dustbins*, Lu. Slow up. Slow *up*. Jesus! That's—'

'Oh, for goodness sake, stop flapping about the bloody dustbins, will you? I've *seen* the dustbins, OK?'

'But you've only got—'

'*Yards*, OK? I've got *yards*.'

There is a hint of a whisper of a suggestion of contact. The lightest of kisses. A sort of muffled 'kerphut'. I don't think he hears it. He couldn't possibly have felt it.

'There!' I exclaim loudly, just to be on the safe side. 'That should do it, I think, then. No problem at *all*.'

I turn round to face him. He is silent and ashen.

'No sweat,' I add. 'So, how was it for you?'

We are half-way down Queen Street before he deigns to speak to me again.

'Hrmmph. I'm giving up smoking anyway,' he says.

Once we've arrived at the office, Iona smiles. 'Giving up smoking again, Joe? Well, that's nice. That's *nice*.' She shunts her glasses on to her head in order to plant a kiss on Joe's scab-free cheek. Then to me. 'He's certainly a trier, aren't you, Joe? Always trying, at least, aren't you, *cariad*?' I should say so. 'And I always say it's better to try and fail than not to have tried at all. Yes, lovely? Now, my Dai, on the other hand – you haven't met Dai yet, have you, Lu? – he's a complete bugger. Fifty a day, every day, and there's not a row in the world that'll budge him an inch. Pah. They'll be the death of him. Anyway, cakes,' she finishes, nodding her glasses back down. 'I've been and bought a bag of ring doughnuts from Gregg's, and I've just put the coffee on the go.'

Joe rolls his eyes and stomps off to his office.

Best place for him. Trier, indeed.

4

'Well, I think you're absolutely bonkers. It sounds like a complete dream. Why would you want to be stuck in an office all day when you can be swanning around in an XJR? You lucky thing! God, I'm *really* jealous!'

By the time I had finished work, prised the car from its wraparound day bed (having pointed out that when a rubber strip of bumper touches a plastic dustbin at 0.0001 m.p.h., there is *obviously* going to be nothing in the way of damage at anything above a molecular level), taken Joe home and driven on to Del's, I had pretty much decided that chauffeuring, even as a temporary career choice, definitely wasn't for me. Even though it was marginally less tedious than translating French boiler specifications, I had decided that (a) the British Isles were *not* the place for cars the size of Wester-super-Mare and (b) I would most probably have to kill Mr Delaney if forced into a confined space with him for too long.

But Del, as was her dear, sweet way, could see only Honor Blackman in plaid slacks and a head scarf, careering up a mountain with James Bond on her tail. (In contrast, all *I* could see was the Gabalfa roundabout and the unbearable smallness of multi-storey car-parks.)

She placed a rubber-gloved hand on the car's back

bumper and swept it squeakingly and lovingly over its contours.

'But he called me a bag. Del. I *mean* – a *bag*!'

She paused to laugh at this, clutching her stomach. Why was everyone *laughing* at me today?

'Well, you most probably were being one, then. You do have a very spiky side to you, Lu. So. Why did he call you a bag?'

'I don't know – he wasn't talking to me at the time. But I presume it was because I wouldn't let him smoke in the car. He muttered it to Iona this morning. He said, "God! She's a bit of a bag, that one." It's been niggling at me all day.'

Del stripped off a glove to rub a spot from the paintwork. Then slipped her arm through mine and led me into the house. She'd been cooking and the kitchen was fragrant and warm. Simeon and Leo were out in the back garden, happily hitting each other with sticks.

'Look, be reasonable,' she chided, rapping on the window and flapping a tea-towel before stripping off the other glove. 'The poor guy has just had a pretty nasty accident. He's probably in shock still. I'm sure he didn't mean it. And if he did, it was probably because you forget he's not a fifteen-year-old with ten Rothmans and an attitude problem. No – *don't* look at me like that. You know what you're like.'

'But—'

'*Forget* it. There are far worse things to be called. And, besides, I have very, very, *very* exciting news.'

Let me tell you something else about my sister. She's completely manic. Not manic in a sectionable sense, of course, but nevertheless fairly exhausting to be around at times. Fortunately, she had had the good sense to marry someone quiet and sensible and generally sane. Though I have to say Ben, who is a doctor, has been

43

seeing a psychotherapist called Mrs MacDougall on a monthly basis for the last nine years. No secret. He's fairly evangelical about her. He started seeing her when Simeon's (complicated, premature) birth had the misfortune to occur on the same day as the clinical section of his FRCS part two examination – which he then failed, and had to retake, and ever since, it was like, Baby! Uuurgh! Exam horror! Help! and so on. A classic negative-association situation. That was the problem he started with anyway. Now I think she's just an all-purpose de-stressing tool. Wish I had a Mrs MacDougall right now.

'Well?' I asked.

'Bingo! We're in!' Del said gleefully.

'In? In where?'

'Well, it's not a one hundred per cent cast-iron certainty in, but almost. And we will be, won't we? How could we not be? Tra-la! Isn't that exciting?'

I sat down on one of the kitchen chairs. There was a pile of still-warm Welsh cakes on the table, and the smell of something wholesome and life-affirming coming from the oven. And I was a bag.

'In where?' I repeated.

She tsked. '*Roomaround*, of course! Look! Here's the letter!'

I took it. Noted the swish TV production-company logo. Oh, God. Of *course*. Oh dear.

'But I thought we decided we weren't going to bother?'

Del sat down beside me, picked up a Welsh cake, took a bite and shook her head. 'No, no,' she corrected me, swallowing. 'We didn't decide that. We decided that there probably wasn't much chance we'd get *on* it, I'll grant you, but that it was still worth a try. You remember.'

I didn't remember it like this at all, but I also knew there was really no point in arguing about it.

'But that was last *year*.'

'I know. Isn't it a lovely surprise? Look.' She took the letter back from me. 'Someone's pulled out, and, as you know, we've been on the reserve list.' I knew no such thing. As *she* well knew. 'We have to call now and confirm that we still want to go ahead, and to arrange for them to come down and check us out. It's all a bit short notice, I know, but are you still up for me doing your living room?'

'Oh, God, I don't know, Del. You're right. It *is* all a bit – ah! There's a thought. We can't do it, can we? What about the couples thing? There had to be the four of us, didn't there? And there's not, now, is there? No Mark any more.'

I'd been seeing Mark for much of the preceding year. He was a teacher too (we'd both taught at the same school), long divorced, and had been sweet, kind and amiable. Sadly, if predictably, we'd fizzled out fairly rapidly after my father had died; when it had become clear that what I now wanted from life (complete career rethink, creative nirvana, to embrace the lost opportunities of my youth, etc.) no longer dovetailed with what he wanted (caravan in Brittany, Renault Espace). But any relief I might now have felt about this development turning out to be the silver lining in the big swell of cumulus that generally constituted what passed for my love-life, was, it seemed, to be very short-lived.

'No,' Del said slowly, as if I was being really, really thick about this, 'but there is *Stefan*.'

'Stefan!' Had I been eating a Welsh cake too I would have choked on it. 'Stefan! You *have* to be kidding, Del. No.'

'Pah!' she said. 'Don't be such a wet blanket. He won't mind. He's an art tutor, isn't he?'

I didn't pause to consider what these two statements had to do with one another, because I was way too busy trying to imagine the conversation. 'Stefan, I know we've only been seeing each other for a few weeks, but would you have any objection to pretending – to fifteen million plus television viewers – that we are a kutchy, suburban, permanently cohabiting couple so that I can have my through-lounge creatively butchered by my sister while you and I spend a week-end emulsioning her bedroom?' The response 'He will mind' seemed pitifully inadequate.

'He won't even know. Because I'm not about to ask him.'

'Oh, come on, Lu. It'll be a laugh.'

'No, it won't. It'll be the end of a beautiful and very promising relationship. He'd run a mile. No. I'm sorry, Del, but no. It's not fair.'

She got up and put on an oven glove. A bad sign. She was obviously regrouping for a lateral attack.

'Look,' I continued, 'it's not that I wouldn't like to do it,' which wasn't strictly true: it suddenly seemed not half so much of a good idea as it had seemed when I first considered it, and I was pretty reluctant even then, 'it's just that I know how it would seem. Quite apart from the fact that he'll think it's stupid, he'll also think I'm trying to pin him down. Monopolize him. Snare him. You know? It's difficult enough, what with . . .' I was forming the words 'me having Leo' but, thankfully, they stuck in my throat. I could not, *would* not, go through life apologizing for my son's presence in the world. I started again. 'What I mean is, well, I'm treading carefully. I don't want to push things along too fast. I'm—'

'You should stop doing that. It's a bad habit,' she said obscurely, waving the glove at me. She pulled open the oven door and her glasses misted up.

'Doing what?'

'Treading carefully.' She mimed it while she wiped them.

'I don't mean I'm—'

'Yes, you do,' she said. 'You *always* do with boy-friends. As soon as you find one you go completely ga-ga over them and become a complete wimp. You should be more assertive. Do what *you* want to do. Be the person *you* want to be. *Be* a bag, if you feel like it. You managed it just fine today with your boss.'

Nice regroup, Del. A full-frontal on me. And an accurate one. She started to smile, but she could see from my expression that today it wasn't going to win any friends and it certainly wasn't going to influence any people. Least of all me.

'Thanks very much. And where does being a bag fit into all this? We're talking about me terrifying a guy I've barely got to know by asking him to play house with me – not having a row about who's going to pay a restaurant bill or something!'

She slammed the oven door on whatever she'd been prodding. 'I know. I know. But come on, Lu. You're going out with him this evening, aren't you? Couldn't you at least ask him?'

'No! Couldn't you just find someone else to do it with? I mean, surely one of your friends would be up for it.' I said this without much conviction. I was quite sure the only reason she had asked me in the first place was because none of them would do anything so rash.

She shook her head. 'Jules *was* pretty interested in the first place, as it happens, but Richard wouldn't hear of it. Anyway, he's working in Germany at the moment, and she's all over the place with her job, so I didn't ask her. I did think we could maybe get Ben's mum to come and stay. Pretend she lived with you. That would certainly count, but—'

'Oh, come *on*. She's eighty!'

She grinned. 'But I knew you wouldn't go for it. So go on. *Pleeease*. At least *ask* him. OK?'

'OK. I'll think about it.'

She pressed the letter into my hand. 'Promise?'

What a bloody day.

I am a bag. I am a spiky bag. And, God, I feel like one right now.

When I get home the telephone is ringing. It is my sometime babysitter, Emma, to tell me she can't sit for me after all. Great. As Emma's mother is the Julia in question, I am tempted to ask her to come to the phone and to offer her an obscene amount of cash to stand in on *Roomaround* for me. But that is the reason Emma can't sit anyway. She has to babysit her brother because her mum has had to go out. Lucky, lucky her.

Bag. Spiky bag. Dateless spiky bag. Great.

But not dateless, at least, as it turned out. When I called Stefan to tell him I was stuck without a sitter he merrily suggested that he'd cycle up to my place instead. Which was both good, but not so good. Good because it meant I'd be seeing him. But not so good in that the couple of hours I'd anticipated spending removing my entire epidermis with a loofah and slathering myself in exotic unguents, I had to spend washing up, dusting, and hoovering the lounge. Not to mention having to bribe Leo to go to bed early enough that there was a half-chance he'd be asleep by the time our little tryst was due for kick-off. Mr Pokémon, I thought, as I came back downstairs, must truly be raking it in.

But it will, I am quite sure, be worth it.

'I'm so sorry to drag you all the way up here,' I say, as I usher him over the doorstep.

'No, no,' he says, blue eyes all a-twinkle and shining. 'This is just fine. Better, even.'

Stefan, who has arrived at my house bearing a large pad of cartridge paper in a Sainsbury's carrier, pulls his arms from the sleeves of his prehistoric tan leather jacket, and hands me a bottle of wine. His hair is hanging loose, and he's a little red in the face. It's a long, long cycle from Canton to Cefn Melin, and most of it is uphill. Still, I quip, at least it will be an easy ride home.

He smiles in such a way as to make it clear that gradient simply isn't an issue for him, and follows me into the lounge.

Del thinks I'm lucky, of course. Del thinks that because I am single and over twenty-one and am not generally considered grotesque by the opposite sex that I have ready access to the sort of wild and wacky sexual adventures that she likes to read about in *Chat*. And furthermore, that I, were I given the opportunity, would take full advantage of my non-married status and shag every buck who happens along.

But it isn't like that. Really it isn't. For starters, I have a child to consider. For the main course, I hardly ever meet any anyway. And for pudding, I have to live with a chronic feeling of sexual anxiety, which reasserts itself with an ever-increasing intensity every time there is somebody new in my life. Not that there have been many. The words 'toddler' and 'torrid' don't sit well together, and though life's long since been no longer nappy- and sick-based, it's still essentially *child*-based.

And this is still my child's home. Which does rather muddy the water somewhat, if I dip into the pool of available men.

And I have never been very good with men anyway. I don't know why. But I just don't seem to be able to get the hang of it.

Actually, scrub that. Why do I think all these things? It just makes me sound like a complete divvy. Which I am most emphatically not. It's just that relationships – oh, I don't know – never seem to pan out, you know?

Anyway, the point is that here I am, half-way to seventy, and I'm all in a flap because a man's in my house. What to wear, what to say, what impression to aim for, whether even, for God's sake, to put the bloody light on or not. Oh, I wish we were at his place. I can't relax here. I feel judged and uncomfortable. Way too exposed.

I am all in a flap, *period*. Del is right, I have gone ga-ga. Just looking at him makes me all gooey. He loops a skein of gold behind his ear and casts an eye over his surroundings. The neatly plumped cushions, the implausibly full fruit bowl and the little dish of Scents of the Sea pot-pourri.

And looks amused. 'Wow,' he says, sprawling himself across my Debenham's sofa. 'Do you clean houses for a living, Lu, or is this just your fetish?'

Which makes me feel awful. And, yes, I'm sure I'd feel like that sitting in my living room if I were him. Not just because he's so heart-stoppingly handsome, but because he's a hedonistic, unstructured, painty sort of person. There is turps in his hair and dried gouache on his denim. I undo the clasp that is holding my hair back and try to pretend I am too.

'Some wine?' I suggest, while he fingers the apples.

'Not for me,' he says. 'That's for you. I'll have some water. D'you have bottled?'

Of course not.

'I think so,' I say gaily. 'I'll just go and see.'

Even though I have not the slightest intention of mentioning it to him, the *Roomaround* question manages to broach itself, because as I turn to go into the kitchen for our drinks, he springs up from the sofa and follows me there. I open a couple of cupboards to make it look like I generally have a stash of Evian about the place, and when I turn to announce that I haven't, he is standing against the washing-machine, reading the TV company's letter, which he has pulled from the board on the wall by the door. He nods at it. ' "Dates for filming," ' he reads out. 'Hmm. Who's the TV star, then?'

'Oh, that's nothing,' I say. 'Just my sister, that's all. She's hoping to go on *Roomaround*.' There. Done. Mission *sort* of accomplished. I open the wine. 'Shall we go back in the lounge?'

'*Roomaround?*' He looks at the letter again. 'I don't think I'm with you.'

'Oh, you know,' I say, herding him back into the hallway. My eyes have alighted on a pair of my pop-socks that must have dropped from the washing when I brought it downstairs. 'The makeover programme on TV. The one where people do up a room for each other. You must have seen it. It's very popular.'

He knits his eyebrows. Perhaps he doesn't have a telly. But then he nods. 'Oh, yes,' he says, sitting back down on the sofa. 'I do know the programme you mean.' He shakes his head as if marvelling at the unbelievability that people actually do that sort of thing for fun. 'Mad,' he says. 'With that designer – what's her name? With the diamanté toolbelt.'

I shrug. 'Africa O'Brien, you mean?'

'No, no. She's the presenter, isn't she? No. The other one.'

'I don't know. I don't watch it that often. It's Del who likes it. Anyway, water all right?'

He puts the letter on the coffee table and stretches out his legs. 'Come and sit by me,' he says.

Which I do, of course, because I am powerless to resist him, but within moments, he's bounded off again. Into the hall this time, to retrieve his paper. He wrestles the pad and half a dozen pencils from the bag, which he folds up and puts on the floor. Then he moves across the room and sits in the armchair instead. 'I thought I might make some sketches of you,' he says, folding the cover back, and skimming through a number of leaves.

'Oh, right,' I say, putting my glass on the coffee table. I feel vaguely embarrassed. 'If you like.'

'Only I've been itching to draw you. You've got a beautiful face and a wonderful body. Very sinuous.' Hmmm. 'Very fluid.' He tests the tip of a pencil. 'Lean back, will you? Loop your arm over the back of the sofa. That's it. And pull your right knee up a bit. *That*'s it. Now turn your body slightly and lean forward a little so your breasts – that's the way. Perfect. Stay exactly like that. *Per*fect.'

I don't think I've had anyone sketch me since we were paired up for an art class when I was about fourteen with instructions to draw each other's faces. On that occasion, I ended up with a girl whom I'd narrowly beaten to the affections of some boy or other, and she'd felt it fair recompense to make the most of the opportunity to highlight every zit on my face. I'd been so distressed that I'd gone home that night and attacked them all with the point of my compass. It

52

was a scarring experience. I looked like a celeriac for weeks.

But this one is a delight. In no more than ten minutes he is back beside me on the sofa and I'm looking at a simple but oh-so-good likeness of myself. The kink in my nose. The way that my hair, which is heavy and wavy, hangs in a scythe shape down one side of my face. My eyes are smiling back at me. I *almost* look pretty.

'Oh, that's lovely, Stefan! Really lovely. Can I keep it?'

He clutches it to his chest. 'Absolutely not!' he exclaims. 'I never give away my sketches.' He lifts his pencil and waggles it at me. 'And neither should you.'

'Oh, I don't,' I say. 'I keep them all tucked up, out of sight, in the loft.'

'Nothing here, then?' He glances around him.

'In my own house? God, no!'

He grins, then leans across and kisses me, lovingly. 'Shall I do another?' he says.

He does five in the end, all posed slightly differently, and I find myself pleased beyond measure that we didn't go out after all. Not to mention pleased that he didn't warm to my original suggestion that I cook him dinner. This is much more fun. I feel like a fashion model. He's still insistent that he's not going to let me get my hands on any of them, but I don't mind. 'Though I'm perfectly happy,' he says, finally returning to his place on the sofa, 'to let you get your hands on me instead.'

Which kind of comment would normally have me twitching and palpitating and getting in a dither, but from him it seems absolutely the right thing to say. He is so very lovely, and so very clever. And so very at home in his beautiful skin.

And mine, too, it would appear. He takes a mouthful of his water and snuggles up beside me. 'Mmm,' he says languidly. 'There's a gap just here. Between your T-shirt and the top of your jeans. Your back's very brown.' He slides his hand along it. His fingers are cold, from the glass, and slightly rough against my skin.

'It's genetic. My mother's side.'

His other hand glides over the top of my head and makes its way down my hair to join its partner, pulling me in towards him. 'Dark skin. Dark eyes. Yet so fair.' He means mouse. 'A fair maiden, indeed.' He kisses me again. This time arching my back a little and easing me downwards. Oh, lummy, I can't breathe for gasping. He takes one hand away. I feel plumped, like my cushions. Then he re-sites it on my breast.

'I don't know about maiden,' I quip, conscious of his quickening breathing and that he already seems to have undone my bra. From the outside. 'I think maiden might be stretching the point just a little . . .'

I tail off here, because Stefan lifts his finger to his lips, then promptly proceeds to undress.

He has only taken off his shirt and, yes, there is a T-shirt underneath it, but it's the deft way he flicks undone the rivet on his jeans that has prudence prevail over lust. I sit up.

'Stefan, I don't think – I'm not sure if it's a good idea to take our clothes off . . .' I roll my eyes and nod towards the stairs.

'Oh,' he says. 'Oh, yes. Right.' He resumes kissing me, we resume our position, and his hands resume their ever more adventurous forays. But within seconds I become aware of some feverish scrabbling in the lower torso region, and this time my own jeans seem to be involved. I disconnect my lips from his.

'Stefan,' I whisper. 'We can't do this. Not here.'

His lips are on mine again. 'Where, then?' he mouths.

Oh dear. 'We can't. Not now.'

'Not *now*?' He pulls his head back. 'You're kidding.'

I blink at him. 'I'm not.'

He looks at me carefully. 'No, Lu. You're not, are you?'

So we have a cup of coffee instead. The hair on Stefan's brow is damp and clinging to his forehead, a little as it had when he arrived here tonight. It's not quite eleven but he has a long way to cycle, and I'm almost glad when he says he'd better push off home. Too much temptation. Too much heat for one night.

'I'm sorry,' I say, 'but you know how it is.'

'So am I,' he agrees, pulling me towards him on the doorstep and kissing me again. 'You may be fair, my lovely lady, but you are very wicked as well. I shall prevail, though. You know that, Lu, don't you? Do you have plans for Saturday?' I shake my head.

'Good,' he says, putting on his jacket. 'You do now.'

I watch him walk round to his bike, feeling tingly and excited in a way that I haven't in a long time. He lashes his pad carefully to the little rack on the back, then gets astride it and turns it round. As he switches his light on, he turns back towards me.

'Just remembered,' he calls out. 'Tia Slater.'

'Pardon?'

'*Roomaround*. I've just remembered what her name is. Tia Slater. The one with the toolbelt. So long.'

5

'SMBC.'

'Pardon me?'

'SMBC. Single Mother By Choice. I've just been reading this article in *The Times*, and I saved it for you. You're one of a new breed – isn't that nice to know? – of women who have babies in the full and certain knowledge that they are going to be bringing the child up on their own. It's rather good. I thought you'd like it. It's an Americanism,' she adds, by way of some sort of explanation.

It's not even eight yet, but as I talk to Del I can already see sunlight sparkling on chrome and am reminded that there is a car parked outside that must be worth almost as much as I paid for my house. Of course, property prices being what they are in north Cardiff these days, I could now sell my house and buy two of them, but it still looks ridiculous in my little drive, which is essentially two strips of badly laid concrete with a dandelion/ gravel/weed strip in between. Like a big stroppy bullfrog sitting on a cow pat. What a curious, curious turn of events.

'Del,' I correct her, 'I am *not* an SMBC. I am an SMBA. No, tell a lie. I *am* an SMBC but only because

56

the A had already happened and the other choice was to SWAB.'

'SWAB?'

'As you well know. Or NHL.'

'What?'

'Not Have Leo. Which might have been an option, I suppose.' I shudder even to think of it. 'But as I didn't discover that SWAB was what I'd actually be doing until I was four months pregnant, then NHL wasn't really tenable, was it?'

'Yes, but *SWAB*, Lu?'

'Yes, SWAB. And you can add another A. Staying With An Absolute Bastard.'

She laughs. 'You sound a bit twitchy this morning. So. *Roomaround*.' It's obviously going to be hard getting out of this one. 'Come on, then. What did lover-boy say?'

I tell Del I'm still at the sounding-him-out stage, and that when I see him again on Saturday evening, I'll do my very best. Lover-boy, indeed. Oh, what a long way away Saturday suddenly seems.

But at least I don't have to pick up Joe this morning. Which is a plus, because I get to drive all the way to work unencumbered by his scathing instructions, and am free to park by means of a twenty-seven-point turn if I so wish. He has gone by cab. Which is because he went to a seven a.m. breakfast meeting, which is the kind of thing people like him apparently do. When I finally get to the office (via Del's, via another row about the bloody Pokémon cards, via school, via the hateful parking space, via the hike up Queen Street, etc.), it is to find that there is an enormous pink teddy on my desk.

'Oh, there's lovely,' says Iona, coming in with the post. 'It's a boy, of course, but I dare say she won't mind.'

I take this to mean that Lily has had her baby. Which would explain why Emma couldn't babysit last night. Lily's husband, I seem to remember, was banned from the labour ward on account of being as much use in a maternity situation as a round of Spam sandwiches, so Julia was on call for the grisly bits.

'Oh, I thought it was yours,' I say, stroking it absently. I'm busy trying to locate the phone number of Swindon police station, in the interests of fending off imminent parenticide.

'It's mine,' says Joe, coming in. He looks alarmingly pale today, and has managed to get his sling integrated with his tie. Iona, without preamble, takes charge of the knotting, in a manner that leads me to surmise that she might also launder his pants, if required. 'Well, not mine, of course. Can you sort it for me? Get it couriered to the hospital? There's a card there as well somewhere.'

'Oh, don't worry,' says Iona. 'I'm off down there myself at lunchtime. I'll pop it along for you, lovely. Bless.'

After Iona's gone I find there is also a note on my desk. *Do the flowers bit, will you? Oh, and while you're at it, I need some more sent. Jeannine Carver. Address in my diary. Ta.*

Joe's handwriting, like his presence, is tall and a bit too full of itself. Doesn't bother with the tedium of lines and so on. His signature takes up almost half the space on a cheque, even given the in-your-face big fat business ones he favours. There is an address in Cyncoed in the diary, which I recognize, having sent flowers there for him a couple of weeks back.

Quite apart from its near illegibility, the minutiae of Joe's diary has suddenly taken on a disconcerting new significance for me. It tells me that while today I have nothing more taxing than his parts store in Ely to negotiate, Friday involves all sorts of uncharted motoring hazards: an appointment for Joe at the hospital (much traffic, little parking, and, *God*, the new multistorey), a meeting with the Luxotel team at the Royal (Lego-sized car park, sneering valet, low-slung arrangements of pansies in stone troughs) plus a trip to make a site inspection in Newport (enough said). I feel like I've just started driving.

I send a blue-themed silk basket to Lily and Malcolm, and a Cellophaned, raffia-tied hostess bouquet of roses, stalks, twigs, etc., to Jeannine. I don't know who she is, exactly, but as her house is called Cedar Folly and is in such a posh bit of town, it strikes me she's probably the sort of woman who'd not be best pleased with a bunch of pinks. 'Who's Jeannine?' I ask Iona, when she comes in with the franking.

She winks at me as she gathers up the teddy. 'We've not been advised, lovely. Not as yet. Hum-de-hum.'

'His girlfriend?'

She laughs at me. 'One of, no doubt.'

But there is little chance of any romantic assignations for Joe today, because tonight I have to deposit him at his house early. Thursday is his access night and though normally he'd drive out to pick up his daughter from the posh red-brick school she attends just outside Newport, tonight his ex-wife, in what he explains on the way is a worrying display of uncharacteristic niceness, is going to drop her round to him after school instead. We are just cruising along Cyncoed Road, when the worry takes violent, high-volumed voice.

'Shit! Shhhiiiiiitttt! Stop the car! Turn it round!'

I pull in, as one generally does when one's passenger is catatonic and spitting. 'What on *earth* is the matter?'

59

He slams a hand against his forehead. 'Oh, *shit*. Oh, God! No! Not there! Go down Bryn Gwyn Road instead. Next right! Go on! Quick!'

I pull out into the road again and take the next turning, while Joe swivels anxiously to see out of the back.

'Shall I stop now?'

'OK. Here. No, go on round the bend there. By that lamp-post. There. Behind that green MG. That's safer. OK. Now, let's think. Think! Joseph, *think*!'

I bring the car to a stop by the kerb and turn, mystified, towards him. He swipes his good hand across his face again and seems to get himself into some sort of order.

'OK. OK,' he says. Then, 'Mobile. OK.'

'OK?'

A car passes. 'Oh, *God*! No. It's all right. We're OK.' He starts punching out numbers then puts the phone to his ear.

'Yes, it's me,' he says then, in an altogether different voice. 'No. Bit of a logistics crisis. I'm on the way now. Should be . . . um, let's see. Half an hour? No. Say three-quarters . . . Yes, I *know*. But these things happen, OK? . . . No. I have not. Lunch! Huh! *Fat* chance. I barely made the meeting. I sat in X-ray all bloody morning!' There is a silence. 'Well, tell the bloody hospital, then!' And another. 'All right! . . . No. No. Where are you? . . . OK . . . No. Still my place . . . No. Five fifteen's fine . . . No. I haven't . . . No. *No!*'

He puts the phone back in his lap and exhales slowly.

'Um,' I begin, 'is there something I've missed here?'

He shakes his head. 'No. Look. Right. It's all right. They haven't left yet. So, let me see,' he looks at his watch, 'right. Change of plan. We have to go back into town. You can drop me and drive around or something while I'm in there. Yes. That's the best plan. Let's do that.'

'Do *what*, Joe?'

He looks at me as if I'm quite, quite mad. 'What do you think? Go to Toys'R'Us, of course.'

Which is, of course, what we then do.

Along with what appears to be the entire population of ten-year-old boys in Cardiff. There is, it seems, some sort of Pokémon trading session in progress and the whole area is teeming with hot-blooded parents vying for the coach-parking space round the side. Which means that by the time we return to Joe's house, it is ten past six. And there is a lavender hatchback parked outside. Joe says, 'Oh, shit,' again, then instructs me to pull up behind it. The passenger door is already opening and by the time I have turned off the ignition a little girl is running towards us and waving. Joe, grunting slightly, swings his legs round and gets out, his expression now softened by a smile. I get out as well.

'Daddy, Daddy, Daddy!'

'Hello, chicken,' he calls. A woman is emerging from the car also. She has Disneyland hair the colour of red pesto, long slender legs and, as near as can be achieved when your features are classic and chiselled and contoured and perfect, a face like a smacked arse.

While Joe attempts a touching air of paternal jollity and bends down to submit to a close inspection of his stitches, the woman glides down the pavement and glares at him.

'You said *five* fifteen,' she says, glancing briefly in my direction. I'm not quite sure what my part in this cheery family tableau is supposed to be, so I walk round to the back of the car and begin pulling packages from the boot.

The little girl, who is really quite striking, with her mother's hair but the same liquid green eyes as her father, pokes him on the shoulder. 'Yes,' she trills. 'You're late. Naughty Daddy.'

'*Very* late,' agrees her mother, then hisses, 'I was just about to ring you. But, then, I presume you think I have nothing better to do than hang around waiting till you deign to show up.' And adds, 'Which would figure, of course.'

Therein hangs a tale or two, I suspect.

Joe straightens then nods in my direction and tuts. *Tuts?* 'Just can't get the staff!' he quips. He is attempting, I assume, to lighten a situation the dynamics of which are writ plain as the microfine ivory residue on his ex-wife's stony face. She looks as unimpressed as I feel. We exchange a look of our own. Joe fails to see it.

'Angharad, this is my assistant,' he continues, 'while Lily's away having her baby. Her name's Lu. Say hello.'

The little girl looks at me warily.

I look pointedly at Joe, before gushing dutifully at her. 'Hi,' I say. 'I'm terribly sorry we're late, Angharad. I had to wrap all your presents up because your daddy can't manage at the moment.' I gesture towards his plaster.

'Yes, and then she went and left them in the office!' adds Joe brightly. Oh, I *see*. I return his conspiratorial wink with a glare.

Angharad nods. 'Oh. Right,' she says.

'Oh, *ri-ight*,' echoes her mother, swinging her key fob.

Angharad gives the parcel in her hand a good

shaking then begins jumping up and down a mite more enthusiastically than the situation strictly calls for, as if this is the role she knows she must play on her birthday, lest her parents descend into squabbles and sulks. 'Presents, presents, presents!' she whoops, as the pile grows on the pavement.

'Hmmm,' says the woman, glancing at me then batting the key fob in the direction of Joe's arm. She lowers her voice. 'And how is she going to get home? I suppose you think I'm going to come out and pick her up again, do you?'

Joe moves himself a little way down the pavement towards her, and the smile leaves his face altogether. 'Unless you expect me to walk her home, I do.'

'Well, I can't. So you'll have to come in a cab with her, won't you? Nine thirty. No later.'

Then she dips to put a kiss on the top of Angharad's head, nods at me briefly and is off up the road.

'So what did you get?'

Del plops herself down beside me at her kitchen table. I can spy a pile of paint-colour cards on the dresser, but the promise of a little light marital discord has diverted her from her *Roomaround* fixation.

'Barbie's Bejewelled Mystical Castle, Barbie's Bike, Barbie's Body Painting Kit, Happening Hair Barbie and Barbie's Four By Four-cum-Surfing Dude's Beach Buggy. Or something. Oh, and Daisy the Horse That Really Eats.'

'Is that what girls go for these days, then?'

'How should I know? I don't do girls, do I? I only know that there wasn't much change out of three hundred pounds.'

'What's new? Pretty much anything desirable toy-wise these days costs three hundred pounds.' She ticks

63

them on her fingers. 'Playstation Two, DVD player, stunt bike. So, did you make it?'

'Barely.' I outlined the Poké-fest details. 'And, of course, we had to stop on the way so I could wrap them all up for him.'

'Poor love.'

'Poor love nothing, Del! Look at the time! And I haven't even been to Sainsbury's yet! I mean, how *could* he? How could he forget his own daughter's birthday? It's not like he's got dozens of them or anything.' Though who knows? He might well have. 'Poor thing. She must have known something was up – her mother certainly did – and even if she didn't it's a pretty poor show.'

'Ah! You met the redoubtable Rhiannon, then?'

'Briefly. They were already there when we pulled up. Joe made out it was my fault, of course, which I thought was pretty bloody cheeky. That he'd given them to me yesterday and that I'd left them in the office. The nerve of the man! I ended up going along with it, of course. How could I not? The poor little girl must have felt like she was in the middle of Beirut. But she's not stupid. And neither is his ex-wife. She knew very well.'

'And probably enjoyed it.'

'I don't doubt it. There doesn't seem to be much love lost between them. And I'm not in the least surprised. It's amazing, isn't it? I mean he manages to go into Toys'R'Us this very morning and get a teddy bear for Lily's baby – a pink one, mind you, even though it's a boy – *and* to whiz some flowers round to some woman or other, yet he completely fails to remember his own daughter's birthday. It's a bit sad, isn't it?'

'Sounds fairly typical to me.'

'Hmmmph. I don't doubt that either.'

'No, darling. Not of Joe particularly. Of men. Period. You do have ridiculously high expectations of them, Lu. It's no wonder you've always had such a job finding one.'

Oh, but Del is so, so wrong. When Leo and I get home there is a bunch of flowers propped against the front door. Makes the place look a little like someone was killed there recently and, admittedly, they are a little limp and listless, but they are for me. And they are from Stefan. Five stems of iris in the most exquisite shade of blue. And there's a message, scribbled on the flowershop paper. It reads: 'Off up a mountain – sorry to have missed you. Saturday can't come too soon! S XX.'

'Yukky yukky yuk yuk!' says Leo, reading it out to me. 'Spew-ee! Is this the man who came round on that sad bike last night?'

'Leo!' I chide, plucking the flowers from his fingers. 'Don't be so rude. They're lovely!'

He follows me into the hall and dumps his bag at the foot of the stairs. 'They're nearly dead. And they smell.'

'They smell *lovely*,' I trill, shoving my face in them enthusiastically. Oh, I'm *so* cheered up. 'Anyway, that's not the point, Leo. It's the thought that counts.'

He pulls a face as he takes off his jacket. 'Well he can't think much of you, then, can he?'

'Oh, ha ha.'

'Are you in love with him, Mum?'

I pause. My little boy is suddenly braced for my answer, and I find myself wondering quite why it is that it hasn't yet occurred to me that he might even *care*.

I'm all out of practice with this stuff. So's he. I ruffle

his hair and poke him playfully. 'Goodness me, no!' I say lightly. 'He's just a good friend, Leo. Someone a bit special. But no love stuff, OK?'

He grins his little grin, and looks again at the flowers. 'Yeah, right, Mum,' he says. 'Just checking.'

6

Friday 27 April

It was raining this morning, so the journey to work added a whole new dimension to the Greek tragedy that was beginning to constitute my relationship with the terrifying car. As with everything else that sprouted from its preposterous dashboard, there seemed to be no end to the options available to the knob-wise driver with a dirty windscreen on their minds. Had it actually been raining with any degree of effort it would have been simple. I had already spent much of the preceding two days getting to know my speedwipe facility: it came into play every time I tried to use the indicators. Today's conditions, however, were falling over themselves to be as difficult and obstreperous as possible. There was just enough wet stuff coming out of the sky to ensure that all the filthy stuff that was lying in the road was liquidized, emulsified, and rerouted to my windscreen, where my speed-wipe facility smeared it obligingly around. And I could not seem to find out where the wash-wipe knob was.

But it was, at least, a learning experience. By the time I reached Joe's house, I had not only established the whereabouts of most of the vast range of wet-weather facilities on offer, but had also discovered that at a constant 42.7 miles per hour I had sufficient fuel on board to make a bolt for Swansea instead.

'Hrrmmmph. So, what's all this arts and crafts stuff about, then?'

It's a little after eleven and we are now on our way to Joe's *real* appointment at the hospital. Such a strange way to be spending the day. Drive to work, start work, stop work, drive somewhere else, hang around, drive back to the office, start work again, stop it again – it's like I can never get to grips with anything useful. Arts and crafts, indeed. This, I assume, is his attempt at chirpy, conciliatory conversation, in the aftermath of our terse exchange earlier about whether ex-wifely placation was really part of my job spec. I negotiate the junction before answering, levelly, 'It's not arts and crafts. It's just art. What about it?'

He reaches out his right arm and makes a grab for the door handle as I turn the next corner. Which, given why the other arm is in a foot and a half of plaster, is just so bloody rich.

'Nothing. I just wondered what it was all about. You know. The night school. The college stuff.'

I am not altogether sure I like the direction in which this conversation is going, and it hasn't even really got going yet. Stuff, indeed.

'What, my *degree*, you mean?'

He raises an eyebrow. 'Is that what you're doing, then?'

'No. Not at the moment. *Obviously*. I'm hoping to start an access course in October.'

'Why?'

'Why October?'

'No. Why an access course?'

'Because I have to complete one – put together a portfolio – before they'll accept me for a degree.'

'Hmmph,' he said. 'Sounds rather peculiar. Anyway, why the degree?'

God! Why do people always *ask* that? Why does it strike people as being such an oddity? You have sixth-formers signing up for master of bloody arts in how to make things out of egg boxes and I get all this grief! We wait at the pedestrian lights for some seconds during which I think grouchy thoughts and a lady with a tartan shopping trolley makes her tortuous way through the by now sheeting (and finally speed-wipeable) grey rain.

'Because I wanted to,' I say, finally. 'I've always wanted to study art. I want . . .' To-be-an-artist. Oh, come *on*.

But I don't have to add anything anyway because he says, 'Yes, I realize *that*. But to what end?'

'Does there have to be an *end*?'

'Well, a point, at least. What's yours? Can't you just paint in your spare time?'

He sounds so reasonable and unruffled that I just know he finds the idea deeply, deeply irritating. I am, I realize, learning fast where he's concerned.

'Because,' I say, patiently, 'I would like to spend three years of my life doing something simply because it is what *I* want to do. So that is what I'm *going* to do. Do you have a problem with that?'

'Not in the least,' he replies mildly. 'It just seems a rather strange thing for someone your age to be doing.'

'I don't see what age has to do with it.'

He ignores this, and grunts as he reaches to flip down the indicator for me. I am going to have to say something about this. I am.

I do.

'Look, this is a dedicated left-turn lane. See? It is therefore not necessary for me to—'

'That's not the point. It's sloppy driving. Always indicate your intention.'

'My intention is perfectly obvious.'

'Not necessarily. You—'

'I am turning *left* at a *left*-hand filter. And,' I check, 'there is no one behind me.'

'That's not the point.'

'Oh, for God's sake!'

He hrruumphs again. 'So what's the night school all about, then?'

I turn left. 'Exactly that. Night school.'

'Learning what?'

'About *art*.'

The indicator stalk flips back. He glances at it. 'But this isn't part of your access course, right?'

'No. It's an interim thing. A one-year course on the impressionists. I'm just doing it as background before I start the access course.'

'A sort of *pre*-pre-course course, then. Uh-huh.'

Put like that, it *does* sound faintly ludicrous. Bah!

'Uh-huh what?' I snap. 'What exactly is wrong with that? Besides, I don't *have* to do it. I'm just doing it because—'

'I know. Because you *want* to.' We join the queue for the multi-storey car-park. The space between the ticket machines looks ridiculously small.

'Uh-huh,' he says, again, nodding.

I turn. 'Uh-bloody-huh what now?'

He shrugs his shoulders. 'Nice life. That's all.'

Because there is really nothing useful I can do while Joe is seeing the consultant, bar driving back into town and reversing into the hateful parking space just in time to have to drive straight back out of it again, I have nothing to occupy me for the next hour or so, apart from being very cross about being told what a nice life I have. (Hey, yeah, right.) Or hanging around the newly refurbished hospital village area catching up with what's hot in the League of Friends shop. Or eating an Eccles cake. Or getting embroiled in a conversation about the female preoccupation with self-justification and its role in the continued repression of women and so on with a complete stranger. Who will doubtless have some grisly communicable disease. But waiting is obviously going to be a feature of my life for the next few weeks so I must remember to plan for it. Next time I will bring a banana, a novel, a sketchpad and pencils, and make like the self-absorbed arty-farty prima-donna he's obviously decided I am.

'Jesus, this hospital's like a bloody Bulgarian airport,' Joe observes.

Here, I assume he speaks from experience. I know from the paperwork that JDL boilers have infiltrated much of the eastern bloc.

'I would have thought someone in your position would have private medical insurance,' I say, a touch tartly, as I scuttle behind him through the shifting throng.

He shoots me a look. 'Oh, I do. But regrettably the bloody king's ransom I pay for it doesn't stretch sufficiently to equip the private hospital with anything as wildly extravagant as an MRI scanner on site when you want one. Theirs is apparently "on tour" at the moment. Abergavenny or somewhere.'

He returns an hour and a half later with a large buff envelope, which I assume holds his scan. He flaps it at me. 'Come on, then. Get up. Let's get going,' he orders. I dutifully gather up my bag and magazine. Then leave the latter behind. There is nothing in *Red* that the likes

71

of me can afford, and the recipes all involve the sort of ingredients you have to live near Harrods to get.

'So, what's the verdict?' I ask him.

'Don't ask.'

'Why not?'

'Grrr.'

'Something bad?'

'Bloody typical.' He starts striding towards the exit. People, I notice, step aside as he passes. It might be the scar but I suspect they'd do it anyway. 'They're not sure the bone is setting properly,' he expands. 'And there's a bit of debris floating around in my elbow that they're worried about.'

'Oh dear.'

'Quite. They're going to give it another week then do another scan. If there's no improvement I'm going to have to come in and have an operation to fix it. And there *won't* be any improvement, of course, because it's always Sod's bloody Law where I'm concerned and I'm sure this will be no different. *And* I've got to come in again on Tuesday to have these bloody stitches out. At eleven bloody thirty again. As if I've nothing better to do. What a bloody shambles. What a bloody – this way?'

I almost feel sorry for him. Almost, but not quite. 'No. That's Maternity.' I point out the car-park. 'Oh dear,' I say again. 'Presumably that will mean you'll be in plaster for longer than you thought.'

'Precisely.'

'Oh dear.'

'Stop saying "oh dear", will you?'

He's walking at such speed that I have to make little skipping movements to keep up with him.

'Sorry. I only—'

'Well, do me a favour, will you, Lu? Don't.'

'Well,' says Iona, when we return to the office – and presumably having read my scowl as a look of anxious concern. 'That's a bit of a blow, isn't it? But never mind, dear, we'll look after you, won't we, Lu?' Will we? 'By the way, Joe, the police called earlier. You have to phone them back as soon as possible apparently. A very nice chap. A Constable Evans. Here's his number.' She hands him a small piece of paper.

Which he takes. 'Nice bloody nothing,' he growls.

The car situation is beginning to look grave. Grave as in that looks like where my precious MG is headed, and grave as in if the woman in the Mondeo has made a statement to the effect that Joe was definitely speeding and that neither car would have been involved in the accident had he not been, the police might take the view that he bears some responsibility. Hmmm.

Not that it makes any difference to me. I had one MG. I will have another MG. The only factor of any consequence here is who precisely is going to be paying for it, the guy with the artic or Joe's unfortunate insurers.

'Oh, no. Not mine,' he explains, as we head back out of the office to the Royal Hotel, which is just round the corner, and where we are to meet with three visiting Luxotel men. 'In theory, it should be completely straightforward. The driver of the artic *was* the one who caused the accident so, according to this Evans chap, *his* insurers should be the ones to cough up.'

I hitch up my skirt a touch, as it is straight and tight, and has not been designed to accommodate the four-foot stride span that is my only recourse if I want to keep up with him without looking like a stressed geisha. 'But supposing the police agree with the woman

in the Mondeo that the damage to your car – *my* car –
was partly your fault?'

He stabs at the button at the traffic lights. Twice.
'They won't.'

'But what if they *do*?'

And a third time. 'Then the insurers on the artic
won't pay out.' He is speaking, for some reason, in an
exasperated tone, as if in response to the questioning of
a small, irritating child.

'Anyway,' I press on, 'it shouldn't make any difference in any case, should it? Because you're covered
anyway. I mean, you'd lose your no-claims bonus, of
course, but I presume you've got one of those policies
that—'

'Hmm,' he says, nudging me out on to the crossing.
The road is clear our way but the little man is still red.
'Not *exactly*.'

'Why not? You've got fully comprehensive insurance,
haven't you? You said you had.' I look at him pointedly. 'You told *me* you had.'

We fetch up at the centre island and he incorporates
a nod into the wave-and-scowl-based traffic-manage-
ment routine that he clearly favours, and which has
been successful in arresting the progress of an on-
coming van – if not the progress of the driver's two
fingers, which are rammed up against his windscreen.
'I do,' he confirms. 'Except when – well, except when
I'm driving someone else's car, apparently.'

'*What?*'

'That's what *I* said. But it seems I was only covered
third party. You only have comprehensive cover if
you're on the owner's policy as a named driver.'

I experience a chilling moment of total recall at this
point. 'Which you weren't. Which you weren't because
you told me you didn't need to be. Because you told *me*

74

that you were insured to drive anything! And you weren't! And—'

'Tsk! Watch that cyclist, Lu, will you?'

I swerve and hobble up on to the opposite pavement. 'Pah! I *knew* I shouldn't have listened to you! I knew it! One phone call! One phone call and all this would have been sorted out. One phone call and it would have been fine! Instead of which, now you don't even know if you're covered at all! God, I can't believe I let you borrow it. I cannot believe I've been so stupid!'

'Look, it's not a problem, OK? You will get your car back – well, another one just like it, though why you'd want another one just like it is quite beyond me – but, anyway, like I said, it's not a problem.'

'Not a problem? Not a *problem*? You're just going to walk into a showroom and buy me a new one, are you?'

He trawls a hand through his hair and steers me through the troughs of mixed bedding that ring the Royal's car-park. 'If needs be. Yes. Of course I will.'

'But even so—'

He holds the lobby door open for me. 'But even so nothing. You'll get your car, Lu. OK?'

Oh, I *see*.

And too bloody right. I *will* get my car. But even so, it was a stupid, senseless, ridiculous thing to have done. Doesn't matter how rich Mr Joe De bloody laney is, it's scandalous to think that he's just going to have to walk into a car showroom and cough up nine thousand pounds for a car. Stupid man.

The hotel lobby is vast, chilly and quietly un-welcoming. We thread past the massed monster holdalls of what I assume is a visiting antipodean ice-hockey team and I wait while Joe makes enquiries of the frosty mannequin at the reception desk. I am not altogether sure why I'm here. I don't doubt that all of these three men are perfectly competent English speakers, or that I will have absolutely nothing in the way of a contribution to make to whatever boiler-related matters they are here to discuss. This, Joe explained on the way, is a meeting to sort out the timescale and schedule for the work he is contracted to do for the Luxotel Group this year. It is, no doubt, a lucrative deal. Luxotel have a hotel in just about every place in France you might wish to fetch up, plus a fair sprinkling around the rest of Europe. Moreover, it seems they are in an acquisitive frame of mind. They are negotiating on five sites alone this month, two of them in the UK. I don't know what the figures are, but there is clearly big money afoot.

Hmm. Which is just as well.

Correction. I *am* altogether sure why I am here. I am here as garnish.

Luxotel's operations director is called Jean Paul Deschamp. He is a tall, stringy man in his forties or fifties, with suspiciously black hair and a mustard linen suit. He looks a bit like a sherbet fountain, and I take an instant dislike to him. It's not something I'm generally given to, but no sooner has Joe made introductions and explained that I speak French than Monsieur Deschamp starts speaking to me in it (very rude – we're in company and, moreover, in Cardiff, not Cannes), and with a content and manner that make it abundantly clear that what he'd most like to do is not thrash out boiler jargon but whip off my blouse and fondle my breasts.

'Look,' I tell Joe, during a lull in which Monsieur Deschamp has gone to take charge of a fax and the other men are engaged in earnest debate about feed vents or zone valves or something, 'wouldn't it be better if I went back to the office and got on with some of the work that's piling up there? It's not as if you need me to drive you back or anything, and you certainly don't need me here to translate.'

He shakes his head. 'I'd rather you stayed,' he says, nodding at the Gallic huddle then winking at me. 'Help oil the wheels and so forth.'

'Oil the wheels *how*, precisely?'

I'm still very angry, and my glance is more pointed, but he either doesn't see it, or chooses to ignore it. The latter, I suspect, because he then says, 'Monsieur Deschamp has suggested that we might adjourn to the restaurant in a while and continue our negotiations over a late lunch. I don't suppose you would care to—'

I shake my head. It is now ten past three. 'You suppose absolutely right.'

'Well, no wonder she bloody left him is all I can say.'

Del, who has been removing the flesh from a cold roast chicken while clucking sympathetically at the many and varied irritations that have punctuated my day, pulls a bone from its bottom and holds it aloft. 'Tsh! Calm down!' she says. 'Make a wish or something.'

I close my eyes and do as instructed: a short but heartfelt one involving Monsieur Deschamp's genitalia and a Magimix. Then say, 'I think I'm going to resign, actually. I really can't see myself driving Joe Delaney around for weeks on end. Can you? He's such a grouch, Del. And we just don't get on.'

'Joe? A grouch? Nonsense! He's lovely!'

'He may be lovely when you run into him at your suburban dinner parties, Del, he may be the dish of the moment wherever he goes – which is all about, according to Iona – but he's not like that at work. Plus he's given up smoking, which makes it doubly bad. Not that I'd know. I suspect he'd be this bad anyway. Look, the bottom line is that he's opinionated and bossy and—'

She clucks. 'Oh, and you *never* are, of course.'

I bristle. 'Not like *he* is, I'm not. And I'm fed up with driving him around.'

'But you *love* driving,' she reminds me. 'And you are driving an XJR, for God's sake. Have you any idea how much that car is worth, Lu? Ben dribbles every time he claps eyes on it.'

'So why doesn't *he* get one, then? He could afford it.'

'Over my dead body. I've got a conservatory planned. Anyway, the point is that it can't possibly be any less tedious than sitting in an office typing up French boiler specifications, can it?' She wipes her hands on a damp J-cloth and puts on the kettle. 'Besides, we're only talking about a few weeks, aren't we? And then you'll get your new car, and then, well, after that it'll only be a couple of months and you'll be off to university to do your access course. It must beat supply teaching, surely?'

I am beginning to wonder if Del hadn't been right all along. That it would have been more sensible simply to continue with the teaching job I had in the first place. This just isn't how I imagined these months would be. I was going to have fun. I was going to work somewhere other than a sprawling comprehensive full of nihilistic juveniles. Spend some time with adults. And not just to squabble over who'd cover who in their non-contact periods. Do lunch in town. Go for drinks after work – on Leo's Tae Kwon Do night, at any rate, I'd figured. But it isn't going to be, is it? It's too late for that. Either I stick with JDL or I have to find another temporary job.

And if I do that, what will happen about my car? And what will happen about *his* car? Especially now it looks like he's going to have to go out and *buy* me a new car. And *when* will he go out and buy me a new car? And what will I do in the meantime? And will he *really* just go out and get me a new one – just like that? I can imagine all the conversations inherent in such a situation and none of them fill me with even a smidgen of confidence. Oh, God, why does life have to be so complicated all of a sudden?

I will worry about it on Monday.

And when I get home, guess what? *More* flowers for me. But this lot – and, oh, yes, *absolutely* to be expected – are from the very same posh florist I was on to yesterday. God, they must be raking it in. These, a confection of lilies and roses and strange hairy seed pods, bear a deckle-edged card with a flowery motif that says: *Sorry for the hassle. Joan.*

7

I was, I presumed, supposed to be impressed. Or, if not impressed, at least mollified a little. Flowers are flowers when all is said and done and, had I not already had the irises from Stefan, perhaps I would have looked upon Joe's overblown offering a little more kindly. But I wasn't and I didn't. Creep. Didn't at all. Not least because he hadn't even bothered to order them himself: he'd obviously called Iona on his mobile after I'd left the hotel and had her phone and do it. *Joan* indeed. And partly because it was a tangible reminder of everything I didn't like about him. His notion that everything woman-related could be solved via forty quid's worth of posh flowers. I pulled out the roses and put the rest in the downstairs toilet. I detest the scent of lilies.

Saturday 28 April

Stefan's flat was on the fourth floor of a crumbling yet rather august Victorian mansion block a short walk from the college. It had big sashed bay windows and a grand pillared entrance, which was flanked by a pair of twiggy, time-expired buddleias. Like much elegant housing that has been purloined by developers and turned into flats, it had the rather sad air of a place

80

gone to seed. But still rather beguiling, in its dignified neglect. Almost as if those who chose to make this place their home were above the garish lure of twentieth-century comforts. On a higher intellectual plane, somehow. I ran my finger down the faded list of names by the doorbells. And there was Llewellyn. I took a breath and pressed.

Stefan, whose one small concession to twentieth-century comforts was a padded saddle on his bike, was wearing a pair of dirty ripped cut-offs and a clean white vest that said *Meat is Murder* on the front. Coils of blond chest hair peeked out of the top, and everywhere, *everywhere*, his sinewy limbs seemed to bulge and contract like beasts held in chains. He took me by the hand and pulled me wordlessly into the hallway, where I half fell over his bike in the gloom. My pulse was going thump, thump, thump in my wrist.

He ushered me into a faintly sweet-smelling room at the front and placed me carefully, as one might a game-show contestant, in front of a very big painting. And then put a finger to his lips and went, 'sssh!'

Obediently, I shushed.

For five whole minutes.

'Hmm,' he said, finally, 'it's way, way from perfect, but I think I have managed to capture the *Zeitgeist*.'

He stepped back a pace and tilted his head to one side. 'Thoughts, then? Impressions? Does it speak to you, Lu?'

We were standing in what I assume Stefan – were he not so endearingly unpretentious – would call his studio. It was large and airy with a floor-boarded floor and a paint-splattered table, and other large canvases ranged around, all facing the walls. And I mean large as in *really* large. As in a good ten times bigger than the diminutive watercolours I crafted so carefully at my kitchen table. Which seemed suddenly insignificant and amateurish by comparison. Not proper art, somehow. The scale here was breathtaking. It put me in mind of a book I'd read to Leo, in which a tiny dragon, not believed in by anyone, eventually grew so large in an effort to get someone's attention that mums, dads, the baker, the milkman, just about everyone, *had* to notice him. Chiefly because he ran off with the house on his back. Was this how art eventually got for people like Stefan? Was sheer scale the barometer of success? Because you really couldn't miss the one in front of us now. It was propped up against two ladder-back chairs, and was the size of a double-bed mattress. It must have used up a hell of a lot of paint. If not a lot of different colours.

'Hmm,' I said, playing for time while I tried desperately to fix my eye upon something identifiable in what seemed, on first inspection, to be nothing more complicated than a pale blue background with a vaguely spherical daub of darker blue paint in the middle. A balloon, perhaps? A puddle? This was simply not fair. I had not expected Pissarro exactly, but how could a man who raved with such fervour about the impressionists do a painting that chiefly consisted of a blue blob? 'Oh dear,' I said. 'I'm not sure I'm the person to be asking, I don't really know a great deal about modern art.'

Stefan drew back his arms and laced his fingers behind his head. 'Mod-*ern* art?' he said, grinning – though, it appeared, a little self-consciously, which helped take the edge off my dismay. 'And what's that when it's at home? *Is* there such a thing?' He dropped his arms again then draped one languidly around my shoulders. 'Look there,' he said, pointing to the (blue) blob in the centre of the (blue) canvas that was marginally darker (blue) than the (blue) area that surrounded it. 'Does that colour,' yep, *blue*, '*really* say "modern" to you? Doesn't it say "depth"? "Weight of repressed humanity" perhaps? "Melancholia"?'

It said blue. Oh dear. Must try to do better. Because he *really wasn't joking*. I tried to remember something of our conversation about colour in class on Tuesday, but all I could think of was how heavy and warm Stefan's arm felt against my neck. Like a python. Like a . . . like a . . . I cleared my throat and tried to think. 'I think . . .' I began '. . . er. It's a beautiful colour. And, er, set against the backdrop of the—'

'Backdrop?' He frowned at this. 'You see that as backdrop?' His arm slipped from my shoulder as he stepped back yet another pace. 'Hmmm,' he said. 'Ye-es. Fair point. Fair point. But do you not get a sense of that area falling away from you somehow?'

He made sweeping movements with his arms to illustrate. I couldn't work out which area was doing the falling exactly, but it seemed that 'falling away' was the impression of choice. So I nodded. 'Oh, *God*, yes,' I enthused dutifully, warming to my task and feeling an increasing (and, all right, almost hysterical) sense of abandon about it. What did it matter what I said? As long as I responded. As long as I – yes! Didn't I read that somewhere? As long as I had a *relationship* with it. I cleared my throat again. It was getting dry from all the intellectual stress. 'Yes,' I repeated. 'When I say "back-drop" I mean as in the sense that, er, space – the universe – is the backdrop to the drama of a black hole. You know? There's that sense, that *obvious* sense, *ob*viously, of the background being deep and impenetrable, and yet the depth of a black hole is – well –' Oh, God. Floundering here a bit. '– well, about as absolute as a falling away can get. You know? Infinite.'

I could hear a fly plopping dolefully back and forth against the window behind us. Perhaps I had enthused too much. It seemed an age before Stefan answered.

'Infinite,' he repeated thoughtfully, pulling out the rubber band that had been holding his hair and sending it skittering across the floor. 'I like that, Lu. I hadn't really thought of it in those terms but I think I can see where you're coming from.'

He *could*? So at least one of us could, at any rate. I turned and nodded, and tried to smile knowingly at him, attempting to convey the impression that where I was coming from was a challenging and mysterious place with a mind of its own and a full set of imaginative and interpretative faculties, rather than where I was actually coming from, which was a place inhabited mainly by butterflies and goose pimples and meringues. He shuffled up close behind me and rested his chin in the crook of my shoulder. Our shadows swayed a little in front of us, deepening the deeper blue and muddying the pale. His hair swung in a fragrant veil against my face.

'You know,' he said, snaking both arms around my midriff, 'I don't know what it is exactly, but there is something in this painting that I find incredibly erotic. Can you sense it? Is it the tonal gradation, perhaps? I wasn't aware of it as I was creating it. But it's there, isn't it? A definite luminosity in the way the blues melt together. Very sensual. Very *organic*. Very *intense*.' He lifted an arm and, collecting one of mine on the way, moved it to draw a slow arc in the air that followed the curve that delineated the central area of colour. 'There,' he said. 'Yes?'

Yes? I tried to get to grips with the intensity of it all,

84

but it was hard. Chiefly because while his breath felt so soft against my cheek, his pelvis felt so hard against my bottom.

'Um. There, you mean? That spot at the edge there? Where all those feathery brush strokes are? Um, well, I—' Oh, God. I couldn't concentrate at *all*.

Sighing, he returned my arm to its original position, tucking his hand underneath my own so that it rested snugly against my ribcage. I could feel a pulse throbbing beneath it. His or mine? It was difficult to tell.

'I'm so glad you like it, Lu. Art – the business of *creating* art – is such a prickly and capricious bedfellow. You struggle to bring something meaningful and valid into being, something that manages both to embody the universal experience and at the same time contribute a unique perceptual energy – you know? But no one ever seems to get the point of anything any more. Not unless you're a Chapman or an Emin – and, frankly, I sometimes wonder if theirs isn't a spurious kind of recognition anyway. But it's *understanding*, isn't it? That's all I really strive for. Commercial recognition would be lovely, of course. Validation would be welcome. But *chiefly* it's understanding I crave. Still,' he moved his head a little so that his cheek brushed mine, 'at least this one has a home now.'

I wondered if he was drunk. And about to present it to me. And how I'd get it in the car. But then he said, 'Exo.'

'Exo?'

I could feel his head nodding against mine.

'The new fitness centre down in the bay?' It rang some sort of bell. Had it been in the papers? 'My friend Lydon,' he went on, 'has designed the interior and he's commissioned some work from me. This study,' he pointed towards it, 'which will hang in the atrium, of

85

course.' It certainly wouldn't work in a chip shop in Splott. 'And a series for the salon and treatment rooms. They've given me a pretty free hand with theme and interpretation, of course, but they're after work that will reflect the post-millennial mindset – you know? So I'm staying largely with the blue end of the spectrum, obviously.' Why obviously? *Why?* 'Lord, I'm warm. Warm and just a little discombobulated. Aren't you? Let me grab us both a drink, yes? Beer OK?'

He released me and, as I turned to face him, looked at me with something almost like shyness, and bent his mouth to my ear. ' "Love me",' he whispered suddenly. '"Not as the girls of heaven love their airy lovers, nor the mermaiden her salty lovers in the sea. Love me",' He paused here and took a breath. ' "And lift your mask".'

My expression must have signalled that I was at a loss to know quite what to make of this, because he then added, 'Dylan, Lu. Right then. Beer.'

Which he then went to get.

He returned a few moments later, carrying a hairy fawn blanket and, as promised, two beers. Kingfisher beer. In bottles that had already coated themselves with a wet dappling of spangly droplets. 'Most thrilling chilled,' the label informed me. I took mine and, at his instruction, sat down on the sofa that was wedged into the bay. It didn't quite fit, and the gap between sofa-back and wall had become home to yet more of his canvases. So many paintings. I wondered what of. I sipped at the beer while he reached out behind me, turned the lock and pushed open the window. A swirl of cool air played on my neck and a penny dropped somewhere, with a clang.

'Dylan *Thomas!*' I announced, feeling rather pleased with myself.

86

His brows lifted in admiration. 'You *do* know it, then!' He swivelled round and sat down beside me, slipping his free hand once again around my shoulder.

'So,' he said, '*your* mask, Lu. Do you feel ready to lift it for me?' He gestured towards the blanket, which he'd dumped on the floor beside us.

I sucked at my beer bottle happily. (It hadn't been the most intractable of puzzles but, nevertheless, I *had* almost said Bob.) I was just about to add that I didn't actually feel I *was* hiding behind one when he said, 'Right. Let's get on, shall we?'

He sprang up and nodded towards the blanket. 'I thought we could have you on this, on the floor in front of the settee – don't worry, it's only old paint splats – maybe semi-reclined. We'll have to see how it works out. Yes? Shall I go and fetch some charcoal and paper while you get undressed? Would that be best for you?'

'*Pardon?*' I said, lowering the bottle from my lips. 'You mean take all my clothes off?'

His face arranged itself into an expression of amused indulgence. He hooked a hank of hair behind his ear. 'Well, of course,' he said reasonably. 'How else can I sketch you?'

Which was, I supposed, a not *un*reasonable point. After all, Botticelli hadn't painted Venus in a tank top. And Renoir's *Nymph* would have looked pretty stupid in a skirt. And, much more to the point, I supposed I *had* come here this evening with a definite clothes-off kind of activity in mind. But take my clothes off *now*? Just like that? Just whip off my knickers and sit on a dog blanket? It wasn't even dark yet. And there weren't any curtains. I processed all these bits of compelling and conflicting data while he looked on with the same indulgent smile.

'Um, yes. I see,' I said finally. 'I suppose – I just hadn't thought . . .'

He leant closer, and took the beer from my grasp. '"Love me",' he whispered again, playing the lip of the bottle against my shoulder with teeny tiny strokes, ' "as loves the mole his darkness. And the timid deer the tigress; hate and fear be your two loves. Love me –" ' his tongue was ferreting about in my ear now ' "– Love me, and lift your mask."'

Bloody hell.

So (fairly inevitably, I guess) we did a bit of kissing and so on, and then he suggested it might be best if he popped off to get some paper and charcoal. He came back in with a roll of what looked like lining paper and an old ice-cream tub.

I had spread the blanket on the floor in front of the sofa, as directed, and had pulled it up so that it covered the front of the sofa as well. Then, feeling just about as stupid and undignified as it was strictly possible to feel when your whole body was throbbing with intense and unbidden sexual expectation (which, as it turned out, didn't feel half as stupid and undignified as I'd thought it would), I had spread myself upon it, lying on my side, with my lower arm bent to support my head. I faffed about with my other limbs for two stressful minutes, before plumping eventually for a knee-over-groin look, plus arm-over-boobs touch and hand on the floor. In this way all that was visible, erotically speaking, were my toenails, which I had painted (oh, happy coincidence!) bright blue. I said nothing. Now arranged and comported, my sexual abandon completely abandoned me – I felt not so much 'timid deer' as 'fat pig on stick'.

Stefan said nothing either. Some way short of nothing, in fact. I had hoped he'd breathe a little more poetry into my ear, but he didn't. In fact he paid me no more attention for the ensuing five minutes than he would have if I'd been an assortment of apples arranged on a table in a Provençal *gîte*. Instead, he busied himself with rummaging in the ice-cream tub, picking out stubs of varying length and thickness and arranging them in a neat row on the table top. Then he went loping off to the corner of the room and pulled out a large piece of hardboard, to which he then attached a length of paper ripped from his roll, using the bulldog that was clipped to the top. Finally he sat down. Then peeled off his vest.

Which, though somewhat startling, was OK by me. Not only because his was a chest of such monumental, tongue-hanging-out, world-beating beauty, but also because it did level the playing-field somewhat. And didn't Mo Mowlam's husband always paint naked? Stefan's torso was lean and quite perfect. Covered in dense curls from navel to neckline that crucifixed outwards across a tawny-gold chest. I lowered my gaze. Wow, I thought. *Wow*.

'Smudges,' he commented, flinging the vest floor-wards. The cut-offs, however, stayed firmly in place.

The silence continued while he made small adjustments to the paper and charcoal, testing the sticks on a scrap of grey card. Embarrassed as I was becoming with this bizarre communication dynamic, I was spared the stressful business of trying to make light conversational parries because he now seemed one step removed from me. As if suddenly inhabiting a private world of his own. I wondered if this was what set real artists apart from pretenders such as myself. This sense of disconnection, of absolute focus. He might have been an actor, reaching inside himself while preparing in the wings. Then he looked at me, with something approaching an ironic expression, and smiled broadly, eyes twinkling. He was so sweet.

'OK?' he said encouragingly. 'Not cold or anything?' He tilted his head. 'Sure you're comfortable like that?'

I wasn't. But the prospect of rearranging any part of my wobbling anatomy was an infinitely less attractive option than blanket-burn and bedsores.

'OK.' I said. Various bits of me were blushing. 'Under the circumstances, anyway.'

He disappeared behind his board for a moment, glanced up and over it, then put it down on the table again.

'Do you mind,' he asked, crossing the room and kneeling beside me, 'if I make a couple of slight adjustments to your pose?'

Oh.

He took my free arm and laid it along the curve of my hip, then gently, wordlessly – as if sculpting spun sugar for a wedding confection – took the weight of my thigh and lifted it upwards and outwards, thus manoeuvring it into the sort of position that would have a gynaecologist poised for approach.

For one pulse of a heartbeat I was stricken with horror, while a light breeze fanned bits for which breezes were rare. Stefan pondered a moment while I studied my kneecap and tried hard to resist the instinct to start up an anxious dialogue with my pelvic floor. Sucking in your stomach was one thing, but . . .

'*There*,' he said, smiling and letting a languid finger trail its way along the inside of my thigh as he stood again. I was tingling from his touch now. 'Better. Much better. Can you hold that, d'you think, Lu?'

I held it. For what seemed like a good half-hour I lay there. Staring into the middle distance while he scratched and scribbled and beavered at his board. I could see nothing below his eye-level, and nothing above his knees. His feet, firm on the floor in a pair of blue flip-flops, looked like the feet of an alabaster god on a plinth. His eyes flicked up and down, back and forth, from side to side. Occasionally a hand would appear above the hardboard, charcoal in fingers, making small measurements, judging. In the distance, a gull, a siren, some laughter, a soporific cocktail of early-evening noise.

Finally he stopped scribbling and sat back, wiping his hands on a bit of rag and pushing the picture away from him. Then he pulled it back against his chest and grinned at me over the top.

'There,' he said, placing the board on the table.

I sat up carefully. 'All finished?'

He stood and stretched. Then he shook off the flip-flops, sloughed off the cut-offs – he was naked beneath them – and crossed the sun-dusted room in three purposeful strides.

'Hardly,' he said, sinking down slowly beside me. 'I haven't even begun to make love to you yet.'

Sunday 29 April

After I had recovered from the vague feeling of anxiety that had been dogging me all night – that the reason I was so keen on doing an art degree was no longer because I had any pretensions to artistic greatness, but because I had become completely infatuated with one of the tutors – I dragged myself from my bed and drove down to collect Leo from Del's. And off we went again. Because Del could see it too.

'You didn't!'

'I did.'

'I can hardly believe it. How erotic. How lovely. How exceedingly romantic.' She lowered her voice. 'And did you shag him as well?'

'Del!'

'Oh, for God's sake, Lu, don't be such a drip. Anyway, I'll take that as a yes. Is he any good?'

'*Del!*'

'At *painting*, you twit! As in with a *brush*?' She waggled a finger in front of my face. 'You, my dear sister, have a one-track mind.' She basked for a moment in the warmth of my blush. 'So?' she asked finally. '*Is* he any good? I've always rather fancied having someone artistic in the family. Anyway, are you going to stay for lunch or what? I have to count my potatoes. Which reminds me, next Saturday. Ben has got it into his head that he's going to invite all his juniors round, so we're having a bit of a party. Absolutely no barbecuing, and we're not talking *coulis* or reductions or anything poncy like that, but I would really appreciate your sisterly support. And you can bring him. No, in fact, you *have* to bring him. Ben has this appallingly dreary new registrar and if you don't bring Stefan he'll monopolize you all evening, mark my words. And there's only so much you can hear about his exploits with an endoscope without wanting to vomit, I can tell you.'

I tried to visualize my beautiful and sensitive Stefan immersed in the sort of physiologically explicit banter that passed for polite dinner-party conversation at my sister's house, and couldn't. Much as I wanted to take him out and parade him around the place, a part of me also wanted to keep him to myself – he was like a rare butterfly: a delicate, precious thing, easily damaged. I wasn't sure how well he'd cope with the culture shock. Wasn't sure that it just wouldn't frighten him off. On the other hand I could simply refuse to go, which would solve the problem altogether.

'Oh, you don't need me here.'

'I most emphatically do. Besides, you'll enjoy yourself. And so, my dear, will he.'

8

Monday 30 April

Sure I will learn to love abstract art. It can't be that
difficult, surely? Surely the only obstacle between me
and a true appreciation of the less readily accessible
forms of artistic expression is a narrowness of imagination brought about by years of having to conjugate
French verbs all day. And spending all the time that
less frazzled people spend on spiritually enriching
esoteric pursuits in going to Sainsbury's and ironing
and so on. And through not having devoted enough
time to stopping and thinking and studying and considering. And will be the same with opera, for sure.

I know nothing about boilers either. This much is
clear. Trouble is, I haven't any sort of yen *to* know
anything about boilers. Heating systems, for me, simply
are. A man comes once a year to open the front of the
one in the kitchen, take calls on his mobile from people
called Bazzer and Dildo and drink cups of tea. Then he
says, 'Tickety-boo', or something, snaps his case shut
and leaves. And heat continues, constant and un-
complicated, in my life. Oh, and sometimes I bleed my
radiators. Though I'm not even sure I have a complete
grasp of radiator bleeding. Why do all mine have a
poo-coloured stain under the little knob at the bottom?

But perhaps I'm being élitist. There are boilers and

there are boilers. I wouldn't want to make any assumptions about the lyrical qualities of commercial heating installations *per se*, and there is no doubt that artistic expression of a kind must inform boiler aesthetics. Mustn't it? Joe Delaney certainly seems to like them. Mind you, I suspect he is a cultural desert.

The kind of boilders JDL made it their business to know about were, it had to be said, clearly in an altogether different stratosphere from the average suburban Potterton. We were talking hospitals, council offices, eight-hundred-room hotels. We were talking constant heat and hot water on demand, health and safety at work, quality-control assurance, BS validation and (most probably) far-reaching networks of those scary metal tunnel systems that house aliens and radioactively monsterized insects, and bad guys with flame-throwers and B-movie spies. I knew this because it said so in their glossy brochure, a copy of which Lily had thoughtfully sent me the week before I landed the spot at her desk.

When I was squinting at the spec sheet in front of me it was difficult therefore to know whether the bits I couldn't get a handle on were merely gaps in my French or things of completely alien origin. Which word for gas valve? *Gaz soupape* or *clapet*? And was flue elbow *really* a *conduite de coude*? So engrossed was I in enlarging my combustion-based vocabulary that when the telephone rang I answered in French.

It was the proprietor of the garage in Swindon, calling to tie up the paperwork regarding what was left of my beloved car. He talked for some minutes about his holidays in Trouville, and confirmed that the insurance inspection had been made. And he wanted to know what to do with Joe's laptop, which, though apparently not working, was still sitting on his desk.

Knowing little about computer hardware and its viability as a salvage item, I told him I would have to get back to him.

'Oh, and by the way,' I asked him, 'did you have any luck finding the Pokémon cards?'

'Do what, my love?'

'I called the other day. To see if anyone had found my son's Pokémon cards.'

There was a pause. Then, 'Do what?'

'My son's Pokémon cards.'

There was another.

'Hmm,' he said finally. 'Not sure I'm with you. What exactly are poky munk hards, when they're at home, my love?'

'No. Pokémon *cards*. Pok-é-mon. You must have heard of them. You know, the film. The computer game. The—'

'So it's a computer game I'm after, is it, then?'

'No, no, just some cards. Like playing cards. They were in the glove compartment. Or maybe under the front seat. But somewhere. About thirty of them. In an elastic band. They belong to my son.'

'Cards, then. Hold on a tick. Let me find a pen. P-o-k-é-m-o-n C-a-r-d-s. All right. Are you going to hold on?'

'Yes. Yes, I'll hold.'

'Right-ho, then. Won't be a tick.'

Iona rumbled past swinging a Matalan carrier. 'Ah, you're *here*,' she announced, as if I might be in another office in a different part of Europe altogether. 'Joe's after you. On the phone. Needs a word, lovely. Quick as you like.' She moved on down the corridor, humming 'Sex Bomb' to herself.

'I won't be a moment,' I called after her. 'I'm just on to the man at the garage about my car. He's gone off to see if he can track down Leo's Pokémon cards for him before it's taken away for salvage.'

Her head reappeared around the door. 'His what?'

'His Pokémon cards. He—'

'Poky what?'

'Pokémon.'

'Poke a *what*?'

'Poké*mon*. It's a game. And a film. And a—' I shook my head. Was there really any point?

Hierarchies have always been a part of my life. In a large comprehensive school, there are hierarchies so complex and unfathomable that they could do with a National Curriculum all of their own. So, though I was almost as ignorant about office politics as I was about boilers, I had an inkling that there wasn't actually a form of protocol that condoned the use of bellowing through an office partition wall as a method of fostering good employee relations.

This was, even so, now happening.

'*Lu!*'

'Just coming!' I warbled back.

Unidentifiable Swindon-based rumblings and whir-rings continued apace down the phone. I waited some more.

'Lu! Are you coming?'

'One minute!'

The rumbling stopped. Then a whine started up. Then a clatter, a thump and, finally, a voice: 'Hello?'

'I'm still here. Any luck?'

''Fraid not, my love. We've got some sort of power lead, a packet of Werther's Originals, and a paperback. Let me see now, called *Virtual Strangers*. No poky-whatnots. He did check in the footwell.'

I made a mental note to mug the next Japanese toy wholesaler I clapped eyes on, then put down my pen and went into the other office. Joe was on the phone, which he now cupped in his hand. 'Don't mind me,' he said, then carried on talking for two minutes. He put down the receiver and started scribbling on a pad.

'Hello,' I said sweetly. 'You wanted to see me?'

He carried on writing for a good thirty seconds. Thirty point-making seconds, if I wasn't mistaken.

'Ah, Lu,' he said, clicking his ballpoint. 'Glad you could make it finally. Amiens. Thursday. Do you think you can do it?'

'Amiens?'

'Yes, Amiens.'

'What – Amiens, *France*?'

He put the pen down. 'Well, of *course* Amiens, France. What other Amiens would I be talking about? Luxotel, Amiens Nord, to be precise. I have to do a site survey and costing for the job there. Plus look at a timescale for the refit in Blois. We'd be back Friday evening. Can you do it or not?'

I gaped at him. 'What – *go* to France?' He nodded. 'With *you*?'

He nodded again. 'Of course. Assuming it's OK with you. *Is* it OK with you?'

'You want *me* to take *you* to France?'

He began to look pained. 'Yes, Lu. I need *you* to take *me* to France. As in,' he did a little one-handed steering-wheel mime, 'you know, *driving* me there?'

'What – drive you to France this *Thursday*?'

He ejected a nicotine chewing-gum from its blister pack and lobbed it into his mouth. Then chewed a bit and said, 'As in the day that generally falls after Wednesday. Yes. Thought it would make a nice change for you. Wouldn't it?'

'Um, well . . . I suppose it—'

'Great. So. I'll need to book us rooms. And the

Eurotunnel. Midday-ish, I thought. But as you're here now, and as I have neither the time nor the inclination to sit and listen to them telling me how important my call is to them *again*,' he tore a page from the pad on his desk, 'you can get on with it instead, perhaps. Yes?'

'But I can't just swan off to France for the night. What about Leo?'

'Ah. That's a thought. Hmm. I know. Why don't you bring him along?'

'I can't do that. What about school?'

He picked up the pen again. 'Hadn't thought of that.' He shrugged. 'Well, I don't know. Can't he stay at your sister's or something?'

'It's hardly – well, I mean, she might have made plans. I can't expect her to just—'

'But she probably wouldn't mind, would she? So why don't you ask her?'

'But I can't just dump him and—'

He looked offended. 'I wasn't suggesting that you *dump* him anywhere, Lu. I simply suggested it might not be outside the bounds of possibility for him to stay at Del's for one night. That's all.'

'Yes, but that's not the point. It's not really fair to—'

He put down the pen again and rolled his eyes. 'Lu, why don't you just call her and *ask* her?'

Where my car being officially dead had lent the morning an air of melancholy, the prospect of being asked to drive my boss all the way to France and back replaced it with one of complete unreality. It had never occurred to me that he might ask me to do such a thing. Which was patently silly. He zipped back and forth across the Channel all the time, so it was hardly a completely outlandish request. But I so hated putting upon Del. She did so much for me as it was.

'Oh, but that'll be absolutely *fine*!' she chirruped,

when I telephoned to outline the unexpected French development for her. 'I'm happy to have Leo for you *any* time, you *know* that. And how exciting! Goodness me, your life's getting very jet-setty all of a sudden! And about time too, I say. Ooh, Lu, I'd give my eye teeth for a chance to – hey! And there's a thought! Perfect!'

'Perfect what?'

'Perfect *timing*! You can get me some stuff for my party! Of course! You'll have time to stop at a hyper-market, won't you? Of course you will. So you can get me some cheese and some wine and – tell you what, I shall sit down and make you a list. Thursday, you say? Perfect, Lu. Perfect!'

So that was all right, then.

'Oh, and by the way, trust you and Stefan are still OK for Saturday? I've decided on St Trinian's. OK?'

'Pardon?'

'My theme. I'm going for St Trinian's. You *know* – white socks, gym knickers, pigtails and so on. Sure you can rustle something up. Anyway, must dash.'

Oh, God.

9

Well. Here we are, then.

So, we drove the two hundred-odd miles to Folkestone and we went through the tunnel, and then we were in France, and it was actually quite all right. Which was an unexpected but pleasing turn of events. After feeling so ambivalent about the whole thing, I was surprised to find myself both enjoying driving the beastie car, and enjoying the prospect of a night in France too. I had not been to France since my grandmother's funeral. And I hadn't been away on my own since Leo was born. And though this was work (and though work was boilers), the thought of an overnight stay in a foreign hotel was not without its appeal. We arrived at the Luxotel mid-afternoon, and though I was a little tired from the driving, I was also in a rather pleasant end-of-term-start-of-the-holidays frame of mind.

Of course, it had been helped enormously by the fact that Joe refrained from grousing, griping and generally being a pain for the entire journey. But, then, he did spend it in the back seat, engaged, for the most part, in tapping quietly but industriously on his new laptop. His infrequent contributions therefore consisted mainly of tuts, ahs!, ri-ights and of courses, most of which were addressed to himself. There was the occasional explosive pah! – this was not a perfect world and we still had to have the radio tuned to Five Live until Folkestone – but as I was no more expected to voice opinions in response to these than to pass judgement on the latest innovations in gas-burner technology, I was able to filter them out and enjoy the view.

The view of Monsieur Deschamp, legs akimbo on a bar stool just off Reception, was a much less pleasing sight. He slithered off it as we came through the entrance and welcomed us (me, specifically) as if we were much-cherished relatives just returned from a lengthy expedition round a salt flat or canyon.

'We are arrived!' he announced, with a smile and a clap and a roll of his Rs, topped off by three mwah-mwah kisses. Fortunately for me, however, there was a serious boiler discussion to be got down to, which meant I could skulk off and lollop around on my own for a couple of hours.

'But later,' Joe suggested, 'you might like to join us. I'll be taking Jean Paul and Claude out for dinner – we generally head into town when I'm here. Up for that?'

Monsieur Deschamp lifted an encouraging brow.

'I'm not sure,' I said, my own knitting slightly in response. 'It's been a long drive. I'm—'

'But I absolutely insist,' the slimy Frenchman added. 'We cannot possibly pass up the opportunity of showing Mademoiselle Fisher a *good time*, as you put it.'

'Whatever,' said Joe, obviously noting my scowl. 'It's entirely up to you.'

It was still way too warm to sit in my hotel room, even by late evening, so after the surprisingly agreeable novelty of a solitary *à la carte* dinner in the half-empty restaurant, I fetched my book – a newly purchased volume about twentieth-century art – then went back down to sit on the terrace. But not before ordering a large brandy, which, with my reliably ill-advised half-litre-of-wine-on-board-already variety of logic, I thought might help me to sleep.

The hotel, situated close to the A6 for the convenience of weary commercial travellers, was in a complex of business and industrial units out on the low hills that circled the town. As ambience went, it would not win any prizes, but in darkness – the sun had finally dipped below the horizon – the vast skyscape dwarfed all the surface-based eyesores, and bathed the fields of young sunflowers and low, stubbly brassicas in a slow-moving gauze of peppermint light. I sipped at my Cognac and opened my book and was soon away somewhere between Post-minimalism and Fluxus. If, admittedly, not much the wiser about either.

'Aha! And what are we reading, Lucienne?'

I had been so absorbed in my book that, half an hour or so later, the voice behind me made me jump. It was speaking in French, so I assumed it was the waiter. But the waft of pungent aftershave (testosterone base with a note of old ashtray) should have alerted me. I turned to find that it was Monsieur Deschamp, obviously back from their beano in town and, judging by his expression, still in full party mood. Joe and Monsieur Dumas were inside, ordering drinks. He puffed on his cigarette and pulled out a chair beside me.

'Oh,' I said, turning down the corner and closing it. 'It's an art book. It's about the—'

'Uh-huh,' he said, nodding, but not bothering to glance at it. 'And clearly very good as it has kept you from us all evening. I was *most* disappointed.' He puffed a bit more, engulfing us both in his fetid emissions, then crushed out the stub in a nearby ashtray. 'So. Why didn't you join us?'

He sat down. I stood up. 'It's been a long drive. I was tired. In fact—'

'But, nevertheless, not yet in bed, I see.' He glanced towards Joe, who was backing through the glass door with a brandy balloon. And leered. *Leered*, the creep. 'And you haven't drunk your Cognac yet, so you must stay for a while. Joe!' he called, switching back to English. 'Here is your assistant. I have found her. Come, persuade her to stay a while longer. We poor men need a little distraction from our drab and charmless world, do we not?'

Monsieur Dumas arrived also, and said something I didn't quite catch, but the word 'python' was certainly there somewhere. The three of them then exchanged a blokey titter, so I assumed it related to the distraction element in their evening's entertainment thus far. I put on my cardigan and did up all the buttons.

'I'm sorry,' I said, and drained the brandy in one swallow, 'but I really am tired. I'll see you all in the morning.'

I didn't go up to bed. Once I had left the restaurant (and finished coughing, hacking, fanning my face, wiping my eyes and recalling, albeit hazily, that it took only one teaspoonful of neat alcohol to kill a perfectly healthy laboratory rat), I decided, as you do, that what I most needed was not to lie supine and misplace my head, but to stride about purposefully for a while in the fresh air. I wandered around outside the lobby for a few minutes, then found a narrow pathway, which wound between clusters of back-lit and aggressively burgeoning green shrub life, and eventually brought me to the large garden at the back of the hotel. From down here, I could hear muffled voices coming from the restaurant terrace above, but I was far enough beneath them that if I didn't venture out on to the lawn, they wouldn't see me.

The hotel pool, which was flanked on one side by gaily striped yellow and white awnings, looked invitingly cool and inky, its surface glossy and fluid, like molten blue chocolate. Slipping off my cardigan – it was still very close – I wove carefully through the huddle of abandoned chairs and loungers (presumably clustered here in case of rain) then slipped off a sandal and poked a toe through the surface of the water. It was cold enough to make me gasp. I shook off the other shoe and sat down on the stone, hitched up my dress and slipped both legs in almost up to the knee. Ripples moved eel-like across the pool, glinting metallically as they peaked and dipped. I picked up my book, but it was too dark to read, so instead I just sat there and thought about Stefan. Which had become quite a thing with me lately, as these things generally do. Since we had slept together, the memory of his torso had an alarming tendency to pop into my mind all the time. That and the way his hair fell in such thick fluid commas on his shoulders, and how the touch of his rough painter's hands made my skin gasp. In an agreeable haze, and caressed by the moonlight, I was, I realized, with no small degree of surprise, rather enjoying myself.

Correction. *Had* been.

'Hello, you.' The voice this time was soft, barely a whisper. And it was Joe's. He had the brandy balloon clasped in the hand with the plaster. It was almost half full. 'Shh, or they'll hear us.' He put a finger to his mouth. 'What are you doing?'

My carnal reveries interrupted, I raised a foot from

the water. Droplets streamed from my toes and danced on the surface. 'What does it look like?'

'I mean, I thought you said you were going to bed.' He held out the glass for me to take then lowered himself carefully on to the ground beside me, and began to unlace his right shoe. I stopped wiggling my legs back and forth and wondered if this might be the moment to do just that. He had obviously decided to join me, and I wasn't altogether sure I wanted him to. Quite apart from the fact that I was quite happy on my own, I wasn't terrifically keen on the idea of being in such an up-close-and-personal proximity to my boss, particularly *sans* his footwear. Stefan's stunningly brown and sculpted feet sprang to mind. Joe's, no doubt, would be pallid and crusty, covered in barnacles and smelly to boot. And not only that: I wasn't entirely sure that this wasn't part of some elaborate and secretly promulgated burlesque they had planned – that Jean Paul Deschamp would soon enter stage left, and start prancing around in a leatherette thong. But, no. It was all right. I could still hear the other two talking above. So I continued to sit. I was cool. I was relaxed. I didn't feel like moving. I supposed he could sit with me if he wanted.

'It's too hot to go to bed,' I told him. 'And I'm not tired enough anyway. I'm not used to having so little to do.'

He continued to fiddle with his shoes. 'You could have come with us. I'm sure you would have enjoyed yourself.'

'Oh, *pur-lease*.' I rolled my eyes and nodded upwards to the terrace.

'Jean Paul? Oh, take no notice. I've known him for years. He's married with five kids, you know.'

'Oh, that's supposed to make a difference, is it? He's a complete lech.'

'You know what I mean. He definitely has the hots for you, I'll grant you that. But he's harmless enough. Look, could you give me a hand here?'

He had removed both shoes and socks (the latter being festooned with little Homer Simpsons – a present from Angharad?), and was trying, one-handed, to roll up his trousers. But struggling a little. Slightly reluctantly, I put down the glass then leaned across and began to do it for him. The hair on his legs was dense and dark. His feet *were* pale, of course (his, unlike Stefan's, being a generally trousered occupation), but surprisingly smooth and undisgusting. I paused mid-roll, concerned for his creases. 'How far do you want me to go with this?'

He grinned at me, teeth very white in the moonlight. 'Oh, ho! Is this my lucky night? But I'm a helpless wounded man, remember. So just be gentle with me, OK?'

'Oh, ho bloody ho,' I muttered, stopping abruptly just short of his shins. He took no notice, and dipped his feet carefully into the water. My own looked tiny and pink beside them. And, though paradoxically, a little bit mer-like, on account of my newly varnished green nails.

'Thank you. Oh, yes, that *does* feel good,' he said. 'Should have brought our bathers, eh?'

I leaned my arms out behind me and resumed my feet-flapping activities. But the brandy was making my head swim. I sat up straight again.

'You can't go swimming anyway,' I said. 'Not with that thing on your arm.' He weighed the plaster in his free hand.

'You're right.' He sighed. 'I'd sink. God, but it's warm for May, isn't it? Couldn't you just slip into that water right now?'

I could. My face was beginning to feel hot. Should have left the brandy. I dipped a hand in the pool then wiped it across my brow. 'I think I will go to bed, actually,' I said. 'Early start in the morning.'

He frowned. His scar, now free of its neat row of stitches, curved in a shiny red line down his cheek. I wondered how much it would fade. 'Oh, don't go up yet,' he urged. 'It's not even eleven. Here,' he fished in his shirt pocket, 'have a nicotine chewing-gum, why don't you?'

He looked so earnest and keen that I felt suddenly churlish. For all its manifest feminine diversions, his must, I supposed, be an essentially solitary life. Just him and his boilers and his once-a-week access. I shook my head and pulled my feet from the water to let them dry a little, but I didn't get up. 'How's it going? Must be hard with those two puffing Gitanes smoke in your face all the time.'

'Ten days now.' He pulled out the packet of gum, then seemed to think better of it and picked up his Cognac instead. 'On this attempt, anyway. I'll get there. May commit murder in the meantime, but I'll get there.' He laughed. 'Or *get* murdered. I know I'm a little difficult to live with at the moment. So if not by you,' he glanced at me as he said this, 'then by Iona, probably.'

He drank a little then passed the glass back to me. My mouth plunged in and took a slurp without doing my brain the courtesy of consulting it first. I shook my head. 'She's too nice.'

'Nice? She's a tyrant. She bullies me relentlessly.'

'Bullies *you*?'

'To keep me in line. I think she thinks I need a firm hand.' He smiled. 'In the absence of having a dragon at home to do it any more.'

I concurred silently. 'How long have you been divorced?'

'Nowhere near long enough. Five years. You?'

'I'm not.'

'Oh. But what about Leo?'

I shook my head. 'I didn't marry Leo's father. I found out he'd been seeing someone else just before I found out I was pregnant. So I . . . Well, telling him didn't seem the best thing to do.'

'Oh. So you dumped him?'

'Exactly.'

'Without telling him?'

'Exactly.' A hint of a pregnant (boom-boom, I don't think) pause, which I could have filled with what occurred to me during it: that I'd sensibly dumped him before what had happened to Rhiannon and Angharad could happen to Leo and me. But I didn't, because I had no fight in me about it any more. Instead I just said, 'Do you have a problem with that?'

'No,' he said levelly. 'I don't have a problem with that.' I wasn't sure I believed him. He swivelled his head to face me. 'So what about Leo? What does *he* know about his father?' His tone, I realized, was entirely neutral for once.

'Apart from the fact that he's a bastard?' He looked at me sharply. I waved a dismissive hand. 'No. He doesn't know *that*, obviously. But not everything,' I said. 'Not yet. I'm kind of hoping that when the time comes I'll have worked out what to say and how to say it. You know?' He nodded, but didn't comment. I swirled the brandy around in the glass and found myself slipping my feet back into the water. 'Not that any of it matters, really. All that's ever going to matter to Leo is that he doesn't have a dad. And there's nothing I can do about that, is there?'

He was silent for a moment, feet moving smoothly back and forth through the water. Then he laughed.

'What's so funny?'

'Well, not funny *really*, I suppose. But what you said about Leo not having a father – it just made me think.'

'What?'

'Rhiannon has the opposite problem. For her the real difficulty is that Angharad *does*.'

'Surely not.'

'Not from a financial perspective. Oh, no. But I think it would suit her far better if I *wasn't* around. I get in the way, you see. Spoil her carefully orchestrated victim image. Pah! As if! Anyway,' he tipped his head back and looked up into the night sky, 'you know what? Bollocks to her. That's what I say.'

I looked up also. There were zillions of stars. Such a big sky. And how tiny we were. The man in the moon seemed to nod his assent. 'Yes,' I heard myself lustily agreeing. 'Me too. Bollocks to both of them!'

The words, which had felt so nice while still on my tongue, boomed from my lips like a salvo of sucked gobstoppers, where they lingered malevolently in the still warm air. Horribly embarrassed, I glanced sideways to find him now staring straight at me. I swallowed some more brandy.

'Um, I mean, when I say, "bollocks to both of them," I don't mean it personally – about your ex-wife, about *Rhiannon*, of course. I mean, I *do* mean it about Patri – about Leo's father. *Oh*, yes. But not about her. I don't know her, do I? She's probably perfectly nice, and it's not for me to make any assumptions about her or you and her or your marriage or – or – or, well, *anything*, really. I was just speaking, you know, generally, *globally* – in a spirit of solidarity and so on. You know?'

I wasn't sure quite why a spirit of solidarity had

gripped me. After all, it was Rhiannon I should be empathizing with, wasn't it? But in any event, I was waving the brandy around somewhat theatrically by now. He grinned and held out his hand for the glass. 'No, no,' he said, taking it from me. 'You go right ahead.' He swallowed the contents. 'Feel free.'

I clamped my mouth shut and looked into the water, muddled and unsure what to say next. I became aware that he was staring at me again. I turned and stared back. He was starting to blur. 'What?' I said.

'What what?'

'What are you *looking* at?'

'You.' His smile broadened. He continued to stare.

'Oh,' I said. 'Why?'

'Why not?'

'Because I'd rather you didn't.'

'I can if I like.'

'No, you can't.'

'Too bad. I am.'

'Well, you shouldn't. It's rude to stare.'

'I'm not staring at you. Just looking at you. Which is not the same thing at all.'

'Yes, it is.'

'No, it isn't. You have a pretty face and I'm looking at it.' He hauled one leg from the water and parked a wet foot on the pool edge in order to sit facing me. As if, it seemed, to endorse the point. 'Do you,' he asked, putting the glass down beside him, 'ahem – have a problem with that?' But I was spared the necessity of answering, because he then said, 'Jesus! What the fuck was that?!'

I started. 'What?'

He pulled his other leg from the water, shaking it wildly as he did so. 'Sorry, but – shit! What *is* that? Jesus, Lu. Look! *There!*'

I did likewise, swinging my legs up alongside me, craning my neck to see what he was pointing at. There was movement and a faint splashing sound at the edge of the water, but our shadows made the darkness in front of us all but impenetrable.

'Good God!' he said suddenly. 'It's a rat! Look!'

He was kneeling by now, and the movement had allowed more light to fall on the water. A small dark shape was moving frantically in front of us, a gloss of wet fur with a small rippling wake. I gathered up my dress and got on to my knees too. 'No,' I decided, peering. 'Oh, *bless*. It's some sort of shrew. Look – it's got a pointed snout.'

'That's one bloody big shrew – Christ! It's coming back this way.' He edged back a foot. The animal, as if sensing our presence, ploughed on with renewed urgency, tiny limbs visibly thrashing at its sides. I looked around for the brandy glass.

'What the hell are you doing?' he exclaimed, as I picked it up.

'I laughed. 'Rescuing it, of course.'

'*What?* Does it look as if it needs rescuing? God, there's a thought! It probably bit me!' He swivelled his leg to inspect his calf. 'Rabid, no doubt.'

'Oh, don't be such a baby!' Still giggling, I plunged the glass into the water. There was enough of a lip around the pool that the shrew wouldn't be able to climb out unaided, but by scooping its back end into the glass I would be able to manoeuvre it forward, steering it towards the edge. I had just got it in place when – on seeing Joe's horrified expression, presumably – it evaded capture and plopped back into the water.

'Ugh! Lu! Leave it!' he hissed.

I threw him a look. 'I can't do that. It'll die.'

112

'So let it! If the bloody thing was silly enough to fall in the pool in the first place, then it bloody deserves to.'

'It didn't *fall* in, stupid. It's a water shrew. But it won't find anything to eat and it won't be able to get out.' I continued trying to scoop it into the glass. 'Anyway, how's it supposed to know the difference between a swimming-pool and a stream? Ah, there we are!' I pulled the glass quickly from the water, and spilled out the frightened contents on to the stone surround. The shrew scrabbled wildly on its back for a moment, then finding purchase, skittered off into the darkness under the terrace, narrowly missing Joe's feet as it went.

'Ugh!' he said again. 'And stop guffawing like that, will you? You wouldn't be guffawing if it was your leg it bit.'

I sat back on my heels and grinned at him. 'Pah! Come on, it didn't bite you.'

'It bloody well did.'

'Where?'

He stuck out his leg. I inspected it. 'Rubbish. There's not even a scratch there. It probably just brushed against it. Don't be such a baby.'

'Hurrmph! You say that now, but you wait. It's in there now.' He gestured to the darkness beneath the terrace. 'You won't be laughing when it scuttles out and climbs up *your* leg. *Oh*, no.'

I shook my head and laughed some more. And carried on doing so, right up until the moment when I decided to stand up and found that my legs had been stripped of their bones while I wasn't looking. I lurched a little, I grabbed a chair for support, then sat down on it heavily.

'Hah!' he said. 'Hah!'

I reached for my sandals.

'Hah yourself, scaredy-cat. Can you pass me my book?'

He was just doing so when the lights went out.

He turned round. 'Great. Must be on some sort of timer. There'll be security lighting, though. It'll come on as soon as we start moving around.'

I wriggled my feet into my sandals and picked up my cardigan, while Joe bent to retrieve his shoes and socks.

I peered pointedly into the blackness. 'Shall I help you put them on?'

He looked fretful for a moment Then, seeing my mischievous expression, he shook his head emphatically. 'No, no. I'll be just fine barefoot, thanks very much.'

He took the shoes from me and tucked them inside his sling and, as the lights showed no inclination to illuminate our progress after all, we began to thread our way unsteadily back through the muddle of garden furniture. Oh, God, my head. My *head*! Up to now it had led me to believe that it would be in control of ambulatory functions once the need arose, but now it had decided to renege on the deal. Behind me, various bangs and scrapes, shufflings and grunts told me Joe's had as well. Either that, or he was being molested by angry rodents.

'God, I feel drunk all of a sudden,' I moaned. I was, I realized, much more intoxicated than I had been in a long, long time. 'This is all your fault. You're a bad influence on me, you know that? I can hardly walk.'

'Me? I like that! You were half cut when I got here. I'm just fine – ow! Damn! Owee! God, I've stubbed my bloody toe now.'

He caught my arm to steady himself, while I reached to move the offending chair out of the way. 'Hah,' I said. 'Hah! And neither can you.'

114

He groaned and stooped to rub his foot. 'Not drunk, Lu, merely incorrectly balanced. Sod it, that hurts. Here, watch that one, will you? Or you'll have us both over.'

'*I* will?'

'For certain.' He tightened his grip on my arm as I led him unsteadily along in the blackness towards the path that ran down the side of the hotel. 'So where are you taking me, exactly? On a bloody shrew-hunt? Or just a whistle-stop inspection of the hotel flues?'

'I wouldn't know a flue from a Frisbee. Back inside, of course. This is the way.'

A branch thwacked his cheek. 'Ouch! Lu, wouldn't it have been simpler to go in via the terrace and through the restaurant?'

'Probably, but then we'd have to go past Monsieur Deschamp again, wouldn't we?'

'So?'

'Well, I told him I was going to bed an hour ago, didn't I? Watch that one. It's got nasty thorns.'

'Ouch! Thanks. I had noticed. So? What do you think he's going to do if he sees you – pounce on you, rip your frock off, and whistle the "Marseillaise" while he ravishes you?'

I must have found this enormously funny because I realized belatedly that I was tittering at him again. 'No, of *course* not,' I corrected, clutching the wall for support. 'But if we're talking things that scuttle around and shimmy up legs, well . . . I just don't like the way he leers at me, that's all. He's so slimy. I have a nose for these things. Anyway – oops! Mind that rock there – we're almost back now.'

We approached the corner, where the enthusiastic landscaping finally gave way to the less daunting prospect of the car-park and lobby. The Luxotel sign cast an eerie green light all around, in which fluttering moths and midges danced.

'You see?' I said, leading him forward. 'Here we are, shrew-free, and all safe and sound.'

'Indeed we are,' he replied, closing the gap between us and peering ahead. 'Civilization at last. But hang on . . .'

I stopped. His arm was still looped in mine. 'What?'

'D'you mind . . .'

'Mind what?'

'If I just . . .'

I swivelled on the path. 'Just what?'

'Just, well . . . just this.'

And then he kissed me. With feeling. Full on the lips.

My head – still, amazingly, on my shoulders, despite its manic spiralling – began to clear. I stared at him, stunned, for some moments. 'Why on earth did you do that?'

He smiled. 'Oh. Did you mind, then?'

I couldn't think what to say. Couldn't even think what to *think*. 'Um. Yes. Yes, I think I did.'

He dropped his arm. His smile vanished. 'Oh,' he said again. 'I'm sorry. I thought you . . .'

I shook my head, fuddled. 'I think—' I began. But my brain could no longer focus. So I turned and, without another look at him, made my way unsteadily inside and up to bed.

Friday 4 May

I didn't make it down for breakfast. It had been almost three before my head had settled sufficiently that it could be trusted on the horizontal, and almost four before my brain gave up trying to remember enough of what had occurred that it could be trusted to give me an accurate account of it in the morning. I was supposed to be accompanying Joe on a full site inspection first thing, but by the time I had surfaced downstairs, it was evidently already over. Both he and his holdall were parked in the lobby, along with a short man in overalls and some fat rolls of blueprints. Joe, who was looking fresh, rested, and ready to paddle enthusiastically up the Amazon should the situation call for it, beckoned me over and made cheerful introductions.

Monsieur Barbusse, it seemed, was the hotel's maintenance manager. It would be he with whom I'd be liaising over the phone. We exchanged a few words about faxes and parts lists, then he left us to check his gauges and knobs.

Joe began to gather up papers. 'Want some breakfast? A coffee?'

I sat down. 'Just water.'

He laughed. 'Hah!' he said. 'It's way too late for that.'

He called for some anyway, which I sipped cautiously. My stomach felt like it had been comprehensively trampled by wildebeest. Which perhaps it had while I'd slept. 'Congeners,' he observed helpfully. 'The darker the drink, the worse the hangover.'

I looked up. Which was painful. 'You seem OK.'

'I have a well-trained and robust liver.'

'You should have called and woken me.'

He patted my shoulder before closing his briefcase. 'Whereas yours, in contrast, is clearly well out of practice. I decided to be gallant and let you sleep in.'

We left the hotel a little before eleven and began the long drive back to Calais and the shuttle. My stomach was settling, but my brain felt like a pea in a whistle. Fortunately, the motorway was all but empty, and the Jag wafted serenely and quietly along it in the sunshine, doing, as Joe had already pointed out to me, what it was best at – driving itself.

Joe himself, now back in the front seat, was in a jolly, talkative mood. The coming year, boiler-wise, looked pretty rosy apparently: the Luxotel Group were already JDL's biggest clients, and Monsieur Deschamp, he told me, had already intimated that once the deal was settled on the next site they were acquiring, yet another heating contract was already as good as his. 'Which is excellent news, because it means I can offer permanent positions to two of the guys I've had on contract till now. Seriously sound characters. Wouldn't want to lose them. Ah, yes,' he stretched, 'a very successful trip, all in all.' He turned to look at me. '*Very*. You enjoy it?'

I said yes, of course, because I'm a polite girl at heart, but my expression must have been less ambiguous, because he cleared his throat and went on, 'Look, er . . . about what happened last night. Bit presumptuous of me, I know. But I thought you were – well, you seemed OK about it.'

Oh. So he *was* going to bring it up. I had been so hoping he wouldn't. I would have to make light of it. 'I was drunk,' I said.

He smiled, too, then snorted. 'Yes, but not that drunk.'

'Perhaps you could tell my head that.'

'Not *that* drunk,' he repeated obligingly. Then laughed. 'Come on. Look, you did kiss me back.'

Oh, God. So it was true. It *was* true.

I shook my head firmly. Which made it rattle. 'No, I didn't.'

'Er, *excuse* me.' He was grinning now. 'You most certainly did.'

Why? *Why* had I kissed him back? And *how* had I kissed him back? Reluctantly? Fulsomely? Had – oh, God! – *tongues* been involved? What on earth had possessed me? Post animal-hospital-routine euphoria? But *surely* he realized . . . I stared out through the windscreen. 'Well, if I did, I really didn't mean to. It was simply—'

'Well, if that was an example of you kissing someone by accident, then, boy, would I—'

He didn't finish the sentence, but instead let it reach what was looking like becoming a very unfortunate conclusion, while he carried on smiling. His whole body was angled slightly towards me. Expectant. Waiting. *Hopeful?* Oh dear.

'*Really*,' I repeated. He was obviously misreading my current reticence as straightforward girly embarrassment. Or was just slow on the uptake. I would have to be firm. 'Look, I'm sorry but I didn't. I don't – I mean, I'm not – well,' I glanced across at him, 'it was a mistake, OK?'

His smile faded abruptly and he moved away a little.

'I'm sorry,' I said, as it finally dawned on me that he really *had* been anticipating an altogether different response, 'but—'

He flapped his hand in the air to silence me. 'No, no. Don't worry,' he said. 'Point very much taken, Lu. Subject most emphatically closed.'

I was back in Cefn Melin a little after six. Del was in their front garden, watering her pots. I pulled up, released the boot catch and got out, a little wearily. She scooted round to the back and started riffling through the bounty.

119

'Oh oh oh oh oh oh *oh*! You are *such* a star, Lu!'

'The Jag,' I said, passing the bags out to her, 'has a very big boot.'

'Oh, and look at these! Oh! How much do I owe you? And you managed to get that cheese with the cumin seeds! Oh, joy! We must try some right now! Anyway,' she took hold of six carriers and headed off up the path, 'we're all sorted for tomorrow evening. About seven thirty, OK? Don't want to make too late a night of it as Ben has a tennis match in the morning. And Leo can sleep over again,' she paused to let me catch up then nudged my arm, 'so that you can take your artist home and have your wicked way with him. Hah! Oh, and I know it's short notice but could you be an absolute angel and bring one of those lovely roulade things you make? I don't want to go to a lot of fuss, but I thought I should at least show willing. Yes?' She kicked open the kitchen door and dumped the carriers on the table. 'Anyway, sit down and let's hear all about your trip.'

I told her about the shrew, and I told her about the hangover, but I didn't tell Del about Joe kissing me. I'd stressed and stressed about it all the way round Auchan (Joe, who clearly wasn't talking to me for the moment, had elected to sit in a café and have conversations with someone else on his mobile while I shopped) but I didn't tell her. Which was unlike me, because I always told Del everything. If this thing was of so little consequence – which it was – then *why* didn't I tell her about it?

It had certainly been a surprise. It had never up to that point occurred to me that Joe might be interested in me romantically. Never. And I was almost as sure it hadn't occurred to him either. And now I had to carry that knowledge around with me, it made me feel rather uncomfortable around him. I even fretted, heaven help me – as if *I* needed to worry about it – that he would feel uncomfortable around me as well. But surely I was worrying unnecessarily. Chances were, given the kind of guy he was, it was a simple case of opportunism. I was there, he was there, we had both drunk a lot of brandy, it was a warm, sultry night and our feet were bare. Situational. That was all. One of those things.

But fancy Joe Delaney being scared of a shrew. It made him seem almost human.

10

Saturday 5 May

Oh, and who cared? Who cared anyway? Who *cared*?

I didn't, for sure. I was way too busy. Busy with my little hand whisk and my Lakeland Plastics egg separator and my novelty bra and briefs apron, and my lemon and ginger mousse roulade recipe safe behind my natty Perspex recipe-book holder, and all was fine with the world. Which is a symptom of what I had clearly contracted: an all-consuming infatuation with Stefan. Believe me, when a person who tends to approach the realm of the Domestic Goddess (baking muffins, sewing, shagging to order) with about as much enthusiasm as a wayward tribal underling being brought to book over the disappearance of a bag of groats, then there is, irrefutably, something afoot. Clearly. Demonstrably. Goodness, I had even tele-phoned Del to ask if she'd like some hand-made truffles as well.

I suppose I should have seen the writing on the wall some time back but, being thirty-five and in hormonal stasis, the word infatuation was not one I'd had recent acquaintance with. As far as I'd known, I didn't *do* infatuation. Infatuation was one of those tedious pubescent afflictions one grew out of, wasn't it? Never-theless I considered myself fortunate. Even with the quantity of washing-up I was creating, infatuation, I decided, made a *very* nice change.

One of the less fortunate side effects of developing a complete infatuation with someone, however, is that it tends to make you hang on every word the object of your affection utters, however ill those words might presage. So when Stefan announced, towards the end of Del and Ben's *soirée*, that he thought the *Room-around* thing might prove to be rather fun, I found myself not only agreeing with him but agreeing with him pretty damned wholeheartedly. I even, God help me, allowed a small but well-upholstered fantasy to take root involving him, me, a sea sponge, a stippler, and a rag-rolling roller, in Del's garden shed. Sad, but true. It was really that bad.

No. *I* was really that bad.

'Oh,' I twittered, 'Del spoke to you about that, did she?'

We were sitting on the low wall that separated the patio from the neatly shorn lawn, him with his King-fisher and me with a mesmerized and (it must be admitted) slightly dozy smile on my face. Though I had resolutely refused to have anything to do with Del's gymslips-and-bunches flight of ridiculous fancy, it was only because I didn't really need them.

It was, however, almost the first time we'd spoken to each other properly since we had arrived. We'd (*I'd* – I never even asked him) elected to come as sixth-formers, which meant our first social exchange of the evening was a stern ticking-off by house-master Benjamin, which turned out to be only marginally less embarrassing than having put a hockey skirt and socks on in the first place. I was *so* mad at Del – you can't *do* that stuff with new boyfriends. It's so *married*. It's so *suburban*.

I'd barely been able to get within six feet of him since. I had also been more than a little dismayed by the amount of attention he had seemed to be receiving from Ben's latest registrar: a tall blonde Australian woman with a nose stud and rings on her thumbs, who had come as a school nurse, and who had greeted me by saying, 'Ah, ind who's this, theen?' before going 'inyway' and continuing straight on with a monologue she seemed to be telling, mainly through her nose, about a sigmoidoscopy and a rampaging bedsore. All the men clustered around her like spermatozoa head-butting an ovum. Apart from Stefan, who had looked on with cool detachment, declared himself on suspension and gone off to the kitchen to help Del with the food. No matter, I'd thought, a few more hours and we'd be back at mine, and then I'd have him all to myself.

He nodded and placed a proprietorial hand on my thigh. Which was nice.

'Mmm,' he said, through the neck of his bottle. 'Indeed she did. I'd always wondered what sort of people subjected themselves to such crass humiliation on national television, and now I know. She's something else, your sister. Very nice, but something else.' He tipped his head in the direction of the dining room we'd just left. Everyone else was still in there, guffawing. About what I knew not. About what I cared less.

'Oh,' I said again, not quite sure how to take this. The dining room was currently decked out to look like a Central American hacienda she'd spotted in a Kuoni brochure – sort of Cancun meets Chitchen Itza meets the *Next* home catalogue. Lots of burnt orange voile and spindly wrought iron. And she'd taken all the knobs off her sideboard and replaced them with rusty hinges. Del had a permanent rolling programme of room redecoration: until a month or so back, it had been Henley regatta, after her protracted Laura Ashley affair. Her and Ben's bedroom (currently a Vermont/Amish fusion involving copious amounts of gingham and corn-dolly knick-knacks) was to be next on the list. And now, it seemed, at Stefan's and my hands. Despite myself, my reservations and the fact that I did not know a toggle from a tin tack, it gave me an unexpected lovely warm feeling.

'It's Del's sort of thing, of course. Decorating,' I said. Then wished I hadn't. Because it made her sound like a bit of a divvy. 'She's very creative with interiors,' I added, to qualify. In case he thought I was being bitchy. It made her sound even worse. 'Not my sort of thing, though. That's why I live in a tip. Ha ha ha.'

He resisted the opportunity to laugh heartily at my decorative shortcomings, and instead traced a languid figure-of-eight on my thigh.

'Oh, and what's *your* sort of thing, then?' he asked.

It couldn't have been much after that that we decided we very much wanted to go home. We said our farewells, left the Jag on Del's driveway, and set off to walk the mile or so back to my place. It was a clear night, and warm enough that I hadn't bothered with a jacket. Stefan's arm, in any case, kept what breeze there was from my shoulders. Here and there, at least. Because he seemed a little strange. Rather skittish, in fact. He kept veering off (as artists do, perhaps?) to pass judgement on various mixed bedding arrangements, sniff flowers and shimmy along front garden walls. It was somewhat erratically, therefore, that we finally reached the junction with the lane that led to Cefn Melin woods. There was an area of grass here and a much sat-upon tree stump. The tree itself had been damaged in a storm some years back and the council had decided to fell it. Stefan, having left me to go and take a closer look at it, now beckoned me over.

'This the way?' he asked. He was squatting beside the stump, putting the lid back on an Old Holborn tin, before lighting a skinny cigarette that he'd made. I hadn't realized he smoked. I said so.

He stood up and held the glowing swizzle out to me. 'Not tobacco,' he replied. 'You want?' I said no. He nodded once again towards the lane. 'In there?'

'No. It's this way.' I pointed. 'That way takes us back up through the woods.'

He took a deep drag on his little cigarette. 'But it does lead back to your house, yes?'

I nodded. 'There's another entrance at the end of my road.'

He started moving, dragging once again on the cigarette, and pulling me with him through the veil of sweet-smelling smoke. 'Then let's go that way.'

'What? Walk home through the woods?'

'Of course. Come on. It'll be fun.'

I looked down at my feet. 'I'm not sure these are really the shoes for it.'

He shrugged. 'So take them off.'

'I'm hardly going to go plunging into the under-growth barefoot. Have you *seen* how many dogs there are around here?'

'Tsk!' he said. 'Tsk!' Then shot off through the dewy grass to the kissing gate, leaving me little choice but to follow.

The moon was still almost full and shed sufficient light that it wasn't too difficult to make out the path. It was flanked by the glossy foliage left by the bluebells, and dotted with wood anemones and low bowers of fern. The scent of wild garlic pricking our nostrils, we tramped gamely on into the trees.

The woods in Cefn Melin are, I suppose, like any other vestige of suburban woodland: diminutive, etched by many well-trodden pathways, and corralled on all sides by back-garden fences and walls. Even so, the natural contour of the hillside remained and, once down in the base of the valley, we could easily, were it not for the much-trampled ground and the buckled Coke cans, have been in some vast forest wilderness. We followed the path's course down the bend of the hillside, the ground stepped, in the steepest parts, with risers of cut logs. Down here the stream opened up into a series of wide shallow ponds that provided the main backdrop to the local primary school's aquatic and conservation endeavours, and much of the filth on many a school sweatshirt as well. It had been dry for some days now so the water trickled rather than tumbled, only half filling the wider pools and moving sluggishly over the twigs, old bricks and other detritus that were daily lobbed into its muddy embrace.

'Well,' said Stefan, treading carefully along a length of fallen tree that thrust out and formed a bridge of sorts over the main pool, 'isn't this just beautiful?' He was, I presumed, an urban sort of person. He released his hand from the branch he'd been holding and took another three careful steps along the log.

I stayed on the bank, not knowing what else to do and feeling more than a little stupid in my sundress and sandals. He seemed to have nothing else to say and the silence was becoming unsettling. 'It's a great place for frog spawn,' I told him. 'We come to these woods quite a lot. Though I don't like to enquire too deeply about what Leo and Simeon get up to when they're down here on their own.'

He reached the end of the tree trunk and stood for a moment, as if listening for something.

'Best not to, then,' he answered finally. 'Little boys in the woods. *Naughty* little boys in the woods. When I was a little boy I used to pull the wings off butterflies and make them funeral pyres in old hollow tree trunks. Hmm. Slugs and snails and puppy dogs' tails. And Jabberwockies.' He raised a finger. 'Best not to know what the Jabberwockies do once the nice human folk are tucked up in their beds, eh?'

His back was still to me, his body now motionless. I continued to hover on the bank, uncertain how to respond. I wondered if he was off on a trip of some kind. I didn't like to ask. It made me feel edgy. 'I don't think we have many Jabberwockies in Cefn Melin,' I said at last.

He took another step. 'Ah, you say that!' he said, reaching the end and turning gracefully on his toes. 'You *say* that. But how would you know? *Listen!*' He put a hand to his ear.

'And as in uffish thought he stood,
The Jabberwock, with eyes of flame,
Came whiffling through the tulgey wood,
And burbled as it came!'

It was difficult enough to follow Stefan's train of thought at the best of times, but even harder when he kept popping poetry into the conversation as well. And more difficult still to think of anything useful to say in response to it. Stefan was very good at stopping ordinary conversations. Should I clap, perhaps? I clapped. 'That's nice,' I said. 'Very atmospheric. I remember it from school.'

He took another step, said, 'Callooh! Callay!' Then

leapt from his tree trunk and pulled me into his arms.

Oh, my goodness me. What *was* it with Stefan and poetry? I couldn't work out whether it was him or me or just me being sentimental and girly or him being so exhilarating and unsettling to be around or maybe it was a Tom Cruise in *Legend* type thing – yes, that must be it. With his little suede boots and his long, long hair. And those unicorns. With their thrusting spiralled horns. Or maybe it was the nodding of the creamy upturned faces of the anemones on the bank or the ivory moonlight or the distant swish of the breeze in the treetops or simply his way of being so romantic and lovely and poetic, or maybe the thought of *him* being so turned on by *me* being so turned on by *him* reciting it to me – was it that? I really didn't know. But it seemed to work anyway. For there was now something very, very sexy afoot. He kissed me fairly passionately for several long lovely minutes, but just as I was about to suggest that we zip home and snuggle under my duvet, he released me and bounded off into the darkness once more.

'Come on,' he called. 'Come down here.' He was just like a puppy.

The ground fell away sharply to the left of the stream here, the water itself moving sluggishly over the slimy green pebbles before tipping itself over the rocks into the pool below. I peered down the bank. 'Come where exactly? I can hardly make you out.'

I heard a snap and a rustle and then he moved back into my vision. I felt his hand tug at the hem of my dress.

'Down *here*. Come on. Let's go exploring, shall we?'

I took his hand and slithered down the few yards of slope that separated us. It was darker down here, dank and dewy and pungent. But what little moonlight could find its way through the rampant early-summer canopy of foliage glittered, beguilingly, in his eyes. He led me carefully through the muddle of young saplings and bracken then pulled me against the lumpy trunk of an oak tree and began to nuzzle enthusiastically at my neck. 'Ah!' he said. 'Can you smell it?'

I sniffed. 'Smell what?'

'The scent of growth, Lu. The scent of glorious verdant excess.' He inhaled deeply and twisted us round so that my back was now against the tree. 'This is such a fertile time of year. Everything consumed with the drive to thrust, to grow, to reproduce. New life everywhere. Fecundity. Abundance.'

His fingers slipped under the straps of my dress. He stroked one aside and bent to kiss my shoulder. An owl hooted.

'Mmm,' I answered. I could feel my heels sinking into the soft earth beneath me. The knobbly protrusions of the bark against my back. His hot sweet breath on my face, and the warmth of his hands, which were now working industriously at the buttons on my dress.

Which went all the way down. He showed no signs of stopping. 'Stefan,' I said, 'it's not far to home now. Do you think we should—'

'What?'

'Be, well, doing this – *here*?'

He stopped fiddling and smiled disarmingly at me. Then stepped back and spread his hands wide. 'Doing what?'

My dress, I noticed, was now undone to the waist. My boobs looked white and alarming in the moonlight. Like beacons. Or a pair of quivering vanilla blanc-manges. 'You *know*.' I glanced around and then pulled the edges of my dress back together. '*This*.'

He stepped forward again, then took my hands and looped them back up around his neck. Then teased my dress apart again and slipped both his own hands inside it, running them ever-so-slowly over my breasts.

His mouth twitched in amusement. 'What – *this*, you mean?'

I nodded. Swallowed a gasp. He was incorrigible. And obviously on a completely different exploratory quest from the one I'd anticipated. 'I mean,' I said, 'lovely though this is, wouldn't we be better off getting back to my house, and, well . . .'

He shook his head and lowered his face to my throat. 'I don't think *I* would be better off. Would you?'

'It's just that I'm not sure I'm comfortable with the idea of . . . I mean I'm *very* comfortable with the idea of . . . oh, Stefan! But I'm not sure I . . . Well, what if someone comes by? Walking their dog or something? . . . Oh, it's just that is this *really* the place to be . . . oh, *God*, Stefan . . .'

He moved his face lower still and lapped at my breasts for some moments, then lifted his head again, scooping his mane of hair to one side. His voice had developed a sudden gravitas and depth. Like a voice-over. Were there gorillas nearby?

'Lu,' he was urging in my ear, 'this is *exactly* where we should be doing it! Amid all this organic bounty. Among the thrusting shoots and stems. Bruising the new bark and crushing the foliage. This, believe me, is where it should *always* be done. Isn't it? *Isn't it?* Can you go with me on this?'

Organic bounty sounded more like a Tesco promotion than sex talk to me, but talking was fast becoming an irrelevance anyway. By this time his hands had evidently decided upon relocation. They were now cruising purposefully up the outsides of my thighs, scooping up the hem of my dress on their way. 'Just say, though,' he was saying to me, quite conversationally, as he flipped it up and scrunched it deftly between our stomachs. 'You only have to say. Is this difficult for you?' He reached behind me and took hold of my bottom. 'Would you feel more comfortable if . . .' I felt his hands slide beneath the waistband of my knickers '. . . if – there we go, now! – if, say, we lay down or something? Would it help if I – hang on—'

And then the talking seemed to tail off. I couldn't hear a great deal, with his face buried, as it was, against the side of my head, but I *could* hear one thing. The sound of a zip.

And I wasn't wearing a zip.

Sunday 6 May

Did I really *do* that? Did I?

We had run home straight afterwards, flushed and giggling and breathless, but Stefan didn't stay. He came in briefly, wolfed down two bowls of Sugar Puffs, then kissed me, got astride his bike and pedalled off into the night. I sat on the doorstep for a good twenty minutes, staring into the night sky and wondering whether I was right to be feeling so disconsolate and agitated.

I tiptoed quietly upstairs, almost forgetting to remember that Leo was sleeping over at Del's – which now bothered me some as well – then stripped off, cleaned my teeth and turned on the shower. I was just about to step in when something caught my eye in the bathroom mirror. Some sort of mark on my bottom. I brushed at it and it dropped on to the carpet. I looked down.

It was a slug.

I slept as I assume hapless villeins used to in medieval times. Uncomfortably, damply, plagued by nameless anxieties, and, as I'd left the window wide open, a plethora of small bewinged wildlife as well. Then woke with the dawn. It was a quarter to five.

As the day in question looked, at least, to be sunny and clear, I called Del early and suggested that, as Ben would be out playing tennis all morning, we take the boys off to the park. I'd seen very little of Leo since Wednesday and if we didn't go off on some sort of shared activity I would lose him for the day to the street life he so favoured at the weekends, whizzing up and down on his stunt bike and swapping Pokémon cards with his mates down the road. And not only that: I *needed* to spend some time with him. Not least because I was beginning to feel it was necessary to reaffirm that I was a grown-up, a mother and a sensible person, not the harlot and wood nymph my actions of the previous night suggested I might be, given half a chance. It wasn't that I had any particular problem with *al fresco* sex generally, or even that I had any specific objection to trees as a location of choice. And it had been fun, hadn't it? But, nevertheless, something uncomfortable nagged at me. It wasn't the dope, but I didn't know what. Why hadn't he stayed? I wished he'd stayed.

'Well,' Del said, getting into the Jag and settling into her seat like a cat on a litter tray, 'I am *pretty* damned excited, I can tell you. I shall call them first thing and confirm that Wednesday's OK for the recce. Ooh, there's a thought. Wednesday. *Is* that going to be OK for you? It'll only take an hour or two and they said they didn't mind making it an early-evening appointment – I told them you worked in the daytime, obviously, and they can always do me first, so—'

'Hang on,' I said, starting the engine. '*This* Wednesday? You mean you've already fixed it up with them?'

She flapped an arm dismissively. 'Oh, Lu, don't be such a *drear* all the time. Of *course* I did. I spoke to them on Thursday. I was going to talk to you about it on Saturday, but then I thought you'd only start whining and fretting again about asking Stefan, so I thought I might as well leave it and just ask him myself.'

Whining and fretting indeed. I backed out of the drive. 'Hang on a minute, Del,' I said, needled, 'did it never occur to you that maybe I should have had some sort of input in this? Don't you think it was just a teeny bit off for you to steam straight in and harangue Stefan about it, without consulting me first?'

She looked at me in such a penetrating way that I wondered for a moment about her nocturnal movements. 'So *don't* you want to do it, then?' she purred.

We set off down the road. 'Well, obviously, now it turns out that Stefan *is* keen on the idea, I wouldn't exactly say *that*. It's just the—'

'The principle, I know. Yeah, yeah. OK. Fair enough. But it also turns out I was right, doesn't it? So we're all sorted, aren't we?' She clapped her hands in her lap. 'Ooh, I can't wait!'

The inexorable march of stark inevitability trotted along my train of thought. 'I was a bit taken aback that Stefan *was* so keen, to be honest. I didn't think it would be his sort of thing at all.'

'Ah, but, Lu, you're forgetting. He's an *artist*, isn't he? A painter. Who *paints*. I told him I thought it might be a good way to get a bit of publicity. Get *noticed*. And he leapt on that one, I can tell you. *Leapt* on it. Bigtime. Oh, I think I've got his measure. He seems very ambitious. So I just hope he's as good an artist as you

134

say he is – I don't want a load of amateurish splattings adorning my bedroom walls. Take note.'

Which strange irony had a decidedly nice feel to it: although, of course, *I* was well able to relate to the deeper resonance that was to be found in work of a more abstract persuasion, I could still appreciate that, to an untutored eye, the word 'splattings' wasn't altogether too far from the mark. But it was a short-lived feeling, because she then said, 'And I have to say, Lu, if you don't *mind* me saying, of course, which I'm sure you don't, that now I've met Stefan I'm not altogether sure what it is that you see in him. He's a bit, well – how can I put this? – *intense*, don't you think?'

'And he wears a lot of sad clothes,' chipped in Leo, as if from nowhere.

'Who does?' asked Simeon.

'Mum's new bloke. He's a dork.'

I threw them both a glare through the rear-view mirror. 'Thank *you*,' I barked, feeling suddenly, inexplicably, tearful, 'and for God's sake, will you stop playing with that window, Leo?' I pressed the 'lock' button. 'What do you mean "*intense*"?'

Del shrugged her shoulders. 'Oh, you know, a bit up himself. All that stuff about the lack of sincerity in western consumerist principles and so on. You can't deny he does have a tendency to drone a bit.'

'He does no such thing. He is just an intellectual. He has opinions about things. He cares. He's—'

'Just a *tiny* bit self-absorbed, wouldn't you say?' She flipped down the sun visor and opened the flap on the passenger mirror. 'Wow, lights! How sweet! And how very useful.' Then up again. Thwack. 'You have to admit that, Lu. He's a bit kind of, well, studiously obscure. You know? Or maybe that's why you find him so attractive. I don't know. You tell me.'

135

'He's just interested in ideas,' I persisted, though with the knowledge that I might as well try to run particle acceleration by her. 'He's a university lecturer, remember. Discussion, debate, aesthetics, philosophy—'

'Aesthetics, philosophy, my backside – while the rest of us just grub around in life's pig-bin, I suppose?' She stroked the walnut on the dashboard. 'Hmm. I *like* that finish. Don't you? Anyway, grubber or otherwise, I just found him a bit superior. And a little strange, if you must know – what's with that risotto thing he brought with him?'

'I told you, he's a vegan.'

'Oh, come *on*. He had milk in his coffee, didn't he?'

And on his Sugar Puffs, now I came to think of it.

'Come on, Lu,' Del was saying, 'don't you think he's just a *little* pretentious?'

'Look, he can't help it if—'

She tutted. 'Well, far be it from me to make judgements about people – but you know me, I speak as I find. Anyway, I'm sure he's very nice once you get to know him. Which reminds me. Where'd you get those fab flowers in your toilet? From Stefan? They must have cost a fortune.'

'Them? Oh, no.' I shook my head firmly, determined to seize the opportunity of making up some ground at last. 'He wouldn't be so showy and insincere. They're from your lovely Mr Delaney, actually.'

'From Joe? Why?' I could hear the boys sniggering in the back.

'He had them bussed round last Friday as an apology for all the grief he gave me last week. Specifically, to apologize for that débâcle over Angharad's birthday, I presume.'

'Well, how absolutely lovely!'

'No, they're not. They stink of corpses. Plus, *really*!' I

pulled up at the traffic lights and turned to face her. 'It's so unutterably naff.'

'*Unutterably naff?* How can you say that? I think it's a really nice gesture. How could anyone not be pleased to get a bouquet of flowers?'

'That's not the point. The point is that it's sad. And inappropriate. And manipulative. *And* pretentious, come to that. And it doesn't impress me in the least. I mean, if he was hard up it would be different. Or if he'd actually gone to any trouble over it – that's the *real* point. It means nothing. It was just a phone call. Send her some flowers and smooth things over. An empty gesture. Which I was not impressed by, I'm afraid.'

Del stared at me for a few seconds, then raised her eyebrows an inch and tutted again. 'Keep your hair on, Mrs Touchy,' she said mildly, patting me. 'I only asked.'

Actually, I *have* felt more charitably disposed towards Joe Delaney since he kissed me because, however unexpected and inappropriate it was, it has at least caused a shift in the power dynamic. Nothing dramatic or tangible, but it has cast a different light over what has gone before, extravagant floral excesses included. But I'm certainly not having Del know that. Not after she's called Stefan strange. And intense. And superior. And obscure. And self-absorbed. And . . . oh, how *dare* she? If only she knew! But, on balance, I'm glad now I didn't tell her about last night.

And thank God I never mentioned the poetry.

Wednesday 9 May

True to his prediction, Joe did indeed need his arm to be rebroken and reset. A bed had been booked for him for the Thursday, and because he was on the morning list and had to be admitted the night before, I dropped him off at the hospital on my way home from work.

'Listen,' he said, as I pulled his holdall from the back seat, 'I need you to do me a favour. I'm supposed to have Angharad tomorrow, and I'm going to be stuck in here. Could you pick her up after school and bring her in or something? I know it's a hassle, but Rhiannon is on some book-club seminar or something and won't be back until seven thirty or so. And she'd like to come in and see me, and – well, yes?'

I handed him the holdall. 'Can't you miss a week?'

He shook his head. 'I missed last week.'

Hmm. 'But surely it would be easier if you saw her at the weekend instead, wouldn't it? You do have her weekends sometimes, don't you? It's not as if you're going to be up to much tomorrow evening anyway. And what about her tea?'

He considered for a moment. Then nodded. 'Yes, you're right. She'll need to be fed. So you could stop at Burger King or somewhere on the way, couldn't you?'

'But how's she supposed to get home again?'

'I thought you could take her, couldn't you? Rhiannon doesn't live far from you.'

'No, I couldn't, Joe. It may have escaped your notice, but I do have a child of my own to look after.' I got back into the car and did up my seat belt.

He stooped to peer in through the window. 'Please? Pretty please? It's not as if it's really out of your way or anything.'

'That's hardly the point. What am I supposed to do with Leo?'

He exhaled and put the bag down. 'Can't you bring him with you?'

'No.'

'Well, I don't know, then. Whatever you'd be doing with him anyway, I suppose. What does he normally do when you're at work?'

'I told you. My sister looks after him.'

'And she wouldn't mind, would she? Oh, come on, Lu. Please? It won't be that late.'

I switched on the ignition. 'It's not *about* that. It may have escaped your notice but the job specification I was originally given did not, as far as I remember, include spending my evenings running around all over Cardiff.' Or playing nanny to other people's children, for that matter. But I didn't say that. Because it would have been mean.

He shrugged. 'OK, so you'll be a bit late. Take the morning off instead. Have a lie-in or something.'

'But I don't want to take the morning off instead.'

'So don't!' He stood up straight again, and snatched up his bag. 'God, Lu, why do you have to make such an issue of everything!'

There's been some sort of spillage on the A469, so that by the time I get home (and still muttering to myself – what a deeply, *deeply* exasperating man), Del's car is already parked outside. Along with Stefan's bike, a small yellow sports car and a van that says Hightime Productions on the side. There is also a cluster of beautiful people in the front garden, hovering in the sunshine like an art installation. They all look on politely while I, cringing slightly, swing the Jag carefully into the drive. *Roomaround*. Oh, God. And I haven't even cleared away the breakfast things.

'*There* you are!' announces Del, in a booming contralto, sweeping down alongside the car and swinging the door open for me. I feel as if I've just turned up late to a party. Everyone else seems to be on happy pills or

139

something. She gushes and flaps and twitters at me. The prospect of impending celebrity has obviously gone to her head – and with rather unfortunate consequences for her relationship with her wardrobe. She seems to be wearing a bedspread. And it is clearly contagious. Stefan, who should know better as he is quite beautiful enough anyway, has put a large diamanté stud in his nose.

Urrgh, urrgh, urrgh. TV people, if this lot are anything to go by, are very, very shiny. They have shiny smiles, shiny teeth, shiny hair, shiny footwear, and astoundingly shiny (and hence rather scary) expressions. The only misfit in this dazzling confection of media-glitz is the resolutely unshiny Damon Denton, whom I recognize immediately, even without his trademark circular saw. He is matt and unshaven and ordinary, and has flecks of emulsion on his jeans. He glides a reverential hand over the bonnet of the Jag, then sniffs and says, 'Well nice. *Well* nice motor. Pretty poky?' Someone else, whom I don't recognize but who is possibly the shiniest of them all, in a gold leather trenchcoat, extends a slim bejewelled hand. 'Lucy!' she purrs at me. '*Lovely* to meet you. I'm Manda Producer.' She says this without a discernible pause between the words Manda and Producer, so it is moments before I realize that it's not that she has a name like a vampish South American soap actress, but that it's actually her job title. She releases my hand and beckons to the others. 'And this is Kit Davis-Donovan, who'll be working with Del, here, and our Tia. Tia Slater, who'll be working with you.'

Tia Slater is not so much shiny as fairy-dust shimmery. She is wearing a tiny powder blue fluffy sweater and jeans that begin about an inch above her crotch. She proffers her own small but very workaday

hand and says (rather predictably, I decide), '*Ciao.*'
Hands are shaken, pleasantries exchanged, and we all
troop off into the house.

Where I have, it seems, an Anaglypta complication.

'The thing about Anaglypta,' Kit Davis-Donovan is
saying, twenty minutes later, 'is that you have to decide
where you stand with it. Do we *go* Anaglypta? Go down
that road? Do we?' The *Roomaround* recce team are
clustered on my three-piece suite, clutching mugs of
tea. Though Manda has yet to take off her coat. There is
a ripple of disconsolate hmm-ing, to which Kit nods an
apologetic acceptance before turning to me. 'Where do
you stand on blown vinyl, Lucy, my love? Have you
had any thoughts at this stage? Been up long? Hmm.
Looks like it. And a touch soiled in places, if you don't
mind me saying?'

I do mind him saying, but I'm sure my sensibilities
have a far rougher ride yet to come, so I shrug and tell
him I have no strong opinions on the matter and that
I'm happy to put my walls in his hands. Heads are
shaken, notes are referred to and, though it is not
actually said by anyone, I feel very much like I've
misrepresented myself somehow. As if I'd made up
some O levels.

And in truth, I'm clearly making light of this. I must
bite the bullet. I do not have an Anaglypta complication. I have an Anaglypta *crisis*. I have a wallcovering
irregularity of mammoth proportions. I have a category-
A logistical disaster. A bad start. A question mark
over my televisual suitability. A difficulty that must
be addressed before my humble abode is deemed
appropriate as prime-time TV footage. In short, I have a
layer of lining paper, a layer of wallpaper, a layer of
blown vinyl, and at least four (three since *I*'ve lived

here) layers of vinyl matt emulsion on top. They will have, they tell me, about seventeen hours.

'Well,' says Kit brightly, 'we could always camp out in the van and get it whipped off tonight, I suppose.'

Hur hur hur, goes Manda. Hur hur hur.

'Or you could leave it,' suggests Tia, from the safe haven of being in charge of Del's biennially steam-stripped and perfectly plastered bedroom. 'Go for retro. Go for kitsch.' She is sitting next to Stefan on my sofa. And their knees are touching.

'Isn't kitsch a bit kitsch, these days?' he asks, very seriously. 'I mean, wasn't kitsch last year's thing?'

'Not necessarily,' argues Kit. 'Not if we put a different spin on it. Ideas, team? Come on! Heads together.'

'You've got pattern here, though, remember,' chips in Tia, casting a disapproving eye over the bit of wall behind the sofa. 'You've got fresco-city. We're not just talking a random wood chip here. I'm not altogether sure you wouldn't just be talking *nightmare* city, scheming wise. It's got to come off. Really it has. Don't you think, Lucy? Wouldn't you like to be shot of it?'

I tut and roll my eyes as if getting shot of my Anaglypta has always been the first, and not the last thing on my mind.

'So how about we just bloody *take* it off and be done with it?' says Manda. 'I'm sure Lucy and Stefan here could make a start, couldn't they? Couldn't you? I don't see any problem with a bare-plaster opening scenario. Do you?'

Kit frowns. 'Bit *DIY SOS*, don't you think? Bit *Home Front*?'

'When's tea, Mum?' says Leo, who has wandered in.

'Fifteen minutes,' I say.

'You said fifteen minutes half an hour ago.'

'No, I didn't. I said it would *take* fifteen minutes. I didn't say I had actually started it. I won't be long. Why don't you and Simeon go and—'

'You'll have to let us have a Twirl, then.'

'I will have to do no such thing. You can—'

'But, Mum, we're *starving*.'

'Which is precisely the way I would like things to remain. Off you go.'

'But, Mu-um—'

'I said no.'

'But, Mu-um—'

'Oh, *come* on, Mummy. Let them have a Twirl. *Go* on,' says Damon Denton. 'Don't be such a meany.'

Meany indeed. I go and get the Twirls.

Because we used to have a hatch, and because we decided to dispense with the hatch by means of a bit of hardboard, a dozen tin tacks and a painting (as us plebeian DIYers are wont to do), I can hear Manda and Kit's summit talks while I'm turning the boys' chicken dippers. As clear as an acid-etched cupboard-front window motif.

'Dump it?' he's saying. 'Go with the oast house, after all? We're only talking a few bricks there. It *is* an option.'

I can hear a pen clicking. 'Not,' she says. 'I spoke to Sal at lunchtime. It's for definite. He's fucked off and is *not* returning. Why the fuck do these dysfunctional couples *apply*? Anyone would think we were a branch of bloody Relate! So *not*, period. Because there's some talk of a writ flying about as well. Though why anyone with a fireplace surround as monumentally grotesque as that would have the slightest inclination to hang on to it is way beyond me. Hur hur hur. And the other couple were such primitives, didn't you think? Did you see her earrings? Don't think I could bear it. Nope. We'll have to push on with this one. Sad but true, kitten. Stout gloves, I'm afraid. Stout gloves.'

By the time I have dished up the children's tea, measurements have been recorded, brows have been knitted, notes have been taken, and Kit Davis-Donovan has pronounced himself full of some '*so* now and radical' scheming ideas for my through-lounge. But it has also been decided (by whom?) that my Anaglypta will definitely have to come off before they begin. There is talk of perhaps sloshing up some magnolia emulsion but, as they finally take their leave, even the *Roomaround* whiz-kids have conceded it's a lot for me and Stefan to fit in in the next six days.

I wave them off and head back to the kitchen with the feeling that I have made a very grave error of judgement. I am not attached to my Anaglypta particularly, but am far less attached to the sort of activity that will end its long association with my walls. That's their job, isn't it?

'Six days! Well, thanks a bunch, Del! Like I haven't anything else to be doing between now and next Wednesday, have I?'

She pours me some wine and puts a reassuring hand on my arm.

'Don't fret,' she soothes. 'We'll all help you. With the four of us doing it – Leo and Sim can help as well, can't they? – we'll soon have it off.'

'Actually, I'm not sure how much of a help I can be,' Stefan counters.

Del tuts. 'Ho! And you an artist! You of all people should be good with your hands.'

He shoots her a look. He seems to have *her* measure now. 'No. I meant that I'm not sure I'm going to be that free over the next few days. I have a full teaching

commitment this week and a big study to finish. So
I—'

'Big study?' asks Del. 'You have a decorating sideline
on the go, do you?' She knows very well that this is not
what he means.

I glare at her. 'Painting. A *painting*,' I say. 'One of the
ones for Exo?' I ask him. He drains his coffee then
nods. We made love three glorious times last night. I
wish I could get his eyes to acknowledge it. They don't.

'But I'm sure I could help out on Sunday or something,' he offers. 'Anyway, must go. No lights with me.'

I follow him out into the hall while Del begins
clearing the boys' tea things. I had hoped he'd stay for
a while, but evidently not. I feel responsible somehow.

'Look,' I say, while he shrugs on his jacket, 'we don't
have to do this, you know. It's not set in stone or
anything. We can always say no. *You* can always say
no.'

He loops his arms around my waist and nods
towards the kitchen. 'What? And have your big sister
after me? I think not. Besides,' his hands snake up
under my jumper, 'I'm quite looking forward to it. And
I'm sorry about the stripping, but I do have rather a lot
of commitments right now. I'll do what I can. OK?'

The arms are gone again. And as he leans to kiss me
goodbye I can smell something fragrant and flowery
and vaguely familiar in his hair.

It is Tia Slater's perfume.

11

Thursday 10 May

Have caved in, naturally, where Angharad is concerned. Not because I'm particularly happy with the
situation, but because I don't want to deny her the
chance to see her father, however much of a truculent
grouch he can be. And also, it has to be admitted,
because I don't want to be considered a person for
whom making an issue about things is an issue.
Though why I should worry, I don't know. Issue,
indeed.

Angharad looks smaller and less confident when I
meet her outside school. Her toffee-coloured hair is
tied in a neat plait down her back and she is wearing
school uniform of a kind not seen in the public sector
since about 1972, involving, as it does, both blazer and
boater, the latter topped off with fat green ribbon.

The teacher, who has obviously been primed to
expect me, shunts her towards me with an encouraging
pat. Angharad looks tense and a little afraid of me.
'Mummy says I'm not allowed to go to the park or
anything because I'm still in my school clothes and I
might get them dirty.' It sounds as though she has been
practising this speech for most of the day.

I smile in reply and steer her towards the car. 'Don't
worry,' I tell her, as I unlock the door. 'We're not going

to the park. I thought we'd go and have some tea in McDonald's and then we'd go straight to the hospital and see how Daddy's getting on.'

Her eyes light up at this prospect, and once encased in the car's familiar leathery embrace, she seems to relax a little. 'I made him a card,' she says. 'At first break. It was wet play so we were allowed to get the colours out and use the paper in the scrap box.' She fishes in her reading packet and produces a folded sheet of pale blue paper, which she places in her lap before putting on her seat belt.

'I was going to bring him a present as well. I had a Bob the Builder Easter egg left because it's white chocolate and I don't like white chocolate and I know Daddy does – he *loves* it – but Mummy wouldn't let me give it to him. She said I couldn't take it because it might get squashed at school and they didn't let you take Easter eggs into hospitals anyway, because of germs.' She looks downcast. 'I wish I did bring it now. I wish I did.'

Such a complicated and distressing business, this sharing of a loved one by people who can't stand one another. So sad.

'Tell you what,' I suggest brightly. 'There's a shop at the hospital. We'll get him some chocolate there. I'm sure it will be all right with Mummy,' I add, seeing her doubtful expression, 'because it's hospital chocolate so it's allowed. Anyway, do you like hamburgers?'

'Nuggets, mostly. I like Happy Meals.' She brightens. 'And I could give Daddy the toy as well.'

As it's getting late and the traffic is beginning to build up on Newport Road, we eat our Happy Meals and bring our dessert – two McFlurries – with us. Angharad, once again, looks worried. 'What about the car?' she says, as we cross the McDonald's car-park. 'I'm not allowed to eat in the car.'

I press the remote control and open the passenger door for her. 'You are today,' I tell her. 'Special treat.'

Joe is on Pasteur Ward, on the second floor, and, having made a visit to the League of Friends shop and Angharad having decided that Joe would probably like the Happy Meal toy better than a box of Roses, we can't find a stairwell, so we join a shuffling group of pensioners and take the lift instead.

Angharad, who has been gaining in confidence by the minute, wrinkles her nose. 'Pooh-ee!' she bellows, as the doors sigh shut behind us. 'Someone in here smells of wee!'

Joe is in the far corner of a ward of four. The other three are at least double his age and snuffling gently, like hibernating voles. I shepherd Angharad past them before she has the opportunity to make any further observations and deposit her at the side of Joe's bed. I feel a little uncomfortable with him, sitting up, as he is, in his green plaid pyjamas with a plastic identity bracelet on his wrist. He, on the other hand, looks completely unconcerned. If a little grey.

'Bleurgh,' he says, to me. 'Bleurgh, Lu. *Bleurgh*. Hello, chicken.' He lifts his good arm out towards her. 'And how was school?'

Angharad pulls a face and throws her hat down on the chair beside the bed. I pick it up and sit with it in my lap. 'Boring,' she says. 'Would you like some of my McFlurry?'

He pulls a face. 'I don't think so. What is it?'

'It's an ice-cream, silly. It's the one with the smashed-up Smarties in. I was going to have the Crunchie one but they ran out. Would you like your present? It's a Snoopy. And you can take his head off. And it has a typewriter and if you put the bit of paper in the back it really writes on it. Can you see? And I made you this

148

card. It says, "Get Well Soon Daddy", and I got Sophie to sign it as well. But I did the kisses and most of the rainbow.'

'It's very good.'

'I'm better at colouring than Sophie. She went over the lines a bit on the yellow but I did the blue and the orange without going over the lines at all. See? What's that thing in your hand?'

He hands me the card and pats the bed. Angharad climbs up and sits beside him.

'It's called a drip. It's got a painkiller in it. It's so it doesn't hurt too much.'

'Will your arm stay bent like that when they take the plaster off?'

'I hope not.'

'Is there a hole in it?'

'I think so. I think they've put a pin in it to help fix it.'

'What, like a safety-pin?'

'A bit like a safety-pin. Only different. More like a nail or a screw.'

'Yuk!'

'Oh, it's all right. It's a special one for arms. It fixes the two bits of bone together and holds them in place.'

'Doesn't the plaster do that?'

'Well, sort of. But this is just to make sure.'

'Doesn't it hurt?'

'A little bit. Not too much.'

'Because of your drip.'

'Because of my drip.'

'Does it really drip? Or does it just pour stuff into your hand?'

'I'm not sure. I think it's called a drip because it only lets in a little bit at a time. So it's not the same as it just pouring in.'

'What would happen if it just poured in, then?'

'I'd have too much. They have to measure it.'

'Why?'

'Because if I had too much it would make me feel bad.'

'Why? If you had more it would make you feel even better, wouldn't it?'

'It doesn't work quite like that. You have to have just the right amount. If you have too much it makes you feel funny.'

'Like beer?'

'A bit.'

'So it's bad for you to have too much.'

'Yes.'

'Does it still hurt when you're asleep?'

'No.'

'Why not?'

'Because I'm asleep.'

'Megan Williams in my class said that things do hurt sometimes when you're asleep. She said her mum had to have the whole inside of her leg taken out and she was asleep when they did the operation and she still felt it. And it hurt her.'

'I'm sure it didn't.'

'It did. She's going to sue the hospital and get lots of money. You could do that. What's that bottle under there?'

'It's for if I need the toilet. So I don't have to get out of bed.'

'Yuk! Why can't you get out of bed?'

'Because of my drip. It's fixed on that stand there. See? And because I've just had an operation so I'm a little wobbly still. So it's best if I stay here for a while in case I fall over or something.'

'Why would you fall over?'

'Because I'm still feeling a bit funny from the anaesthetic.'

'What's the anaesthetic?'

'It makes you go to sleep.'

'Like if you have too much of the painkiller drip?'

'Not quite. It's supposed to make you go to sleep. While they do the operation.'

'So they have to measure it like the painkiller drip?'

'Yes.'

'So they probably measured Megan Williams's mum's one wrong, didn't they?'

'Um . . .'

'I expect so. But yours was OK, wasn't it? Because you didn't hurt.'

'Um . . .'

'Is it hurting now?'

'Ug . . .'

'Oh, Daddy! What's the matter? Oh, yuk! Oh, *yuk*!'

Oh, *yuk*.

He's not *hugely* sick, but quite violently so, and there is fall-out all over my trousers. But the main thrust, as it were, is on Angharad's tunic. I call for a nurse then scoot her off to the toilet, her wails of horror growing more voluble with every step.

'It's not a problem, Angharad. It will be just fine, *really*.' I stand her on the step stool that's in there, then flip the tunic front up into the sink and run the hot tap over it. 'Look, it's all coming off now, see? Come on, don't worry. Don't cry. Mummy will understand. It's only wet now – there, see? And I'll explain to her all about it. She won't mind. She really won't mind. And I'm sure you've got another school tunic, haven't you?'

She is cheered somewhat by the novelty of drying her clothes under the hand-dryer, but is nevertheless a bit traumatized. As I would be if I were her. Once she's only damp rather than dripping, I take her back to the ward, where a pair of nurses, bent with their mop pails and Marigolds, are finishing the cleaning before re-making the bed. Joe himself has been dispatched to the chair, where he is sitting, looking better now, and twirling Angharad's school hat in his hand. It is twenty past six and I want to go home.

'Well,' he says brightly, as we shuffle up alongside him, 'trust me! Fancy Daddy being sick all over you!'

Angharad brightens a little at his jocular tone but elects to keeps a prudent four feet from him. As do I. It will be half past six by the time we get outside. Twenty to seven before we're out of the car-park. Five to seven, driving slowly, before we hit Cefn Melin. Seven by the time we reach Pontprennau, where Rhiannon lives. Half an hour still to kill, then.

'Well,' I say, 'you've certainly got a bit of colour back. Daddy's looking much better, isn't he, Angharad?'

She nods. 'Did they put too much painkiller drip in?'

One of the nurses pauses, plumped pillow in hand. 'Your daddy,' she tells her, 'had a glass of Ribena. Told him not to – didn't I? – but the thing is with daddies that mostly, my lovely, they simply won't do as they're told.'

'Look at the state of you!' barks Rhiannon, an hour later.

With a little directional assistance from Angharad I have pulled up in front of a neat modern semi, one of many of its kind, and very recently built, set high at the end of a rambling close. Because it's been built on the side of the hill, some are set down from it, and others set up. This is of the latter kind, with a curled herringbone path that leads up through a rockery, and a flight of three steps leading up to the door. Which means that Rhiannon is looking down at me now, in an oyster-grey suit and a pair of excruciatingly pointy reptilian skin boots. There is a smile of sorts on her face but she is otherwise making little attempt to disguise her irritation. With Angharad, with me, but mainly, it seems, with Joe.

'Daddy was sick.'

'Sick! Dear God, is *that* what it is?' She wrinkles her nose and takes Angharad's hat from her. I hand over her school-bag as well.

'One of those things,' I suggest helpfully. 'It couldn't be helped.' She shoots me a look to say that, far from it not being able to be helped, she is quite convinced that it has been carefully arranged and scheduled with her annoyance uppermost in mind. Right down to the lurid purple effect. 'Some people don't take anaesthetics very well, do they?' I go on. 'It's all over my trousers too. Still, no matter. We got cleaned up as best we could, didn't we, Angharad? No harm done. As I said, just one of those things. Well—'

'Well. Well, thanks anyway. For bringing her home and everything. Say thank you, Angharad. Typical of him to cause all this fuss. And all of it entirely un-necessary. I don't quite know what he was thinking of – which is nothing unusual, mind you. I *told* him he didn't need to bother this week. My friend could just as easily have had her. It must have been a *huge* hassle for you.' She scoops a hand around Angharad's head and pulls her in over the doorstep. The hallway beyond is tastefully bare. 'In and get that lot off and into the washing now, young lady – mind you, every-thing's a huge hassle where he's concerned, isn't it?' Her eyes flick up and make contact with mine. '*Every-thing.*'

She laughs. A conspiratorial laugh. I suppose (particularly now that I'm conversant with her version of the facts) that I should agree, and wholeheartedly so. But it doesn't feel right somehow. So I shrug instead.

She shifts her weight on to one foot and crosses her arms. 'And how *is* the wonderful world of combustion these days? As scintillating as ever?' She makes combustion sound like sewage. And I can't help thinking there is a slur on me buried in there somewhere too. I wish I could tell her I'm actually an ex-teacher soon to be mature art student and so on. But that would be childish, so I can't.

'Oh, it's not that bad. Not *quite* the same job I started with, but, well . . .'

She peers past me to the car and back. 'How much longer have you got to cart that oversized slug around?'

I'm not sure if she means Joe or the car. 'It'll be another six weeks, I suppose. Longer, perhaps. I don't really know. I'm only working for him temporarily anyway—'

She waves my long-term plans aside. 'I must say, I think you're incredibly tolerant. I would have thrown the book at him if it had been me. And no way would you catch me ferrying him around like you seem to. You're supposed to be a secretary or something, aren't you? But that's him all over, isn't it? Don't worry about anyone else. As long as he's all right. Are you from around here?'

Or something indeed. 'Er . . . Cefn Melin. Not far. Anyway, I guess I'd better get back and pick up my son.'

'Oh,' she says. 'You have a child too, do you?'

'Yes, and one who I'm sure is beginning to think his mother has abandoned him. I'd better go. See you. 'Bye.'

As I drive off I ponder, for a while, about Joe's

154

insistence on the necessity of my bringing Angharad to visit him. By rights, I should be very cross with him. It hadn't been necessary at all. But then I think about Leo and how I would feel if I were in Joe's shoes, were my parenting time apportioned and rationed in such a way. I recall what he said about Rhiannon in France. I wonder about their marriage. I wonder about his infidelity. I wonder about their divorce. She and I, it would seem, share common ground where Joe is concerned. By rights, I should roll my eyes with her at him. But I'm glad I didn't, somehow. Glad, in fact, that I went.

Sunday 13 May

Stefan arrived just after lunch and by early evening we had managed to strip all but the wall with the fireplace. Leo, who had spent the latter part of the afternoon, which had been rainy, holed up in his bedroom cataloguing his Gym Leader cards, appeared in the doorway. 'Can I go out and ride my bike now?'

'No, Leo,' I said. 'You have homework to do. In fact, why don't you go up, get it done, have your bath, get your pyjamas on, and then we'll be straight down here and you can watch TV for half an hour before bed? OK?'

He looked at me with exasperation. 'But I don't want to watch TV. I want to ride my bike.'

'Then you should have done your homework this morning, when I asked you, shouldn't you? Homework, bath and bed, young man. School in the morning.'

'But it's only ten past seven.'

'No buts, Leo. Now, come along, scoot.'

He scooted, as instructed, closely followed by Stefan,

who loped behind him as far as the door then closed it quietly.

'Come here,' he said, taking my hand.

'What?'

'Come and look at my creation.'

He pulled me over to the other side of the room, where he had contorted a couple of scraggy bits of wallpaper into some sort of raggedy free-standing sculpture. He stood them side by side on the window-sill. They looked vaguely bovine.

'What are they supposed to be?'

'Can't you see? They're representational. Look harder.'

'Goats?'

'Goats!'

'Some rabbits, then.'

'*Rabbits?*' He separated the pieces and adjusted their position on the sill. 'There. That help?'

'Um – are they human?' I asked him.

'Human*oid. Of* humanity. As I said, representational.'

I nodded. 'What do they represent, then?'

He tutted. 'Sloth, on the one hand. Lechery, on the other. See?' He gestured. I considered making some jocular comment about him putting it up for the Turner or something, but with Stefan you could never be sure he wasn't being serious, so I decided against it.

'Very nice,' I said instead. He scrumpled up his masterpieces in his hand and gestured towards the living-room door.

'Sloth and lechery. Lechery and sloth.' He stretched and wound his arms around my middle. 'Which is my point.' He nodded. 'That son of yours, is he likely to be long up there?'

'Depends whether he has any problems with his homework or not. Why?'

156

'Oh, just wondered. I've been scrabbling away at this bit of wall all afternoon and I thought it was high time I had a scrabble at something a little more yielding.'

He had, in fact, been scrabbling fairly intermittently. And he'd gone off for a quarter of an hour a little while back, because I wouldn't let him open his Old Holborn tin in the house.

His hands now found their way under my T-shirt with unnerving speed and accuracy, and I felt a familiar surge of heat diffuse through my stomach. 'Oh, really?' I answered, allowing his hands to linger a while and curling my own around his neck. 'You did, did you?'

He grinned. 'Indeed I did.' He lifted a foot and brought it down speculatively on the pile of wallpaper we had heaped up at the foot of the wall. 'Something yielding and soft and spreadeagled on some Anaglypta, ideally. Come on,' he urged, pulling me against him and opening his mouth to kiss me. 'Let me strip you to your naked brickwork and sugarsoap your nooks. Mmmm?'

I wriggled free and picked up his scraper for him. 'Here. Have patience. If we give it another hour or so that son of mine, as you call him, will be tucked up in bed and fast asleep.'

He looked at me petulantly, and drew me against him again.

'It's been a long afternoon and you've been jiggling about in those slinky jeans of yours like some smoky-eyed siren. What is a man to do?

    ' "Now, therefore, while the youthful hue
    Sits on thy skin like morning dew,
    And while thy willing soul transpires
    At every pore with instant fires . . ."

157

'Lu,' he urged, covering my lips with his own as he spoke, 'I really don't know if I can wait another hour.'

I twisted a lock of his hair around my finger. 'Well, you'll just have to, I'm afraid. I'll go and make us another cup of coffee, shall I?'

He followed me into the kitchen. 'There's a thought,' he said, sidling up behind me and cornering me against the washing-machine. I could feel his pelvis pressing into the small of my back. '*There*'s a thought. How about I just slide up your T-shirt, like so, and then undo your bra – like *so* – and—'

Excited but a little unsettled by his persistence, I prised his hands from my breasts and tugged my T-shirt down again. 'Stefan! Stop that! Leo might come in.'

He was breathing hard. He *was* hard. He pressed himself even more firmly against me. 'No, he *won't*,' he whispered into my ear. 'He's doing his homework. You said so.'

I swivelled around to face him. 'Which is no guarantee he won't come down here wanting to know how to spell Merthyr Tydfil, I can assure you. So put me down, will you, and let's have that cup of coffee.'

'I don't want coffee. *I* want to do some homework. I want to extend my carnal knowledge. I want to pop you up on to that work surface and peel off those jeans and—'

'Come on. You're being silly.'

'How so?'

'Because we can't make love in the middle of my kitchen. Not right now. Got it?'

'Yes, we can.'

'No, we *can't*.'

'Yes, we *can*. And what's more, Lucienne, my lovely lady, you will enjoy it hugely. Look,' he took hold of one of my hands and steered it towards the front of his jeans, 'I need to make love to you now. I really do. Here. Now. *Right* here. *Right* now.' He was fiddling feverishly with the button on *my* jeans now. '*Come* on, live dangerously, why don't you?'

How I wanted to be able to live dangerously for once. There was a moment – a tiny moment – when the logistics of our situation seemed suddenly, enticingly, exhilaratingly compelling. That being pinioned against the Formica in a shuddering, spontaneous explosion of passion was the best, indeed the *only*, way to bring this situation to its natural conclusion. I was breathing hard also. I was scarily randy. Stefan's ardour, which had thus far made speedy progress – my jeans were undone now and he was *yanking* them off me – was pricking at my few remaining shreds of sanity. And, before too long, were I not to resist his advances, something would be pricking at my knickers as well.

But it was only a moment. There was, in that instant, another kind of pricking. The pricking of a nerve-janglingly shrill maternal conscience. That would not, it assured me, be able to stomach or countenance the picture of me, jeans awry, legs akimbo, jammed up against the toaster in red-faced abandon, while Stefan's smooth little bottom pumped me into the wall. And then Leo walking in. Oh no oh no oh no oh no.

'No, Stefan!'

'Oh, *yes*! Yes, yes!'

'I said *no*!'

'You meant yes!'

'I meant *no*!'

'No, you didn't!'

'I *did*!'

'No, you *didn't*!'

Punctuated, as these breathy utterances were, with a

159

frazzled and inelegant ballet performed between my (frustratingly, increasingly irresolute) hands and Stefan's (steadfastly resolute) willy, it was odds on that, before long, a climax would loom. And I was not having that, for him, me *or* the toaster, however many poems he panted in my ear.

'God, it's *Leo*!' I hissed.

It was a lie, of course. And it worked like a charm.

'I'm sorry,' I breathed, moments later, my modesty whipped safely back inside my clothing and my frenzy of arousal slapped back firmly into place, 'but I thought I could hear him coming down the stairs. Look—' Stefan had turned away. He seemed to be having some difficulty with his flies. 'This is just way, way too stressful for me. But,' I stepped away from the cupboard front and slipped my arms around his middle, 'I am now almost *beside* myself. Truly. So let's get finished in the other room, and I'll get Leo into bed, and then you can make love to me any which way you want to. On my worktop, under the stairs, draped over the occasional table, whatever. Indeed,' I kissed the back of his neck, 'I shall *demand* that you do.'

Which was quite a forward speech for a quiet girl like me, I can tell you, so it made his response altogether less than welcome.

'We'll see,' he said, shrugging me off him. 'We'll see.'

Monday 14 May

I don't like Mondays. Actually, that's not strictly true. I *do* like Mondays – I certainly like them much more now than I used to, at any rate. But I don't like *this* Monday. I hate this Monday.

In the end, Stefan didn't stay long enough to ravish

160

me, because Leo did indeed need some help with his homework – ostensibly only a handwriting exercise, but in reality, via grunts, denials, shouts, tears and eventual conciliatory hugs, also the draft cover design and introduction for the project on Antarctica he was supposed to have started a week back. By the time he had been properly dispatched to bed, Stefan (astonishingly, given his earlier work-rate) had finished the last of the stripping and was standing in the hall, putting on his jacket. He had got to get back before nine, he said, as he had a couple of students dropping off portfolios or something. He hadn't mentioned it before, and I seriously doubted its authenticity, but as my repertoire of seductive behaviours did not extend to a bold and unsolicited shedding of either my clothing or inhibitions (standing, as I was, holding Leo's dirty socks and pants), I had little with which to hold him except my disappointed and wide-eyed blinking. And it failed. Utterly. He had evidently been telling the truth earlier, then. He kissed me goodbye, but with little enthusiasm. It seemed I had missed my moment.

'See you at class on Tuesday, then?' I asked forlornly, as he straddled his bike.

He pedalled up the drive and turned into the road. 'Expect so,' he threw over his shoulder.

So here I am at work, and it is Monday, and it is drizzling, and I feel like the pits, and I *look* like the pits, and there is a postcard on my desk. It is a postcard of Cardiff Bay by night: lights twinkling gaily, barrage resplendent, landmark buildings proud and clawing the skyline. I turn it over. It says, simply, *Sorry*. And then, underneath, in a scrawl at the bottom: *God, I could kill for a fag!*

Yes, OK, I know. I *know*. I know I shouldn't have. And I know it was silly of me even to think it. But I really had thought Stefan had sent it. I don't know why I should have thought this. This is Monday, that was Sunday. Post doesn't happen that fast. And it was only for a moment. A tiny fragment of a moment. But enough of a moment for my heart to do such a joyful little leap and a cartwheel. But it was closely followed by another moment, this one so jam-packed with horrible recollections and feelings that it felt like the best part of a month. I have got things all wrong. I have displeased him hugely. What a horrible start to the day.

'There's lovely,' remarks Iona, who has obviously recognized the writing. 'I saw it when I came in. He's not so bad, really, our Joe, is he? He can be very thoughtful when he puts his mind to it. Um. Er. What's . . . er . . . he apologizing for?'

Oh, I really, really don't want to talk about Joe. 'Nothing terribly dramatic,' I tell her. Her brows twitch a little. 'No. *Really.*'

I tell her about what had happened at the hospital (she isn't in the office on Fridays) and reassure her that Joe is doing fine. Then I pop the postcard into my desk drawer and get back to the job I suspect I will be spending the day on: feeling bloody miserable and fretting about Stefan.

The rest of the day was spent on the laborious translation into French of various parts and assemblages, topped off by a call from the lizardly Jean Paul, who wanted to discuss the specifications of some new power system and to let me know the date of some big dinner in June. Even down the phone he made my skin prickle.

'I love listening to you speaking in French,' smiled Iona, once I'd put down the phone. She obviously hadn't quite caught the thrust of my tone. 'It has such a lovely lilting ring to it. It must be lovely to be able to speak another language. And useful too.'

'I don't know about that. The only use it's ever been to me has been to chain me to a frustrating and unfulfilling job for the last fourteen years.'

'Ah, but it must be nice. Being bilingual, like. I would have loved to learn a language. To travel.'

Iona, I knew, came from Carmarthen, and was a fluent Welsh speaker. 'You are bilingual,' I told her.

She snorted. 'No, lovely. I mean a proper language.'

'Welsh *is* a proper language.'

'And about as much use as a chocolate teapot. Nick – our lad – went to Welsh school, you know. Complete waste of time. We had hoped he might make some use of it. Join the BBC down at Llandaff or something – he's a bright lad and they like native speakers for the telly – but he didn't, of course. He went into public relations. He works for an international charity.'

'There we are, then. It must come in useful sometimes, I'm sure.'

'Not really. He's just moved to Hemel Hempstead, lovely. Bought a house with his boyfriend.' She looked crestfallen.

'Oh.'

Just as I was leaving Joe called. 'Don't panic,' he said. 'I'm not going to drag you up to the hospital or anything. I'm already home. I got a cab. But I'll be needing a lift in tomorrow. That OK?'

'Fine,' I said. 'How are you? Is everything OK now?'

'Well, they scanned it this morning and made confident-sounding noises about it, so, yes, I suppose so. Bit of a bitch to be back at square one, though. Still, it was entirely my own fault, so I shan't bang on about it. Eight-ish OK?'

'Fine,' I said again. 'Oh, by the way, you know I mentioned about that TV makeover thing? *Rooma-round*? I forgot to mention on Thursday but they're planning to film it this week so I'll be needing to take Wednesday and Thursday off. I know it's short notice, but is that going to be OK? The brochure translations are all up to date, and I can finish off the parts catalogue tomorrow.'

'I'm sure we'll manage.' He paused for a moment. 'You sound like you're *really* looking forward to it, Lu. I don't think. Everything OK?'

Was it really that obvious? 'Yes, fine,' I said again.

I was just heading out when a man was heading in with a bouquet of lilies. 'L. Fisher?' he asked. 'Glad I caught you. Late order. Enjoy!' And with that, he was back off down the stairs.

Flowers. *Again.* I took a look at the message. It said, *You're a star.* Not from Stefan, then. No.

12

Tuesday 15 May

Another grey day. Joe has been out for most of it as there has been a minor conflagration in the basement of the law courts, which he's been busy sorting out with one of his engineers. Iona, currently, is cleaning the computer. She has been sent a trial pack of some specialist brushes that attach to a miniature vacuum-cleaner, which she has been applying with vigour to much of the office electrical equipment. I have spent much of my own dreary boiler-drenched doldrums hoping Stefan will telephone and recite me some poetry, but even as I'm thinking this I know it won't happen. He teaches undergraduates all day on Tuesdays. And he doesn't have a mobile because of microwave rays.

Or whatever. Joe is back in at four, a little stressed, a little grubby, and understandably anxious that Cardiff's penitents are not incinerated prior to their cases being called. I remember to thank him for the flowers, which I've arranged in the office, and he tells me my timing is absolutely perfect. He needs to replace some pivotal knob or flange or rivet or other, so could I please, pretty please, drive him out to his parts store?

'That's OK,' I tell him. 'But I absolutely *have* to be away by quarter to six. My class.'

'Class?' he asks, poking a pencil up his new plaster. It is covered in a layer of mesh, as protection. In shocking pink, because he promised Angharad he would. 'Oh, yes,' he says. 'Your painting class.'

I try to discern an element of sarcasm in his tone, but I don't think there is one. Even so, I still feel instantly rattled. We don't paint. It's not a *painting* class – it's a learning-to-*understand*-painting class. And painters – artists. Understanding artists . . . but I don't bother. I don't think he'd know the difference anyway. And in any case, to be honest, I think it's probably just me. I spend so much time gazing in awe at great painters, yet I'm not altogether sure what I hope to achieve. All it makes me feel is useless. As if anything I might attempt will be risible. I've not finished anything since I started these classes. Not a single picture. God, it's been weeks since I've even got out my paints. Is that what it's supposed to be like? Is that what I'm *supposed* to feel? I've learnt so much about other artists – truly great artists – but what on earth is that going to qualify *me* to do? So why *do* I go? Why do I bother? Maybe he's right. Maybe I *should* be at a painting class. Maybe I should just be sitting at home painting. Would that make more sense? Oh, he makes me so mad.

He puts down the pencil and riffles through his Filofax.

'What time does it finish?'

'Seven.'

'Actually, that'll suit me even better,' he replies. 'It'll be getting on for that before I'm finished at the courts. I'll walk over and meet you and you can drop me on your way home. Whereabouts will you be? Somewhere on Park Place?'

I shake my head. 'No. We're having a lecture in the museum.'

'Even better. I'll be just across the road. I'll meet you there about seven, then?'

'That's OK. But it mustn't be any later. I've got to pick Leo up, remember.'

I haven't spoken to Stefan since Sunday evening and we're a good half-hour into the class before he speaks, in any meaningful sense, to me. But he seems to have got over his huff, at least.

Stefan has given us a lecture on Monet tonight, about his water-lily phase. Apparently Monet did eighteen studies of his lily-pond at Giverny, and I'm now sitting in front of one of the three that are owned by the museum in Cardiff, trying to get my head around the essence of his motifs (or something), trying to make notes on his brushwork (or whatever) and trying (mainly, and very, *very* hard) not to track Stefan's movements like a sniper. He spends what feels like an age with the pneumatic young Cerys then squats down beside me and peers over my shoulder. I have written nothing. I have drawn nothing. I have done nothing.

'Everything sorted out for tomorrow, then?' he asks.

'I guess so,' I say. 'As sorted as you can be when your home is about to be invaded by Cefn Melin's answer to the style police.'

His hand, reassuringly, is moving over my shoulder as I speak, pausing briefly to commune with the base of my ear. 'Good, good,' he says, nodding. 'I thought I'd get over to you early. Bring some stuff round.'

'You could come tonight, if you like,' I suggest, suddenly hopeful. 'I could come down and pick you up, maybe. If it would make things any easier.' But his head has started shaking before I can even finish the sentence.

'No, no,' he replies, rising, and patting me on the

head with his clipboard. 'No need, really. And I've got things to do tonight. Just as easy to make an early start.'

'Whatever,' I say lightly, trying to swallow my disappointment and wondering what kind of activity constitutes 'things'. 'It's up to you,' I add. 'It was only a thought.'

Towards the end of the lesson, I notice that Joe is already in the museum, strolling up and down and pretending to look at paintings, but in reality, I suspect, eavesdropping on Stefan. Then I see them deep in conversation as I go down to fetch my bag and coat. They are standing in front of an abstract by John Hoyland. Stefan is pointing. Joe is nodding. By the time I've been down to the cloakroom and returned, Joe is alone, and now looking at the painting opposite. It's a recent work, by a Welsh artist called Kevin Sinnott, an exuberant oil, full of light and colour, in which two running figures are set against the backdrop of the apex of two steep valley streets. I know it well.

'This is one of my absolute favourite pictures,' I tell him, as I draw up alongside him. 'The thing that's always struck me about it is that you can't be sure who exactly is who. It's called *Running Away With the Hairdresser*, you see. The guy who painted it studied at Cardiff, you know. And don't you think it has all the qualities of a great impressionist work? I mean, I know I'm no expert, but don't you think it's reminiscent of Cézanne, somehow? The quality of the light. The way it's so intense, you know. That sort of acuity you get when it's about to pour down, but the sun's still hanging in there. And the brushwork. It's so immediate, isn't it?'

'Mmm,' he says, turning and studying me for a moment. 'Right, then. You ready to go?'

We head down the front steps. The air is warm and

full of pollen. Despite my disappointment about Stefan and his 'stuff', we have at least communicated. As they have, it seems.

'Dear me,' Joe observes chattily, as we head across the road and into the gardens beyond. 'What a wanker that guy is.'

I stop in my tracks by the Rossi's ice-cream van that's habitually parked there. 'I beg your pardon?'

He tilts his head back towards the museum. 'That tutor of yours. I mean he obviously knows his subject but, well, *what* a wanker, eh?' He glances at me, then chuckles to himself.

I continue walking. And say nothing for some moments. 'Really?' I venture finally. *'Why*, exactly?'

'Oh, come on, Lu. You've got to admit it. I mean, I know you're into all this art lark and everything but you surely can't take all this stuff *that* seriously, can you? I mean, I'm as in awe of great art as the next man. But when all is said and done, some of the paintings in there are, well, quite beyond me. How can anyone stand there and be so bloody metaphysical about something that could have been done by a five-year-old, for God's sake? Or a load of stripes? Dear me, is that what you get up to in your classes? Learning how to spout that sort of élitist bilge?'

'Different things,' I say haughtily, 'appeal to different people. Just because you do not personally respond to some forms of artistic expression does not make them any less valid, you know.'

The smile dies on his face and he looks at me sharply. 'Oh, *absolutely*,' he agrees. 'But the same, therefore, can be applied in reverse, can it not?' There is now an edge to his tone. 'Which is exactly what I'm saying. Just because someone – me, for instance – does not get the point of something does not, by inference,

169

make them a pleb. Just because someone has not made it their business to memorize huge chunks of pretentious and largely meaningless artsy psycho-babble, does not mean they lack the necessary tools to make an informed judgement about artistic merit.' He puts much of this in verbal quote marks. 'Or lack of, for that matter,' he finishes, gruffly. 'A fact that *that* wanker,' he jerks his head back towards the museum, 'would do very well to remember.'

We reach the end of the gardens and wait at the crossing while the early-evening traffic streaks past us.

'That *wanker*,' I tell him, as the lights turn to red, 'just happens to be my boyfriend.'

There is a longish pause, which I try to savour as I walk. Which I *would* be savouring as I walk were it not for the fact that declaring Stefan as my boyfriend makes me feel like I've just put a bad spell on myself.

'*What?*' splutters Joe. '*Him?*'

He turns and walks backwards for a few paces as if a second view of Stefan might crystallize the reality of the situation in his brain.

'Yes, him,' I say.

'You mean, you and he are – he and *you* are – good God! Ooops! I see. Sorry about that.'

'No need to apologize,' I say stiffly. 'You weren't to know.'

He looks at me pointedly. 'Because you never said.'

Much as I am aware that there is an underlying accusation in his tone, I refuse to acknowledge it. Wanker indeed. 'I wasn't aware it was in my contract that I had to keep you informed of the details of my private life.' Such as it is right now.

'Yes, but, well, you never said,' he says again. 'So you can hardly blame me for—'

'Calling him a wanker? No. I can't.'

'But I'm sorry, anyway.' The smile is creeping back now.

'No, you're not.'

'Yes, I am.'

'Oh, yeah? Only because if you'd known he was my boyfriend you would have kept your opinions to yourself. It wouldn't have changed them any, would it?'

'Well, I don't know about that. If I'd known he was your—'

I whirl round to face him. He stops with a judder.

'It doesn't make any difference! You think he's a wanker. On the evidence of a five-minute conversation with him you have decided he's a wanker. Fine. End of story. But I don't *care* what you think of him anyway. Your opinions don't matter a fig to me, OK? Or to him, for that matter, I'm quite, quite sure.' I resume my walking. 'Why should *he* care what someone like *you* thinks of him?'

He catches me up. 'What do you mean, someone like me?'

'Someone,' I say acidly, 'who clearly hasn't a modicum of artistic intelligence. Someone who obviously has the intellect of a gnat.'

'That's hardly fair.'

'It's *perfectly* fair. If it's acceptable for you to breeze around deciding people you don't know from Adam are wankers, then it's *certainly* fair for me to make the observation that you obviously have the intellect of a gnat. In fact, I would even go so far as to suggest that the two things might not be entirely unrelated.'

'Not true, actually.' Is he *grinning* now? God! 'I can call him a wanker because it's an opinion. *My* opinion. Which I have every right to.'

We reach another junction and I turn to waggle a finger in his face. 'Hang on. Hang *on*. You just told me you were sorry you called him a wanker, did you not?'

He waves his plastered arm at me. 'I'm talking hypothetically. Anyway, as I said, that's a *value* judgement. An opinion. Whereas your comment about the extent of my intellect is not. Intellect, as far as anything of that kind can be measured, is a quantifiable thing. I could, for example, produce evidence to support the fact that I do not have the intellect of a gnat. So it's not the same thing at all, is it?'

I set off across the road. 'And can you?'

'Can I what?'

'Produce some evidence. Come on, Mr Smartass, let's hear all about your credentials, shall we? Let's see what qualifies you to call Stefan a wanker. Let's see how much *you* know about art, shall we?'

He stops on the opposite pavement and stares at me. 'Lu, that isn't the point at issue. Look. The point at issue here is that I called that guy – Stefan, was it? – a bit of a wanker, which—'

I continue round the corner into the lane where the Jag's parked. 'Not a *bit* of one,' I correct him. 'Just the definite article.'

'And you've gone completely bloody potty! Look, I'm sorry, OK? I opened my big mouth and stuck my boot in it. I don't know him. It was just an observation. A throwaway observation. Which I would most certainly not have made if I'd known who he was. And I'm sure if I did know him I'd have cause to revise my opinion. Or not, as the case may be. But, as you say, I didn't know he was your boyfriend, and now I do—' He stares at me. 'Oh, God! Now you're crying! Oh, God! Look, I've got some tissues in my case. Hang on and I'll—'

'I don't want your bloody tissues!' I fish the car keys

172

from my bag and stab at the remote. 'Just get in the car, will you!'

'Look, is there something—'

'Yes! No! Look, just leave me alone!'

We drive, in a cold and foggy silence, for the twelve minutes it takes to get from his parking space in town to his house in Cyncoed.

'Look, Lu,' he begins, as he undoes his seat belt, 'I—'

'Goodbye.'

'Er . . . well. Good luck for tomorrow, then.'

'Goodbye.'

See you Friday, then.'

'Goodbye.'

'You're pre-menstrual, my darling. That's all it is. Come on. Pour yourself a nice big glass of wine and curl up in front of *Millionaire* or something.'

I already have a glass of wine. I have a glass of wine and a thumping headache. The kind of headache that is usually demonstrated in aspirin advertisements by means of exploding craniums. The kind of wine that would be better employed dressing a salad in a Little Chef. And were Del in the room she would doubtless observe that I have a bit of a face on as well.

'I'm not pre-menstrual, actually,' I correct her. 'I'm just very pissed off. Why am I doing this, Del? Why? I'm sitting here in what looks like a Nigerian field hospital after a locust attack and I've just told my boss to fuck off.'

'You didn't!'

'I did.' I sniff. 'But only after I drove off. I don't think he heard me.'

'So, no harm done, then. But should I enquire why?'

'Because he called Stefan a wanker.'

'Ri-ight. And when was this?'

'Tonight. After my class.'

'And would this be for any particular reason?'

'Oh, I don't even know. Something to do with something he said to him about some painting in the museum. I'm not even sure what. He didn't realize Stefan and I were going out with each other. And he was taking the piss, Del. Oh, I'm just so bloody *angry*.'

'So I can hear. I thought you were a bit peculiar when you came to pick up Leo. Why didn't you say something?'

'I couldn't trust myself to speak.'

'Well, I wish you had. If I'd known you were in such a flap I would have whipped out my ironing-board and given you some of Ben's shirts to take it out on. But, as I said, no harm done. And I suppose he is entitled to his opinion.'

'*Don't* say it!'

'Say what?'

'That you agree with him.'

'I wasn't about to.'

'But you do, right?'

'No comment. I'll leave all the *faux pas* to Joe, thanks.'

'Grrr! That's *exactly* what makes me so bloody mad at him. Who does he think he is? I'm a bag. Stefan's a wanker. What right has he got to hurl his abuse all around the place wherever he bloody chooses? Huh? He's a horrible, pig-headed, arrogant man and I don't care if he bloody knows it!'

'I'm quite sure he already does.'

'And I'll tell you something else. If he sends me another bloody bouquet of his bloody stinking flowers, I tell you, Del, I'll shove them right up his bloody arse! Oh! Leo! What are you doing downstairs? Look, Del, I'd better go.'

'Hang on a tick. There was a reason why I called you. Two things. One was to say that we'll be over first thing. They'll be coming to yours first in the morning because they want to do the opening link at the end of your road. And the other was a favour. Weekend after next. I was wondering if you could have Simeon for me. I've got a date for getting my eyes done. Well, one eye done anyway. It's on the Monday, in Bristol, but as Ben's at some conference in Bath I can stay over with him, and then he can drive me home. There's some dinner-dance too. Just Saturday to Monday. That OK with you?'

'Oh, the laser thing, right?'

'Yep. Can't wait. I'll say yes, then?'

'Yes. Fine. No problem. I'd better get Leo back to bed.'

'Get *yourself* to bed too. Early start in the morning. Sweet dreams, sweetie-pie.'

I wish I did have some shirts to iron. I wish I had someone to iron shirts for.

13

Wednesday 16 May
8.22 a.m.

'Hello! And welcome to *Roomaround*! I'm Africa
O'Brien and today we're in Cardiff, capital of Wales –
hang on. Should I bother saying that, Mand? That
it's the capital? I mean, doesn't everyone know that
already? What? No, no. Just checking. OK. OK, Bill?
OK.'

'Hello! And welcome to *Roomaround*! I'm Africa
O'Brien, and today we're in Cardiff, capital of Wales.
Specifically, in the beautiful village of Cefn Melin – no?
Cef-in Melin? No? What's that? Cev*in*? As in Kevin?
Kev*un*? Kev*en*? Oh, OK. Cev*en*. OK. Ce-ven. Right.

'Hello! And welcome to *Roomaround*! I'm Africa
O'Brien and today we're in Cardiff, capital of Wales.
Specifically, in the beautiful village of Cefn Melin, a
place whose main claim to fame is a pub that boasts no
less than Oliver Cranwell among its – Oliver Cr*a*nwell?
Who the bejesus is *he* when he's at home? Shouldn't
that say *Crom*well, Mand? *Surely* they mean Cromwell. Sorry, guys. We'll have to go again. What?
Yes? Definitely Cromwell? Tsk. You just can't get the
staff.

'Hello! And welcome to *Roomaround*! I'm Africa
O'Brien and today we're in Cardiff, capital of Wales.

176

Specifically – oh, I don't *believe* this! Typical! Bill? Anyone? Umbrella?'

Don't believe everything you see on the telly.

Africa O'Brien is just the latest of the thirty-seven-odd people who have been descending on my home since something like a quarter to seven this morning. There are runners, carpenters, carpenters' mates, soundmen, cameramen, design assistants, makeup artists, people with giant Frisbees for reflecting the sunlight, people with small clipboards for telling them to, people with lengths of cable slung over their shoulders, people whose job seems to be to hold coats for other, more important people, and people who don't seem to have any jobs at all yet, except standing around drinking coffee from polystyrene cups. There are five vans and a lorry parked up on the street outside, all open-jawed and spewing out stuff. Paint, power tools, wheelbarrows, toolboxes, panelling, timber, sheets of MDF, big lights on stalks, small lights on wires, things in bags, things in boxes, things in strange-looking crates. There are two people erecting gazebos in my garden and another erecting tables and benches for drills. There is someone else busy stacking a rickety trestle with tea urns and cool boxes, tea bags and Coke. There is even, I'm told, at this very moment, a large catering lorry parked up by the sports field, which will cater for any and all culinary whims.

Am rather impressed.

9.18 a.m.

Am no longer impressed. Am amazed, appalled and horrified, frankly, that I forgot one very important fact. Fact that guest couples on *Roomaround* are expected to act as a lumpen foil to the glittering celebrity contingent, and to spend the entire two days in an XXXL *Roomaround* T-shirt and jogging bottoms combo, colour dependent upon season. The latter, clearly the benchmark in clothing-as-contraceptive, feature an elasticated ankle cuff, drawstring and mock-fly detail, plus large interior swags of redundant pocket lining, which make one's hip region reminiscent of the Pennine Way. As it is summer, the choice is between 'sea' (dark blue – thus already nabbed by Del) or 'sand'. For 'sand' read 'yesterday's washing-up water', or 'chicken korma' or 'pork-scratching puce'.

'Slip them on, my love, so we can shoot the opening link,' urges Africa. Someone comes and combs her hair while she speaks to me.

'But these won't fit me,' I explain. 'They're a size sixteen.'

She clucks, which I take to be Irish for 'Tough, mate.' 'Well, you know what it's like,' she says. 'End of the series and so on. All we had left. And better too big than too small, I always say. Think Carol Vorderman! That dreadful *suit*! Ugh!' She pats the top of my head. 'Don't worry. They'll look fine once you've got the T-shirt on over the top.'

I get the T-shirt on over the top. I look like a cot mattress.

I tuck the T-shirt in. I no longer look like a cot mattress. No. I now look like I have seventeen ferrets down the front of my knickers and a guinea pig glued to each buttock.

'There!' she says, smiling. 'You look great, Lucy! Great! And you get to keep them too, you know!'

The leviathan that is *Roomaround* has finally lumbered into being, and after waving a fond farewell to Del and Ben for the camera, we have relocated to their house with our overnight bags (plus Tia, Damon, Manda, Africa, about ten other people, most of the vans, more gazebos, urns, power tools, workbenches, stuff in bags, lights, Frisbees, etc.), and Stefan and I are finally allowed our first taste of the awesome creative capability that has been brought to bear on Del and Ben's bedroom, in which we are now standing. Tia's vision is illustrated by means of a watercolour and ink sketch, surrounded by little fabric swatches and dabbings of paint. It looks very professional.

'So, Tia, what's your main angle?' says Stefan, who is naturally quite at home with the strange, amorphous language of the truly artistic, and who has, I suspect, found a like-minded soul.

'Well,' she says, lobbing a hair hank behind her and stabbing a French-polished fingernail at it. 'Look around you. Angles. Dormer. North-easterly aspect. Tate Modern.' She pauses for effect. 'What else?' Oh, indeed. Just what *I* thought. She casts her hand around and waits for our murmur of approval. 'Screams it, doesn't it?' Stefan nods gravely. 'Plus it's very now. It's very in-yer-face. It's very strong. It's very *statement*.'

It's very statement? Stefan nods gravely again.

'But,' she goes on, 'it needs a different spin. You know what it's like. You can find yourself with a very sixties/early-seventies colour scheming thing going on once you go down that road, and I felt Del and Ben weren't really aqua/taupe/mustard kinds of guys. Am I right, Lucy? Hmm? So I've gone down an entirely different road here and come up with something that I

179

think will draw together the kind of elements I want the room to be defining, but still keeping within the framework of their particular lifestyle parameters. So it's really a sort of Tate/Quality Street fusion thing.'

And she has, too. She turns over a leaf of her big important cartridge pad and on the second page there is a selection of Quality Street wrappers – real ones, both shiny and Cellophane – all carefully stuck down in neat little rows. There's the toffee penny one, the long yellow swizzle, the purple one with the hazel in caramel inside. The red one – Montelimar? – that's always still there after Christmas, and the new turquoise one, whose filling escapes me but which sits very well with the green one next to it. They look very pretty. I'm not entirely sure Del would approve of being described as someone with a mass-market festive-chocolate-selection lifestyle parameter. But they do look very pretty. Very Del, in fact.

Stefan nods gravely again. 'Absolutely,' he says. 'Uh-huh. I'm into your drift, here, Tia. We're talking juxtaposition, aren't we?'

Ah! I know that word.

She nods enthusiastically. Evidently she does too. '*Exactly*, Stef.' Stef? 'Juxtaposition it is. Which is where your paintings come in, of course.' Paintings? What paintings?

She spreads her fingers, and flicks them one by one. 'I'm going weighted voile panels. I'm going canopy. I'm going minimalist window treatment. I'm going glass finials. I'm going light. I'm going shadow. I'm going maximum contrast. I'm going *Utilitarian* stroke *Embarras de richesses*. I'm basically going Jewel Colour, Tate Attitude. Yes?'

Oh, yes. I see. Like it says on her pad.

I don't know what they are talking about.

But my not knowing what they are talking about is obviously an irrelevance.

After we've removed – *sans* Tia and Stefan, who have gone off to look at said paintings – every last vestige of the US eastern seaboard from Del and Ben's bedroom and relocated it to the various rooms, gazebos and storage boxes that the *Roomaround* crew decide will best facilitate the unhampered progress of TV persons through dwelling (which has its own curious protocols and has already necessitated the temporary removal of Del and Ben's front garden gate) we have to shoot the paint bit.

The five tins – which have been arranged on some newspaper in the middle of the bedroom floor – are from one of those manufacturers who have cottoned on to the fact that people will often pay a little bit more if informed that the shade of their choice is an almost exact match to one that was last seen distempering the walls of a late Edwardian toilet in Chippenham. Tia, who has armed herself with a large screwdriver, bids us come and squat expectantly around them.

'Right,' she says, after someone important-looking called Sheena has irritably silenced the six other people in the room – who are scrubbing and sand-papering and barking each other's shins with step-ladders. 'I think you're going to like this.' She prises open the lids with deft jerks of her hand and smilingly – she already has a book out on the subject – exposes her colourist's credentials.

There are three shades of pink. One of purple. One of turquoise.

'Lovely,' I say.

'Perfect,' observes Stefan.

Tia grimaces. 'Oh, *cut*,' groans Sheena.

'I'm going to have to stop you if I may,' she says, batting the man with the sound boom away and joining us on the floor. 'The thing is, sweeties, we need a little more reaction.' Tia is nodding her agreement. 'Teensy bit of shock, perhaps? I mean, like you were expecting something a little quieter, perhaps? The odd expression of doubt and anxiety maybe?' She nudges Stefan. 'Conflict. The punters expect it, sweetie. Makes for better telly.'

Stefan adopts a petulant expression. I am beginning to realize he sees himself as one of these people, and being called 'sweetie' by a woman with a light meter and a pencil in her hairdo does not make him feel very 'in'.

'But I *like* them,' I say. '*They* will like them.' In fact, Ben won't much care as long as no one interferes with his aerial point, and as for Del, well, pink is so her. If it had occurred to Del to decorate her bedroom in chocolate wrappers I'm quite sure she would have. And she's been very canny. She's droned on about 'naturals' at every opportunity, in the confident expectation of a slick double-bluff. Looks like it paid off.

'Well, whatever,' says Tia, popping the lids back on again. 'But you do get the drift, guys, yes?'

11.07 a.m.

'Ooh, I really like that one. Don't you, Stefan? But I'm not sure about that one. It's a little . . . um . . . *bright*, isn't it? I mean, I know you can't tell till it's on the wall, but, ooh, I don't know . . . hmmm . . . don't you think – oh, my *God*! *Oh, my GOD!* Is that *turquoise*? I'm dead.'

Et cetera. This is really very silly.

Lunchtime. And I have found a Welshman.

'Oh, but you must know it! Just past Carmarthen. You take, let me see now, the road up to Pontwelly. It's about five miles past Rhydargaeau, just south of where the Duad meets the Gwili. Lovely place. Just the one pub. And the chapel, of course. My great-great-uncle Trevor's buried in the churchyard, as it happens. Dreadful bronchitis. Collier, of course. Finished up with lungs like two festering cess-pools. Enough phlegm to plaster a wall.'

Lunch is in two sittings, presumably so we can't get together and develop any mutinous tendencies, and we are to be the first. The van, from which a not unpleasant smell (up to now, at any rate) of gravy and onions is emanating, is staffed by a genial man in his sixties, called Frank, and a brace of young girls who look as if they've been misrouted from the *Blue Peter* studio. The menu is liver and mash or mixed vegetable mornay. I note that they very kindly microwave Stefan's Tupperware box of couscous.

But note it from a distance. Because Stefan is sitting on the bank with Tia Slater. And I am sitting with Will, who does the carpentry (*Roomaround* is big on carpentry) that is deemed not exciting enough to merit any footage, but that is nevertheless essential if Damon's to have sufficient time to misinterpret Tia's sketches, get bolshy with Kit and do phallic things with his jigsaw. Will, who used to be a set maker for the BBC, and who is a sort of session musician of the TV home-improvement world. Will, who needed me to come in his van with him, in case he got lost on the way.

As did Tia, of course. It can be no more than a ten- or

fifteen-minute stroll from my house to the sports field, but as one is never too far from a shower in Cefn Melin, it was decided that walking was too much of a risk factor. Tia, naturally, needed a navigator in her little yellow sports car, and Stefan was quick to volunteer. Her *two-seater* little yellow sports car, moreover. I'm not feeling very happy with Stefan right now.

While I'm waiting for dessert, she slides across with their empty plates and helps herself to a cup of hot water, into which she dangles a little herbal tea bag that she has taken from a pocket in her toolbelt.

My banana fetches up. She smiles a little smile. 'Oh,' she coos, 'you put me to shame, you do, Lucy. And two roly-polys, please, Frank.'

7.37 p.m.

Do not care that Tia Slater has the hips of a twelve-year-old boy. Do not care that Tia Slater has a BAFTA for services to B and Q paint sales or whatever. Do not even care that Tia Slater has a way with a wood chisel that has grown men weeping. But care very much that she has developed an interest in the Abstract Expressionists. Because Stefan is now going out.

'What, *now*? Where?' I ask him, shocked.

We had spent most of the afternoon painting. Del's bedroom is now pink and purple with a smart turquoise dado rail, and my hair is similarly hued. At five on the button Sheena announced that they would 'wrap' for the day, and within thirty minutes every last one of them had gone. The house is now empty and quiet and cool, and though the whiff of gloss paint is almost all-pervasive, the scented candles I'm lighting will soon deal with that. I am laying the table. I have

184

plans. I have planned our evening meal. I have planned our evening. I have planned our *night*.

He looks at me guiltily as I blow out my match. 'Back to mine,' he says, and for a moment I think he means for the night. 'But not for too long,' he adds, hurriedly, obviously seeing my expression. 'Just that I have to pick up some more board and paints. Brushes as well.'

I don't know quite what sort of creations he and Tia have planned for Del's bedroom, as their discussions on the subject have not included me. But as they are to comprise the Tate Attitude component, I doubt they'll be watercolours of steam trains or rabbits.

He is fishing in his holdall for his bike light.

'Don't be daft,' I chide. 'I'll drive you. It'll take for ever if you go by bike.'

He shakes his head. 'No, no,' he says. 'Don't worry.'

'I'm not worrying.'

'No. I mean, I'd *rather* cycle. Need the exercise.' How? Why? We have barely drawn breath all day. 'And I might, well, try to pull something new together while I'm there as well. I've got a couple of unfinished canvases that I want to take a look at so . . .'

All this for Del and Ben's bedroom? Why? 'That's OK,' I say. 'I don't mind waiting. We can eat later, can't we? It doesn't make any difference to me.'

In fact, I am rather warming to the idea of spending a quiet hour or two back on Stefan's lumpy sofa. Watching him work. Sipping something. Feeling slinky. But the expression on his face wipes the smile right off mine.

'Look,' he says. And his tone leaves no room for discussion. 'It's better that I go down on my own, Lu. Really. And the sooner I get away the sooner I'll be back, won't I?'

'If you'd rather,' I say forlornly. 'I just thought . . .'

He reaches out suddenly and pulls me to him roughly. 'Come here, my lovely lady,' he growls, hands clasped firmly against my bottom. 'You,' he says, 'really don't get it sometimes, do you? How on earth can I concentrate on work with *you* there, eh?'

He shuffles me backwards till we meet the kitchen doorframe then kisses me hungrily for several minutes. The stubble on his chin scratches my face. His breathing becomes increasingly ragged and for a moment I wonder if he's going to make love to me now, right here, against the door. But he pulls away. 'Right,' he says. 'I'd better go if I'm going.'

'I wish you wouldn't.'

'I must. Don't worry about dinner. Just keep *yourself* warm for me.' He nods upstairs. 'I will be back in an hour.'

Thursday 17 May
7.48 a.m.

I wake to the sound of raindrops pattering against unfamiliar surfaces, and wonder where I am. But when I open my eyes they are greeted by the familiar view from Del and Ben's spare-bedroom window: the towering horse-chestnut, heavy with candles of creamy blossom, glossy leaves running with rain.

I remember. Stefan. Of course. I turn my head. The bed is empty except for me, but there is an indentation in his pillow, and when I slide my hand across the sheet, there is a reassuring warmth.

But not *that* reassuring. Where the hell did he get to? I track him down eventually in the garage. He is painting. Miles away. Doesn't hear me come in. I'm fearful of speaking in case I make him start. I don't want to make him cross. So I cough, very lightly, instead. He turns.

'There you are,' I say. I'm still in my Tigger nightshirt. I feel suddenly silly. 'What time did you get back last night?'

He had called me, just after nine, to apologize. Said he'd become rather engrossed but that he wouldn't be much longer. I'd gone to bed, finally, at midnight, when my eyes wouldn't stay open any more.

He shrugs. 'Don't know. Didn't look at a clock.'

'You should have woken me.'

He's still painting. With small, dabbing strokes. The paint is the colour of blood. His hair is held back with a length of pink ribbon. 'No, I shouldn't,' he says. 'You were sleeping like a baby.'

My first night in bed with a man for God knows how long. My first night in bed with *him*. And I didn't even know he was there. And I was in a silly nightshirt.

'This morning, then.'

'Ditto.'

I move across the garage towards him. The floor is icy beneath my bare feet. 'I wouldn't have stayed asleep for long, I can tell you.'

He stops painting now and points the tip of his brush at me. 'Is that so?' His eyes move the length of my body and back. He winks. 'Tell you what, then, why don't you go make us both a cup of tea while I finish off here, and then we'll take it back up to bed?'

The doorbell goes just as the kettle starts whistling.

'Lovely day for it, eh?' observes Will.

187

As it has stopped raining, I have been detailed to go
into the garden and cut five shades of voile into
what looks like the entire mainsail assemblage of a
nineteenth-century tea clipper. I have been allocated
the far gazebo, and have a sheet of not-very-helpful
instructions from Tia: they are both obscure and
obscured, having had a half-cup of coffee spilt on them.
There are midges everywhere. The scissors aren't sharp
enough. The day is deteriorating fast.

Tia is inside, filming with Stefan. A bit, apparently,
on his paintings, about which everyone – *every*one –
has been droning all morning. I know this is accepted
behaviour. I know TV people tell everyone everything
is lovely all the time, but nevertheless it is getting
on my nerves. I'm sure I shouldn't feel like that. But
I do.

Africa trots across the garden towards me 'How's it
going?' she asks. 'Tsk! What terrible slippery stuff this
is!' She scrutinizes the drawing and tsks again. 'This is
going to be the bed canopy, right?'

'I think so.'

'All these triangles and rectangles and so on fit
together, do they?'

'In theory.'

She parks the drawing under a pin-pot and pulls a
pair of scissors and a tape measure from her dungarees.
'Typical Tia,' she says, finding the bag with the purple
voile in. 'Never can do anything straightforward.
You've to sew this as well, have you?'

'Oh, I hope not. I'm completely useless with anything
involving a needle and thread. I think she said *she*
would.'

'*I* would, more like.' She laughs. 'Anyway, no matter.

Sure it'll look great once it's up there. You think your sister will like it?'

'Actually, yes. Yes, she will. For definite.'

Her scissors slice effortlessly through the fabric in front of her. 'And your man's paintings? Quite a contrast, eh?'

'Er, Del's not really into abstract art,' I tell her.

'And you?'

'Me? Oh, yes. I *love* it.'

1.11 p.m.

I don't know quite why I said that, because the first thing I see when I go back inside to track down the girl who put the sewing-machine to bed for the night is the red creation Stefan was working on this morning, propped against the inside of the front door. And it is just a red rectangle. That's *all*. Big deal. Now the sun looks like staying it's gone quiet inside. Damon is busy in the garden making the fretwork wardrobe doors that Tia intends backing with pink satin, and much of the crew have gone to shoot stuff at my house, before we all break for lunch. However, there is still activity upstairs. Someone, I know, is sorting out some concealed ceiling lighting, under which our patchwork canopy will go. I head up the stairs in search of sewing-machine clues.

There seem to be people moving about in the loft, and as I mount the stairs I peer upwards hopefully. But then I hear something else. The sound of conversation in the main bedroom. It's Tia's voice.

There is a large trestle just inside the open door, on which stands Del's chest of drawers. So from my vantage-point, three stair treads from the top, I can only see her from the legs down. She is standing in front of the window, sideways, and Stefan is standing nearby. They are considering his paintings, obviously.

'No,' she's saying. 'I don't agree. I think the Förg needs to go on the back wall. See the way the shadow falls there? That diagonal from the dormer? I think that'll work better.' I take a step, but then wonder if Bill and Co. are quietly filming, out of sight across the room. Best not to interrupt.

His feet move back a pace. 'Yeah, but here,' he says, 'you'll get the benefit of the downlighter on it. Which, given that this is a bedroom, makes it a much more practical bet. Night, remember. People go to bed at *night*.' He moves back to where he was.

I hear Tia laugh. 'In Cardiff they might do.'

Stefan laughs too. 'I meant *mainly*. I meant to *sleep*.'

'Ah,' she says, 'but what about when they're *not* sleeping, eh? You don't think the right atmosphere – the right *evocation*, even – is every bit as important at those times too?'

She takes a step in his direction and crouches in front of the painting. Suddenly I can see right to her shoulders. Her corncob hair falls in a heavy loop down her back.

Stefan moves too, crouches beside her. His jogging bottoms are doing him no favours, I note. 'Oh, I'm all for the right evocation,' I hear him murmur, standing again. He seems to be leaning to look out of the window. I see him turn. 'But summer's lease hath all too short a date . . .'

Oh, my Lord. He's at it. He's bloody at it! I'm transfixed now. Horrified. Rooted to my stair tread. She says nothing, but stands up as well. Then they turn, face each other and sort of meet in the middle.

There are no cameras here. No big furry boom head.
I slip silently down the stairs.

3.46 p.m.

I have no evidence. No real evidence. I saw nothing –
heard nothing – that counts as such.

'Getting there,' observes Africa who, true to her
word, has spent the last hour turning the heap of voile
shapes into a large swathe of shimmering colour. Tia
and Damon are fixing it up now. Stefan is screwing
crystal knobs on Del's cupboards, and the room is once
again full of people and coffee cups and step-ladders
and mess. And I am trying very hard to be jolly.

'It looks lovely,' I agree. 'Way, way better than I
imagined it would.'

Tia pauses in her pinning and glances down at
me. 'Shame on you, Lucy.' She laughs. 'You should
have a little faith. You should trust me more. I'm a
designer.'

5.20 p.m.

Funny to be back in my own house again. It feels like I
left it ages ago. Africa, who is most insistent that we do
not open our eyes until instructed to do so, shepherds
us over the front step and into the hallway and has us
wait with her there until the sound check is finished.
'This is it,' she whispers, squeezing my hand. 'Bet you
can't wait to see it.'

I've decided I really rather like her. I can hear Kit
Davis-Donovan's voice coming from the kitchen. I can
feel someone brushing my hair.

'OK,' calls someone, and we begin to troop in. 'Don't wander out of shot,' she reminds us.

When I open my eyes it is to find myself in a room much, much larger than the one I used to have. A pretty room. Apple-fresh. Welcoming. Sunny. A room with mile upon mile of pale strip wood flooring that is softened here and there by big fluffy green rugs. It puts me in mind of an orchard in spring, and had I not something more important to try not to cry about, I'm quite sure my eyes would be pricking.

6.10 p.m.

They've chosen to do the closing link in my garden rather than Del's because they've already disassembled the gazebos and trestles. Some chairs are brought round from the catering lorry, and expensive champagne is brought forth from a cool box. There's just one hitch, Sheena tells us. 'They've got a problem with the film and we're going to have to shoot Kit and Africa's last link again,' she explains. 'Won't take long,' she reassures us. 'Come on, sweeties. Let's get this done.'

Someone opens a bottle of champagne anyway, and we cluster in the doorway watching while they rewind the TV clock to half an hour back. The champagne is cold against my dusty throat, and the bubbles go up my nose. I gulp down half a glass. I would like to get drunk.

'There's lovely,' says Will.

'Quiet!' someone barks from behind me.

'Well, Kit,' says Africa, 'you're *way* over budget as usual. Pleased with yourself?' He does his *faux*-guilty shrug. 'So,' she says, 'what are you going to call it?'

Kit swivels on the sofa and glances at the camera,

then the floor then the camera again. 'I kind of thought – wait for it – "Lucy Gets Laid"!'

It is funny in its way, I suppose. It is certainly ironic. I have nothing against Kit. I have nothing against Africa. But as this is my absolute last chance to insert anything like a modicum of control on the proceedings (and as I am feeling more and more miserable by the minute) I cough, loudly, and step over the camera cable.

'Look, do you mind if we stop?' I ask miserably. He looks quizzically at me.

Manda goes 'Tsk!'

'Because my name *isn't Lucy*! OK?'

Kit, as it happens, is mortified.

'Why didn't you *say*?' he entreats. 'I feel awful. *Awful*. Look, d'you want me to check through the rushes before we go into production? Bit of editing, here and there, and I'm sure we could sort it.' He's so apologetic about it that I wish I'd never said anything. And when he tells me that the inspiration for the room came partly from my very own watercolour, which Del got down last week from my loft without my knowing, and which he has put, centre stage, over the fireplace, I have to rush to the loo so he can't see me snivelling.

It's another hour before my house is my own again. Del and Ben have gone back to supervise the striking of camp at their own place – Tia Slater, thankfully, with them – and Stefan is outside straightening the garage. But once I've cleared the last of the debris in the kitchen and gone back into the living room to gather up mugs I find that Stefan is in there and, moreover, donning his jacket.

Again. Oh, *hell*.

'Oh,' I said. 'Are you going?'

193

He nods. He has, I noticed, made fast work of exchanging the sweatpants for his jeans. 'Yeah,' he confirms. 'Got to make a move. I'll leave my bike and my paints, if I may. Tia's dropping me.'

I can feel my stomach falling off a ledge somewhere. '*Tia* is? Dropping you where?'

'At my place.' He doesn't look at me.

'Oh.'

'She wanted to see some of my Abstraction-Création 2000 studies. And it's on her way, so—'

'Oh. Right.'

He pushes his hands into his pockets. 'She's got a friend who's opening a ceramics café in Bristol, apparently, and she—'

'What, *now*? I thought we were going to Del and Ben's for supper.'

Now he does look at me, but guardedly, and only briefly. As if he has already decided that looking at me for any length of time might just bring him out in exploding boils. 'I know,' he says, gathering his hair into a rubber band and sliding his eyes away again. I can hear a car pulling up outside. He swivels his head round to look out of the window. 'But, well . . . now this has come up . . . Look. I'd better make a move. We'll talk later, OK?'

I have trodden so carefully and for so long with Stefan that even though what I most want to do now is tell him what an absolute and utter bastard he is, I seem unable to find words that will take us on to more suitably combatorial zones without my dignity being run down by a loose chariot on the way. He is only, after all, skipping a meal with me for her. Not whipping her off up an aisle. Plus he doesn't know what I know. And I'm not going to tell him. My dignity is precious to me.

'Right,' I say. 'Fine.' And begin straightening cushions.

'Fine,' he says back. Then starts off to the doorway.

There's a voice. But not mine.

'Stef? Are you coming?'

'OK,' he calls back. 'I'll be there in a moment.'

We're now twelve feet apart. He walks out. Makes it twenty. And the moment, such as it's been, is now gone.

14

Oh, woe is me. Oh, woe. Oh, *woe*. Headache, dyspepsia, MSG-induced dehydration, loneliness – oh, such loneliness! Much misery, much regret, *such* remorse. Plus niggling undercurrent of anxiety and guilt about dreadful, infantile, rampage of carnage that performed on Mark Rothko *et* bloody *al* last night. Will go to hell, for certain sure.

'Look,' says Joe. Quite without realizing, I seem to have picked him up, for he is sitting in the passenger seat and talking at me. Perhaps it's all true. Perhaps Jag *is* a pussy. Perhaps Jag will now drive Joe and me into work.

'Look,' he says again, as he puts on his seat belt, 'I don't want to start you off all over again or anything, but can I just say – can I *just* say – how sorry I am that I upset you on Tuesday? I feel really bad about it. It was a flippant, throwaway, meaningless comment, and if I'd had the slightest idea – the *slightest* idea – about you and him then I wouldn't have dreamt of saying what I did. Which is not to say that I wouldn't have thought it, of course – as you yourself said, I would have carried on thinking it anyway because the guy wound me up like you wouldn't believe but, as I said, I am very, very sorry. I was completely out of order and you were quite

196

right to berate me for it – who am I to venture opinions about him? I'm sure he's a very nice guy, once you get to know him, and, well – I hope I didn't upset you so much that you are going to remain in this state of icy aloofness for the rest of the day. I'm not very good with moods. I don't do moods, Lu. I've been at the receiving end of enough moods to last me a lifetime. So I hope we can leave it at that. Can we leave it at that? Yes? So. How did the TV thing go?'

My hands move to turn the key in the ignition and the car somehow moves itself into the road. My mouth then opens and a voice issues forth: 'You're right. He's a wanker,' it says.

I cried a fair bit on Thursday night, of course. Bastard.

After they'd gone, I sat in my new through-lounge and wept hot snotty tears all over a small green cushion. Which made me feel at least sufficiently rejuvenated that by the time Del returned from collecting Leo and Simeon from her friend Julia's to pick me up to take me back to their place for the evening, I had relocated Stefan's bike to a spidery corner of the garage, relocated the hateful jogging bottoms to my Imperial Cancer Research bag and relocated much of my mascara to a tissue in the bin. Had I had so much as a shred of self-esteem left I would have rolled it into the shape of a marlinspike and relocated it up his backside to boot. But I didn't. All I had left was the horrible feeling that the moment I'd *really* cocked up on by missing was the one, back in February, when I could have written 'cancel' on the enrolment form.

'Humph!' said Del. 'Humph! Well, that's charming, that is! I even made him a pine-kernel pilaf! As if I haven't enough to do! Well, in that case I think I'll just

197

shove it all in the freezer and order us a curry in, don't you think? Or is he planning to come back later to bore us anew about his glittering career?'

She looked at me sharply to gauge my reaction.

I fashioned a what-the-hell-who-gives-a-stuff! one. Then twittered it. 'What the hell! Who gives a stuff?'

In the end, we opted for a Chinese, because the boys wanted chicken balls. And two bottles of red that Ben had been saving for some Wales/Norway friendly, most of which we consumed with the hot and sour soup in a kind of hysterical, demob relief.

But I could never keep anything from Del for too long. Once the boys were ensconced with Ben watching football on telly, we took ourselves, plus a wine bottle, up to her bedroom, where I outlined the sorry gist of me-and-Stefan's demise. For demise, whatever agenda he might be working from, was what it most emphatically was. I had had a dull ache in the pit of my stomach all evening – and it was nothing to do with the egg foo yung. It was a horrible way to feel, and I remembered so acutely how it *did* feel. So whatever Stefan's motivation for casting his net in the direction of Tia Slater (and cast it he had – emphatically so) it didn't really matter. One thing was for sure. I wasn't going to be made to feel that way again.

'Humph!' she said. 'What a toe-rag he is! And what the hell's a ceramics café when it's at home? Sounds completely implausible and contemptibly fashionable.' She poured me the last of the wine and put the bottle down on her new bedside table. It rocked slightly.

I sighed and sat down on her bed. I felt used up and grubby. 'I haven't a clue,' I said. 'A café where you can buy pots or something, I suppose. Anyway, I presume it has an ambience that she thinks might be enhanced by his efforts. I don't know. And I don't much care.'

She looked disdainfully at her bedroom walls.

'Huh. Should have let her take these, then. Ugh. They're so gross. D'you know? I don't think I can even bear to spend the night with them. In fact, why don't I just have the bloody things down and be done with it?'

She walked across to the wall and yanked the largest one from its hook above her bed. 'And what's with this disgusting orange? Was it the dregs of a couple of cans of emulsion or something? It looks like cat sick.'

'No, no,' I corrected her. 'You should consider yourself privileged. He did them specially for you.'

'Is that right? Aren't I the lucky one, then? But come on. What was he thinking? I nearly had a fit when I saw it. This room is pink, Lu. And this painting is orange.'

'Tia said it was a trendy combination.'

'Lu, "trendy" is not something I generally strive for. This is a bedroom. Not a branch of Dorothy Perkins. I'm sorry, but you don't put an orange painting on a pink wall.'

I took another mouthful of wine. 'Oh, but it *had* to be orange. It's orange because it's after Still. Clyfford Still, I think it was. Abstract Expressionist. They're all,' I gestured expansively with my glass, 'after Abstract Expressionists, you see. Which was apparently a terrifically important school of abstract art. In New York. In the late – oh, well, I don't know, whenever. But definitely *terrifically* important. That one over there – that maroon one? That one's after Rothko.'

She pulled it down and scrutinized it. 'Is that right, Lu? My dear, it is a piece of board that has been painted red. If I'd paid good money for this I'd be after him too. It looks like a carpet tile.' She slung it on the bed.

I picked it up and looked at it morosely. 'He killed himself, you know.'

'I'm not in the least surprised. Ugh. And as for *this* one . . .' She plucked the third from the wall and glared at it. 'What's this one after? A bucket of paint stripper? A smack in the gob?'

I squinted at it. 'Oh, that's the Förg,' I told her. 'Which means it has – now, let me see if I can remember. Yes. That's it. "A simple beauty that evokes a wistful and spiritual longing." Apparently.'

She lobbed it disgustedly on to the pile. 'Is that so? Hmm. All it evokes in me is a heartfelt desire to throw up. So perhaps it would like to take itself off and evoke it somewhere else. Perhaps,' she took down the last painting, 'it would like to take this monstrosity along with it. Then they can be wistful and longing together. Come on, my darling,' she flopped down on the bed beside me, 'repeat after me, "He's a rat-bag, a toe-rag, a scum-bag and a shit-face, and I'm better off without him." Yes?'

Yes. Ben dropped us back, and after I'd tucked Leo and Pikachu into bed, I took the paintings from the rubbish bag Del had put them in and propped them in a corner of the garage, with the absolute, absolute, *absolute* intention of giving them back to Stefan when he returned, which he presumably would at some point, to pick up his paints and his bike. But, looking at them now, I had a thought. It occurred to me how much I'd learnt over the last few weeks. How much knowledge I had acquired. How much I'd come to understand about art. About impressionism, cubism, surrealism, op-art. And how much I had learnt about their creation as well. How it was that, at the hands of a great artist, a simple square of uniform colour could, if one were to approach it in the right frame of mind, become imbued with the power to explain, to enhance clarity, to help one connect with one's inner life. To act as a metaphor – was it De Kooning who said it? – for relationships, a metaphor for life. I arranged them against the wall, side by side. There was, I had to admit, a certain compelling quality about them. A certain representative resonance. What was it Stefan had said about colour? About the hypnotic quality of tonal juxtaposition? About the essence of the power of colour in abstract art being in its powerful contemplative facilitation? I stood, thus, for ten, maybe fifteen powerful, facilitated, contemplative minutes.

Then I picked up the red one and bashed it to bits.

'Ah. So I was right, then,' Joe says, when we reach the traffic-lights a few minutes later. 'He *is* a wanker.'

I nod my head. 'Yes.'

'Uh-huh. I see. And do you want to talk about it?'

I shake my head. 'No.'

'Are you sure about that?'

I put my head on the steering-wheel. 'Yes.'

'Fair enough,' he says equably, and pulls out some gum. 'Anyway, the main thing is that we've got a busy week coming up and I have to get the rostering sorted today. Oh, and we've also got to get some ads in the paper. Big developments while you were away, because Luxotel have given us the contracts for Bath and Edgbaston – no, no, no need for congratulations or anything – which means I'm going to have to get a big push on, recruitment-wise, and start thinking about expanding on the parts front. Isn't that excellent news? Light's gone green, by the way.'

Light's gone green, indeed. Lights never go green in my life. Never. It's red, amber, red with me, every time, *always*. And by the time we get to his parking space, and he has rambled on in similar jocular fashion, it occurs to me that my life would be so much simpler if I could just let go of all my fanciful artistic and romantic notions and develop a full-time fascination for boilers.

'Oh, and by the way,' he says, as he opens the back door and reaches for his case. 'I've got something for you. Might cheer you up.' He clicks open the case and pulls out a (oh, God – yet another!) painting. It is a picture of chickens and flowers and dolphins and stars, carefully painted in bright poster colours and liberally plastered with green and gold glitter. At the bottom, in tiny joined-up handwriting, are the words 'To Lu. Thank you for my tea, from Angharad Delaney XXXXX.'

'Oh, bless her,' I warble at him. 'How sweet of her. Bless her.'

He beams happily, crumpling his scar as he does so. 'And entirely unsolicited, I might add, in case you were wondering. Which you were, of course, weren't you? But, no, she brought it round with her last night. Oh, and this, too.' He hands me something else. It's a little woven bracelet. 'It's a friendship band,' he explains. 'All the rage, apparently. She – oh, my Lord. Lu! Don't tell me you're at it again!'

This time, I take the tissue he's proffering and blow mightily into it, as if I might manage to expel something of the pain in my head along with the unbidden outpouring of misery.

'I'm sorry,' I mumble. 'I really didn't – I really *don't* want to bother you with all this stuff. I'm all right. Really.' I slide the bracelet over my wrist. 'Could you put the picture back in the car for me, please? I don't want to scrumple it up in my bag. I'm all right. Really, I am.'

He looks doubtfully at me, but does as instructed. 'Tell you what,' he suggests gently, 'let's go for a coffee and a croissant or something, shall we?'

'No, no.' I sniff again. The last thing, the *very* last thing I want to do is slosh around in the mire of my hopeless love-life, particularly with someone with chest hair and androgens and six bloody girlfriends on the go. Particularly with someone who just wouldn't understand. 'You said we were busy. Let's just get to the office, shall we? You know. Get on.'

He looks at me carefully. 'Are you absolutely sure, Lu?'

'Quite sure.' I snuffle.

'Well, OK. If you say so.' We start walking up the lane to the lights. 'Oh,' he says suddenly, 'almost forgot. Your car. They wanted to know if you had any preference numberplate-wise. Won't be too long now, eh? Oh, and which type of hood you were after. There's a choice apparently. I've got all the gen back at the office for you.'

I suppose I should be pleased. I suppose I should be pleased and relieved that Joe has, contrary to all my expectations, simply got on quietly with the business of organizing my car. I wonder if he's paying for it too.

'Oh. I didn't realize there was more than one type. Isn't it just up when it's raining and down when it's sunny?'

But who cares, anyway? There isn't any sunshine in *my* life. Ever.

In the end, I submit to being taken for a coffee, because Iona has brought in Lily's daughter, Aurélie, to see Joe for half an hour, and as it's such a nice day – meteorologically speaking, at any rate, which is something, I suppose – she suggests I might like to walk up to the castle with them at lunchtime and have a sandwich while Aurélie feeds the birds.

We grab a couple of cappuccinos from a café on St Mary Street, and head off towards the castle, Aurélie pushing her teddy in the buggy. If Iona has noticed that I'm not quite myself, she is obviously going to make no mention of the fact. Which is absolutely fine by me.

'She seems very fond of you,' I remark, as we sit ourselves down on a bench.

Iona rolls up the sleeves of Aurélie's jacket and produces a plastic bag from underneath the buggy. 'Oh, and I of her, lovely,' she answers, tearing the bread inside into little pieces. 'There we are! She's a poppet, aren't you, sweetie? It's a privilege to be able to spend time with her.'

I watch as she toddles off, the bag clutched tightly in her pudgy little hand. 'And it must be a big help to Lily right now, with a new baby to look after. How is she doing?'

'Oh, she's a real natural, that one. Well, you've only to look at little Aurélie here to see that. Good as gold, she is. Always has been.'

'I suppose you've known them for quite a while.'

She nods. 'Lily came to work for Joe when Aurélie was, oh, couldn't have been more than a few weeks old. She'd given up her job – she taught French at night school – and I think she'd hoped to stay at home for a bit. But they couldn't afford it. Not on Malcolm's money. They'd set their hearts on a little house, see. And they don't pay teachers terribly well, do they?'

I shake my head. 'Tell me about it.'

'Oh, of course, you'd know all about that, wouldn't you? How on earth have *you* managed all this time?'

'Oh, we got by. My father helped me out with a deposit for a flat, and once Leo started school I was able to buy a place near my sister. She's been so fantastic – she looks after Leo after school for me. Simeon, my nephew, is an only child too. They're more like brothers than cousins. I don't know how I would have managed without Del, to be honest.'

'That's the thing, isn't it? Having family around. But no one seems to stay in the same place any more these days, do they? That's half Lily and Malcolm's problem. They've no one really. Lily's mother's in France, of course, and Malcolm's parents live in Snodland. They do what they can, of course, but it's not the same, is it? Not the same as having them close by. It's a bit of a struggle at times. So I like to help out.'

I pull off my cardigan to give the sun a chance to breathe some warmth into me. 'Do you look after Aurélie much, then?'

'Oh, nowhere near as much as I'd like. But, well, work and all that. Have to earn a crust. But I try to babysit when I can – give them a chance to get out a bit. It's no bother, what with Dai working nights most weekends. I look forward to it.'

'I'm sure she does as well. You must be like a grandmother to her.'

She smiles a happy smile. 'I'd like to think so. Not that I'd want to take the place of her real grandparents or anything. Of course I wouldn't. But I think it's good for a little one to have someone, well, someone like me around – do this sort of thing with them. Bit of time. Few sweeties. Outings and everything. Always too busy when your own are little, aren't you? You must find that yourself, I should think, what with being on your own and having to work full time.' I nod. 'And then all of a sudden they're all grown-up and you wonder where the time's gone. Suddenly they're adults and they don't need you any more. And then you start thinking how lovely it'll be once they have little ones of their own.' She sighs. 'Oh, I know you shouldn't, but you do, don't you? It's only natural. But it doesn't always work out that way, eh? Still, I get to borrow little Aurélie here, so I count myself lucky.'

'Nick's your only child, is he?'

She nods. 'And he's a lovely lad, Lu. Lovely. We're both very proud of him. And his boyfriend, Howard – he's a teacher, too, funnily enough – seems like a very nice lad as well. Very polite. Very friendly. And they seem settled. That's the main thing. We went to them for Christmas last year. And it was a proper home. No babies, obviously, but two *enormous* great dogs. Played hell with Dai's chest, but it's nice to see. And I'm used to things now. Come here, sweetheart,' she calls, 'let's look after Nonni for you, shall we? Don't want him getting pecked, do we?'

Aurélie gives her the teddy and I suddenly realize it's the one Joe bought for the baby. But then something strikes me. He hadn't bought it for the baby at all. He'd bought it for *her*.

Iona starts rootling in her bag. 'Anyway, let's have a look at what we've got in here, then, shall we?' She smiles at me. 'Lily's packed us a little picnic.' She pulls out a small plastic box. 'Let's see. Ooh, quiche. Would you like some? Lily makes lovely quiches. And you look like you could do with something inside you.'

I'm not really hungry, but I realize I haven't eaten anything since yesterday evening, so I accept the thick hunk of quiche she proffers.

She gives me a piece of kitchen roll to go with it. It has a pattern of little blue hens on the edge. 'Now,' she says, through her mouthful, 'I've been *dying* to hear all about it. Did you have a lovely time making the television show?'

*   *   *

When we get back to the office, there is a man on the floor fiddling with the photocopier and a faint whiff of smoke in the air.

'Hello, what's happened here, then?' asks Iona. She narrows her eyes. 'You haven't been smoking, have you, Joe?'

'No, I bloody haven't!' he growls. 'I was just sitting in my office, minding my own business when *that* bloody thing blew up!'

'Blew *up*?'

'Well, not blew up in a particularly explosive sense, but was certainly on fire. I'd set it to run off some application forms. Lucky I hadn't gone out or anything, or God only knows what might have happened.'

The man on the floor grunts then teases something out and sits back on his heels. 'As I thought,' he remarks, holding it up and scrutinizing it. 'Foreign body in the jiminy-doodah [or something].' He gestures to Aurélie and winks knowingly at us. 'You've not let the little one loose around here, have you? Looks *very* like a dolly's hairbrush to me.'

Joe was meeting up with a friend after work and didn't need to be taken home, so when Leo and I got back it was still fairly early. And still light, so I conceded to his request to be allowed to go and get his bike out for half an hour while I made dinner. But so immersed was I in my melancholic thoughts that I had completely forgotten there was a certain important something that I had forgotten to do first. Moments later he was back in the kitchen.

'Mum! Mum! Come and see what's happened in the garage! You will *not* believe it!'

Oh, shit.

By the time I'd cleared the last of the debris into a bin-liner, it was almost nine. And by the time I managed to persuade Leo that, no, we had not been the victims of a frenzied hammer attack and that, no, these bits of painted canvas and board were absolutely nothing to do with the pictures Auntie Del had had put up in her bedroom by the people from the television, and that, well, yes, OK, I knew he *wasn't* a complete derr-brain and that, OK, I *had* been telling a fib, they *were* Auntie Del's paintings and, yes, they *were* the ones that had been done by Stefan, and that though, yes, it *did* look rather like someone had attacked them with no small degree of enthusiasm, this *wasn't* in fact the case, and that the truth was, regrettably, that Auntie Del had decided they didn't really go with her bedroom after all and that she had given them back to me to give back to Stefan and that, oh, deary me, I had had a bit of an accident, in that I had put them down on the garage floor and somehow driven the Jag over them by mistake and made a terrible mess and that it really would be best if he kept it to himself because, after all, Stefan wouldn't know they weren't still hanging in Auntie Del's bedroom anyway, and that there was no sense in upsetting him needlessly, was there? . . . It was almost ten.

I was quite, quite sure he didn't believe a word of it, but needs must where parenting is concerned and, anyway, I also knew that he would have forgotten all about it in the morning.

'Joe?'

It's by now almost ten thirty and I'm busy considering whether the director's cut of the *Texas*

Chainsaw Massacre (with previously unseen footage, etc.) might be a therapeutic way to draw the week to a close when my internal debate is interrupted by the jangle of the phone.

'Yep,' I hear him say. 'Sorry – crrrrrrrrch – to both – crrrrrrrrch – you. I've – oh, hol – crrrrrch – n—' I can hear muffled scrapes then a bang.

'Where are you?'

'On my mobile. In the pub. In the Flag and Fulcrum to be precise. Just *outside* the Flag and Fulcrum now, in actual fact. Just had dinner. There's only so many varieties of ready meals you can stomach in a week. There, that's better. Can you hear me OK now? Yes? Anyway, you OK?'

The Flag and Fulcrum is a pub down in Queen Street. A very trendy pub. The sort of pub where young-buck management types gather to eat tapas at lunchtime, and again to drink pints of Export at five thirty most nights, before stumbling home with a typist if they're lucky, or a takeaway curry if not. The sort of place I had once fondly imagined *I* might find myself sitting outside after work sometimes. Sipping Sauvignon blanc. In a well-cut suit from Next. With a girlfriend from the office. Iona, maybe? No. I wonder what he's doing there so late. I wonder what kind of friend he was seeing.

'Yes,' I tell him. 'I'm fine. Is there something up?'

'No, no. Just thought I'd give you a call. I remembered I've got to meet with one of the engineers first thing Monday. Got to go on site with him. Wondered if you could pick me up a little earlier, that's all.'

It occurs to me that this is a strange time to be calling to sort out what's happening next Monday. 'Yes, that'll be OK,' I tell him. 'As long as it's not too early. What sort of time?'

'Oh, I don't know. Seven thirty? Something like that? If you can manage it. Anyway—'

'I'll check with Del. But I'm sure that'll be fine. Anyway . . .'

There is a short pause. Then he says, 'What are you up to?'

'Nothing much. I was just about to go to bed, actually. Long day. Anyway—'

'Oh, I'm sorry. Did I call a bit late?'

'No. That's OK. Anyway—'

'And *are* you all right?'

'Yes, I'm fine, Joe. Anyway—'

'Good. Only I thought I should just check. You haven't seemed, well, yourself. And, well, with what you said this morning about that tutor of yours, I just—'

'Not "of mine" Joe. Anyway—'

'Exactly. So I just wanted to let you know that—'

'Joe, I *told* you. I'm OK. You really don't need to worry. My shambolic love-life is really something you shouldn't concern yourself with. It's very sweet of you and everything but, well . . . Anyway—'

'Sweet!' He laughs. 'I don't think I've ever been called that before. I've been called plenty of things in my time, believe me, and "sweet" has never been one of them. So I'll take that as a compliment. Doing anything nice this weekend?'

'Cleaning my house. Buying food and so on. Washing. Anyway, if that was all, then—'

'Lu, hold up. One question.'

'What?'

'Why won't you talk to me?' he says.

Just like that.

And I don't even know. 'Look, it's not *you*, Joe,

particularly,' I lie. 'I just don't really want to talk to anybody right now. I'm just tired, OK?'

There is silence for a second.

'Fair enough,' he says. 'Night.' And the line goes stone dead.

Inexplicably, I feel guilty. And it makes me cry.

15

Tuesday 22 May

Six o'clock. Class time.

I thought about not going. Thought long and hard about not going. Thought long and hard about giving up altogether, because I don't wish to put my stomach through any more mangles. But in the end I decided that I had paid good money to be guided in forming my impressions of the impressionists and was not going to have some bloody tousle-haired sex-maniac goblin git hippie low-life preventing me from doing so. So mad at myself about Stefan. So mad about the fact that I've been duped. *Again*. So mad about the fact that I'm still so immature and stupid and utterly gormless that have been unable to see what has been staring me in the face from day one. That I have been merely a diversionary sex-conquest project. A shag, for want of a more poetic expression. Now filed, no doubt, under D, for 'done that one'. Not to mention 'dingbat' and 'dodo' and 'dunce'. Or Dylan, for that matter. Dylan bloody Thomas. No offence, Mr Thomas, but *poems*, indeed.

Then I thought something else. I thought about *him* not going. It occurred to me that there was every possibility that Stefan would not appear to take the class anyway. That the best course of action in the face of having angry rampaging cast-off on day's horizon would surely be to call in sick and have someone else take the class. The more I thought about this the more likely it seemed. Were I Stefan, I decided to myself as I marched up Park Place, I would keep *well* out of my way for a while.

It was with surprise, therefore, that I arrived at the museum, not only to find him sitting outside with his clipboard, bold as you like, but leaping up and scootling over to greet me – arms open wide, smile full of sunshine, hair full of an unseasonal Cardiff-based mistral and circling his head like a basket of snakes. But then again, not such a shock once I thought about it, because the one person who didn't know about me-and-Stefan's demise was, it occurred to me, Stefan. How would he?

'Hello-ee!' he sang, flicking the mane to one side. How girly. How sad. 'How you?' he enquired.

This was Tuesday. I hadn't seen him since the previous Thursday. Not a sniff of a phone call for the best part of a week. Perhaps I had missed some fundamental shift in relationship dynamics, because if his current manner was anything to go by, this was obviously to be considered normal behaviour. There was, it seemed, nothing up between us. Nothing at all. He put a hand on the small of my back, rubbed it around a little, then slipped it southwards and started directing me back towards the museum. Just like that. Bastard. Hello-ee indeed.

'So,' I said, shunting my bag to my shoulder and knocking his palm off my bottom, 'did she like them?'

He blinked. 'Did who like what?' he asked.

I considered responding, 'That bitch off the telly' and 'What d'you think, arse-face? The size of your nuts?' But I didn't. Because you don't. Instead, I smiled and said, 'Tia Slater, of course. Your creation-abduction series, wasn't it?' I loaded the words with as much haughty disdain as I could manage, but he was obviously having none of it.

'Oh *those*,' he said, smiling broadly and shifting his clipboard from one hand to the other. 'My Abstraction-Création series. Yes. Yes, she did. Very much, as a matter of fact. Looks like I might have a few sales on my hands there. She's going to arrange for me to go down and meet up with the owner. Take some smaller studies for her to look at.'

I watched another student walking carefully up the far side of the steps. And I thought about the smaller studies that were residing in a bin-bag in my garage. Substantially smaller studies, in fact. 'Is that right?' I said, feeling an unexpected smile cross my face. 'Well, that's nice, isn't it? So it's been quite a productive exercise for you, then, hasn't it? Good for you. Are we going straight in?'

He turned around at the foot of the steps, blocking my route.

'Have you got the car with you?' he asked.

His hand was sliding up the sleeve of my jacket. A very intimate thing for it to be doing.

I ignored it. 'Of course I have.'

'Excellent. I wondered if you could run me back with you. Pick up my bike and stuff. And if you hadn't any other plans, I thought we might, well, I don't know. It's a nice evening. How about we stroll down for a walk in the woods or something? I don't know. What do you think?'

I looked him square in the eye. 'You, me and Leo, you mean.'

'Um. Er. Well, yes. Yes. Why not? Or we could maybe just go back to your place and . . .'

And? And? *Well?* He shuffled about on his feet and

214

scooped his hair out of his face again. Why didn't he just have it bloody cut?

'Actually Lu,' he went on, 'I wanted to ask you a favour. I had a call from Mand yesterday.'

Oh! *Mand*, is it? First-name terms now, are we? Big luvvie pals, eh?

'And it seems she's got a friend who's a commissioning arts editor for the BBC and who's looking for artists to profile for a new documentary series they're making. Charting the influence of the major twentieth-century movements on the work of contemporary artists, and Mand's told her about *my* work and, well, actually, I was wondering if your sister would mind if I had my Abstract Expressionist paintings back. I know it's a little cheeky of me, but it turns out they could be – well, anyway. I could find her some others, of course. Do you think she'd mind?'

Oh. I *see*.

Hmm. I stopped ignoring the wheedling-hand dynamic and placed one of my own on his arm. And squeezed it affectionately.

'How *exciting*,' I cooed. 'You'll be hung in Tate Modern before you can say Pollocks. And I'm *sure* she wouldn't mind. And of *course* come up. That would be *lovely*. Tell you what, we can ask her when we stop off to pick up Leo, can't we? Oh, look, there's Cerys.' I glanced at my watch. 'It's gone six. Shouldn't we go in?'

Well, now. Wasn't he just the man of the moment? Wasn't he just the bright young thing? Damien Hirst? Yesterday's fishmonger. Tracey Emin? Get back into your bed. Move over, you guys, because Stefan Llewellyn is about to take Brit Art to dazzling new levels of blobby creativity. Come marvel at his new spin on Crustacean Extrusion! Let Ablution Expulsion get under your skin! That was about the size of it, anyway. Encouraged by my apparent enthusiasm for his impending elevation to minor iconic status (and the four million plus expected viewing figures) he burbled his narcissistic bollocks for most of the way to Del's. Though shrewdly (and luckily – I had not hatched a plan yet), elected not to come in. He'd leave Del to me, he said, and wait in the car.

Which was what he did. And it was just as we were almost home and swinging into my drive that Leo, obviously beside himself with glee, decided to pipe up.

'Oh, Stefan,' he said brightly, 'did Mum tell you about—'

'Leo!' I hissed at him. 'Belt up, will you!'

'Tell me about what?'

'Um . . .'

We got out of the car.

There is a point in any potentially confrontational situation where one has to take stock and weigh up the odds. In my case, in *this* case, it was a question of dignity. Dignity versus what I knew would be a deeply satisfying and cathartic encounter.

We're back with Patrick, of course. Boy, had I done dignity with him. On the day I discovered I was pregnant with Leo, I spent a lot of time rehearsing. I'm going to have a baby. I'm going to have *your* baby. I'm going to have *our* baby. I have something important to tell you and I need you to be completely honest about how you feel about it. That kind of thing. It had been a sunny day. A day not unlike this one. A day that had fallen exactly eighteen days after the day when I found out about him and her. It had been a long and thoughtful eighteen days. There had been indications of his infidelity for some time, of course, but the twenty-five-year-old me had elected to ignore them. The twenty-five-year-old me had been anxious to ascribe them to work-stress, or misinformation, or crap. The twenty-five-year-old me had been such an optimistic, hopeful soul.

But also someone with dignity. He was due to come round for supper that evening. We generally ate at either his place or mine. On this day I hadn't bothered to get anything in. Instead I had zipped down to Boots in my lunchbreak and bought a Clear Blue pregnancy test. Being over a week late I had used it at tea-time, straight after I had returned home from work. I'm having a baby. We're having a baby. What's all this about – and tell me the truth, now – what's all this about between you and her? I could have said something sooner, of course. Had I said something sooner it would have been easier. Eighteen days. Any of which might have played host to the ending of our relationship. As it was, I still had a relationship with him and now I had two bits of data to impart. That I was having his baby. And that I knew he was cheating on me.

He arrived. I said, 'We need to talk, I think, Patrick.'

He said, 'Oh.' He said, 'Oh? Right. OK. What about?'

I said, 'Us, Patrick. Us. About how things have been going. About the fact that I think we've reached the end of the road.'

He said, 'You do?'

I said, 'Oh. Don't you think so? I'm sorry but, you see, I don't love you. I don't love you and I don't want to see you any more.'

Or something like that. I was brief, at any rate. Because I can clearly recall sitting on my little sofa in front of *EastEnders* soon after, twenty-seven unmarked

French tests beside me, while someone on screen –
Michelle? – shouted the odds.

I sometimes wonder if it wasn't about dignity at all.
Maybe it was actually about fear. Sometimes I wonder
how the conversation – had I let it happen as it might
have – would have panned out. But not for long,
because however it might have (and there were count-
less permutations and possibilities), all the options had
me cast in a role I hadn't planned on playing, and the
child in a bit-part it didn't deserve. So, in acting as I
did, I never had to be the victim. Didn't have to own up
that I knew he'd been unfaithful to me. And never had
to see the horror on his face when I told him I was
going to have a baby that I knew he wouldn't want.
Didn't have to deal with any of it. And I got to keep my
dignity.

So here we are in the kitchen. As life events go this is
small fry, of course. Just some jerk. Just some minor
relationship. Nothing to get worked up about. Thus the
dignified thing would be to engage autopilot, tell him
sorry, but no, he couldn't have the pictures, and then
send him, politely, on his way. But something in me
has decided to have none of it. Thing is, where's
dignity ever *got* me anyway?

'Did you tell me about what?' he asks again.

Leo, whom I have denied the pleasure of en-
lightening him, has gone upstairs, at my instruction,
to get on with his homework. I fill the kettle with
water and plug it in. 'About your paintings,' I answer
levelly.

'What about them?' he asks.

I fold my arms. 'Your paintings are gone,' I say
gravely.

'*What?*'

'Del couldn't stand the sight of them, you see, so she gave them back to me.'

The words feel nice. He winces slightly.

'And?' He has now adopted a slightly gladiatorial stance: arms across chest, legs apart.

'Cup of tea?' I suggest, crossing the kitchen and pulling mugs from the cupboard. 'Or perhaps you'd like something stronger. I think I have a couple of Kingfishers rolling around at the back of the fridge. Yes, indeed I do. Those ones I got in specially for you last week. Beer?'

'No. No, thanks, actually. Look, Lu, what do you mean "gone"?'

'Well, not gone, as such. More sort of *evolved*. Or would that be *de*volved? Hmm. Yes. Devolved. Tell you what,' I say, and beginning to tire of his increasingly irritating presence, 'I've got an awful lot on tonight, actually. Come along.' I take him by the hand and lead him out through the back door and into the garage. His palm is clammy. And I have, I note, moved now from schoolgirl to matron. I pick up the bin-bag and hold it out to him. It's not too heavy, but slightly unwieldy. There are some shards of board – hues various – poking out from the sides. He doesn't take it. Just stares at it. 'Here you are,' I say. 'I think that's all of them.'

'All of what?' He is looking mightily confused.

'All of the bits, of course.' I jiggle the contents to illustrate.

'Bits? Bits of what?'

'The bits of your Abstract Expressionist paintings.'

'My *paintings*? Why are my paintings in bits?'

'Because I *broke* them into bits.' I say this very slowly, enunciating every word.

'*Broke* them?' He gapes. 'Why on earth did you break them?'

'I had to.'

'Had to?'

I nod at him. 'No choice.'

'What the hell are you on about?'

'I just couldn't stop myself, Stefan. Because,' I explain, smiling, 'they were absolute crap.'

There is no scene. Because he is mute with distress. Thus, ten minutes, some muttering and a few flounces later, he has pedalled off down the street and out of my life.

And, gosh, I feel *so* much better.

16

Saturday 2 June

Doesn't last, of course. A euphoric, watershed, satisfying moment to be sure, but nevertheless a transient one. If I look at things life-wise, tot up the points on the Fisher Happiness Index, I'm not doing so great. What I really feel is bloody lousy. And you can't persuade yourself out of feeling bloody lousy any more than you can persuade yourself out of a cold. Which new delight is what I now seem to have contracted, quite possibly as a result of a low white-cell count, quite possibly as a result of a depleted immune system, quite possibly as a result of feeling so *very* bloody lousy. In any event, it's with less than unbridled enthusiasm that I contemplate the prospect of trailing round the zoo all day.

'Aren't we going to have fun, boys?' I gush anyway, because that's what you have to do. Young boys, I've learnt, are a bit like lawnmowers. Get them up and running and they're generally away. Leave them to their natural propensity for scowling lethargy and dissent for any length of time and their flywheels tend to get stuck.

'Yes,' agrees Del, whose base levels of enthusiasm know no bounds at the best of times, and who today, of course, is almost effervescent with it. Dinner-dance, hotel, the prospect of unassisted vision on the horizon. Why wouldn't she be, bless her?

I give her a hug. 'Have a fab time,' I tell her, 'and don't hurry back on Monday. I can hang on to Sim for as long as you like.'

'Hmm,' she says. 'Might take you up on that, darling.' Ben toots the horn and points to his watch. 'Anyhow, must off. Have a fab time yourselves, guys. And you make sure you behave yourself, Sim. I don't want to hear you've been playing Auntie Lu up, especially with her being poorly.' She reels him in for a cuddle and blows me a kiss.

'I'm *fine*, Del. Go *on*.'

I'm just waving them off when I hear the phone ringing.

'Aha! Caught you!' trills the voice at the other end.

I finish blowing my nose. 'Joe?'

'The very same. I was calling to ask you a favour.'

Except when I've been driving him to work, I've seen little of Joe for around ten days now, as he has been on site overseeing a new installation. As my French is of little use in the bowels of North Pentwyn Community Centre, he has been driven around by one of his engineers. I reach out to shut the front door and switch the phone to my other hand. 'Oh,' I snuffle, 'what kind of favour?'

'I wondered if you had any plans for today, that's all.'

'Why?'

'We-ell, it's just that I have Angharad for the weekend and it's a lovely day. And I only have the one arm, of course. And no car. And I really don't think I can face Claire's Accessories. And, well, I wondered if you might do me a tiny favour and drive us somewhere. The beach or something.'

Oh, he did, did he? 'I can't Joe. I'm busy,' I tell him.

'Oh. Oh, right.'

He sounds like it never occurred to him I might be. 'Sorry,' I add.

'No matter,' he answers. 'Doing anything nice?'

'Depends on your definition of "nice", I suppose. I'm taking the boys to Bristol Zoo. I've got Simeon for the weekend and Leo's got a project to get done and—'

'Perfect!' he replies. 'Can we come with you?'

Just like that. 'With *us*?'

'To the zoo. Yes. Can we? Come on. Take pity on me. Take us to the zoo.'

'But—'

'But what, Lu?'

The problem is that there isn't really a 'but' with which I can address the situation. No space in the car 'but', no time 'but', no logistics 'but', no inconvenience 'but'. There *is* the small but important 'but' of not particularly *wanting* to, of course, but it's a sorry little 'but', with no basis in logic, and therefore completely useless as artillery. But then again, as 'buts' go, it *is* valid. Do I *really* want to spend all day having to make polite conversation with Joe? No, I do not. I already have a plan for our outing to the zoo. A plan that will involve the boys frolicking gaily in the sunshine, while I trail around all day on my own, staring bleakly into cages and feeling sorry for myself.

'Come on,' he coaxes. 'Take us with you. After all, you don't want to trail around all day on your own feeling sorry for yourself.'

'Who said anything about feeling sorry for myself?' I snap.

'Well, you're certainly not living up to your name right now.'

'What?'

'Light of the Morning, wasn't it?'

'Oh, how very droll. I have a cold.' I cough, to illustrate. 'And who said I was going on my own anyway?'

'No one,' he says brightly. 'You are, though, aren't you? Just you and the kids and your runny nose. Which seems a shame when I could come along as well and cheer you up. Come on. Be nice to me. Take us to the zoo.'

I'm not entirely sure that I *want* to be cheered up, and even if I do, I'm far from sure that Joe Delaney is the person to do it. But there is something so childlike and hopeful in his manner that for a moment I almost forget that I don't much like him.

'All right,' I decide, sniffing. 'You can come to the zoo.'

Leo, however, was deeply unimpressed. 'That's so totally skank, Mum,' he moaned, while I packed up the sandwiches. 'And I suppose it means I have to sit in the back now, do I?'

'Yes, Leo, you have to sit in the back.'

'Well, I'm not going in the middle. I'm not sitting next to *her*.'

'Nor am I!' chipped in Simeon.

I zipped up the backpack. 'Well, one of you will have to,' I told them both. 'Unless you'd prefer to travel in the boot.'

'Yeah! Wicked! We'll do that, Mum! Yes!'

'Now you're just being silly. You will sit in the back and you will be nice to Angharad – got it? Or we don't go at all. OK?'

Leo's face brightened perceptibly. 'We don't care. We don't want to go anyway, do we, Sim? Why do we have to go to the stupid zoo? The zoo's pants. Why can't we go bowling? You said last week that we could go bowling this weekend. We want to go bowling, don't we, Sim? Can't we go bowling instead, Mum?'

I took the picnic into the hall and put it on the floor by the front door. They skittered around behind me hopefully. 'No,' I told them sternly. 'We cannot go bowling instead. It's a lovely warm day and we should be out in the sunshine. And you have a project to finish, young man. Remember?'

Leo rolled his eyes. 'Mum, we do *not* need to go to the zoo to do my project. We can just get a book from the library and do it.'

'No, we can't do that, Leo, *actually*, because every book in the library that is anything remotely connected to anything south of the equator is already on loan. To parents of children who were sensible enough to have told them they were doing a project on Antarctica when they were told about it by their teachers three weeks back. Now, go and get your sweatshirts, please.'

He spreads his hands. 'So why don't we just *buy* one, then?'

'Because I am not going to waste good money on a book you will never so much as glance at again.'

'It'll cost just as much to go to Bristol Zoo. If we didn't go to Bristol Zoo we would have enough money to buy a book *and* go bowling.'

'Leo, we are *not* going bowling, OK? We are going to Bristol Zoo. Now. Who needs the toilet?'

'Well, I'm not sitting next to *her*.'

'*Her* name is *Angharad*, Leo. And, Leo, you will sit – atchoo! – where you're told.'

So lovely to be out on a family outing. Such lovely, enriching *quality* time. God, what is it with children, these days? When I was ten I would be beside myself with excitement at the thought of being taken on a trip to the zoo. *Beside* myself. I blame Steven Spielberg.

When we arrive at Joe's house they are already waiting outside for us. Angharad is skipping along the pavement (so at least one child in this trio is exhibiting some signs of enthusiasm) and Joe is perched on his front wall with a pair of sunglasses on his head and a candy-striped cool-bag parked between his legs. He stands up and waves cheerily at us.

'And that's another thing, Mum,' Leo starts, as Joe advances with it. 'Why do we always have to take a picnic? Why can't we eat in the restaurant like everyone else does? I hate sitting in that picnic bit. You get bird poo on your head. Everyone else eats in the restaurant. Why do we have to have smelly sandwiches all the time?'

I swivel in my seat and fix him on the end of a particularly virulent species of glare. *Get in the back,* I growl.

'Well,' says Joe, once everyone is in and belted up and we are off, once more, on our jolly travels, 'isn't this nice? Must be years since I last went to Bristol Zoo. Do they still have Wendy the Elephant?'

They do indeed still have Wendy the Elephant, but she rarely does the walkabouts she used to, being rather elderly these days. Having managed to find a parking space on the top of Clifton Down and only a twenty-minute precipitous trail back down to the entrance, we obtain our family ticket (oh, irony), gather up our maps and bags and head on out into the gardens. At least Joe has managed to break the ice somewhat, by recounting to the boys with much graphic detail how, as children, he and his brother used to follow Wendy around on her twice daily excursions, in the hopes of being witness to her frequent emissions of grapefruit-sized nuggets of steaming brown dung. 'There was a keeper who used to follow along behind with a wheelbarrow and shovel and collect it all up,' he tells them chattily. 'They used to save it, you see, for manuring the roses. I expect they still do.'

'Wicked!' says Simeon, much enthused by the subject matter and skipping along brightly at his side. 'We went to the zoo in Jersey last year, and the gorillas there used to poo in people's faces if they annoyed them.'

'That's stupid,' mutters Leo, marching along on Joe's other flank and obviously anxious to reclaim the conversational impetus. 'They can't poo *at* people. You can't poo *at* things.'

Simeon rolls his eyes. 'They didn't actually poo *in* people's faces, stupid. They would do a poo in the grass then pick it up and throw it at them. We saw it.'

'Liar.'

'We *did*. They would—'

'*Thank* you, Simeon! I don't think we want to hear any more about gorilla toilet habits, if you don't mind. Now, what shall we go and look at first?'

Angharad, who is a girl – and can therefore be relied upon not to take part in such infantile displays of toilet humour – is doing what girls do best: walking sensibly beside me with her Groovy Chick mini-rucksack on her back and carefully studying the complimentary map and animal-encounter itinerary in order to plan our day. 'Ah!' she exclaims. 'Look! They have gorillas here as well now. Shall we go and see the gorillas?'

Which turns out to be a shrewd move, as the hippo enclosure, which we are now passing, seems to be the place of the moment. It is six deep in spectators. There is an animal encounter scheduled here any time now, and the animals themselves seem anxious to oblige: they seem to be having an encounter of their own.

'Ah, the spring,' says Joe, as we skirt around the excitable throng. 'When a young hippo's fancy . . .' He points towards the water. 'Don't fancy yours much, Leo.'

Fortunately, the mammals we're after are housed on an island, the moat for which, comfortingly, looks more than wide enough to put paid to any shot-putting activities. But the gorillas are all holed up inside so we carry on round to the indoor part of the enclosure, which fetid environs they share with Wendy herself. She, though, is outside being scrubbed down in the sunshine, but the evidence of her recent passing hangs like a miasma in the still warm air. The boys, somewhat deflated by the general lack of primate activity, and the keeper's insistence that beating one's chest is an absolute no-no when there are silverback males in the vicinity, console themselves with the fact that one of the females has her bottom in the air.

'Western Lowland Gorilla,' reads Joe. 'That's *Gorilla gorilla gorilla* to you scholarly types. Gorillas, it says here, are great apes – as are humans, take note – from Africa. And despite their enormous strength and vicious-looking teeth, they are – oh, and this is good to know, kids. This *is* reassuring. This enclosure,' he goes, 'which was officially opened in March 1999 by Mrs Moira Bugle, secretary of the Friends of the Zoo Society, incorporates state-of-the-art surveillance and security technology, thereby ensuring the safety and well-being of both gorilla and visitor. Though it does point out that, like most gorillas, these are a *particularly* unaggressive family group, and that they haven't actually dismembered any small boys since the unfortunate mauling incident of nineteen eighty-four.'

They both swivel. 'The *what*?'

'Goodness, did you never hear about that? You never told them about it, Lu? I'm surprised you missed it. It was in all the papers. It was a pretty grisly attack, apparently, though not as bad as it might have been, because at least they were able to re-attach the severed arm. Groundbreaking surgery, by all accounts. Though they couldn't do much about the fingers, obviously.'

'What fingers?' says Simeon, wide-eyed. 'What happened to the fingers?'

Joe sticks two of his own towards his mouth and leans towards them. He beckons them closer. 'Straight through and out the other end,' he whispers.

The boys digest this horror for a moment, then Leo's brow creases. 'You're making that up,' he says. 'You are, aren't you? You made all that stuff up.'

Joe's face takes on a look of incredulity. 'Making it up? Why on *earth* would I make something like that up? Leo, these are dangerous animals. Think about it. Why else would they have a fifty-billion-volt fence around them?' Then he shrugs. 'You can ask the keeper if you don't believe me.'

Simeon pushes his hands into his jeans pockets and glances around, as if weighing the temptation to ask the keeper and expose Joe as a fraud with the unpalatable possibility of being made to look like a complete twit. I try to keep my lips from twitching. 'You are, though,' he says finally. 'Leo's right. You're making it *all* up, aren't you?'

Angharad, who has been absorbed, up till now, in the task of trying to get a picture with her disposable camera, trots across and rolls her eyes at her father. 'Of *course* he's making it up, silly. Tsk! He *always* does. And don't you know *anything*? Gorillas are vegetarians.'

'I *did* know that,' Leo persists, as we set off again in search of a place to eat lunch. It is now past midday, and people are laying claim to patches of lawn with alarming speed, but Joe has declined my suggestion of a bench. He has, he tells me, a plastic-backed blanket rolled up in his bag, and is more than happy to sit on the grass.

'Of course you did,' he says now, to Leo. 'Though I have a feeling they do like the odd termite. Does that count?'

'I'm not sure,' says Leo. 'Do vegetarians eat insects? But I did know you were making it up. Simeon didn't.'

'I did!'

'Anyway, *I* knew you were lying.'

'Telling fibs, Leo, *please!*' I say.

'Because that electric-fence thing in the moat is four volts. Not billions. I know because it says on them. And I've touched one.'

'You haven't.'

'I have. They've got them at Longleat. And it makes you jump six feet into the air and all your hair goes on fire.'

'No, it doesn't.'

'Yes, it does!'

Strangely, *strangely*, I appear to be having fun. The sun is warm on my back, and the children are behaving themselves, and despite my glowing nose and molten sinuses, my mood has lightened considerably. I find I'm almost happy that we brought Joe and Angharad along.

'You look *much* cheered up,' reflects Joe, who has obviously noticed, and who is trying to deal one-handed with the ring-pull on a can of Diet Coke. The children have cantered off to the play area, having laid waste to most of the contents of both picnic bags.

Which, in Joe's case, has consisted mainly of Jaffa Cakes, sausage rolls, jam sandwiches and crisps. He gratefully accepts a cheese-salad roll from me, with the observation that Angharad had taken charge of the picnic, and that he'd been happy to let her, because her mother fed her mainly on gruel.

'Indeed, I consider it a parental responsibility,' he adds, while I deal with the can for him. 'Left in Rhiannon's hands the poor child would reach her dotage without ever having tasted an oven chip. And, besides, I rather enjoy the chance to expand her cultural horizons. I don't want her to grow up into a middle-class deb who only eats bread if it's got wood shavings in it, and can quote E numbers like share prices. How dire. And – good Lord! Hello!'

He puts down the Coke can and lifts his hand to wave. An elegant woman, whom I judge to be in her late fifties or early sixties, is coming across the grass towards us.

'It *is* you, Joe! I thought it was.' She puts her hands on her hips and shakes her head. Her clothes – a sprigged dress and long tailored jacket – look well made. 'I saw you earlier,' she says, 'and I did a bit of a double-take, and I thought, It *can't* be, and then I saw your arm and – well, well, well! Anyway,' her smile includes me, 'how on earth did you come to do that?'

Joe stands up, knocking over the Coke can. 'Hello, Liz,' he says, pecking at the cheek she has proffered for a kiss. He takes off his sunglasses and lifts the plastered arm for her. 'I was involved in an accident last month. Broke it in two places. Nothing major. How are you?'

I don't know whether I should stand up as well, so I stay on the rug and dab at the spillage.

She nods. 'Fine. Absolutely fine,' she says. 'Oh, and it's *so* good to see you, Joe! But ouch,' she adds, tutting, '*that* looks nasty.' I look up, unsure what she's referring to, and realize it's Joe's scar. I'm so used to it now that it barely registers any more. She reaches out and touches it gently. 'You *have* been in the wars. Angharad did tell me about it, after a fashion but, oh, you poor thing, I'd no idea it had been this bad. Where is she, by the way? Is she here?' She glances around.

'In the play area with Lu's son and nephew,' Joe tells her. Then turns to me. 'This is Lu Fisher, by the way. She works with me. Lu's being a bit of an all-round hero right now. I can't drive, of course, so she's been ferrying me around a bit. And she very kindly let us gatecrash her trip. Lu, this is Liz.' The woman smiles at me, and now I do stand up to shake her hand She seems very nice.

'Lovely to meet you,' she says cheerfully. 'And isn't this such a perfect day for it? Well,' she goes on, checking her watch, 'better go and round up the gang for some lunch. And I'll go and say hello to Minnie Mouse while I'm at it. Mind you, once the twins know she's here I doubt I'll get a minute's peace. Poor David's already looking like he needs a stiff drink, bless him. And all he's got is a max-pack of disgusting coffee. You must come over and say hello, Joe. Catch up later for a cup of tea, perhaps?' She engulfs Joe in a warm embrace and I can smell her expensive perfume. We agree on a rendezvous at four thirty.

'Who was that?' I ask, as she heads off towards the play area.

'An ex of mine,' he responds, a twinkle in his eye as he sits back down again.

I do a double-take of my own.

'Really?'

'Ex-mother-in-law.'

'Goodness! As in . . .'

He nods. 'The genuine article. As in Rhiannon's mother. David's her husband – Rhiannon's dad, of course – and the twins are Rhiannon's nieces. Her sister's two girls. They must be, oh, six or seven. Something like that. I think Liz looks after them a couple of days a week.'

'She seemed very pleased to see you,' I observe. Genuinely pleased. Which I can't help but find odd, given whose mother she is.

He looks at me sideways and lifts his black brows. 'You mean, she didn't rush over with a rolling-pin and beat me about the head with it?'

I laugh. 'Something like that. You've got to admit, it's not the way things usually work out. I mean, I wouldn't have imagined you'd be her favourite person under the circumstances.'

'Why?'

'Well, you did leave her daughter, after all. And it's not as if you and Rhiannon have one of those trendy amicable-divorce relationships on the go, is it?'

He laughs this time, but without much humour. 'Oh,' he says. 'You spotted that, did you?'

'And in that sort of situation the last thing you'd expect—'

'Oh. And what sort of situation would that be, Lu?'

There is now, suddenly, a distinct edge to his tone. But his pointed use of my name makes my hackles rise slightly. As if I'm being patronized, somehow. 'Well,' I say, 'given what happened between you, it – well,' I shrug. 'A woman scorned and all that. I suppose it's only natural to assume—'

'Is that so?' He looks at me sharply then takes the bag of Jaffa Cakes out of their packet, crushing the latter in his fist. Moments pass. 'D'you know what?' he says at last. 'I think you've made rather a lot of assumptions where I'm concerned, Lu.' He leaves the words to press their point for a few seconds, then adds, 'And what exactly do *you* know about it, anyway?'

I'm not quite sure how to respond to either of these statements. I feel as if I've suddenly been dumped in the middle of an argument I didn't know I was having, and I'm aware that the confrontational tone is still very much in his voice. I flounder uncomfortably under his gaze for a few seconds and reach for a tissue to blow my nose. 'Sorry,' I say eventually. 'It's just what I'd heard. I thought you'd left her for another woman. I thought—'

There is a tic at the corner of his jaw, and I have the uncomfortable feeling that I've trodden on eggs. That I'm about to be upbraided. Which makes my hackles rise further. Because I know all about infidelity. But just as I'm squaring up to defend my corner, his expression suddenly softens.

'Men, eh?' he observes.

'Pardon?'

'A woman scorned and all that?'

'I wouldn't say—'

'Yes, you would,' he says, twisting open the half empty Jaffa Cakes bag. He takes one and offers them to me. 'I don't know quite what's happened with you exactly, but I think I've grasped that much. So I don't imagine any of us are going to get a very good press with you at the moment, all things considered, are we? Want one?'

'No thanks.' I don't know how to answer him. I'm not sure I want to. His conciliatory turnabout has thrown me. 'It's nothing to do with that,' I say, stiffly. 'It's just that I thought you and she . . . Well. It's none of my business, anyway. And I think it's very nice that you and her parents manage to—'

'You're right. It *is* none of your business, any more than your love-life is any of my business either, as you've already made clear. But for what it's worth, I imagine it was all for the best. I'm sure you can do better than that.'

How on earth did we get on to *this*?

I start clearing the picnic things. 'And what would you know about it? What would you know about *him*?'

He gives me a cool appraising look. 'All that I need to, I suspect. And I certainly don't hear you telling me he's flavour of the month. Not this month, anyway.' He starts to help me, gathering crisp bags and cartons. I'm torn, inexplicably, between a sudden desire to tell him all about it and another to tell him to sod off. So I clamp my mouth shut and say nothing.

'It's OK,' he goes on. 'And you're quite right, as it happens. There *was* another woman involved. So, yes, that is probably what you *have* heard. And I can see you've reached your own conclusions about it.' He flips his sunglasses down on to his nose. 'But let's just say that where tar and brushes are concerned, I suspect you're a bit of an expert anyway.'

I take this in, feeling indignant and guilty in about equal measure. The word 'assumptions' drifts across my consciousness. The word 'bag' bustles along to join it. And, I regret to note, seems to have the edge. 'Look,' I say, 'you've got me all wrong here, Joe. I didn't mean to sound disapproving or anything. I was only making an observation, for God's sake. That's all.' I snap shut the clip on my backpack and catch my finger in it. Which hurts, so I stick it into my mouth.

'Ouch,' he says, noting my wince and unzipping the cool-bag he has just zipped up. 'You bleeding? I've got some tissues.' I shake my head and he does up the bag again. 'And look at the state of your nose, Miss

Fisher. As red as a baboon's bottom. Come on. Let's go and find the children, shall we? Go make this visit to Antarctica.'

So, bloody hell, here I am feeling bad again. Feeling bad about what I said to Joe. Feeling worse about what he said to me. Assumptions, indeed. Tar and brushes, indeed. But, oh, God, the dreadful thing is that he's right, isn't he? He *is* right. Who am I to pass judgement on him? I don't know the first thing about it. I don't know the first thing about him, really. I certainly don't know the first thing about his marriage. I don't know anything about him or her or him *and* her or him and the other woman – women? – or why I feel so angry with him. *Why* do I feel so angry with him? And do I feel angry with him, really? Or do I just feel angry with men? Or do I really feel *so* angry with *men*, or is it just the one man? And what the hell did I ever see in Stefan? And what did he ever see in me? And isn't it *me* that I'm angry with, really? Am I ever going to get it right? Am I? Sod and damn and blast it. I don't know the first thing about anything, really. Except that my head hurts again.

Bristol Zoo's latest visitor attraction is a Disneyesque confection of rocky Antarctic outcrops, with lots of heavy-duty decking, cutesy wooden cabins and thoughtfully placed coils of thick, oily rope. Scummy water slaps at the pebble beaches and mock-rock, and the animals – sea birds, fur seals and two kinds of penguin – plough over us, under us, backwards and forwards, tracing well-flippered routes through their miniature world.

We file along a watery tunnel, Angharad clutching Joe's hand and muttering nine to the dozen, with the boys, flushed and damp-necked, zig-zagging behind them, cavorting and shouting in the way that boys do. Ironically, it seems Leo and Angharad have had some words of their own. About what, I don't know, but there's certainly some frost in the air.

Though Joe, disconcertingly, is all jolly smiles once again. 'Gran find you OK?' I hear him asking Angharad. 'That was a nice surprise, wasn't it?'

Angharad nods happily. 'And guess what, Dad? She said she'd buy me a Magnum later.'

'And us as well,' Simeon is quick to remind her.

'Might,' she retorts. 'She said only if your mummy says so.'

'But my mum's not here, is she?'

'So tough, then.'

'My mum is,' says Leo, 'and she'll say it's all right, won't you, Mum?'

'We'll see,' I say. 'Now, come on, Leo,' I add, rummaging in the backpack. 'This looks like a good spot. How about you make some notes on all this information here. Look, there are details on all the different animals that live here, and – oh, look, here's some information about all the ones that are en-dangered species. And maybe we can get some pictures of the penguins, and—'

'You can't use my camera,' says Angharad.

Joe puts his arm around her shoulder and pats it. 'Now, come on, chicken. Don't be unkind,' he remonstrates, meeting my eyes and rolling his a little. 'You've got lots of film in there. I'm sure you can spare Leo a couple of shots.'

'We-ell. OK, but only—'

'It's all right,' I say. 'I've brought my camera too.' But it comes out all wrong. As if I'm being touchy about it. 'But thanks anyway, Angharad,' I add quickly. 'That's *very* kind of you.' She gives me a slightly hostile look, which I return with the widest smile I can manage. 'Now, here you are, Leo. Here's your pad. And here's a pen. Why don't you start over there?'

'Mum, do I *have* to do it right now? I want to go with Sim and look at the seals. Can't I? I want to go and—'

'Leo, don't *start*. We came here with the express intention of getting some stuff for your project, and I told you that once we'd been for a play in the play area we would have to get on with it. Why does everything always have to involve an argument? Why can't you just do as I ask?'

'But, Mum, they're going to be feeding them soon.'

'Which is all the more reason to stop arguing with me and get on with some work, isn't it?' I snap.

'But, Mu-um—'

I become aware of a hand lightly brushing my arm. It's Joe's. 'Leo,' he says, 'come on, mate. Do as your mum says, eh?'

And he does. It's like magic. Which makes me feel even more of a bag.

Simeon and Angharad skip off soon after, to go and save us a good spot for when the seals get fed. Joe, who is being almost painfully helpful, directs Leo to all the most useful bits of conservation information, then comes across to watch the penguins with me while my suddenly industrious son stands and makes notes about the information film they're showing in what looks like Captain Scott's hut.

Joe rests his plaster on the thick wooden fence rail beside me and with the other hand pats the backpack on my back. 'Can I take that for you?' he offers. 'I'm sure it'll fit inside my bag. Save you humping it about all afternoon in the heat.'

'Don't worry. It's fine. There isn't much in it now, anyway.'

We stand and watch the penguins gliding by for a while. The sun is making millions of little spangles on the water.

'I'm sorry,' he says suddenly.

I turn from the rail to look at him. 'Sorry?' I ask. 'Sorry for what?'

'Sorry for being so tetchy with you earlier. It wasn't fair. Am I forgiven?'

Irritation at myself wells in my throat. 'There's no need to apologize. Really,' I answer. 'It's me who was being tetchy. And you're right. I was making assumptions. All of them unwarranted. My fault, not yours. So the apology should be mine.'

And, of course, I wish now that I'd got down off my carefully constructed pedestal and been the one to make it. Why didn't I *do* that?

'No, no,' he persists, as if aware of what I'm thinking and anxious that I don't. 'I was winding you up. I was being grouchy with you. It was a perfectly valid observation and you made it in all innocence. So I'm sorry. Friends again?'

He's now standing in front of me, plaster aloft and holding out both arms towards me, and for an instant I have a mind to surprise him and step into them. It feels like so long since anyone's given me a proper hug. But something stops me, and the moment passes. God, why is it that I can never *do* this sort of stuff?

'You don't have to do this,' I say instead. 'You're always apologizing to me. Being generous. When it's me who's at fault here. You were right, you know. I *was* being sniffy. I was—'

'Whoa! Enough!' The arms go up in the air now, so I've missed my chance to have them round me anyway.

'*I*'m the grouchy one round here!' he says sternly. '*My* job, got it? So stop muscling in on my territory, will you, woman?' He lifts a finger dramatically. I notice a couple of heads turn nearby. He winks. 'And, good *God*,' he booms, 'can't a man have a stab at a bit of a grovel without – oh, my Lord! You're not about to start bursting into tears all over me again, are you?'

'I'm not! I'm not!' I pull my tissue from my pocket and shake my head wildly. 'I'm just . . . I'm just . . . aah . . . aah . . . at*choo!*'

Now his arms do go round me, in some sort of fashion, though the plaster goes 'thunk' against my right ear. 'Well, thank Christ for that!' he says firmly.

I don't know if it's the fish in the aquarium that pinched them, but by the end of the afternoon, the scales seem to have fallen from my eyes. By the time we arrive for our tea date at four thirty, Leo and Angharad seem to have got over their little spat (an incident, Simeon confided to me earlier, involving access to, and denial of, the curly-wurly slide, some shouting, some taunts and a lightly scratched forearm) and it's Magnums all round and a pot of tea for four. Joe's nieces (ex-nieces?) are whisked off into the wood-chipping paradise with our three, and conversation of the news-and-weather kind ensues. We are properly introduced (he a retired corporate accountant, she a part-time occupational therapist) and Joe explains that I used to be a teacher and that I'm only working for him temporarily before taking some time out to pursue my real ambition, which is to do a degree in fine art. And he says it smilingly. Nicely. As if he approves of the idea. Which makes me want to burst into tears, for some reason, even more so when David enthuses so wholeheartedly about it and wonders why more people don't consider doing likewise, then tells us both, with unabashed, genuine pleasure how he's currently engrossed in his second year OU course and how fired up about geology he is.

'Mind you,' confides Liz, *sotto voce*, 'that may have more than a little to do with the fact that there's a rather luscious forty-something attending the tutorials too. Charlie Simpson, Joe? You know her, don't you? Married that GP recently?'

Joe smiles and nods. 'Adam Jones,' he says. 'Yes, of course. And didn't someone tell me they had some sort of wedding blessing in the Himalayas?'

All of which reminds me that it's Joe they're here to see, and I don't want to dilute their evident enjoyment in doing so, much less their chance to catch up after what is clearly a long while, so I suggest that, if Joe wouldn't mind keeping half an eye on the boys for me, it might be an idea if I go off to the gift shop to plunder the postcard stand before the last-minute rush.

'I know what you're thinking,' he comments, as we begin the long hike back up to our car-parking space on the top of the downs. 'You're wondering how two such lovely people managed to produce Rhiannon, aren't you?'

I listen for traces of antagonism, but, of course, there are none. Why do I see these things everywhere anyway? 'I wasn't, actually,' I tell him, 'because it's never that simple, is it? I don't doubt Rhiannon has all sorts of fine qualities,' he inclines his head slowly at this, 'but that she simply didn't turn out to be the woman for you.'

'Or vice versa, perhaps?'

I'm aware that he's turned and is watching me as I walk, and I can't help but feel there is still a great deal

241

that I don't know. But I don't want to revisit that territory again today. However cheerful his tone. And neither does he, it seems. He volunteers nothing further. 'Whatever,' I say lightly. 'But what I was *actually* thinking was how very sad it all is. You know, families and so on. Break-ups.'

He swings the empty cool-bag up on to his shoulder. 'Sad's about right,' he agrees. 'I'll have to tell you all about it sometime. But not right now, huh? Wouldn't want to spoil such a beautiful day.'

By the time we get back to Cardiff, there is a palpable air of celebration in the air, as it has come to light on the journey home that not only does Angharad have Tomb Raider Three for her PC, but that she also has a Scalextric set, laid out, just like in storybook families, on a huge landscaped table in Joe's loft.

'Wow, that is just *so* mega!' exclaims Leo. Through the rear-view mirror I can see Angharad's glowing expression. She is practically puffed up with pride. 'Can we see it? Can we? Can we? Can we play on it? Can we?'

'Leo! Simeon! How many times have I told you? We don't invite ourselves into people's houses. It's very rude and you're both old enough to know better.'

'Oh, it's *fine*,' says Joe. 'But it's up to your mum,' he adds diplomatically. 'She may want to get you home. She may want to get home herself. It's been a long day and she's got a cold and—'

'And Joe might have had about enough of you two for one day, don't you think?'

'Not at all,' he replies. 'You're more than welcome. But,' he turns to me, 'if you'd rather not, that's fine, Lu. You've already let us hijack your outing as it is, and—'

'Nonsense, Joe. We didn't mind in the least. We've

had a lovely day, haven't we, boys?' They obediently mumble assent. 'But I'm sure the last thing you want is these two thundering up your stairs, and laying waste to—'

'No, no, Lu,' he continues. 'It's up to you. It's up to your mum, boys, OK?'

Oh, rats rats rats rats *rats*. I *hate* this. Why do children *do* this sort of thing? It's so embarrassing. And, God, how I loathe these conversations. What does he mean 'she may want to get you home'? Does he mean that he wants us to come in or that he doesn't? And when he says 'if you'd rather not' is he dropping a hint or just being polite? Or what? Does he or doesn't he? Should we or shouldn't we?

Angharad leans forward in her seat and taps Joe on the shoulder. 'Daddy, *tell* them,' she says. 'Tell them they've got to. You've got to come in,' she explains to the rest of us, 'because Daddy's already got tea for us all.'

Ah. Well, at least I'm embarrassed on someone else's account now. Which is something. And, boy, is he embarrassed! He's not blushing as such, but I just know his toes are curling. Oh, bless him.

So in we crunch, on to his pea-gravel, pillar-flanked, in-and-out drive, and the Jag seems to purr like a cat by a fireside. If it could speak I'm quite sure it would be saying, 'Ah! Home! And about bloody time, woman!' Except it wouldn't, of course, because it's a car of good breeding and would consider it impolite.

I haven't been inside Joe's house before, but straight away I can see it's the kind of place that, were it for sale, would merit a full-page colour ad in the 'Homes of Character' slot in the local paper. For it is huge. And what people tend to refer to as 'well appointed'. I don't know what 'well appointed' means, quite, but it has bronze plug sockets and bronze door plates and deep skirting-boards and ceiling roses everywhere. I picture Rhiannon and I wonder if they lived here together as a family, because it feels very much like a family home. It has a square central hall with a big chandelier in it, a wide turning staircase and dozens of doors. Well, OK, not dozens, but my initial sweep takes in at least seven, one of which is actually two doors – of the kind people used to fit in the arch of their through lounge so they could say they had a separate dining room. We hover here in quiet humility for some seconds, the boys finally calling their manners to order and awaiting instructions about trainer deposition, until Angharad flings her own footwear back out on to the doorstep and Joe says, 'Go on, then,' which leaves only us.

'Shall we sit in the garden?' he suggests.

He opens the double doors on to a spacious living room. A room for which the *Roomaround* budget would barely have stretched to redecorate a corner. Two sofas, two armchairs, all leather and squidgy, plus another set of double doors that opens on to the garden.

It's then that I notice the painting. *Oof!*

Not that you could fail to. It hangs above the stone fireplace, elegantly framed, and with a little brass hooded strip-light fixed above it. It's a print, of course, because the original hangs in the museum. At the far end of gallery sixteen.

Joe is standing behind and slightly to the right of me. I can smell grass and sunshine. I can't see his grin but I can hear it in his voice.

'Do you like it?' he asks. 'It's called *Running Away With the Hairdresser*. And the thing that's always struck me about it is who exactly is *who*, you know?'

Oh, God. 'Uurgh. I'm so embarrassed,' I say.

He laughs his big laugh. He is finding this far funnier

than I am. 'No need,' he assures me, tugging off his jacket, 'but blush away. It suits you.'

As if I have a choice. 'But you never said you knew it. That you *had* it.'

'Er, correction.' He chortles. 'You never gave me a chance.'

'Oh, rubbish!'

'You were far too busy enthusing at me. Which was fine, Lu.' He puts a hand on my shoulder and grins at me. 'I didn't mind. And by the time you'd finished enthusing about it, well, it would have been very churlish of me to own up, wouldn't it? I didn't want to embarrass you.'

I turn round, nettled at his relentlessly mirthful tone. Were the boot on the other foot . . . plus I don't quite recall it like this. And I certainly recall the conversation we had straight after.

'Well, I'm embarrassed now instead,' I retort. 'You must think I'm—'

'In need of a reviving cup of tea after a very long drive.' His hand is still on my shoulder and he squeezes it gently. He doesn't want to fight about it. Why would he? 'So why don't you sit in the garden, while I go and put the kettle on, eh?'

'I'll come and help you.'

'No, no. I can manage.'

'Yes, but wouldn't it—'

'I can *manage*, Lu.'

The terrace outside the living room (drawing room?) is cosy and decked and full of scrambling climbers. Clematis, passion-flower, honeysuckle and ivy, all rising from indigo-glazed terracotta pots. There's a circular teak table and two robust-looking steamer chairs, the latter plump with expensive stripy green cushions. Once I'm out here, I can see the full extent of the garden, which rolls down and away from the house, and is reached via a short flight of steps that are set into the grass.

And it's some garden. There is a wide sweep of neatly cut lawn, edged with shrub-filled borders, and another, much larger, patio area below and to the right of us, strewn with the abandoned evidence of Angharad's occupation: a football, a skipping-rope, a little silver micro-scooter, plus more garden furniture, this time in slightly moss-fuzzed white plastic, including the sort of table you could get a rugby team round. Not that he does, I suspect. For all its size and opulence it has the look of a garden that has been left quietly to itself, that has matured, with little input, for quite a long time. There aren't any flowers except the ones on the terrace, no gay lines of bedding, no baskets, no pots.

I sit down in one of the chairs and gaze out over the fuggy Cardiff skyline, a little tired, a little agitated, a little awed and out of place.

Eventually he clatters in with two mugs in one hand and a packet of chocolate biscuits clamped under his arm.

I get up to take the mugs from him. One is slopping over the side a little and on to his hand. 'Oh, Joe, you should have let me give you a hand with those.'

'I told you. I can manage.'

I put the mugs down on the table for him and take the biscuits from him. 'And I hope you haven't gone to a lot of trouble. There was really no need.'

He sits down heavily beside me and parks his plastered elbow on the arm of his chair. 'No trouble.' He glances at me. 'So don't fret. Just got a few cakes in and so on. She's a sociable soul, my little girl, and she wanted to have a tea party. And, well, what with her being my only child, I like to indulge her a bit. Anyway,' he picks up his mug, 'cheers! Thanks for a lovely day, Lu.'

'It's been a pleasure,' I say. I sip my tea, and, goodness, I find I mean it. Who would have thought it, eh?

Which makes what happens after such a bitch. *Such* a bitch. Oh, why does life have to be so unfair? OK, I know it's a cliché, and I know it was never written anywhere that life wasn't going to be unfair from time to time, but haven't I had my fair share of it? Haven't I? And, OK, I know that makes me sound like I'm feeling sorry for myself when I have no particular right to, and I know it was my own fault anyway, mostly, and I also know that I deserved it. But, oh, damn. Damn and blast it.

'Crisis,' says Simeon, who has suddenly appeared at the French doors, small scarlet Marlboro Maclaren in hand. 'The track came apart at the bank by the grandstand, and Angharad didn't know how to fix it all back. And Leo said he did but he doesn't, and now a bit of the chicane has come undone too, and Angharad's crying and says we can't play any more, and could you fix it, please?'

Joe parks his mug then pulls himself upright. He smiles at me. 'All in a day's work,' he says.

After ten minutes have passed I wonder quite how much time Angharad actually spends playing with her Scalextric set, and how much more time Joe probably does. When Angharad herself appears and plonks herself down beside me, her expression confirms it.

'Has Dad fixed it?' I ask her.

She takes a biscuit from the packet and nods. 'They're *all* playing on it now,' she says, with the air of someone for whom the dreary inevitability of boring cars and boring boys and there being no fun to be had from either was only ever a matter of time. 'I'm no good at racing,' she adds. 'I always go too fast and crash.' A little like Joe, I think. A lot like me. 'So,' she goes on, 'I thought I'd come down and see you instead. Shall we have tea out here?'

'Yes, why not?' I follow her back inside and into the kitchen.

'I decided we'd have scones,' she says, bustling straight into action. There are two little pink spots on her face, one on each cheek. 'I wanted to make some,' she tells me. 'We did them at school last week, and I know how to make them, but Daddy said it would take too long so we bought some in Sainsbury's this morning instead. Do you like scones? We got some strawberry jam and squirty cream to go with them.'

'That sounds lovely,' I say. 'Now, what would you like me to do?'

There are all sorts of packets of things on the work-top. As well as the scones there are mini rolls, chocolate fingers, grapes, little bridge rolls, packets of Hula Hoops, yet more Jaffa Cakes. She gathers them all up out of the way, and gets out a breadboard and knife.

'You could put stuff on plates, I suppose,' she says. 'They're in the cupboard over there.'

And near the cupboard, in the corner, there stands a bucket. And in the bucket there is water. And in the water there are flowers. Lots of flowers. Tightly furled peachy roses and lemon lisianthus and cream Brompton stocks, all standing to attention in their Cellophane bags.

'Gosh, look at all these,' I remark, getting the plates out. I know, even then, that something is amiss.

She pauses in her cutting. 'Oh, those,' she says. 'They were supposed to be for you. Daddy got them as a thank-you present. But it's all right.' She glances at me. 'I know you don't want them.'

My mouth drops open. But while I struggle to make sense of what she has just said she goes back to her work, carefully splitting each little scone round and lining them up in a neat row on the bread board. There is a flush spreading across her cheeks. She puts down the knife and turns to look at me. 'But *why* don't you want them?' she asks forlornly. 'Is it because you hate him?' There are tears welling up in her eyes now and I don't know quite what to say or do.

I cross the room, plates in hand, and put my arm around her. 'What on *earth* makes you think that, Angharad? Of *course* I don't hate him. I like him very much.' I hug her. '*Very* much.'

She looks visibly relieved. So much so that I wonder how much hate for her father she has to live with on a daily basis. I put down the plates and pull off a piece of kitchen roll for her.

'Leo said . . . Leo said that if Daddy gave you those flowers you would be really cross with him. He said you said you'd shove them up his bottom.'

'Oh, Angharad, that's ridiculous! Why on *earth* would I want to do that? They're *lovely* flowers. And it was very, very thoughtful of Daddy to get them for me.'

She sniffs and wipes her face with the kitchen roll. 'That's what I said. He's just being a stupid boy, isn't he?'

'Exactly,' I agree. 'I don't know what he thinks he's on about. Did you have a fight or something?'

She picks up the knife again and scowls at it. 'Just because I said he couldn't play on the Scalextric any more. But I wanted us to play in the garden. I wanted us to have our party. But all they want to do is play with stupid cars all the time.' I am trying to work out how this appalling conversation has come about and can't. Oh, God. What on earth has he *said*? 'And now Daddy's up there playing with them and nobody wants to play with me, and—'

'Come on, Angharad. Take no notice. They're *all* stupid boys, aren't they? Come now. Dry your eyes and let's get this lovely tea made and then I'm sure they'll be down like a shot. In any case,' I reassure her, 'there's no harm done, is there?' I gesture to the bucket. 'I'll be pleased as punch when Daddy gives them to me, I can tell you. Pleased as punch. Really I will.'

Her eyes start to swim again and she shakes her head sorrowfully. 'But he won't,' she sobs, 'and now he's all cross.'

'Oh, Angharad—'

'Because I already told him.'

17

You wouldn't know anything was up, of course. If you were nine, like Angharad, or ten, like Leo and Simeon, you wouldn't know at all.

They were down minutes later. We'd laid out all the scones with their swirly cream hats, put the chocolate fingers in fans, made a tower of mini-rolls, transferred crisps into bowls and little sausages to sticks. Then we'd taken it all outside, with the requisite lashings of lemonade, on to the table on the little patio. Angharad had been down and fetched up some more chairs – pink and green plastic ones – a little too small for them, then she handed round napkins and passed round the goodies and we all sat down and had tea.

A very nice tea, if tea's your particular bag. Lots of merry chit-chat about gorillas and race-tracks, and with Angharad and Leo's little spat all made up. And nothing to suggest that there was any sort of atmosphere. Like I said, you wouldn't know.

You wouldn't know, that is, unless you were me. Unless you were me at that point on the doorstep when feet were wriggled back into trainers, 'thank you for having me' and 'you're welcome' exchanged, and the flowers in question, at Angharad's bubbling insistence, duly presented, together with the obligatory fulsome and delighted thanks.

They say you can convey all sorts of emotions with

your eyes, and, over the top of my sweet-smelling armful, I attempted to fashion a sort of oh-shit-this-is-so-embarrassing-and-whatever-she-told-you-it-really-wasn't-how-it-was kind of look.

Joe's fingers were thrumming out a tango on the door jamb. And his eyes, glittering so green in the early-evening sunshine, were way, way better at communication than mine. They said, 'Sod off.' No question.

'Safe journey home,' he incanted. 'Goodbye.'

And the silly thing is, the most *frustrating* thing is, that I would have been thrilled with the flowers today.

Attack is the best form of defence. That's the rule, isn't it? But it hadn't been what I'd intended. Oh, no. No, what I'd *intended*, from the point at which Leo had made his sparkling little *faux pas* to the point at which I had wrested the flowers from their wrappings, mixed my little sachets of flower food with water and arranged the lot – carefully and lovingly – in my biggest vase, was that I would phone him up and explain what had happened. That I would do the decent thing. That I would apologize to him.

So that was what I did. I had to look up his number in my address book. I'd never called him at home before.

'Delaney,' he said. As if he was at work. Had he forgotten he wasn't?

'Is that you, Joe? It's me.'

'I know,' he replied. His voice was as cool as a mountain stream, but without the health-giving mineral component or the high-altitude leisure connotations. Just the kind of environment you wouldn't want to plunge your foot in.

'And I wanted to call and, well, tell you—'

'Tell me what?' He sounded bored too.

'That, well, that I'm sorry about earlier. I don't know *exactly* what Angharad told you, but I'm really sorry, and—'

'Sorry about *what*, Lu?'

There it was again. *Lu*.

'About the fact that she told you that Leo told her that I'd said that if you gave me those flowers I'd shove them up your backside. And . . . er . . . so on.'

'Oh, that. And did you?'

'Did I what?'

'Did you say that?'

'Um. Yes.'

'Fine.'

'Yes, but that was *ages* ago. *Ages*. And it was taken out of context. It was said in anger, you see. And certainly not for Leo's ears. And he obviously thought it would be very clever to repeat it to Angharad and, well, I'm very sorry.'

There was a silence. Then he said, 'Said in anger *when* precisely?'

'Oh, Joe, does it matter? I can't even remember.'

'Yes, you can. When?'

'Oh, when I was cross with you. When you called Stefan a wanker, if you must know. When—'

'What's he got to do with it?'

'Well, nothing now, less than nothing. But pretty much everything at the time.'

'No. I mean how'd you get from that to flowers?'

'Oh, I don't know. It was just—'

'No, really, Lu. Humour me. I'd really like to know. What has the one got to do with the other?'

'Look, it was just one of those things you say. I was talking to Del, and I told her what had happened and I just said that if you thought you could get round me by – well, you know. Just one of those things you say when you're angry.'

'Get round you by sending you some flowers, you mean.'

'Yes. I suppose it must have been. Yes.'

'From which I presume I can infer that you assumed I might.'

Pardon? 'Um. Yes, I suppose.'

'And if I *had* sent you some flowers to apologize, that's how you would have responded, yes?'

'Yes. No! Oh, I don't know. I was cross. I don't know. Maybe I would and maybe I wouldn't. But, on balance, I suppose. Yes. Look—'

'It's OK, Lu. I get the message.'

'*What* message? There's no message! I was phoning to apologize, Joe! I'm sorry, OK? I'm appalled and embarrassed and I'm sorry!'

'But you still think it's sad.'

'What's sad?'

'*I*'m sad.'

'I never said that!'

'I never said you did. But, then, you didn't need to. I took the point anyway.'

' "Took the point"? What are you *on* about? I never *said* that!'

'But it's true nevertheless. Even though on this occasion I can't fathom it.' What other occasions had there been, for heaven's sake? 'What's so sad about a guy buying a woman some flowers? What's so sad about *me* sending *you* flowers, Lu? *Why* is it sad? Why does it offend you so much?'

'It *doesn't*, Joe. It's just that in some situations, in *some* circumstances – and *not* today's circumstances, so *please* don't misunderstand me here . . . It's, well, if

254

you must know, I just think that sometimes men think it's an easy option—'

'Ah. We're back with men, then.'

'No! It's just—' Oh, what was the point? I'd already jumped into the pit he'd dug for me. 'Well, *yes*, in fact.' I sighed. 'It's just that some men seem to look upon it as an all-purpose answer to everything. A sop. It's nothing personal, but it just happens to be what I think.'

'A sop?'

'Sometimes. Yes. You must be able to see that. And, well . . . well, it's not like *you* don't make a habit of it, is it? And it's so easy for you to do – you know, pick up the phone, or get *me* to pick up the phone, or get Iona to pick up the phone, then reel off a credit-card number or whatever – and, well, it devalues it, doesn't it? Do you see? Do you understand what I'm saying? I'm not trying to make a point here. I'm just being honest with you. And it's basically why what happened today happened, that's all. It was such a lovely gesture and it was ruined because of it, and I'm sorry, but you did ask, so I've told you. So . . . so . . . Joe?'

The line hisses back at me for so long that I begin to think he's hung up. But he hasn't.

'I'm still here,' he says at last.

'Look, I'm sorry. That wasn't fair.'

'No, no. You're right,' he says quietly. 'My fault. I'll take myself off to the bottom of the class. Must try harder.'

'Joe—'

'Goodnight.'

It's true. I am a bag.

Cannot believe I just did that. How could I be so horrible? How could I be so unkind? God, if I was Joe and Joe was me and he'd just spoken to *me* like that I'd be crying by now, no question. How could I be so *hurtful*? And now I can't get a picture of him out of my mind. Of him sitting by the telephone, hurt and wounded and crying. Except he wouldn't be crying because men don't do that stuff. He, of all people, wouldn't do that stuff. Stefan might do that stuff, but then Stefan's not a proper adult anyway. No. There is a natural order to these things. Women like me go around blubbing about everything, and men like Joe send bouquets of flowers. And have stiff upper lips and don't cry. Women cry. Men send flowers. God! I'm right back with the tar and the brushes. And the assumptions. It's true. I'm a bag.

Monday 4 June

'Oops,' observes Del, when she telephones on Monday afternoon.

It's been a strange day, one way and another, because having been so sure I'd be seeing Joe and then *not* having seen Joe (he called Sunday evening to say he'd be on site in Acapulco or wherever, but Leo had taken both the call and the message – I'd been in the bath and he'd said not to bother me) I've been feeling all agitated and chopsy and irritable. And I keep jumping on the phone in case it's him. And Iona hasn't been herself either. She started her day with a big row with Dai, apparently, because she'd told Lily they'd have Aurélie and the baby for them overnight next Saturday evening so they could go to some dinner, and Dai had said no, because he was tired and fed up with playing nursemaid to a yowling sprog and so on, which has completely thrown Iona because she'd never realized he felt like that (and so on). So we're both feeling a bit sorry for ourselves. Still, at least Del's operation went

OK. She feels like she's got a bag of pistachios in her eye, but already, she says, she can see so much better. She's already booked in to have the other one done in July.

'I know,' I say, 'and do I feel five kinds of cruddy about it. He must think I'm such a stuck-up, opinionated cow.'

'I don't know about stuck-up, but opinionated, certainly. I've always thought that was one of your most enviable qualities. You tell the truth. You speak as you find. There's no harm in that.'

'But there *is*, Del. I'd intended to apologize to him, and instead I ended up giving him an ear-bashing. Just trampled all over his feelings. Like the bloody cow I am. I know I have. But you know what I keep hoping? Do you know what – *bizarrely* – I keep hoping? I keep hoping the buzzer will go and it'll be someone clutching a big bouquet of flowers for me. Isn't that silly?'

'Er, under the circumstances, I'd certainly say it was highly unlikely. I think you're probably the very last person on earth that Joe would consider sending flowers to today, don't you? If, indeed, ever again.' Which made me wince. 'Besides, *why* would you want him to do that?'

'I'm not sure. I guess I'd like him to do it just to make the point that he'll do what he bloody well likes, whatever I say. A sort of horticultural two fingers at me. A kind of shove-these-up-your-*own*-backside gesture. You know? The sort of thing I'd *expect* him to do. All the product of a guilty conscience, I suppose. So I can feel less bad about myself. Less like I've hurt his feelings so much. Less horrified about the fact that I'd obviously never really credited him with even *having* any feelings. You know, he's right, Del. I am a bag, aren't I?'

'Of course you're not. Not most of the time, anyway. But if you feel that guilty about it, then why don't you turn convention on its head and send *him* some flowers instead?'

'Now you're just being silly.'

'Tsk! So are you, sweetie. So are you.'

I did roll the idea around my head for a while. Because it occurred to me that that was essentially what it was all about. Convention. Assumptions. Men sent flowers. Women liked getting them. And that had obviously been the assumption he'd been working from. And why the hell shouldn't he? And what difference did it make that he could so easily afford to? Why did that make it a less worthwhile gesture? And why did the fact that he made such gestures often make it seem to me as if therefore they didn't count? Surely, when you thought about it, the opposite was true?

But today there weren't any flowers and neither was there any Joe. And when I popped my head round the door to let Iona know I was leaving to pick up Leo and Simeon from school, she told me he'd called, and that he'd asked her to let me know he wouldn't be needing a ride in tomorrow either. He was off to Birmingham in the morning with Monsieur Deschamp and wouldn't be back in till late Wednesday.

18

Wednesday 6 June

I had been looking forward to going to my class on Tuesday night. Looking forward to swanning around and letting Stefan know that I'd gone off him, big-time. That I didn't fancy him any more. Mand, indeed. BBC, indeed. Commissioning art editor, indeed. With a penchant for poetry, perhaps? Well, more fool her. She was welcome to him. And all sorts of other stuff along those lines. It felt good. *I* felt good. Or if not exactly good in a 'wey-hey!' sort of way, at least, way better than expected. Just a little repointing around the edges of my confidence, and I would soon be able to get back on track with my life.

But I couldn't go to my class as it turned out, because Del's eye was still painful. As Ben was out speaking at some meeting or other, I insisted that I keep Simeon for one more night. And you know what? I didn't miss class for an instant. Not a single instant. Which is another huge weight off my mind. The one good thing about infatuations, it seems, is that they can be as transient as they are intense. *Really* can't think what I saw in the guy. A wanker, as Joe said. Though, speaking of which – no, speaking of *whom* – I'm not sure he hasn't had more than a teensy bit to do with my road-to-Damascus conversion. In any event, one thing I *do* keep wanting to do is pick up the telephone and call him. Have another stab at apologizing to him. Perhaps get it right this time.

Which is a slightly unsettling turn of events, but doubtless simply down to guilt overload. Suspect that my guilty conscience, having been buried for so long in the dusty depths of my bag-like persona (and only surfacing here and there for global crises, BBC Children in Need, etc.), has decided to make up for lost time.

And at least my cold is better. Which is something to be grateful for, because we are busy beyond belief with sorting all the job applications Joe's recent ads have elicited, and there is no time for the weary application of Vick Stick to nostril and even less for the kind of self-indulgent introspective analysis that has commanded so much of my attention these last days.

'Look at this,' says Iona, who I suspect wouldn't give a cold the time of day anyway, and who is still in feisty enough fettle that only the most reckless kind of virus would dare run the gauntlet of her white cells. She is not happy. Although she has apparently wrestled a compromise from Dai – in which she gets her way on the babysitting front as long as he gets his in the matter of the rugby on Saturday afternoon – a perennial flashpoint *chez* Williams by all accounts – relations are still on the strained side. Mainly, she says, because he's being a complete grouch at the moment: snappy and miserable and irritable with her, and spending most of his time sprawled in front of the TV. She thinks he's having a late male menopause.

'We've got an invite, Lu,' she goes on, 'for the launch party of that health club they're opening down in the bay.'

I glance at the card she is brandishing at me. 'Oh, Exo,' I say, taking it. 'How come?' It's in the form of an enormous, silver-edged, loosely cross-shaped postcard with a pop-up facility and a raffia bow. The word 'Exo' is emblazoned in silver across the middle, and is fashioned from tastefully monochrome images of thin people with towels round their necks. They are mostly engaged in energetic (and, therefore, presumably life-affirming) pursuits. Though not those – if the one who is modelling the 'X' is representative – that one would attempt without benefit of a stout panty-pad. It says 'Mr Delaney and guest' in the corner.

'Because we did the heating, I assume. Didn't you know?'

I shake my head. I didn't know that, though I do know all about Exo, of course. I know particularly that they're anxious to reflect the post-millennial mindset and that, consequently, they're staying largely with the blue end of the spectrum et cetera. And that they have an atrium, of course. And doubtless, by this time, one with a very big picture of a blue blob hanging in it. (Is there a place for me in the art world? *Really?*)

'Well,' I say, turning the card over and noting the stylishly scrawled address. 'It sounds very posh.'

'Ooh, I wouldn't know, lovely. Not my sort of place at all. I don't hold with all this cavorting and leggings. But I'm sure it'll do very well down there. Now they've got the assembly sorted and that hotel and everything. And at least it's a bit of a do. Lord, I don't think I've been out in months! D'you know? I've a Lurex two-piece in my wardrobe that hasn't seen the light of day since the last Five Nations. And I *mean* Five Nations, lovely. The last Six Nations I hardly saw hide nor hair of him for best part of a month.' I assume she means Dai. 'And if he's not propping up the bar in the Old Arcade he's flat out on the settee. As much get-up-and-go as a plate of tripe just lately.' She gives

261

me a nudge. 'Ooh, I'd go to the opening of an envelope right now, especially if there's free nibbles and a glass of something. And, ooh, *that* sounds tidy – they're having sushi, it says here.' She rhymes it with 'mushy'. 'Come on. Come with us. We'll have a laugh, eh?'

'Oh, am I invited?' I point at the card. 'Joe will want to go, won't he?'

'Oh, we won't worry about that, lovely! They're hardly going to refuse to let us in, are they? They'll want us to sign up for aerobics, won't they? Let me see, next Wednesday. Not long, then. There. Something to look forward to. Isn't that nice?'

She goes back to her office, and when I hear the phone ring five minutes later I take little notice. There are three lines coming into the JDL offices – two that ring in the main office, where I am, and a third, with a different number, that goes straight through to Iona's room. It's the number the engineers use to call in on. About work schedules, pay queries, parts and so on.

It's only when I hear Iona's sudden exclamation that it occurs to me something might be wrong. I get up and walk through. She is sitting at her desk staring into space, and the colour has drained from her face. Both of her hands are clamped to her mouth, and the receiver is back on its rest. Something is obviously very wrong, and for one horrified moment I imagine Joe in another pile-up on the motorway. 'Iona? What's the matter?'

She looks at me vacantly. Then at the phone, then back at me again. She takes her hands from her mouth and balls them into fists.

'Oh, *cariad*,' she whispers, her face crumpling in distress, 'it's Dai. It's my *Dai*. He's collapsed. He's in an ambulance on his way to hospital. They think it's his heart. Oh, *cariad*, my Dai!'

262

I move quickly around the desk and put my arm around her shoulders. I can feel her body trembling through the fabric of her blouse. 'Right, then,' I tell her, while I try to gather my thoughts. 'Then we must get you down there as soon as we can. He's on his way to the Heath, then, is he?'

'Er . . . I think. Yes. Yes, the Heath.' She rises, looking distractedly around her.

'Right,' I say. 'You wait there while I go and get your coat. Then we'll go down and get the car and I'll drive you there, yes? In fact, no. It'll take too long to walk down to the car. We'll pick up a cab on St Mary Street.'

By the time I have found her coat for her, she is still deathly pale, but her expression has pulled itself together somewhat.

'I'll be all right,' she says firmly, as she takes it from me. She pushes her arms into the sleeves. 'You can't leave the office unattended. There's things to get done. There's the wages and everything. I'll be fine, lovely, really. You stay here and . . . and . . .'

Then she folds into an ungainly heap on the floor.

'Joe? It's me.'

'Oh,' he says. 'I'm in the middle of a meeting. Can it wait?'

In other circumstances I'd be dismayed by his tone. But there is no time for my piffling disappointments right now. 'No,' I tell him. 'It can't, I'm sorry. Look, I'm in the back of a cab, on my way to hospital with Iona. Dai's—'

'What? Slow down. I can't hear you.'

'On my way to the Heath. Dai's had some sort of collapse and he's gone by ambulance, so I'm taking Iona down there. I just wanted to let you know that

263

there's no one in the office at the moment. And I didn't know how to put the phones on divert, and poor Iona's fainted.' I squeeze her hand as I say this. 'And, well, anyway – what?'

'I said, is she all right?'

'She's OK, Joe. She's just shaken up, aren't you, Iona? I don't know how long we'll be, but I'll call you and keep you posted, OK?'

'Oh dear,' he says. 'Oh dear.' He is beginning to sound like me. 'Right. Yes, OK. I'm leaving here about two so I should be back by four-ish. Let me see. I'll go straight back to the office, then, shall I? Yes. I'll see you there. Let me know what's happening, won't you? Oh, and Lu? Give her a hug for me, will you? Tell her I'm sure everything will be OK.'

I don't know how old Dai is – I have never met him – but I assume he must be in his fifties or sixties, and as we arrive at the Accident and Emergency entrance all I can think of is my father's death. And how swiftly – how cruelly quickly – he went. And how here we were, Del and I, right here at this very hospital, stand-ing, shell-shocked and uncomprehending, while they wheeled him inside. We had both travelled in the am-bulance with him, and he'd already gone. DOA. Dead on Arrival. Oh, please, God, don't let Dai be already dead.

I pay the driver and help Iona out of the taxi, then take her inside through the floppy double doors and up to the desk. The woman behind the plastic partition looks up, smiling yet incurious, at me.

'Dai Williams,' I say. 'Came in recently, by ambu-lance? I've brought his wife. Iona Williams.' I watch while her finger moves smoothly down her list.

Her expression changes to one of professional

concern and I brace myself for the worst. Iona, too, is rigid against my arm.

'Ah,' she says, nodding. 'All right, lovely. He's in with the medics now. If you'll just take a seat I'll go and find someone who can look after you. Won't be a tick.' She slides off her swivel stool and heads off out of the back of her office, while I pull my arm tighter around Iona's shoulders. Not dead then. Not dead. My relief is so immense I feel like crying too.

'There,' I say, growing anxious at Iona's increasingly disconnected expression. 'Everything is going to be fine. Come on, let's sit you down, shall we? I'm sure someone'll be with us in a moment.'

'Mrs Williams?' A young female doctor has appeared in the waiting area. 'Do you want to come with me?'

Iona, who has just lowered herself into a chair, begins to rise. I rise with her, but she puts a restraining hand firmly on my arm. ''S all right, lovely. I'm all right,' she says.

'I'll stay here, then, shall I? I'll be right here, OK?'

As I watch her being led away round the corner and out of sight, I wonder again at the admissions clerk's words. She said all right. She didn't say *he*'s all right. I wonder fearfully what Iona is about to find. As I gaze unseeing into the middle distance, I become aware that a man is approaching me. He's short and bearded, with a grim expression, and has an identity tag swinging from a clip on his jacket pocket.

'Hello,' he says, proffering a large hand. 'You Lu, by any chance? Bill Keeley. Came in the ambulance with him. You bring Iona in, then?'

I nod. 'What happened?'

'Heart-attack, by all accounts. They've got him on a monitor at the moment. And help with his breathing, like.'

265

All of which sounds serious. I stand up. 'Is he going to be OK?'

He shrugs. 'OK for the moment, they said. Hanging on in there. But I don't suppose they'll know for a while yet, will they? Thank Christ he wasn't on the road, eh?'

I nod again. 'Where was he, then? With you?'

'Back in the office. He'd just finished taking a fare out to Penarth and he said he needed to take a bit of a breather. Wouldn't get off home, God love him. But he's not been right for a couple of weeks, truth be known. Tired, like. Not himself. Works all hours, does Dai, love him. But he's not been himself. We've all said.' He shakes his head sadly. 'A bad business.' He glances at the clock on the wall. There is a poster beside it which says, 'Don't go breaking your heart.' 'Anyway, I'd best get back, now you're here. You all right for getting Iona home, are you, lovely?'

'Yes. Yes, of course. I said I'd stay.'

'Anyway, she said to ask if you could let their Nick know what's happening. You know. Sooner rather than later, like?'

'Of course. Yes, I'll do that. I'll get on to it now.'

But I don't have Nick's number. And I'm not sure how to go about finding it either, because I can't even think of anyone I could ask. But find it I must. Find *him* I must. I presume Iona thinks I have it. If she's thinking at all, which is doubtful. I'm just considering whether I should ask one of the nurses if perhaps I could have a quick word with Iona herself, when the theme from *Star Wars* starts tootling gaily from my bag. I use my phone so infrequently that it's a moment or two before I even register what the noise is. That and the fact that Leo's always changing the ring tone. Last time it rang it was 'Boogie Nights'. Which might have been marginally worse.

Conscious of the looks I am attracting, not to mention the large signs informing visitors that mobiles in hospitals should be turned off at all times, I hurry outside to fish it out and answer it. It's Joe. No preamble. 'What's the latest?' he asks me. His voice is accompanied by a low thrumming sound, which I assume means he's now on the train coming home.

'He's had a heart-attack,' I tell him, 'and that's all I know at the moment. Iona's in with him. I said I'd wait. She's been gone, let me see, about three-quarters of an hour or so.'

'That sounds bad,' he decides, 'though not entirely unexpected. He had one a couple of years back. Jeez,' he says. 'Nothing like something like this happening to remind you why you gave up smoking, is there?'

'Joe, I—'

'Lu,' he interrupts me, 'I *wasn't* being flippant, if that's what you were about to tell me.' I wasn't. I *wasn't*. 'Just making an observation. Poor guy. Poor Iona. God, life's a bitch sometimes, isn't it? Makes you realize just how precious . . . Anyway, I'm just coming into Worcester now, so I should be back in Cardiff a little earlier than I thought. I'll see you back at the office, shall I?'

'Actually, Joe, I was just about to call you. You don't have their son's number, by any chance, do you? I said I'd call and let him know what was happening but I don't have it, and I – oh, hang on. I think I can see her now. I'll call you later, OK?'

I push the swing doors open and see Iona casting about anxiously for me. Her expression tells me little other than the amount of pain she is going through.

As if it has seeped in through her pores. She looks suddenly older. Suddenly smaller.

'I'm here, Iona,' I call, threading my way towards her through the sea of anxious people. So many crises for one ordinary Wednesday. So many traumas and tragedies going on. She scans the room to find my voice, and makes her way across to me.

'Oh, *cariad*, thank you so much for staying.' Her voice is small, too.

'How's he doing?' I ask, steering her to an empty chair.

She shakes her head. 'Not good. They've got him stable. But they don't know. The first forty-eight hours. That's the thing.'

'They told you that, did they?'

'Didn't need to, my lovely. We've been here before. I know the drill.' She clasps my hand and grips it. 'Oh, *cariad*, what'll I do? What'll I do if I lose him?'

'Come on,' I tell her. 'Let's try to be positive. He's in good hands. In the best place. I'm sure everything will be OK. Come on, let's get you a cup of tea, shall we?'

She nods, her eyes brimming with the tears she's fighting so hard not to shed in front of me, and I feel suddenly so aware of how little we know one another. A few weeks, that's all. Barely three months. I'm not the person she needs right now. I wish Joe was here to comfort her instead. 'We need to get hold of Nick, don't we?' I suggest, while we wait in the queue for the tea.

'I just remembered. He's in Bristol this week,' she tells me. 'A conference or something. I can't remember. We're supposed to be driving down at the weekend to see him. Oh, Lu . . .'

I put my hand firmly on hers. 'But he'll have a mobile, surely?'

Hers is shaking. 'I don't know the number. It's at

268

home. It's in my book. I don't have it with me or anything.' She looks panicky.

'So we'll go home and get it. Or I'll go home and get it for you. How about that? Or – hang on – what about his boyfriend? What about Howard? He could tell us. Do you know where I can get hold of him, maybe?'

I pay for our teas and find a vacant table.

'He'll be at work,' she says, sitting down heavily. 'We'll have to wait till he gets home. Oh, *why* didn't I put Nick's number in my bag? I'm so stupid. And now his dad's . . . Oh, I'm so *stupid*. And now he might . . .' The tears start swimming in her eyes again, spill over and track down her cheeks. I move round the table and sit down beside her, gathering her into my arms.

'I'm sorry,' she whispers. 'I'm terribly sorry . . . '

'Sssh,' I murmur. 'Sssh. It's OK. It's all right.' Her hair smells of peaches. I rock her against me for ten minutes, her sobs gentle shudders against my chest.

Finally, spent, she pulls away a little. 'I'm so sorry,' she tells me, hauling her handbag on to her knees and pulling out a packet of tissues. 'What must you think of me, Lu? I don't know what came over me. I'm all right now. Sorry.'

I want to tell her that she doesn't need to be sorry. That there's nothing wrong with needing a cuddle in a time of crisis. I want to tell her that I'm sorry it's only me. That I feel for her, having to share her distress with someone who knows her so slightly. With whom she feels awkward about crying. Most of all I want to get her son here, and quick. 'Right,' I say briskly, conscious that I mustn't crack the veneer of control she's managed to reassemble. 'Come on, Iona. Think. Where does Howard work? He's a teacher, right? So what school does he teach at? Is it a secondary or a primary?'

'Primary,' she confirms. 'Near where they live. Except I can't think – he did tell me. Oakridge? Oakdale? Oh, I wish I could remember. Or was it Beech something?'

I pull some paper and a pen from my bag and write down the list of possibilities, as well as his surname, which is Ringrose.

'Drink your tea,' I command. 'Then we'll get you back to Dai. And I shall go outside and call Directory Enquiries and track him down, OK?'

She nods at me mutely and does as instructed. And the steam from the tea makes her glasses mist up.

There must be any number of primary schools in Hemel Hempstead, I imagine, but after a couple of attempts, I manage to get the number of one that sounds hopeful – an Ashdale Primary, on the outskirts of the town. I thank the operator and dial the number, and am rewarded by a voice that confirms Howard does indeed work there, but that he's out on the field taking PE right now. So I explain why I'm calling and give the woman there my number. She promises she'll call him in and have him ring me back.

It's chilly, standing outside A and E. The area is covered – it runs under the building – and what little light's shed there is reflected off grey. Grey concrete pillars that hold up the roof, grey roadway, grey pavement, grey trolleys, grey faces. The only colour is the yellow of the criss-cross road markings, and the startling neon of the paramedics' jackets as they come and go, cutting through the damp air with their chatter. I remember those most. It's not a nice place to be.

But it's only a few minutes before my phone rings again, and not much longer before I'm talking to Nick himself, who sounds reassuringly calm when I tell him the news. 'OK. I'm on my way,' he says. 'Shouldn't be more than an hour. Tell Mum I'm coming, OK? Tell Dad.'

It's a strange hour, one way and another, because sitting alone in the draughty A and E waiting room it's like the whole of the past year has melted away, and that I'm enveloped once again in the undiluted horror that was the morning when my own father died. I remember the wail of the ambulance siren, the charcoal-tinted world that streaked, uncaring, past the windows, the clatter as the wheels of the stretcher were lowered, and the terrible emptiness that cloaked itself around me as we waited for someone to tell us what to do. I remember us clinging together like children under the patient ticket machine, but not needing a number. No longer requiring a place on the list. But most of all I recall that sense that nothing would ever be quite right again, because I never had time to say goodbye to my dad. I feel suddenly vulnerable. Suddenly so mortal. Every time someone walks into the waiting room I expect it to be Iona, face contorted with distress, to tell me it's too late. That Dai has gone too.

But by the time the hour has passed, I must, in fact, have travelled miles from this place, because I'm alerted to Nick's arrival only belatedly, when I hear him say his name to the woman on the admissions desk. He is tall and tanned, with dark wiry hair, and the sort of effortless good looks gay men often seem to have. I hurry across to greet him.

'Thanks so much for getting in touch,' he says, shaking my hand rather formally, which reminds me again that I'm only an onlooker in this particular drama. That my own is done and gone now. 'And for waiting with Mum,' he adds. There is hardly a trace of Iona's Welsh lilt in his voice. 'That was really kind of you. Where is she?' He glances around. 'With Dad?'

I gesture to the stairwell. 'You'll need to go upstairs. They've transferred him to ITU now,' I tell him. 'I didn't want to go till you arrived, but now you're here I'd really better get back to the office. Will you let her know that if there's anything I can do, well, just to call?'

I watch as he hurries off to find his family, feeling suddenly claustrophobic in these woe-flecked surroundings. That I need to escape. I'm just shouldering my bag when a hand slips over my shoulder. 'Hello, you,' says a voice.

It's Joe's.

And I'm *so* glad to see him.

He is ruffled and train-weary and has taken off his tie. His overnight case is standing to attention beside him, and in the curve of his plaster is clamped a rather heavy-looking basket of fruit.

'Oh,' I say, reaching to take it for him. The action has become almost automatic, I notice. 'I thought you were going back to the office.'

'Changed my mind,' he tells me, nodding at the basket. I wonder how he has managed to procure such a thing at such short notice. 'Thought I'd cab it straight up here and see how he's doing. Plus I guessed you'd still be here. So not much point in me schlepping back to the office – anyone needs me that badly they can get me on the mobile, can't they? Get hold of Nick in the end?'

He looks tired and pale against the still-red stripe of his scar. I wish I could read something warm in his expression. 'He's just arrived,' I tell him, 'so I was about to head back. I'll do that, then, shall I, while you go up and see them? And see you back at work later?'

272

He glances at his watch. 'Oh, no,' he says. 'No rush. I won't stay long if Nick's already here. Just say hello. Give him that.' He nods at the fruit basket and his eyes narrow slightly. I can't be sure if his faint smile is accusing or not. I hand it back to him. 'So,' he adds, 'why don't you wait for me down here and then we'll go back together? I'll only be a few minutes. Yes?'

True to his word, he is back within a quarter of an hour and we make our way out to the cab rank outside. He, like me, seems happy not to be staying any longer.

'He doesn't look good,' he comments, as he holds a rear door open for me. I shunt across the seat to make room for him beside me, but he puts his case there instead, then clunks the door shut and walks round the car to get in the front with the driver. 'But then,' he adds, doing up his seat belt, 'he wouldn't right now, would he? But they seem reasonably happy with his progress so far.'

'I hadn't realized he already had heart problems,' I said. 'Iona had never said. It must be like living with a time bomb.'

He nods. 'Exactly. But at least she has Nick with her now. He said to thank you, by the way, for being there for her.'

'Poor Iona,' I say. But I'm talking to the back of his neck.

When we get back to the office it is almost four thirty and the telephone in Joe's office is ringing. He goes off to answer it while I start trying to schedule some interviews for all the applicants who've written. But I can't seem to concentrate. All I can think of is how Iona must be feeling, sitting there contemplating the possibility of being widowed. Being alone. With her only son living so far away. And I think about Leo, all

273

the hopes I have for him. How I want him to see the world, do things, have adventures. And how my own life will change when he no longer needs me. How much of it I've put on hold. How well I've prescribed for the needs he has now. I try to imagine myself next year, knee deep in oil paint and canvas, the smell of turps sharp in my nostrils and the dry feel of clay in my hands, but the idea, which I've held dear for so long now, seems insubstantial and silly and, well, not really the answer, somehow. When I go to start franking the mail I notice that the Cona machine's still on. This morning feels like an age ago and, as if to remind me, it's snapping and hissing, and what little coffee there was when we left is now a sorry round stain in the base of the pot.

By the time we leave the office the shops on Queen Street are already shut, and even though the sun has now muscled its way through the cloudbase and is winking gaily off the swirly rainbow puddles on the pavement, the world feels a markedly more melancholy place. And me with it. It has been many months since the loss of my father has visited me so acutely – so physically – and I'm anxious to get home and put my arms round my son. But I recall that Del took Simeon and Leo swimming after school this afternoon and won't be back until eightish, and that the house I will be returning to will be empty. No family to enfold me in its reassuring bosom. I wonder if Joe feels that way at times too. We're both of us going home to no one tonight. I wonder if he feels that way *now*, perhaps. I wonder if, like me, he'd rather have some company for a while. As we approach Starbucks I almost find myself saying, 'God, you know what? I could kill for a coffee. Shall we grab a coffee? I mean sit down and have one.

Here? Together? We'll be sitting in traffic for half an hour in any case. What do you think?'

But I don't. I rehearse it in my head about six times, but I can't seem to do it. Because he might say no. Because his stride is too purposeful. His expression too impenetrable. Plus I'm aware that he keeps glancing down at his watch.

And, as it turns out, I'm quite glad that I haven't. Starbucks goes by, then the bank, then the cake shop. Then we get to the car, get in and set off. We're just heading out of the city when he says, 'Take a left up ahead into Llandennis Avenue, would you?'

'Oh,' I say, as I do so. 'Are you not going home, then?'

He shakes his head. 'No. Drop me up on the right there. Past that car over there.'

'The white Fiesta, you mean?'

'That's the one,' he confirms. 'Great. Thanks. That'll be fine.'

So he does want some company tonight, but not mine. He takes out his suitcase and, as I drive off, he waves. Then heads up a path to a house I remember. I haven't been there myself, but it's called Cedar Folly, and I certainly know of some flowers that have.

19

'So, anyway, he's all right for the moment, at least. No further episodes overnight, and when Joe spoke to Iona this afternoon he was still doing OK. But it was all a bit traumatic. Brought back everything with Dad, you know? Made me feel quite tearful, in fact. And lonely, somehow. It's so strange being thrust into the middle of something so personal. I kept thinking about how awful it would be if he *had* died. How Iona's memories of the day would always be that the only person there to comfort her was someone who'd never even met him. And it's not as if I know *her* terribly well, is it? I was really pleased to see Joe, I can tell you.'

'Ah,' says Del. 'And has he forgiven you for last Saturday?'

My, but she's quick. 'I don't think so. He didn't say anything about it. Didn't say much about anything, really. And he was off round his girlfriend's straight after work so I didn't get a chance to bring it up anyway.'

'Hmm,' she goes. 'Hmm. And do I detect a note of mild reproach in your voice, sister dear?'

She opens a bag of Kettle chips and shakes the contents into a bowl. We're at my place this evening, doing good deeds for the school. Specifically, for the school fête, which takes place this coming Saturday, and which, round these parts, is generally organized to within an inch of its life, and for which we, along with the half-dozen or so mums who are due here in an hour, are preparing and freezing about two hundred Welsh cakes at the behest of one Caryl Phelps, whose word here is law.

I'm not on the PTA myself but I have agreed this year to become one of the merry band of PTA helpers, which inspired category of inclusion is perfect for the likes of me: it means I help out when I can, which up to now hasn't been often, but that I'm spared the obligation of attending the meetings. (And, this being Cefn Melin, they are many and lengthy and involve bullet points, flip-charts, action plans, profit projections, parent-preference profiles, in-depth event cost/benefit analysis and, most stressfully, Caryl Phelps's homemade cinnamon snaps.) But those are just the meetings. Nothing else in Cefn Melin seems to be done without recourse to wine, which is much more my scene. Plus as I see so little of the other mums it will, I've decided, be a good way to make friends.

I rip the top off some Pringles and swallow another mouthful of wine. As social events go, it's hardly the pinnacle of groovy action, but it's the best I have right now, so I intend making the most of it.

'Not at all,' I tell her indignantly. 'Why would you think that?'

She lifts the bowl from the little stack in front of her and reaches for a bag of pretzels. Then looks at me pointedly. 'Well, correct me if I'm wrong, but you do seem to be exhibiting a certain irritation at the developments in his love-life right now. And given . . .'

She pauses to consider. I don't wait. 'Given *what?*'

'Well, given that Joe Delaney has been your number-one topic of conversation these last few weeks, I can't help but wonder if you aren't developing a bit of a thing for him, Lu. That's all.'

I spread the Pringles in a little arc round the edge of a plate. 'Oh, don't be ridiculous, Del.'

'It has been known. He is, after all, a *very* attractive man. Or hadn't you noticed?'

I decide not to comment. 'That's as may be,' I say, 'but I can assure you I'm developing nothing of the sort. I don't deny that now I've got to know him a little better I like him a *lot* better. And I don't deny that I feel pretty awful that I've given him the impression that I – well, that *he* – oh, I don't know. I just don't like that he's being so off with me, that's all.' That maybe now that he's got to know *me* a little better, he likes me a whole lot less. Which I don't say.

'But is he?' she asks.

'Being off with me? Yes, he is.'

'Sure it's not just that he's not being *on* with you, particularly? Decided he's not going to bother?'

'Bother? Bother with what?'

'Bother with *you*, sweetie. Romantically, that is.'

There is a twinkle in her eye that I don't like the look of. It has nothing to do with the surgery.

'Bother with me *romantically*? What on earth are you on about?'

I'm not sure why I say that. I'm not sure why I feel the need to come over all incredulous about this because the notion of Joe Delaney having, at one point, been interested in me romantically is hardly news. Not to me, at least, even if Del doesn't know about it. It is fact. *Was* fact, at any rate. In a minor, spur-of-the-moment sort of way. But not *that* interested. Clearly. I know because I checked. 'Since when,' I add innocently, 'was Joe Delaney interested in *me*?'

'Oh, come *on*, Lu! You know he was.'

Yes, *I* do. But she doesn't. Does she? She pops a pretzel into her mouth and crunches it, grinning. I find I don't like the fact that she says 'was' too.

'I know nothing of the sort,' I lie, wishing she'd tell me something else. Has she seen him or something? And has he mentioned me to her? Has he said something about me? 'Besides,' I point out, 'he's been seeing this Jeannine woman since I started there. If it's any concern of mine. Which it's not.' Once or twice a week, in fact. Three lots of flowers.

'Hmm,' she goes on. 'Methinks the lady doth protest too much. Anyway, it's funny you should mention it, because I ran into Julia at the doctor's yesterday. She was asking after you and I'd been telling her all about your chauffeuring exploits – and she mentioned that she'd seen Joe at a party on Sunday and she'd said he was with someone. Said she didn't know who. Tall woman? Blonde?'

Which reminds me *exactly* why it is that I don't want to own up to any sort of anything. On either his part or mine. My fingers are still smoking from the last time I burnt them. My fingers have been smoking for half my life, I think. 'I wouldn't know,' I say lightly. 'I've never met any of his harem.'

'And you don't much care anyway, right?'

'Precisely.'

'Precisely it is, then,' she sings, by way of answer. 'Now. Almost eight. Shall I take these on through?'

What am I to make of all this? What am I to make of the fact that my sister thinks she can detect something in my voice that makes her think I have a bit of a thing for Joe? What am I to make of the fact that when he arrived at the hospital yesterday what I really wanted him to do was put his arms (OK, arm) around me? What am I to make of the fact that I know, I just *know*, that had he done so I would have felt so much better? What am I to make of the fact that his manner – his 'not bothering', as Del would have it – is getting to me so much? What am I to make of the fact that I have started blow-drying my hair in the mornings?

I don't know. But there is one thing I do know.

That all of it makes me feel anxious and funny in a way that I can't quite articulate, somehow.

Friday 8 June

'We're going to need a temp,' says Joe.

I have a headache. Which is what you get if you roll Welsh-cake dough out till one in the morning. Which is what you get when you drink red wine from a plastic bottle. Which is what you get mainly when you don't sleep a wink because your brain refuses to obey your instruction that it will cease its relentless dissection of everything a certain man utters or does.

I look up. 'A temp?'

'Yes. A *temp*,' he repeats, patting his forehead and grinning. 'Doh! A temp while Iona's away. Someone who can do the payroll this week, at the very least. You don't do PAYE, do you?' I wish I did suddenly. 'No. Thought not. So can you get on to the agency for me and see if they can sort something out? They've got a woman, Clare something – they'll know who I mean. See if she's available. Anyway,' he says, 'better crack on. When's the next one due in, by the way?'

By 'next one' he means the next engineer on the list. I've organized six interviews for today and another six on Monday. He has five posts to fill for the Bath and Birmingham jobs and needs three of them available for the beginning of July. The first, a young guy with a ring

280

in his lip and a sheaf of dog-eared certificates, has been deemed a 'possibility' and given an asterisk. The next is due half an hour from now. I give Joe the form and he trots back to his office while I pick up the address book and reach for the phone.

Oh, it's all go without Iona. Which is good, because much as I would enjoy the chance to stare out of the window and watch the seagulls for a while, it would, I suspect, lead me down avenues of speculation that would be seriously bad for my health. Despite my conviction that to do so is folly, I am, rather stressfully, *noticing* Joe today. Like Del with her new laser-beam vision, I'm suddenly *seeing*. With a great deal more clarity than I have up to now. I'm seeing the way the hair at the back of his neck forms little glossy question marks against his collar. I'm seeing the way his shoes are so shiny. I'm seeing the way his right eyebrow is always arched slightly higher than the left one. How it makes his expression look ironic somehow. I'm seeing how when he smiles, the groove on his forehead is replaced by two little clefts at the edges of his mouth.

This is pathetic indeed. This is ditsy behaviour. And this is all my sister's fault.

If it wasn't for my sister I wouldn't be behaving like this. I know I wouldn't. I wouldn't even be feeling like this. I certainly wouldn't be . . .

'Lu?'

I look up from my desk. He's back in my office again. All six feet two of him. All tensile and honed, and capable of hefting an AVH Excelsior-six eleven heavy-duty . . . Oh, God.

'Hello, you,' he says, dipping his head to smile engagingly at me. 'Er, anybody in? Just remembered. Next Thursday. Suppose we should really get things organized, shouldn't we?'

'Thursday?'

'The Luxotel development meeting. The one in Birmingham. Had you forgotten? It is in the diary. Meant to remind you about it last week, but with one thing and another – anyway. It's just going to be the one night again. Not going to be a problem for you, is it?'

I had not forgotten at all. Oh, no.

'Um. Oh, yes,' I said. 'I'm not sure. I'll have to see if it'll be OK with Del. Shall I call her?'

He nods. 'So we'll have to get the temp in Thursday morning, ideally. I have to be at the hotel by three for the meeting. Oh, and there's a dinner, by the way. Did I mention that to you? Black-tie thing. Bit glitzy. Better bring a frock.'

There are lots of things in Joe's diary. Lots of appointments, lots of squiggles, lots of impenetrable acronyms. Several mentions along the lines of 'J – 7 p.m.' and so on. (Though no mention of a party on Sunday 3 June. Just a coffee ring straddling the whole weekend.) What there is, of course – and has been for some weeks now – is an entry for this coming Thursday, because I was the one who put it there, but since the events of the past few days my attitude to it has shifted considerably. Where once it was just a date (and one that at the time I hadn't assumed would have much impact on me – I thought he'd be driving himself by then) it has, this week, taken on a distinctly looming quality. Much as, in fact, a real date would. Would he ask me to take him? Would he not ask me to take him? And, much more to the point, if he did, would I go?

Dinner, indeed. Glitzy indeed. *Frock* indeed.

In *my* diary – which is not a diary at all, but a *Lion, the Witch and the Wardrobe* calendar full of dental appointments and swimming lessons – there is, conversely, just the one thing. And it is the Cefn Melin Primary School Fête, which this year is taking the form of a medieval extravaganza. Truly, can there be another school in Britain that sports a jousting arena by the bric-à-brac stall?

And Del, who is always depressingly proficient with a Singer and a selection of bargain-price remnants, has provided me with a very fetching costume, in which to lure unsuspecting punters towards my sugar-sprinkled, raisin-studded delights. So here I am, in a persistent drizzle, crouched over a Baby Belling in a length of mock-sacking, slapping Welsh cakes around and saying, 'Prithee, my lordship! Prithee, my lady! Fare thee quite well on this exceeding fair morn? Wouldst thou like to make merry with my fine bakes today?'

Which is no bloody way to spend a Saturday, I can tell you, but the hierarchy at PTA plc dictates that it will be so. By the time I'm eligible for the dizzy heights of bar duty, Leo will be old enough to hire a car in Cadiz. Have given him enough money to make a bid for control of the entire Pokémon empire, and have neglected to remember to eat any lunch. But do not want a Welsh cake. Do *not* want a Welsh cake.

'Oooh! Welsh cakes!' says a voice. 'Now that'll be a treat!'

The voice (one of many expressing similarly effusive sentiments – I sometimes feel the Welsh cake is a deeply overrated bakery item) is one that I recognize. For it is that of Liz, Joe's glamorous ex-mother-in-law, who has fetched up at my stall with a similarly smiling friend.

'How much are they?' Liz enquires. Then, 'Oh, hello! Thought I knew you! It's Lu, isn't it? Goodness! Did you make all these yourself?'

'Not quite all,' I admit, impressed that she has remembered my name. 'Only the first three hundred thousand. How many would you like? I give discounts for bulk purchases.'

She turns to her friend. 'Lu works for Joe, Pam,' she explains, 'while his regular girl's on maternity leave. And look at you,' she continues admiringly. 'As if you're not busy enough, you're giving up your Saturday for the school. Well done, you!'

Liz, it turns out, is at the school fête today because her grandchildren – Rhiannon's sister's children – are pupils here. As Angharad herself was, apparently, before moving to the private school. She comes every year, she tells me. Which, after her comments, puts me to shame because that's certainly more than I've managed. I wonder if Joe used to come to them too.

'And what about Iona's husband?' she says. 'I hear he's had a heart-attack. How is he, do you know?'

I update her on his progress and promise to pass on her good wishes. And they buy thirty Welsh cakes between them. They then declare themselves in need of some fortifying tea, so I direct them to the Ivy Bush Tavern (or so says the sign on the adjacent classroom door). Something that would be of no consequence whatever were it not for the fact that minutes later, as I trot across in search of a tea-towel, a name I recognize floats from the rumble of their genial dialogue. They are, I realize, talking about Joe. As I steer a route past them I catch the tail end of it.

'It's great,' Liz is saying. 'And I think he's on top of it.

And it's certainly lovely to see him looking so well, arm notwithstanding, of course.' She lowers her voice. 'Did I tell you, by the way, Pam? He's back with Jeannine again. Bless.'

It's difficult to elicit what Pam's thoughts are on this subject, without looking as if I'm waiting for a bus. It's difficult to elicit what this subject is, period. God! Pam. Liz. Iona. Uncle Tom tall blonde woman flipping Cobbleigh. Why does everyone but me seem to know everyone else?

I will just have to reach my own conclusions.

Wednesday 13 June

Paralysed as I was with the stress of trying not to spend my every waking moment leaping from conclusion to conclusion like a demented hare, the last thing on my mind was the Exo opening party, but Iona called mid-afternoon to remind me, and to check that I was still going to go. She'd spent all afternoon at the hospital and the last thing *she* wanted to do, she told me, was get the bus home to an empty house. Nick had driven back to Hemel Hempstead that morning and wouldn't be returning till late on Friday. I didn't want to let her down.

'Oh, I'm *so* pleased, *cariad*. And guess what?' she said, with awe in her voice. 'Nigel Walker is going to be there!'

The name meant nothing to me whatsoever. 'Nigel *who*?' I asked.

'Tsk!' she said, shocked. 'You mean you've never heard of him?'

'Er, no,' I replied. 'So who is he, then?'

He was, she explained, a sportsman. An ex-Olympic

athlete, in fact. And, more to the point, an ex-rugby-player too. An ex-rugby-player for Wales, specifically. Which, in these environs, meant as near to deification as it was humanly possible to be. And probably why his existence on Planet Icon had, up till now, passed me by. I don't much do sport as a rule.

'He's doing the opening, apparently, so I thought I could get his autograph for Dai. Oh, he'd be so chuffed, bless him. See you later, then, lovely. You never know. Perhaps we could get you one too.'

We'd arranged to meet up with Joe there. He'd had some sort of business to attend to down in Penarth and said he would make his own way. He also had another J – 7 in his diary, so I wasn't sure that he'd show up at all.

Iona came up to meet me at the office. Despite her sparkly blouse and her upbeat demeanour, she looked drawn and hollow-eyed and as if what she really needed was some rest, but I think she needed company more. Lily had been in to visit, she'd said, and Dai's sister from Maesteg had brought him a fatless sponge. He was, she said, looking more like himself. As much like himself, she commented wryly, as could be expected with half his heart buggered up. As we walked down to get the car I marvelled at her stoicism. How did she live with that kind of fear all the time?

Exo was based in the fashionable new retail development they'd recently opened in Cardiff Bay. A throng of achingly trendy people had already spilled out on the pavement, all braying at each other in newsreader voices, and holding foot-long blue-tinged champagne flutes. We drove round and put the car in the new multi-storey, then made our way back across the road.

'Well,' remarked Iona, as we were ushered in and

handed our glasses. 'I'm certainly glad I didn't bother with my two-piece. What a dreadful bunch of scruffs this lot are!'

With the champagne we'd also been given more publicity material. The number three seemed to be the thrust of the theming. That and insects. Exo was short for Exoskeleton, apparently, and the trio analogy was evident elsewhere: head/thorax/ abdomen, mind/body/ spirit, past/present/ future, and, rather bizarrely, I thought, the Oasis-inspired directive of be/here/now. But strangely, given that this was essentially a posh beauty parlour, no cleanse/tone/moisturize. Too last-century perhaps.

We edged our way slowly inside. The salon itself was on the first floor, blue lit, and reached via a long sweep of blond wooden staircase with a wall on one side made of pale blue glass bricks. It felt a little like the inside of a toilet cistern. And, as befitted a place with such an esoteric bunch of mission statements, even the stair treads had attitude, each one etched, as it was, with an uplifting quote. 'Why worry?' said one. 'Is as does', said another. I skipped over 'Read a poem a day'.

Once we reached the top, Iona – who was standing on 'The worst almost never happens' which seemed spookily apposite – spied the object of her affections within seconds. 'There he is, lovely. See? Isn't he something? Oh, and there's Joe, too.'

And there *was* Joe, too. Across the room, looking lovely. And deep in conversation with a man in a skirt. My heart went bing-bang-a-bong as I spotted him. And bing-bong again, as he spotted me. We caught each other's eyes and for a second it was as if there was no one else in the place. No, *really*. He was *looking* at me. Looking at me intently. One brow slightly arched.

Saying something to me with those piercing green eyes. I didn't have the first clue what they were trying to transmit, but who cared? He shouldered his way towards me through the sea of bobbing heads. Was this what it was going to be like from now on? This rush of endorphins every time we clapped eyes on each other? That we were destined, like two excitable molecules, to go fizz! bang! pop! every time our eyes met? Oh, me, oh, *my*. What a turn-up. What a thing.

'Hello, you,' he mouthed, beckoning me to come a little nearer. He leaned closer still and put his lips to my ear. 'Done a lot of nude modelling?' he whispered.

'. . . and so I looked up, and there it was. About twenty feet high. I couldn't believe it! Hanging there. Right slap bang in the middle of the salon. Right in the atrium. I nearly died, Del. I nearly *died*.'

We hadn't stayed terribly long.

Because it hadn't been terribly much fun. Whatever mesmeric delights had been occasioned by that piece of singularly divvyish misreading of Joe's expression were wiped out in an instant. Because there's only so much indignity a girl can take.

So I took Iona (plus precious autograph) back home to Grangetown and was back at Del's to collect Leo by seven. My face, by that time, was still only marginally less terracotta than the nasturtiums and pelargoniums that sprang enthusiastically from her pots. She followed me into the kitchen and tutted. '*What?*' she demanded. 'What was twenty feet high?' She put down her trug and pulled out a chair for me to sit on. 'Whoops. Spaghetti hoops. Hold on. There. Come on – what?'

'The painting! The painting Stefan did for Exo, of

course! It wasn't the blob! It was supposed to be the blob!'

'What blob? You're not making any sense, girl.'

'The blob painting! The one he showed me! You know – I told you. The one he was supposed to have done for Exo. The painting he'd done for the atrium. But that's what I'm saying! It wasn't! It wasn't the blob painting at all! Del, it was a painting of *me*!'

She sat down, too, and raised her eyebrows enquiringly. 'Of *you*?'

I put my head on the table and groaned. '*Three* paintings actually. It was a triptych, made up of three separate panels. To tie in with the insect allegory, I suppose.'

'*Insect* allegory? What's that when it's at home?'

'Oh, you don't want to know. Some pretentious crap. Anyway. So it was three paintings, three *huge* paintings, all in a row, side by side. All hung on wires. You know, head, thorax, abdomen and so on. So I was chopped up into three. Lying down. Three panels. One with my head and shoulders, one with my – God, my whole *body* in it, and one with the legs. God, he even did the blue nail varnish!'

'You've lost me, I'm afraid.'

'The picture, Del! The picture he did of me. The *naked* picture he did of me! The charcoal. You know, the one he did of me when I went round there that time. He's obviously used that instead. He's obviously made an oil painting out of it. A *huge* oil painting. *Three* oil paintings!'

'Well, well,' she said, grinning. 'And are they any good?'

'Good! Good! They were *abominable*, Del! God! I was *soooo* embarrassed! Well, you can imagine, can't you? I walk in there and the place is *heaving* with people and right there staring down at me is, well – me! A *huge* me, a huge, distorted, *slavering* me, with enormous drooping boobs and my knee sticking up in the air, and an expression on my face that, well – well, I looked like a centrefold on heat! Oh, it's too, too horrible. I shall have nightmares for ever more. Oh, there was *acres* of it, Del. Acres and acres of pink flesh and wibbly bits, and well, you know . . . *pubes*! Mine! All swirly and sprouty and I *mean* – ugh, ugh, ugh!'

'What a hoot!' she exclaimed, clapping. 'I'm going to have to go down and pretend I want to join. What *fun*! I don't know what you're making such a fuss about, Lu. I think it's brilliant! And I'm sure it can't have been that bad. I mean, it is a fitness place, after all. Besides, on the evidence I've seen, you should consider yourself lucky you didn't morph into a lobster or a plank of wood or something. I take it it was a pretty good likeness, then, yes?'

I nod, slowly. 'Oh, yes. Absolutely, horrifyingly, unmistakably me. I mean even with all the frantic brushwork and mad hair and the leer. Oh, yes. It was a good likeness, all right. It was the first thing Joe saw when he walked into the place. He said he was gobsmacked. He said he nearly choked on his champagne.'

'Ah, but did he *like* it? That's the point.'

'Point? *Point?* God, I'm still in shock that he's even *seen* it! Oh, it's so embarrassing. All those people! All those *hundreds* of people! Oh, Del, how will I ever live it down?'

'Oh, I wouldn't worry if I were you. I'm sure no one else even noticed.'

'Joe did.'

'Yes, but he already *knows* you, doesn't he?'

And more intimately than most now. Oh, God.

'Anyway,' she goes on, 'it's not like you're going to be down there cavorting around with your clothes off on a regular basis, is it?'

'No, but there were a couple of photographers there and at least one of them took a picture of it. I'll probably be a double page spread in the *Western Mail* in the morning. What a cheek! The nerve of him! I mean, can he *do* that? I mean, shouldn't he have to ask my permission or something?'

She got up to put on the kettle. 'I don't think so. I mean you already gave it to him, really. You did pose for him, after all. Seems to me he can do what he likes with it. Seems to me he already has. Was he there?'

'Oh, yes. He was there all right. Prancing around with a stupid hat on and guzzling champagne and slapping fish rolls in his mouth. Oh, and he was so *full* of it! He said he'd been meaning to give me a ring and tell me about it. I'll give him *ring*. I told him I'd half a mind to wring his bloody neck.'

'Wring whose bloody neck?' asked Leo, who'd walked in.

'Language!' I snapped.

'What a laugh!' observed Del.

20

'What a laugh!' observes Joe, popping gum from his packet. 'I mean, you've got to see the funny side, haven't you, Lu?'

Oh, ha bloody ha. And which funny side would that be? The image of my prostrate form came, rather distressingly, to mind. It was true that once I'd established that the combined media machine of Cardiff had deemed the Exo opening party worth little more than a couple of column inches and a rather grainy photo of Nigel Walker, I had calmed down a little on the exposure front (and, well, fair enough, I was quits with the rat-bag at least) but, even so, the tag 'funny' was not one that came naturally to mind.

And now we're on our way to Birmingham, Joe and I, and the last thing I want is for him to remind me of anything about it. That I'd . . . that *Stefan* and I'd . . . that we'd . . . What mania had possessed me? Ugh, ugh, ugh.

'Have I?' I answer stiffly. 'Well, I haven't yet, I can tell you.'

'But you will,' he says consolingly. 'It's not every girl who gets herself that kind of publicity.' He chuckles. 'And you can't deny you *looked* like you enjoyed modelling for it, can you?'

I can see from the corner of my eye that he's looking at me. Looking at me, I'm sure, in a completely new light. I keep my eyes on the road. 'That,' I say, finally, 'isn't the point. The point is that if I'd had even the *slightest* notion that the result might be hung in a public place I wouldn't have *dreamt* of letting him do it.'

Even 'letting him do it' sounds seedy, somehow. But he laughs. Ho ho ho.

'It *was* a good painting, Lu. I mean, fair play, the guy may be a dipstick but he does have a talent.'

Oh, yes. For the seduction of witless maidens.

'Oh,' I say, shocked. 'You mean you *liked* it?'

'Very much. And so did everyone else I spoke to. It was quite a talking point, in fact.'

My twenty-foot, naked, slobbering self? 'Well,' I concede, 'evidently he does, then. But, like I said, that's not the point. I wasn't posing for the benefit of the clientele of Exo, was I? I wasn't posing so that half of Cardiff could ogle my breasts. I was posing because . . . because . . .' Uuurgh. 'Well, anyway,' I say, sniffing, 'it was personal and he shouldn't have done it. He had no right.'

Joe takes his gum from his mouth and wraps it carefully in some tissue. 'Lu,' he says sternly, 'you're ranting. Why can't you just chill out about it? God!' He exhales extravagantly. 'You always get so *indignant* about everything. And what's the point? It's up there now, and it'll doubtless be staying. So there's no point in railing against it. And why worry anyway? You looked great. The business.'

Great? The *business*? What *planet* is he on?

'Oh, *great*, for sure. Great as in megalith bottom. Great as in—'

He turns his head. 'Lu, you're a woman, not a pretzel.

293

Great as in *great*. Great as in *sexy*. And the only reason you can't see it is because, as ever, you're too busy getting on your high horse about it.'

'Hruumph. And why wouldn't I? How would you like it if it had happened to you? How would you feel if it were *your* genitalia wanging in the breeze up there? Ho ho I *don't* think.'

He smirks and falls silent. Indignant, indeed.

Oh, why does he say things like that to me? Why?

OK, I will concede that his observation that I looked great, the business and sexy to boot *was* moderately uplifting, but his observation that I was always indignant about everything was more than moderately annoying. How dare he? What did he know about it? And why couldn't he say something completely unequivocal? Like 'I fancy you, Lu.' How hard was that? But he said nothing more for the next twenty minutes, and I was still feeling ranty when we pulled up at the services. We'd been narrowly beaten by a coachload of tourists and had to make a dash for the restaurant. I'd had no time for breakfast and my stomach was rumbling. Could one politely eat chips before noon?

Could one politely eat chips ever again, in fact, when one's five-acre stomach was aloft in Cardiff Bay? I pulled out two trays and handed one to him. But he shook his head. 'Er, no thanks. Nothing for me.' He patted his stomach. 'Just coffee. Get me a big one, will you? I'll go and grab us a table.'

I went up to the counter and, as I was now to be eating alone and under scrutiny, I decided to forgo the fries and opted instead for the small bowl of fruit and a wizened white roll. I got him a cappuccino, which he fell upon, wincing.

'Heavy night, then?' I asked.

He pulled a face. 'Um, ye-es.'

'So it was a good party?'

Now he shook it. 'Oh, I didn't stay long at the party. Went out to dinner.'

Oh. Oh, *that*. I recalled the 'J – 7' that I'd seen in his diary. Oh, yes. *That*. I don't know what possessed me to utter the words I said next. A kind of masochism, maybe? Exasperation? Who knows? All I know is that it suddenly seemed the right thing to do. Jump off the express train to disappointment I'd started riding. Move on, move out, move up. That kind of thing. Oh, if he would only drop a bit of *his* sex-life into the conversation now and again, instead of making reference to mine all the time, then I'd be denied any reason to hope, and could therefore get on with the next bit of my life. Was it so much to ask? That he offered up a casual 'Jeannine my girlfriend', or something? 'That tall, blonde woman I'm seeing' or whatever? But he hadn't. And out the words popped. Just like that.

'Oh,' I said, melon ball teetering on spoon, 'with anyone nice?'

The 'nice', to my utter dismay, came out with quote marks attached. He blinked at me. 'What?'

I plopped the melon ball into my mouth and sucked it in what I hoped was a nonchalant manner. Then said, in what I hoped was a similarly disinterested one, 'Last night. Just wondered, that's all.'

He slid his coffee cup back and forth over its saucer a few times before lifting it to his lips and sipping cautiously. Then his left eyebrow inched quizzically upwards a fraction. 'Why d'you ask?' he enquired, looking at me over the spirals of steam.

I moved in on a grape. He was still looking at me.

I couldn't read his expression at all. 'No reason,' I said.

He put the cup down. 'Yes, there was.'

Just like that.

'No, there *wasn't*.' I put the grape in my mouth and bit into it. Pips. I swallowed them. 'Just making conversation.'

He moved his saucer a little to make room for his plaster, then parked it on the table and lifted the cup again. 'No, you weren't, Lu,' he said. 'You don't do "just making conversation". And no, as it happens. No one desperately nice. With the maintenance manager for Tower 2000. Business.'

I scooped up a brown shard of apple and considered it. Was he lying? 'Oh. Right,' I said.

He shifted a little in his seat. Something like a grin was playing at the corners of his mouth. 'And was that the answer you wanted to hear?'

I shifted in my own seat. 'What?'

'That I wasn't out with "anyone nice" last night?'

Uuurgh. 'It's of no consequence, Joe. I told you,' I said, 'I was just making conversation. OK?'

'OK,' he said, smiling as he put down the coffee cup again. 'Then supposing I told you I *had* been out with someone "nice" last night. What then?' He was looking at me pointedly now.

I made a big show of shrugging. 'Then nothing. Like I said, I just wondered.'

He lowered his head and blew a little furrow in the foam on his coffee. 'Oh, right,' he said.

And I wish I wish I wish I *wish* I hadn't said that. Why had I said that? Why hadn't I seen it through? Why hadn't I asked him what I really wanted to ask him? Why hadn't I said that it *was* of consequence? Why hadn't I said that I *wasn't* just wondering? That I

296

really wanted to know. That I *cared*? That I wanted to know who the hell Jeannine bloody Carver was once and for all. Why hadn't I said that I was suddenly all at sea about him and that if only he'd tell me she wasn't his girlfriend, that what I'd really like to do was to take back everything I'd previously said/done/ thought/ *assumed* where he was concerned. And start again. From that kiss, maybe? So why didn't I?

He leant across the table and narrowed his eyes. 'It's only,' he went on, 'that you seem very interested in my comings and goings all of a sudden. I wondered if there was any reason for it.'

I shook my head and started ferreting in my bowl again. More melon, some orange. A glacé cherry. He continued to look at me. Even with my head down I could feel his gamma-ray pupils boring little green holes in my head. But I couldn't find the words.

Half a year or so passed. I finished the fruit salad.

'Suit yourself,' he said flatly. 'Shall we go?'

This is not good progress. This is crap progress. Del is right. I *am* developing a bit of a thing for Joe Delaney. But I don't know quite what to do about it. I don't know quite what to do about it but at least I now know what *not* to do about it. What not to do about it is to sit there like some po-faced bloody baggage and pretend I couldn't give a f**k.

Because he's got the hump again. Because he's got his scowly face on again. And because, when all's said and done, one thing is certain. Del's right. Whatever praise he might have heaped on my image, he's clearly not bothering with the flesh-and-blood me.

Clearly not.

The meeting, for which a large group of Gallic hoteliers had gathered, was to go on till six. And didn't require my presence. Which meant I had three hours to get ready for the dinner. Which would have been an amusing irony were it not that I felt so bloody miserable about it. Three hours I could either spend primping and preening and trying to make myself beautiful, or slap on some slap and read the paper instead. In fact, I spent the first of them holed up in the bathroom, neck deep in Body Shop tangerine bubbles, and knee deep in conflicting irresolute thoughts. Which to do? What angle to take? Round and round I went, getting precisely nowhere. Because much as I wanted to let Joe know how I felt about him, as soon as I envisaged the actuality of doing so, there was JC before me, tall blonde JC, and Joe, saying, 'Sorry, but . . .' I couldn't bear that. The very idea made my toes curl. On the other hand, if JC was JC *as in non-romantic item*, as evidenced by my small but growing store of hope-giving moments – he had said it, he had, he'd said I looked sexy in a pointed kind of way – then why didn't he simply make some sort of move? Obviously because he *wasn't that interested anyway*, so why even *think* about letting him know I was? Why put myself through that? Why suffer the humiliation? Hadn't I already been humiliated enough?

I poured myself a glass of wine from the little bottle in the mini-bar and, quite soon after, it became apparent that my makeup bag was having none of my dithering in any case. If I was going down with the ship of failed romances, it seemed to tell me, then I was bloody well going down sparkling and flawless. Thus prettified and glowing, I sat on the bed with the rest of the bottle and a towel round my bottom, and watched Ainsley on *Ready Steady Cook*. Then *The Weakest Link*, so that I could divert myself from feeling petulant about Joe by getting cross with Anne Robinson while

I painted my nails. Scarlet, on this occasion, because I'd brought my best dress with me. It was a blood-red designer-label devoré and satin affair that I'd picked up in Howells' last-but-one January sale. And a pair of spindly, strappy, quite ridiculous stilettos. The most appallingly uncomfortable shoes I'd ever owned. And I'd be setting off this confection of seduction tonight with an attractive mock-leather organizer handbag, in fashionable black with contrast frayed stitching, and leaked-biro detail on front. Courtesy George, House of Asda.

There'd been a text message on my phone when I'd risen from the bathtub. From Leo. *'Hi Mum! Luv U! Any Pok packs?!!!!!! Forgot A. Del's Eve bag! Oops! XXX'*

Bugger.

But what the hell? Why was I doing all this stuff anyway? He wasn't bothering, was he?

Clearly not.

'Ah! The lovely Lucienne!' said Monsieur Deschamp, snogging my cheeks like a toilet plunger and clasping both my hands in his. 'And looking, if I may say, even lovelier than before. Quite breathtaking, in fact. Don't you think so, Joe?'

Joe, who had responded to my appearance in the Outrigger Bar with about as much enthusiasm as a bald man contemplating a matching brush and comb set, muttered, 'Mmm, yes,' as if admiring a trifle, then put his face back into his lager. He was wearing a cream tuxedo, one shoulder of which was slung casually across the arm with the plaster. The shirt underneath was crisp and blue-white. The bow tie was cream satin. And a real one. Not clip-on. How on earth had he tied it, I wondered. He looked fabulous. Swashbuckling. Heart-stoppingly gorgeous. But I certainly wasn't going to say so. Even *look* so. *Oh*, no. 'Mmm, yes', indeed. *Fine*.

'And she's mine, I might add!' added Jean Paul, with a flourish. 'I 'ave sat you by me, *chérie*,' he added with a simper. '*Entente cordiale. Entente très cordiale*.'

And, well, sod Joe, I thought. Sod him. At least someone was showing me a bit of interest around here.

'Lovely, Jean Paul.' I simpered playfully, accepting the gin and tonic he was proffering and smearing it with lip gloss. 'You can tell me all about your new erection in Blois.'

Which, as it turned out, set a tone of sorts.

I don't know if it was simply a function of my determination to starve Joe of my scintillating company, but with two glasses of wine and two gin and tonics inside me, Jean Paul seemed as charming and attentive a dinner companion as any girl could wish for. Plus it transpired that he knew my mother's home town of Béziers rather well, having himself grown up not far away in Perpignan. Thus we chatted and laughed our merry way through the starter and best part of yet another bottle of wine.

And I guess that's partly how these things come to happen. In any event, it wasn't till the main course that his hand on my forearm and lascivious expression made me realize his chit-chat had a definite agenda. That while I was busy making inroads into my dinner, Jean Paul was attempting to do likewise with me.

We had moved on somehow to the art world. An area about which Jean Paul evidently knew a great deal more than I would have expected. He waxed lyrical for some moments about his great love of Degas and how perfectly he thought he captured the female form. No surprise there. Little girls, ballet dancers, women *après le bain. Naked* women. I'd been there. I shuddered.

'And, Lucienne,' he hissed, arresting the northerly progress of a small spear of broccoli I had wedged on my fork, 'Joe tells me you dabble a little yourself.'

For one horrified moment I thought he'd told him. 'He does?' I asked cautiously.

'Oh, but yes,' he went on. 'You are an art student yourself, I understand.' He gave my wrist a little squeeze before giving it back to me. His eyes flicked to my cleavage. His mouth curled in a smile.

'Excuse me,' I said. 'Got to powder my nose.'

He looked blank. 'Call of nature,' I said. He looked blanker.

'Little *girls'* room.'

He leered. It figured. I went.

The toilets in the new Luxotel Birmingham Sud were located some way distant from the function room we were in. Once outside, I slipped off my shoes and padded there barefoot, my toes burying themselves gratefully in the soft, yielding pile. As I came out, I noticed that just beyond them was another function area, this one dark and empty. 'The Orangery', it said in script over the door. Anxious to retain a bit of distance between me and the hotspot of expectation I seemed inadvertently to have created, I thought I would duck out of the dessert, and send Leo a text message instead. I tried the double doors. They sighed open unresistingly, so I padded in for a nose around. It was a room of similar grandeur to the one we were occupying, with a part-glazed vaulted roof and tall windows on three sides. The flooring was stone – giant diamond-shaped quarry tiles – and the room was full of potted palms, yuccas and citrus plants. There was a faint scent of lemon and compost. I plonked myself down on one of the vast cane sofas and fished out my phone.

It's a fiddly mode of communication, text messaging. Especially when you are sitting with nothing in the way of illumination but your little green display. And a cheap pay-as-you-go phone that doesn't light up the numbers for you. 'Hi! Msg 4 Leo. Love U Lots & lots.' Which was probably why I didn't hear him. 'Have U done H Work???!!! If Y then 2 Packs Pok!!!' Probably why I wasn't aware that he was standing two feet from me. 'C U tomorrow. Give S & A D & U B my love.' Probably why the touch of his hand on my bare shoulder sent me six feet in the air.

It was Jean Paul.

'Ooh, la!' he chirped, giggling. 'My apologies, Lucienne! I didn't mean to startle you, *chérie*.'

He was swaying a little. He was probably flammable. *Chérie* indeed.

'Oh! Goodness, Jean Paul! Well, you certainly did!'

He flopped down beside me on the sofa and waved an expansive arm into the darkness. 'You like it?'

I switched off my phone and reached down to pick up my bag from the floor.

'It's very nice,' I said, rising. 'Very grand. Anyway. Better get back.'

His hand, which he'd taken away when he'd startled me, now slipped into mine. He gave it a tug. 'Don't go,' he coaxed, with a glassy-eyed pout. 'No hurry, is there? Stay awhile with me here. So. You like our 'otel, do you?'

I glanced around, conscious of the pressure of his fingers wrapped around mine. I pulled them away, which he didn't resist, then opened my bag and slipped the phone into it. The hair was prickling at the back of my neck.

'Yes, yes, very much. I just thought I'd come in and take a look and, well, just sending my son a—'

'Ah.' The hand that had been holding mine now began moving along the outside of my thigh. He smiled encouragingly at me. 'Then perhaps I can find some more places to show you. Shall we go outside? We 'ave all kinds of ducts.'

Ducts? *Ducts?* What the hell would I want to see them for? This was pushing the allure of combustion too far. I stood up. At least I was free of the sofa. But I couldn't see my shoes anywhere. Where *were* they?

'No, thank you. That's very kind of you, Jean Paul, but I think I'd better get back. They'll be—'

'Oh, come, come,' he urged, rising unsteadily to his feet. His hand, which was now warm and damp, slithered across the back of my neck and around my shoulder. 'Worry not, my Lucienne. They will be busy reconvening in the bar. Come. Let me show you the ornamental fountains. And the queck-quecks! It is a beautiful night.' He tried to coax me forward.

'No. *Really,*' I said, wriggling free of his embrace and stooping to see if I'd accidentally kicked them under the sofa. Quack-bloody-quacks indeed. 'Ah, but *chérie,*' he said, instantly re-establishing it as I straightened. 'What about our *entente cordiale*, hmm? You and me, I think, we have an understanding about these things, don't we?'

'We do?' Where the bloody hell were they? Perhaps I should leave without them. 'And what sort of understanding would that be, Jean Paul?'

His lunge, when it came, was so sudden and unexpected and sure of itself that I lost my balance and barked the back of my ankle against the coffee-table leg. His hand was like a vice against the top of my arm and his hot smoky breath poured in a rush against my neck. 'Ah, Lucienne,' he urged, 'just a kiss. *Un petit bise.* Come on. Don't tease me. You always tease me. You and I, you know, we have a—'

'A *mis*understanding, Jean Paul! What we have is a *complete* misunderstanding. So I'd rather you didn't do that, if you don't mind.' I wriggled myself out of his grasp.

'But I *do* mind, Lucienne!' he entreated, gusts of buttery breath billowing between us. 'You are so cruel with me. *Cruel!* I am very anxious that I—'

'And *I*'m very anxious that you pack this bloody nonsense up,' I snarled. 'So you can stop that right now!' I tried to swing a slap at him but as soon as I raised my arm to do so, he grabbed both my elbows and pinioned them at my sides. He was alarmingly deft for a lush.

If a little unfocused. His mouth lurched towards mine and made hot squelchy contact with my cheek instead, chomping its way, mole fashion, through the sparkle dust and blusher, towards what I assumed was its goal of my lips. Yeuch! Not in this lifetime, matey. I yanked my head back and his tongue fetched up against my throat instead. It sounded like a bath emptying.

'*Chérie*, come *on*,' he breathed. 'Why resist? Why resist?'

He pressed himself against me, all knobbly bits and groanings, pawing at my chest now with feverish hands. Which made me stumble backwards and, what do you know, I found my shoes at last. One of them, at least. Because it kindly made its presence felt by viciously spiking the ball of my foot. There was a sharp snapping sound and a fire in my instep, which had me yelping with pain and right back where I started. On the sofa, knees up now, with Jean Paul on top.

He wasted not a second in trying to play his advantage.

'Ah, *chérie!*' he cried. His was clearly not an extensive vocabulary. '*Chérie!* Come on! Kiss me! Kiss me now!' He was half on the sofa and half on the floor now, hands flailing madly and scrabbling at my dress. I heard a rip.

Jesus Christ. A situation, or what? This was fast becoming more than just difficult. He was drunk and incapable and as floppy as a rag doll, but he was intent on a grope and he was not going to stop. I was almost too incredulous to draw breath. Almost but not quite. There is a moment when resistance, as they say, is useless. When it needs to change tack. To a full, take-no-prisoners, McNab-style attack.

'Get *off!*' I bellowed at him. 'Get *off* me, you animal! Get your filthy hands off my tits, you great oik!'

I had his forelock in my fist and was just drawing my knee up to hammer seven bells out of his scrotum when all of a sudden he was whisked to his feet.

'Hey!' barked a voice. 'What the hell's going on here?'

Joe's voice. *Joe*'s voice. Oh, thank God. It was Joe. My heart was hammering in my chest. My right leg had gone dead. I had a scribble of slimy black hair in my hand.

'I *said*,' growled Joe, 'what the hell is *going on here*?'

Jean Paul bared his teeth. He was breathless and panting. The air was taut with his anger and fuggy with fumes. I struggled to my feet and unswizzled my dress.

305

'I don't think,' he spat, 'that it is any of your business.' He scooped his hair back into a clump. Joe's hand was still firmly attached to his jacket. He yanked it free and batted Joe's plastered arm away aggressively.

'Is that right?' said Joe. His voice was low and measured and infinitely threatening. 'Well, that's where you're wrong, mate.'

Then he lifted his fist, drew it back like a bowman, and slammed it – ker-pow! – into Jean Paul's astonished face.

It was just like on *Batman*.

I don't think. I *don't* think. Because real violence is not in the least like cartoons. There was, instead, a horrible sickening thwump. I felt like I was going to throw up.

'*Christ*, Joe!' I yelled, as he squared up for an encore, eyes flashing, body tensing, expression one of cold determination. He advanced towards Jean Paul again. 'Stop it!' I flailed at him. 'What are you *doing*?'

But there was neither need nor opportunity for a double whammy. Jean Paul, once propelled, had travelled some distance backwards and had had his fall broken by a large Lloyd Loom chair. He groaned a little. One of his shoes had come off and blood was oozing from his nose. He was going nowhere. Let alone the distance with Joe. I plunged shaking hands into my bag and pulled out a scrap of tissue.

'Oh, my God,' I mumbled, sinking to my knees and dabbing anxiously at his face. The enormity of what had just taken place began to sink in. I was shaking. 'You didn't need to do that! You might have broken his nose, Joe! Oh, God. Oh, God, Joe!' I turned to look up at him. 'You idiot!' I hissed, horrified. 'You Neanderthal! Look what you've done to him! Look what you've *done*!'

He was standing there just like a mannequin from Moss Bros, flexing and unflexing his fingers and thumb. Then he looked down and said coldly, 'So what *should* I have done, Lu?'

Then he turned on his heel and marched out of the room.

21

Great. *Grrrreat. Now* what was I supposed to do? What the hell was I supposed to do? Jean Paul was beginning to stir in his chair.

'Joe!' I yelled. 'Joe! Come back here this *instant*!'

'Uuuugh,' gurgled Jean Paul. 'washafug sappen?' I rose to my feet and lobbed the tissue at his lap.

'Don't move!' I barked. 'Don't *move*, you hear me?'

Then I snatched up my bag and sped off in pursuit.

I caught up with Joe in the foyer. The contents of his pockets were strewn across the top of the cigarette machine, and he was standing in front of it, slamming in coins.

'*There* you are,' I said, rather needlessly. '*Joe!*'

He raised his head. 'Don't start, Lu,' he said.

'Don't start? Don't *start*? And what on *earth* are you *doing*?'

He glared at me. 'Lu, I am *buying* some *fags.*'

I slapped his hand away angrily. A shower of loose change exploded all over the floor. This aggression was becoming contagious. 'Oh, no, you're not!' I barked. 'You're coming right back in there to sort this mess out.'

He leant down and started gathering up his money.

'Joe,' I said, 'listen! There's a man in there with a broken nose, and blood everywhere, and – and – God! Will you stop *doing* that? You're coming with me *now*!'

I started retrieving his scattered belongings and lobbing them into my handbag. 'We've got to sort this thing out. *Now*. God, his *nose*, Joe! He might need to go to hospital! He might need an operation! We need to call an ambulance! Oh, God, Joe! Why d'you have to go and punch him like that?' He began feeding the coins in again. 'Joe! You are *not* going to stand here and buy a packet of cigarettes. D'you hear me? Not! Don't you *realize* what you've done?' I jabbed a finger angrily in the air. 'That's your best client in there! Your best *client*! Don't you see what this means? Joe, you have to come and sort this out! You are going to come with me right now, d'you hear? Right now!'

He pressed one of the buttons and the machine started rumbling. A packet of Marlboro plopped into the tray. I was trembling so much I could hardly focus. I reached down to grab them. 'And you are *not* having a cigarette.'

He beat me to it. 'No? Just you watch me,' he said.

His face was like thunder. Right then. *Rrrright*, then.

'Right, then,' I snapped at him. 'Sod you. Do you hear me? You can sort it out yourself. I'm going up to bed.'

But how could I go to bed? How could I? There was a man not a mile away supine and bleeding (to death, quite possibly), and the person responsible was – hey-de-bloody-ho – calmly buying a packet of fags in the foyer. Men. Men! I stomped off back to the Orangery.

It was puddled with moonlight, and still in darkness. And I could just about make out Jean Paul's shape in the chair. I pushed open the door carefully and tiptoed towards him. He was still sprawled where I'd left him, feet splayed on the tiling, and with splashes of blood decorating his shirt. The tissue, however, was no longer in his lap. It had been carefully twizzled into the shape of a bung, and was currently sprouting from his now crusty nose. And he was snoring. Snoring like a horse.

'See?' whispered Joe. 'Drunk as a skunk. Drunk as a bloody skunk.'

I whirled around, startled, and he put his arm up to shush me. The packet of cigarettes was still unopened in his hand.

'Oh. *Right*,' I snapped. 'And I suppose you're Mr Lime and bloody Soda, are you?'

But his anger had obviously dissipated. 'I didn't say that, Lu,' he said reasonably. 'Here, let me have a look at him.' He slipped the cigarettes into his pocket and crouched down beside the chair. Jean Paul snuffled a little and smacked his lips together. His right eye was swelling. Joe ran gentle exploratory fingers over the bridge of his nose.

'Hmm,' he said. 'Doesn't look very broken to me. Looks more like I got him on the cheek, to be honest. Look. Here's the mark. By here. Think I did more damage to my fist than his face.' He flexed it, and smiled wryly. 'It wasn't *that* hard, Lu. Honest.'

'Well, it looked pretty hard to me!' I hissed. 'You lobbed him half-way across the bloody room!'

'It wasn't, *really*. Look, I don't make a habit of this sort of thing, you know. He was just roaring drunk and went flying. He's fine. Chances are he won't even remember in the morning. And anyway,' he shrugged, 'it's done now, isn't it? So I guess I'll just have to deal with the consequences.'

Consequences. There would be many, I was sure. Not least the possibility that the Luxotel Group would probably decide to put their boilers henceforth in less volatile hands. What a stupid, needless mess. 'So what do we do with him now?' I asked.

Joe shrugged and stood up. 'You think I much care?' he said levelly. 'Leave him to sleep it off, I suppose.'

'But we can't just leave him here all night!'

He glanced down at Jean Paul and considered. 'He'd bloody well deserve it if we did. But, no, I guess we can't. No rush. I'll go and see if I can dig Claude out of the bar. We'll get him up to bed. Don't worry.'

'But what about,' I gestured, 'his face and everything? What will you tell him?'

'Claude? The truth, of course. What else can I do?' He set off across the room, then turned in the doorway and said gently, 'You go on up, if you like. Leave it with me.'

As I picked up my shoes, I could hear Jean Paul snorting. Like a truffle pig truffling. As Joe had said, there was *every* chance he'd have forgotten it by morning. But what if he hadn't? What then? I watched as Joe disappeared from view.

Then I walked back to Jean Paul and took out his bung.

It is dark on the fifth floor. Dark and a little cold. I work my way around its labyrinthine passages and eventually light on room 507. I'm still shoeless. Because I am minus one heel. It is twenty past twelve. I tap gently. 'Joe?'

I listen carefully. Hear nothing. I tap again. 'Joe! It's me! Lu! Open up!'

This time I hear something. The sound of a chain being drawn back. The sound of the door being unfastened. He opens it. 'Oh!' he says. 'Lu! You still up?'

Up and still dressed in fact. Like he is. And he looks like he's just stepped off a film set. Bow tie hanging down, shirt undone, tumbler in hand. What with me in my spangles, we make a right pair. Except I suspect I

311

don't look quite so arresting. Not as if I've been dragged through a hedgerow exactly. No. I look worse. I just look like the hedge.

'Alka-Seltzer,' he observes, noticing the direction of my gaze. He gestures to the chair, then sits down on the edge of the bed and swallows the rest of it. 'Couldn't sleep?'

If only he knew. If only he knew how much sleep he's been stealing from me just lately. This is just one more lost night among many. I sit down and shake my head.

'I wanted to talk to you. Before morning.'

'Oh?'

'Just so you know how to play things tomorrow. To tell you that everything's all right. You know, with Jean Paul.'

He sighs. 'Well he's tucked up and sleeping like a baby, at least. And tomorrow's another day, as they say. We'll just have to hope it all pans out, won't we?' He puts his hand across his eyes and pinches the bridge of his nose. 'Christ, Lu. I can't quite believe I did that. I bloody decked him! This might take some sorting.'

'No, it won't,' I say. 'Because I've already sorted it.' He lifts an eyebrow. 'I mean, you don't need to worry. Because you won't be hearing any more about it.'

He tips his head back and laughs, but without much mirth. 'You sound like you've got a contract out on him.'

I wish. 'I woke him up. While you were off finding Monsieur Dumas I woke him up. Just to be sure.'

'Sure? Sure about what?'

'To be sure that he *would* remember in the morning. Because it seemed to me that what he'd be most likely to remember was that you'd hit him. Especially as he'd be waking up with a black eye. But I wasn't so sure he'd remember *why* you'd hit him. So I thought I should remind him. So I woke him up. And I told him *precisely* why you'd hit him, and I showed him the rip in my dress. And I told him that he was very very *very* lucky that he wasn't spending the night in a police cell on a charge of attempted rape. And that I'd had every intention of making sure that was exactly what he *would* be doing, and that the only reason he wasn't – the only reason he'd got away with it, so to speak – was because *you*, his friend, persuaded me not to. I think it did the trick.'

That and the slap. This aggression *is* catching. But I'm certainly not about to run that one by him. He stands up and puts his glass on the table. 'Well,' he says. 'You are one brave lady. And that was exceedingly shrewd thinking, Miss Fisher. No wonder he looked so contrite. I'm impressed. Well done.'

I'm not sure if I should stand up now as well. Stand up and shuffle off to bed, perhaps. I stand up. My foot hurts. I sit down again. I don't want to go to bed. Not yet. 'And there was something else, Joe. I wanted to say I'm sorry.'

'Sorry? Whatever for?'

'Because I never said thank you.'

'You didn't need to.'

'And for calling you an idiot.'

'I *was* an idiot.'

'And a Neanderthal.'

'Ditto.'

'No, you weren't Joe. God, I should *never* have said that. That was really crabby of me, and I didn't mean it. I *didn't* mean it, Joe. I was just frightened. God only knows where things would have got to if you hadn't come in. I was so stupid! I should have known what might happen. If I hadn't put myself

313

in such a ridiculous position in the first place, then—'

'It wasn't *your* fault, Lu! Jesus! *Don't* think that!'

'But it's true, Joe. I behaved like a complete idiot. I knew very well that he was coming on to me. I should have realized . . . And I should never have gone in there. If I hadn't none of this would have happened. I'm just so grateful you turned up. You were so heroic – there you were, with that great hunk of plaster up your arm, and you still managed to leap in and save the day, and—'

'Oh, *please*, Lu! Enough. All in a day's work for the knight in shining armour about town,' he says ruefully. 'No thanks necessary.'

He puts up his arm to wave away the heroics. There is a nasty gash oozing on the side of his hand. I hadn't noticed it before. Why hadn't I noticed it before?

'Joe! You're bleeding!' Suddenly, more than ever, I want to kiss it better. I want to kiss *him* better. I want to kiss *him*. 'Let me take a look at that,' I say instead.

He holds out his hand for inspection. 'Caught it on the lift door when we were taking him up to bed. Bastard.' He laughs. 'He bloody got me, after all!'

'Well,' I say, scrutinizing it. 'It needs a proper clean-up. And it definitely needs a plaster.'

'I haven't got one.'

'No,' I reply. 'But *I* have. I'm a mother, remember. I *always* have plasters.'

In this case, as it happens, because it's a brave, brave woman who ventures out in such shoes as I was wearing with nothing between her and the threat of complete exfoliation of seven layers of dermis. But who cares? I've got one. I can be of some help here.

'OK, Mummy,' he says, grinning and sitting down on the bed again. 'I'm all yours. Do your worst.'

As luck would have it, I also manage to find an antiseptic wipe. And some wasp cream. A relic from our trip to the zoo. We decide against the latter but he is mightily impressed by the contents of all my little organizer pockets and I'm absurdly grateful that the God of Forgotten Handbags stepped in earlier today.

'It's my grandma,' I tell him. 'I think it must be genetic. She always had everything you needed in her bag. Colouring pencils, Parma Violets, handkerchiefs, safety-pins. So I'm a bit like a Girl Guide. Always prepared. Plus Leo doesn't have a grandma, of course, so I kind of feel it's important, you know?'

'How come?' he says. 'What happened to your mum, then?'

'She died. A long time ago. When I was nineteen. She was only forty-three. She had breast cancer. I don't think my dad ever really came to terms with it.'

'He died last year, didn't he? I remember Del telling me.'

I nod. 'I think that's why – no, I *know* that's why I've been so determined to leave teaching and do something else with my life.' I stroke the wipe gently around the edges of the cut. 'My mum always had such amazing energy – such a lust for life. And then there she was, all of a sudden, gone. I think it was a huge sadness to my dad that I never . . . Well, that my circumstances were such that it was so difficult to, well, make anything of my life, really. He knew I wasn't happy teaching. You know? Well, anyway. You don't want to hear all this. Lift your hand there so I can dry it. What about you? What about your parents?'

Joe holds up his hand obediently. It is warm to the touch and surprisingly soft. I expect it's hormonal or genetic or something, but touching his hand is making my head swim a bit. 'My parents live in Spain,' he says.

'In a little village just outside Javea, called – wait for it – Jesus Pobre, of all things.' His accent is faultless. 'We stayed there in a villa when I was nine or ten and they fell in love with it, basically. Bought a place when I was in my early teens. They moved there when I was seventeen.'

I dab carefully at the cut, cradling his palm in mine. 'But you didn't?'

'I'd left school by then. Got an apprenticeship, had some money, friends. I had no intention of going anywhere, least of all some dozy hamlet in the middle of the sticks.'

'But what did you do?'

He shrugs. 'Stayed behind. It wasn't such a big deal. They had no plans to sell the house in the short term. At first, they'd just go over for the summer, and sometimes in January. They didn't settle there permanently till I was in my early twenties.'

I have a riffle through my plasters and can't find one big enough. It'll have to be two. I start to pull them from their wrappers. 'But all that time, I mean while they were away, you just stayed here on your own?' I picture the seventeen-year-old Joe looking after himself, and though I don't doubt his capabilities, I wonder how he managed back then, all alone.

'It made sense. It meant I could look after the house for them. And I was always,' he smiles, 'an independent little soul. And that's where Liz and David come in, of course. They were our next-door neighbours, you see.'

Which explains things. I do see. About them, at any rate. 'You've known them a very long time, then.'

'They were my parents' best friends. Known them for most of my life.'

I stick the plasters on and he flexes his hand.

'And ditto Rhiannon, I guess.'

He looks at me carefully. 'Right. And Rhiannon.'

'So what *did* happen, Joe?'

His forehead creases. 'What often happens, I suppose. I was busy building up my business. I was very driven. And away a lot. Providing money, but little else. She did her thing. I did mine. Once Angharad came along, and she was stuck at home all day, well . . .' he shrugs '. . . it just didn't work any more. We'd fallen out of love way before then, I think. We just replaced it with mutual resentment. That's all.'

I don't say anything, and he must think I'm waiting, because he then says, 'And, yes, I *was* unfaithful. Just the once. It was mindless and I'm not about to justify it. But neither am I beating myself up about it any more. It wouldn't have made any difference in the end. It could have been either of us. Anyway,' he says, rising, 'that's life, sometimes, isn't it?'

I pick up the plaster wrappers and scrumple them into a little ball between my fingers. I wish he would say more, but then it occurs to me that there is probably little more of value *to* say. I feel sudden admiration for Liz and David's wisdom. It's pointless to blame. It was just another marriage that didn't make it. Culpability apportioned, guilt decided – whatever the circumstances, whatever the catalyst, whatever the detail, what does it matter really? It's all history now.

I watch his expression shake off the past and regroup.

'Well,' he says, looking at his watch and stretching. 'What a very long night it's been, eh?' He crosses the room and starts rummaging in the little pot on the tea tray. He hasn't got his sling on and his plastered arm hangs awkwardly. I wonder, watching him, how he manages *now*.

317

But time to go, clearly. 'Yes,' I agree briskly, suddenly deflated by his change of gear. 'Yes, you're absolutely right.' I start fishing around in my bag for my keycard. 'Early start in the morning. Better push off to bed.'

He turns around. 'I didn't mean *that*, Lu,' he says. 'I didn't mean I wanted you to go. I was going to make us a coffee. Stay and have a coffee.' He pulls out some sachets and waggles them at me. Does he mean it? I wonder. Does he really want me to stay? Or is he just being polite? Jeez, we're been here already. And I don't seem to be getting any better at it.

'Or tea, maybe?' he says encouragingly. 'Earl Grey? English Breakfast?' He starts riffling around again and brandishes some little packets. 'Bourbon biscuit? Custard cream? Ginger nut, even?'

Yes, he *does*, I realize. He *does* want me to stay. He throws them on the bed and advances with the kettle. I don't know if it's those puppy-dog eyes, or just the notion of Joe having been so sad in his life, or simply that for the first time since the zoo he's looking at me with something approaching interest in his eyes, but whichever it is, a slow stirring of something is percolating through me. A delicious something. A powerful something. They say that inside every woman another, different woman is struggling to get out. One with balls and ambition. One who knows what she wants. Or maybe they don't. But that's certainly what seems to be happening to me. Perhaps, even now, my brazen image down at Exo is transmuting, Dorian Grey-style, into the me who stood here a few moments ago.

'Oh, I don't know . . .' I say, but I say it without conviction. With such an absolute absence of any sort of conviction, in fact, that I might just as well leap on him now and have done with it. Which does not go unnoticed. He takes another step.

'How about an Alka-Seltzer, then?' he suggests instead, meeting my eye and reflecting the glint there. His own arc like jewels – like lime diamanté. 'Can I tempt you,' he goes on, his smile growing wider, 'with my extensive selection of antacids, perhaps?'

I smile coyly at him. 'In the morning, perhaps.'

And another. There is now very little space between us.

'A glass of water, then?' he offers. 'I have some nice Eau de Tap.'

Very little between us except my organizer handbag – and my few remaining pretensions towards girlish propriety. And they are certainly few. Because the other Lu Fisher has got out at last, and has some sort of plan on the go. Oh, gosh.

Oh, *golly* gosh, in fact.

'All right, then,' I say, smiling now. 'I'll stay and have a coffee.' I place my bag, very purposefully, back on the bed.

He follows the movement then his eyes flick back up to meet mine. And we stand there looking at each other for what seems like an age. We are no more than six inches from full-on nose-to-nose contact. One more step and we would be close enough to touch. A small tremor goes through me. What should I do now? He looks hesitant but, then, he has no arms available. Should I put mine around him? Should I reach up and kiss him? Or should I wait? *What?* I wish I knew what he was thinking. I wish he'd *do* something. Give me some encouragement. I wish he wouldn't look so undecided, all of a sudden. His lips part in a half-smile, but he holds up the kettle. 'I'll just go and fill this up, then,' he says.

I can't recall what kissing Joe was like the first time, because I was way too drunk, but if how I feel right now is anything to go by, it will be a glorious, electrifying, wonderful thing. It's all in the pheromones, of course. That much is clear. Pheromonal, and hormonal and genetic and psycho-sexual and diurnal, and didn't I learn way back about long-day breeders or something? Red deer, wasn't it? That's it. We're approaching the longest day of the year. Is that an equinox? No. That's in spring, isn't it? Well, whatever. Anyway, that must be what it's all about. Must be. How else can I explain it?

Except with reference to evolution, of course. That's it. It's all well and good all this post-modern identification with the male and his quest for his feminine side and so on. But I have the sneakiest, *sneakiest* feeling that there isn't more than a little of the good old-fashioned 'Me Tarzan, you Jane' factor at play here. Not remotely PC but there you go. Oh, and Snow White, of course. She's always in there. Can't get away from biology. Can't. He hero on horse, flaying sundry villains at random, she, *ergo*, in major-league swoon. She lump of putty in his white-begloved hands.

Or was it short-day breeders? Who knows? Who cares? Whatever the biology, one thing's for certain: there's only so much a girl can achieve via swooning. Got to be, *got* to be proactive here.

But as it turns out it's all academic anyway. Because while Joe is in the bathroom, my eyes light upon the packet of Marlboro, which are still wrapped in their Cellophane and sitting on the desk. Beside them is a big box of nicotine chewing-gum, one blister pack broached, and minus one square of gum. Which reminds me, of course, that I still have Joe's things in my bag. Which is either a bitch or a blessing, depending on which way you look at it. Depending on which way *I* look at it, at any rate. And I don't really want to look.

I reach for my bag again, and start rummaging for his stuff. His wallet, a heavy, warm, slippery thing (which, OK, I will confess to holding fondly against my face for some moments), his packet of chewing-gum, and his phone.

His bloody phone.

Pretty swanky, is Joe's mobile. And slim, because size matters. And switched on, because what else are mobile phones for?

There is a little phone icon on the display. I shouldn't. I mustn't. I *will* not. But I do.

I press the green button.

The display lights up.

And it changes.

And now it says 'Missed call. Jeannine.'

And then he's back in the room with me. He has washed up his coffee cup as well.

'Black or white?' he asks beguilingly. 'Decaf or ordinary?'

I put the phone down on the bedspread. 'Joe, I've changed my mind,' I say. 'Thanks all the same. But you're right. It *is* late. I'm going to get off to bed after all.'

'Oh,' he says, staring at me. 'Right. If you want, then.'

And that's the image I take away to bed with me. Joe poised by the kettle with his Nescafé sachet, looking puzzled and weary and saying, 'Oh.'

22

Friday 15 June

Forgive my French. But bollocks, bollocks, bollocks.

I lay on my bed for a while, unable to sleep – unable to fathom quite why I had acted as I did. Who the hell cares who Jeannine is anyway? I sometimes wonder if I'm going mad. Why am I so insecure? Why?

This is such a terrible affliction. I am thirty-five. Thirty-*five*, damn and blast it. Why don't I know better than this? Why the hell didn't I do it? Why didn't I just go right ahead and kiss him while I had the chance? That was all he needed. Just one tiny affirmation from me, that's all. And I didn't quite do it. I couldn't quite bring myself to make the first move. I should have made the first move. But every time I set myself up to try to believe that it's all right to do this stuff, as soon as I even *contemplate* doing it, I'm all of a dither.

Patrick, damn him, has such a lot to answer for. Oh, I know it's pointless and stupid to blame him for everything, but sometimes I just can't help it. This is *his* legacy. Forget the three Rs. It's the Ds that are the problem. Seems like all my adult life, my *whole* life since Patrick, I've been dogged by a stupid, useless dogma that's entirely of my own making. A dogma that's really of such questionable use. The D for

Dignity, which I have done *ad nauseam,* and the D for Damage-limitation. Done that one to death.

So I have made a decision. I have decided that I don't actually give a monkey's cuss who Jeanine bloody Carver is. I'm going to take my heart, my head, my whole bloody bagload of pathetic insecurities and I'm going to give them a damn good shaking. Because he *was* interested, he *did* want to kiss me, and had I not gone careering off in my usual pathetic scared-rabbit manner then he doubtless *would* have kissed me, and I would have kissed him back with so much conviction that it would be absolutely clear that whoever Jeannine bloody Carver is, she's not only missed that particular moment – she's bloody well missed the whole boat.

It is with this kind of mindset (Dignity indeed! Damage-limitation indeed! I fly in the face of them both) that I shower, dress, and approach the breakfast buffet.

But it doesn't last long.

Because, oh, goodness me, *what* a surprise! Joe is being off with me again.

And now Jean Paul is as well.

Which is, I'll grant, perfectly understandable under the circumstances. He is probably wary of getting within twenty feet of me. Which suits me just fine, as I'm quite sure I can smell his breath even over the oily whiff of eggs and baked beans.

But he certainly doesn't seem off with Joe. They are already sitting at a table when I get there, talking in urgent but entirely unaggressive tones, and tucking into breakfasts the size of tennis courts. Both look up as I enter the dining room, Jean Paul with an expression of wary uncertainty, and Joe with the most cursory of cursory nods. Then, having acknowledged my presence, they simply resume their chat.

I wonder what curious code of social ethics exists in the world of combustion, and decide that to wonder is as pointless a business as pondering the craters on Jupiter's moons. Then I collect some fruit juice, two rolls and a croissant, and go and sit down somewhere else, on my own.

By the time I had finished my breakfast Joe and Jean Paul had long since left the restaurant, and I made my way back up to my bedroom without bumping into either. When I arrived back downstairs, Joe was already at the reception desk, checking out. His suit-carrier and case were parked beside him. I put my holdall on the floor beside them and he turned. 'Ready to go?' he asked. I nodded. There was no sign of any of the Luxotel people, except those who were currently in its employ at Birmingham Sud. No sign of Claude, no sign of Jean Paul. It was almost as if I had dreamt them all up.

'So?' I enquired testily, as I traversed the decidedly frosty air in his wake as we made our way out to the car park. 'What happened, then? What did he say?'

Joe put our cases in the boot and clunked it shut. 'Not a great deal,' he answered flatly, walking round and getting into the car. 'He was fairly mortified. He wanted to apologize to you, but I told him you were pretty upset and that it probably wouldn't be a good idea to approach you until you'd cooled down a bit. So he asked me,' he went on, doing up his seat belt, 'if I thought it would be a good idea if he sent you some flowers instead.' He turned to look sharply at me. 'I told him no. Obviously.'

I was reversing out of our parking space as he said this, so I could see that the small smile on his lips was not complemented by one in his eyes. I felt tired and depressed.

'Yes, but what about *you*?' I said. 'What about your Luxotel contracts?'

'Oh, don't you worry about me,' he said.

'What do you mean "don't worry about you"?' I retorted. I swung the car out of the car-park. He was busy fiddling with his wretched gum. 'Well?'

'Like you said, it's sorted. Jean Paul is sorry. I am sorry. No harm done. Case closed.'

'Just like that?'

'Just like that. Just like you said it would be.'

So my small-hours rant had worked, at least. Though it didn't make any difference. He was still off with me, and looked like remaining so. In perpetuity, at the very least.

Because it was Friday, and there were engineers to be paid, we were on the road before ten. And by ten past his phone was ringing. He pulled it from his jacket pocket and answered it.

'Oh, hi . . .' he began, in a voice entirely dissimilar to the one he'd been using with me thus far this morning, '. . . In the car, driving back from Birmingham. Had a meeting up here yesterday, and . . . I know, I *know*. I just forgot. I'm sorry . . . Oh dear. I'm sorry. I had it in my diary for . . . I know. And I meant to call you yesterday morning, but what with one thing and another, and Iona being away, well, it just went right out of my head. Did it mess things up for you? . . . No, you *know* I don't think any such thing. It's just that sometimes . . . Well, I'm not sure. How about this evening instead? . . . 'S OK. Let me know later, yes?' And then he said, ''Bye.'

Hmm, I thought darkly. Jeannine.

He switched off the phone and I glanced sideways at him. 'Hmm,' I said lightly. 'Rhiannon?'

So much for my early-morning decisions, then. I was

325

clearly unable to sustain a positive mindset for long. He shook his head and pushed the phone back into his pocket. The little tic was starting up in the corner of his jaw. 'No,' he said. 'Not Rhiannon. Someone else. I was supposed to be somewhere last night and I forgot to ring and cancel.'

Someone else indeed. 'Uh-huh.'

'So I'm in the dog-house, that's all. No big deal.'

He didn't elaborate. He didn't explain. We drove on for an hour with the radio on.

Just before we get into Cardiff, my own phone starts ringing. Joe, who borders on the phobic where in-car clutter is concerned, bends an arm round to fish my handbag from the floor in the back. By the time he has retrieved it, I have missed the call. 'It's Del,' he informs me, reading the display. 'You want me to call her back for you?'

'Don't worry,' I tell him. 'I'll wait till we get to the next tailback. Sure it's nothing that important. Expect she just wants to know how last night went.'

'Hmm. You'll have plenty to tell her, then,' he observes, with some asperity. 'You got a pencil in here?' he asks, as he goes to put my phone back. 'This wretched thing's driving me mad.'

But even had I intended to regale Del with last night's three-act drama (which I hadn't – not all of it, at any rate), when I call her back during a go-slow at Newport, I am, it seems, unlikely to get a word out for some minutes.

'Ah!' she says. 'Got you at last! Why haven't you called? Did you not get my message?'

'What message?'

'The message I left on your mobile this morning. Didn't want to ring too early in case you and Joe were –

326

well, anyway,' she giggles, 'you can run all that by me later.' Oh, yeah? What *is* it with her? I press the phone a little closer to my ear. 'Anyway, I wasn't calling about that,' she goes on excitedly. 'I was calling to say *have you seen it*?'

'Seen what?'

'Seen *you*, you great noddle! You're in the paper, my girl!'

Paper? What's she on about now?

'But I checked, Del,' I tell her. 'I'm not in the papers.'

'Then, sweetie, you're reading the wrong ones,' she says.

23

As soon as I got back to the office I telephoned Del.

Clare, who had made short work of the payroll, was busy putting payslips into envelopes, and as there wasn't any coffee made, I suggested I might slip down to get us all one, which gave me a chance to get the Pokémon cards I'd promised for Leo (and forgotten, which made me feel awful as well) and to pick up the dreaded paper.

And there I was, in glorious, wobbling, monochrome splendour. In a feature on one of the arts pages.

'But *The Times*, Del! It's completely mind-boggling!'

'Believe it,' said Del, who was stifling giggles. 'It's right there in black and white and various shades in between.'

'I know!' I said, the paper spread on the desk in front of me. 'I'm looking at it right now!'

It was an article about the Nude. It was called 'Naked Ambition', and was discussing the depiction of flesh and its role as a cultural barometer throughout the last century. The sort of analysis that would inform my artistic studies. The sort of article I really should be reading. But don't.

I scanned the page. My own modest breasts were in opulent company. There was one by someone called Schiele – all scarlet nipples and lipstick, and two big-bosomed women arranged on a couch. And a photo of something that looked like a sculpture and appeared to be a man having sex with a tree. And me. I started reading.

'God, Del!' I spluttered. '*God*, Del! Did you read this bit? This bit on the right?'

'I haven't got it in front of me. Which bit in particular?'

'*This* bit! *This!* Listen. "Stefan Llewellyn's breathtakingly intimate portrait eschews traditional physiological emphasis and instead makes its purpose to capture the essence of the erotically charged atmosphere that is inherent in the form. Cutting through the notion that fine art, first and foremost, serves a higher purpose than to sexually excite, it instead draws us straight into the mind of his subject.

' "For Llewellyn's model asserts" – wait for it – "– a *powerful* sexuality." ' Uuurgh! ' "Reminiscent of Schiele's models (Schiele was, of course, imprisoned briefly for 'making immoral drawings'), Llewellyn's subject is" get this! "*an overtly sexual animal. A willing participant* in the carnality of the creative process, her state of" and *this*! God! "*extreme sexual arousal* is fundamental to the study, and contributes to the erotic charge the work undeniably possesses. Which begs the question—" Oh, God! Oh, Del! This is *awful*!'

She sniggered. 'Yep. I did. And it seemed like quite a pertinent analysis to me.'

I slapped the pages back together in disgust. 'God! We might just as well have hired the millennium stadium and sold tickets! But how on *earth* – *why* on earth? How did they get *hold* of this? I mean, the Exo do was only on Wednesday, for goodness' sake.'

'Well, I suppose they must have got it before then. Have you spoken to him yet, by the way?'

'Who? Stefan?'

'Yes. He rang here an hour or so back. I told him to try you at work this afternoon.'

Oh, he's all about now, isn't he? I don't think I've ever been in such demand. He rings again, at the office, an hour or so later, but I'm with Joe, running through contract amendments, and Clare tells him I'll have to call him back later on. And then again, when I'm home, but I'm busy with spellings, so I tell him I'll call him once Leo's in bed.

Stefan's voice, always his primary organ of seduction, pours like warm toffee down the phone line to my ear. It is not impressed. I move the receiver away slightly.

'I know,' he drawls languidly. 'It's pretty cool, isn't it?'

I'm not sure that 'cool' would be my interpretation. 'No,' I say acidly. 'It's not cool, Stefan. It's very embarrassing. And how did it end up in *there*? I mean, I did half expect there to be something in the *Echo* – which would have been bad enough, quite frankly – but *The Times*? Were they there?'

'No, they were down two weeks back,' he says grandly. 'Mand organized it. You know—'

'Yes,' I snap. 'I course I know who Mand is!'

'Well, I told you she had a friend at the BBC, right? Well, Saskia – that's her name – her partner is a feature writer for them and, of course, there's not much doing at this time of year, and as he was doing a piece on the Nude, he asked Saskia if she could suggest any up-and-coming contemporary artists he could feature and, of course, she's got all my stuff.'

Yeah, yeah, yeah. 'Stuff?'

'Mmm.' I could hear him drawing on a cigarette. He exhaled audibly. *Junkie*. 'And, of course, he loved *Supine Five*.'

Supine Five? *Supine* Five? This is my epitaph, is it? And who the hell were *Supines One* to *Four*? I wonder. And who has he lined up to be *Supine Six*? Cerys? One of next term's new cohorts? Oh, I wish I'd taken a look at some of those canvases at Stefan's. Perhaps, had I done so, I would have exercised a touch more caution before slinging my knickers to the four winds.

And he's still droning on at me. '. . . and he was *really* keen to feature it, particularly once he knew it was going in Exo. They're in talks now, as it happens. About rebadging their two existing centres and developing a new logo. You might just find yourself the new image of Exo, you know.'

'Oh. Right. And I'm supposed to be *pleased* about that, am I? That my naked body is going to be slapped across all their brochures? That I'm *Supine* bloody *Five*?'

'That is the title of the study,' he replies loftily.

'I know it's the title!' I bark.

He says nothing. I can hear him puffing again.

'So?' I hiss. 'You wanted to speak to me. What about?'

'About the documentary, of course.'

This was becoming tiresome. I couldn't think of a single thing about it that would be of interest to me. 'So?' I said again. 'What about it?'

'Well, they want your number, obviously. So I wanted to check if it was OK to give it to them.'

'Mine? Why?'

'Because they want to interview you, of course.'

'Interview *me*? What on earth for?'

Which is, patently, a very stupid question, as his little sigh of irritation suggests. They want to interview me about the carnality of the creative process, of course. They want to interview me about the

331

erotically charged atmosphere that is inherent in the form. *Obviously*. They want to interview me, basically, about Stefan and me. They want to interview me about shagging.

Tuesday 18 June

Which pretty much puts the lid on things, really. Didn't Tracey Emin crochet a tent or something, sometime? With all her sexual adventures embroidered in the lining? And didn't some French guy make an installation once? Of tins of his own excrement, arranged in a pile? So *is* there a place in the art world for me? Somehow, I think not. Not that one, at any rate. Doesn't matter how much I try to convince myself otherwise, it turns out it's not quite the world I imagined. And the thought of spending the next three years of my life holed up in a classroom (lecture room? studio? creative space?) with people like Stefan and his blobs and his supines is beginning to fill me with a nagging unease. I know it's a generalization, and I know there are probably going to be plenty of perfectly ordinary people there, doing perfectly ordinary art, but *how* many? How many, really? For the first time since I embarked on my career as an artist, I feel like a dinosaur. I feel like I'm *old*. I don't want to be made to feel old.

But before I can address the small question of my entire life-plan rethink, I have to address the more pedestrian matter of taking Joe to the hospital to have his plaster removed. As we sit at the lights on Allensbank Road, I realize that in less than a week I'll be picking up my new car. Less than a day and he'll be able to drive this one. I wonder what will happen in the meantime. Will I still borrow his? Or will he hire one for me? It will be strange not driving the big pussy any more. Strange and a little sad. Not so much because I've been given an opportunity to drive a car most people can only dream of. It is just a car, after all. Not a lifestyle. Not a life. But I've grown quite attached to it. It's like a warm comfy armchair that just happens to move. I've driven a fair few miles in it now, and we've kind of got used to each other's little ways. I even fancy that Joe has got used to me driving. At least he isn't trying to do it for me any more. I curl my fingers fondly over the steering-wheel. The leather is soft and warm to the touch. The walnut behind it is gleaming.

I become aware of a sound. It's Joe. And he's laughing. 'Hello-ee?' he says softly. 'Er . . . the light has changed, Lu.'

Joe, strangely, seems to have stopped being off with me. Although I haven't seen much of him since I dropped him home on Friday, what encounters we've had have been increasingly confusing. He has been talkative. Friendly. Normal, even. I am sure this is partly because he has heard from his insurers that his precious no-claims bonus is safe after all (this is of some significance – I have seen his premiums), but even so, I'm not sure I like it. It makes me anxious again.

'By the way,' he says now, as I pull into the drop-off bay at the outpatient entrance, 'I talked to Iona earlier. She's back in tomorrow, so I—'

I pull on the handbrake. 'Iona? Back in work? Already?'

He nods. 'Dai came home yesterday. All's as well as can be expected. She doesn't want to take any more time off. So—'

'But how? I mean, doesn't she have to stay home and look after him for a while?'

'I'm sure that in an ideal world that's exactly what she would be doing. But she needs to get back to work, doesn't she? It'll be weeks before Dai's fit enough to work again himself – assuming he even wants to, which is by no means certain – so she needs to get back.'

'But surely she wants to be able to take—'

'And no. She's not interested in taking any more time off, Lu. I have offered her that option, and she's going to reduce her hours. Do three mornings a week. It's what she wants to do, Lu.' He looks at me pointedly, as if to forestall my disapproval. Am I really such a bag? Am I really so judgemental?

'Joe, I wasn't—'

'Look,' he says, turning in his seat and checking his watch, 'I'd better get to my appointment. But the point is that I've – well, I've got to go to France again on Thursday, and as Iona's going to be back, I was wondering if—'

'Thursday?'

'If you'd drive me there, yes.'

I stare at him, confused. I don't recall him mentioning this before. But then I realize why not. Of course. His arm. 'Hang on,' I say. 'You're just about to have your plaster taken off. You can drive yourself there, can't you?'

But he looks sheepishly at me. 'Apparently not. Not for another week. I have to give it time to settle before I start using it properly. I've got to have a couple of sessions of physiotherapy to build up the muscles. Anyway,' he goes on, 'it'll be just the one night. I know it's going to be a hassle for you, but it *is* fairly important, Lu.'

'*This* Thursday?' My heart does a little jink-a-jink, quite without my permission. Which makes me feel all cross with him again. 'Joe,' I retort sternly, 'it's hardly fair, is it? I mean I can't just expect Del to drop everything and look after Leo again for me. She might be busy on Thursday. She might—'

'I know, I know, I know,' he agrees, nodding. He has, I note, adopted a rather baleful expression. An expression I assume is designed to carve a little chink from my own stony one. And he changes tack. 'Jean Paul won't be there, if that's what you're worrying about. It's the Blois survey,' he adds, as if to convince me. 'And, like I say, Lu, it *is* fairly important. *Very* important, in fact. Please?'

'But couldn't you fly this time?' I suggest. 'Couldn't I take you to the airport or something? I'm sure I could manage that.'

He climbs out of the car. His plaster has become rather raggedy over the weeks, and the edge where it meets the base of his fingers is fluffy in places and moulting. I wonder what sort of shape his arm will be in when it's released.

'Yes, you're right,' he concedes, crouching down to speak to me through the open passenger door. The sun is behind him and his face is in shadow. With his dark brows and white teeth and the scar, he looks like he should be on the high seas. 'I *could* fly,' he agrees. 'Of course I could. But I'd rather not. I can't speak French, can I? Look, the thing is, I have to spend some time with someone pretty important there, who does speak some English, I'll admit, but who most of the time I can't make head nor tail of, and, well – would you at least think about it? Would you at least ask Del?'

I watch as he strides off towards the outpatient entrance, broad-shouldered, purposeful. And then he swivels suddenly, and jogs back towards me. I slide down the window and look enquiringly at him. 'Almost forgot,' he says, fishing in his trouser pocket. He pulls something out and passes it to me. I take it. It's three packets of Pokémon cards. 'For Leo,' he says. 'I was in the sweet shop this morning. They'd just had a new batch in. And I remember you telling me they're like gold dust, so I thought I'd grab him a couple of packs before they all go.'

I'm so touched by his thoughtfulness that I don't know what to say. 'Oh, he'll be thrilled, Joe,' I manage. He taps his hand on the car roof and moves away again, waving.

'See you,' he calls out. 'And don't forget, Lu. *Del.*'

I drive on to my class feeling all agitated again. It's the last *Impressions of the Impressionists* tonight, and I had imagined this point as being something fairly special. The end of my apprenticeship back into study. The end of the springboard. The take-off point for my brand-new career. Instead, it just feels like any other Tuesday. I don't seem to care much any more.

We're in the museum again this evening. To do the whistle-stop tour that I recall Stefan mentioning a few weeks back, of our impressions of the works we've been studying this year. I'm still half an hour or so early, and there's a heavy shower looming, so I go inside to look around for a while.

Almost without meaning to I find myself at the far end of gallery sixteen, drawn, as ever, to my favourite picture, letting it coax me into its exuberant planes. And, as always, marvelling at its strong, vibrant colours. Feeling awed by its richness, its compelling sense of place. The way the characters in it are so brimming with life and vitality. What are they running away from exactly? I wonder what the artist decided as he painted it. Did he have some idea of where they were running to? Did he have a plan for them? A happy ever after? I do something I've not done before. Not on my own. I sit down in front of it. Cross-legged on the floor. For a moment I'm lost in silent contemplation. But when someone else wanders in, I feel silly and self-conscious. I can't even do that without feeling out of place. And I find myself wishing I was back in Joe's house. Just me and him, and this beautiful painting. The man and the woman, hand in hand, in the foreground. Which one *is* which? I'm quite sure Joe would know.

And even surer that Stefan would have some half-baked, metaphysical, nonsensical views about it. Interpretations that would be completely at odds with my own. After class finishes, I go straight down to the cloakroom, leaving him to accept the fond farewells the class are anxious to bestow upon him. I wonder if it's like this every year. The nubiles and hopefuls all got through slowly, leaving, come term end, just the male and the elderly, and the ones he's got lined up for seduction next term. And as if by magic, once that thought has occurred to me, I'm joined by Cerys, pink and breathless from her jog down the stairs.

'Did you hear?' she says, in reverential tones as she unloops her jacket from the coat stand. 'Stefan's going to be on the television.'

I push my arms into my own. My cynicism is beginning to dismay me. 'Is he?' I say.

'Yes,' she says excitedly. 'He just told us. They're doing a documentary about him. Oh, we're so lucky to have him for a tutor. I'm definitely enrolling for *Renaissance, Renaissance* next term. Are you? I'm sure it'll be really exciting.' She hefts her heavy bag under her heavy arm. 'Did you see that article in *The Times*

337

last week, by the way? He's got one of his paintings in that new Oxo club in Cardiff Bay, you know. It's mega.'

I don't bother to correct her. I even think I prefer it.

'And there's been lots of interest in him,' she prattles on breathlessly, as we make our way back out to the stairwell. 'It's going to be on BBC2, you know. And not just BBC Wales. All over Britain.'

'Oh,' I say. 'That's nice. You've seen the painting, then?'

She nods enthusiastically. 'Not the original. But there was a picture in the article. He's so talented, Lu. We're amazingly lucky to have him.' I nod. So why worry, eh? *She* hasn't noticed. She hasn't noticed it's me at all, and we've been sharing gallery space for months now. I mentally strike it from my list of things to fret about.

We take the stairs back up to the main hall and start heading across it. I go to push the revolving door but she lingers. 'Oh. Not going just yet, then?' I ask her.

'Nah,' she says, looking faintly uncomfortable. 'Not yet. Er . . . meeting someone. You know.'

'Fine,' I say. 'Well, I'll see you around, then. Best of luck with everything.'

'Oh, you too,' she says happily. 'Good luck with college.'

Outside the museum the sun is still high in the sky. But a lot of rain has fallen: the pavement is strewn with wide puddle mirrors, in which high raggy clouds scoot through deep iris ponds. The air is humid and thick and smells intensely of leaves. I breathe deeply. It makes me feel a little light-headed. I look back to where I've come from. And there they both are.

Arm in arm, giggling. *Supine Six*, then. For certain.

Good luck to her, I think. Good luck to both of them. I feel suddenly, unaccountably, free of it all.

*   *   *

Except freedom, like Welsh cakes, is *sooo* overrated. One bite and you find yourself thinking, This it? Thanks to my father's legacy, I have sufficient money in the bank right now that I could do pretty much anything I want to. *Anything.* Take Leo on a six-month tour of every theme park in America if we felt like it. Or a world cruise. Or we could build an extension. Or buy a new house. Or a holiday cottage in Tenby, like Del has. But I don't feel like it. I had everything planned and now, all of a sudden, I'm not even sure I should have left teaching. At least there I had a framework to rail against. At least, as a teacher, I could daydream a bit. Now I'm not even sure what I'm dreaming for, really. The notion of 'Doing Art' seems rather pointless.

'Well, *I* think you should embark on a career as a nude model,' suggests Del. As it's such a lovely evening, she's insisted that Leo and I stay for supper, and while Ben footles round the kitchen making kebabs for a barbecue, she has fetched out some deck-chairs and made up some Pimm's. She pours me one, lobbing in big nuggets of fruit. I want to hug her. 'You could put an ad on the university noticeboard,' she goes on. 'Sure you'll get loads of enquiries once the TV thing goes out.'

'Stuff that!' I retort. 'I told him exactly where he could shove his bloody TV show, I can tell you. As if! No. I'm going to get an OU prospectus and have a bit of a rethink. The courses don't start until February, so I'll have plenty of time to decide what to do. I think they offer an arts foundation course. I might do that instead. Or something else, maybe. We'll see.'

She graciously doesn't make a told-you-so face at me. 'And in the meantime? What happens when you finish working for Joe? Are you going to get another job of some sort?'

I look across the garden, to where Leo and Simeon are sitting cross-legged on the lawn with their carefully catalogued piles of cards. 'Some sort's about right. Oh, I don't know. I'm not going to worry about it for the moment. I've decided I'm going to book a holiday, actually. A proper holiday. Just me and Leo. I'm going to blow a disgraceful amount of money and take him to Disneyland.'

I imagine Leo's face when I tell him we're off to Disney at long last. Life's been a slog for him too. In all sorts of ways. The idea of doing so makes me feel suddenly excited. Why didn't I think of it before? Why? Such a little treat, really, but he'd never even asked. And I, all the while, was so busy with my grand schemes, my grand plans – with *me*, in fact – that it never occurred to me he deserved a few too. I feel overwhelmed with love for my son.

Del nods. 'That sounds like the best idea you've had in a long time,' she observes. 'You could do with a break. You both could. And you're right. What's the rush? You may as well just sit tight at JDL and bide your time till you've made some decisions. Lily's not due back till the autumn, is she? And you'll have your new car next week and everything will get back to normal. Or what passes for normal in your case, at any rate.' She grins. 'I'm sure Joe would be pleased.'

'Which reminds me,' I say, as if I'd forgotten, 'Joe's asked me if I'll drive him to France again.'

'Well, that's nice,' she says. 'When?'

I take a sip from my glass. It tastes of summer and green lawns and weekends and birdsong. A happy drink. I swallow some more. 'This Thursday.' I sigh, recalling Leo's gift. 'But I wish he hadn't. I don't want to go.'

'Why ever not?'

'Because I don't. It's a hell of a journey, Del. And besides that, it's really not fair on you.'

'But there's no problem with Leo,' she says. 'I'll have him for you. You know I will.'

'I know. You're an angel. But it's not the point.'

'And you love driving.'

'That's not the point either. I just think that the sooner I extricate myself from the situation with Joe then the sooner I'll be able to get my head together.'

She laughs. 'The day you get your head together pigs will start sprouting wings. Besides, you have to.'

'No, I don't.'

'Yes, you do. It's what he's paying you for, isn't it? You did agree to the job in the first place, after all, Lu. Seems a bit mean to let him down. It could be something really important.'

I nod. 'He says it is.'

She sips her own drink and considers me for a minute. Then says, 'Extricate sounds a bit dramatic. Why extricate, exactly?'

'Because it's doing my head in.'

'Hah!' she says. 'You sound like a fifth-former.'

'I feel a bit like one. I'm all jumbled up about him and it's bad for my health. Chin-chin.' I raise my glass and take another gulp of Pimm's.

Del does likewise. 'Only because you won't do anything about it,' she says.

'What's to do? It's a complete non-starter.'

'Because of this Jeannine woman.' It's a statement, not a question.

'Partly, I guess.'

'Wholly. I know.'

341

'Actually, no. It's not just that, Del. I mean, yes, that *is* a big factor from my point of view. But . . .'

She shifts her weight in the deck-chair. 'Why is it a big factor? Either he is or he isn't seeing her. What difference does it make? Does that not make him eligible? Have you decided you're only dating virgins these days?' She's smiling, but there's an edge of exasperation in her voice.

'Don't be stupid, Del. That's not what this is about and you know it. I just don't want to get myself emotionally involved with someone who's *already* involved, that's all. I just can't stomach all the hassle.'

She puts down her glass and flicks off her sandals. It's a beautiful evening. A low moon is just rising from wisps of lobster-pink cloud.

'Lu,' she says, 'get real, will you, sweetie? This is not *Grange Hill*. We are all grown-ups. If you hold out for someone who's not been involved recently, then you will no doubt net yourself someone with all the drive, commitment and libido of a slug. Or a psycho.' She looks at me sharply. 'Lu,' she says, 'so what if Joe *is* seeing someone at the moment? So *what*? If he starts seeing you, I'm quite, quite sure he'll end it with her pretty sharpish. I think I know him that well, Lu.'

I'm sure she does. I'm sure I do too. 'Of course he would. But that's not really the point, Del. I'm really not that convinced he *is* interested in me any more.'

'Rubbish!' she says, with conviction. 'Of course he is. You're just so insecure you can't see it.'

'I'm not so sure. He's had plenty of opportunities to let me know.' I swivel round to face her. 'But he hasn't taken them, Del. So I can only conclude—'

'Psh!' she exclaims, picking up her drink again and swilling it around in the glass. 'You sound like you're making a speech on the council. And why conclude anything? Why not *do* something instead? You know what?' She takes both my hands in one of hers. 'You could do something really *avant-garde*. Really groundbreaking. You could tell him.'

'Tell him what?'

'How you *feel* about him, stupid! Why not? What's the worst that can happen?'

'Uuurgh! I'll tell you the worst that can happen. The worst that can happen is that it will be the most embarrassing, most humiliating, most—'

'There you go!' She sighs extravagantly. 'That's exactly your problem! That's exactly why you're in the situation you're in now!' She pokes me. 'Lu. Let me tell you. The worst that can happen is that you get rejected. And if so, then so be it. But you never give anyone a chance. You push people away all the time. Yes, you're right. If you don't stick your neck above the parapet then, fair enough, you won't get shot at. But is that really any way to live your life? Yes, you get to keep your dignity. Yes, you get to leave the battlefield with your feelings intact. Yes, you live to fight another day—'

'Exactly,' I insert. '*Exactly*.'

She snorts. 'But what kind of life *is* that? Lu, if you want someone to love you – if you want someone to love you like *we* all love you, and I'm quite sure you do – then you have to let them know that you love them too.' Where did all this love stuff come from all of a sudden? I retreat uncomfortably into the top of my glass. 'Lu,' she says sternly, 'has it never occurred to you that he might find it difficult too? Has it never occurred to you that *he* might have been hurt? That *he* might be wary? Lu, has it ever occurred to you that he might be worried about getting rejected by *you*?'

By *me*? *Joe*? I shake my head emphatically. 'Oh, no,' I say, remembering our encounter in Amiens. 'He's certainly not that. Far from it.'

'Well, I wouldn't be so sure about it.' She reaches for the jug and scoops a piece of orange from it. 'But then, *no*,' she decides, sucking it. 'I guess it *wouldn't* have occurred to you. You're so busy fretting about your own feelings all the time that I doubt you have a moment to stop and consider anyone else's, least of all his.'

My mouth drops open. 'Well, that's charming, Del. Thanks.'

'Lu, it needed saying because it's true! You know it is! Look, I know you feel vulnerable. I know you've had some bad experiences. But think about it for a moment. You carry on all the time as though the sole responsibility for you two having any sort of relationship rests with Joe. But maybe it's a responsibility *he* doesn't want either. Maybe he's fed up with trying to second-guess how you feel about *him*. I don't think you realize how frosty you can be at times. How well you do the whole "hands off – fragile goods" bit. I mean, look at you! It's glaringly obvious that you're completely smitten by the guy, but how's he supposed to know that? How's he going to know that if you don't tell him? Lu, for once in your life grasp the nettle, can't you? Make a bit of an effort, for goodness' sake.'

'Well, thanks very much I don't think!'

She pats me. By way, I assume, of softening her words. 'Lu,' she says, 'you know what I'm saying. I know you're wary of putting yourself through any more romantic traumas for a while. But you can't spend the rest of your life like a bloody seed pod.'

'*Seed* pod?'

344

'Yes! Waiting for conditions to be absolutely right before you deign to pop your bloody case and interact with the world.'

It's such a ridiculous analogy that I almost want to laugh. She does laugh. 'Del,' I say sternly, 'it isn't as simple as that, and you know it. And that's exactly my point. I can't go plunging from one disastrous relationship to another all the time. I have responsibilities. I have my *son* to consider. Or had you forgotten about Leo in all this?'

'Oh, for *God*'s sake, Lu, not that old chestnut again. It's nothing to do with Leo, and you know it. You just use him as a shield to protect *yourself* from getting hurt. But it doesn't wash with me, I'm afraid. Leo is not going to be scarred for life just because you happen to fall in love with someone. Leo is not going to become a crack pimp just because you have a man in your life. Leo is fine. Leo is happy and well adjusted. *You*'re the one that's making dysfunction a career.'

'Thanks a lot.'

'You're very welcome. Ah! Ben! Perfect timing! Shall I fire up the coals?'

Dysfunction, indeed.

But Del's right, of course. Del is always right. Always, *annoyingly*, right. Being annoying and right is her job as my big sister. Just as never listening to her is mine. Has been up to now, at least. Perhaps I should wash my ears out.

When Leo and I get home, the phone is ringing.

'That'll probably be Auntie Del to check we're back OK,' I tell him. 'Run in and grab it for me, will you?'

He does so, and is back outside a few moments later. 'It's not Auntie Del. It's Joe,' he tells me, panting. I lock

345

the car. My heart is twizzling itself into sheep-shanks. 'And don't worry, Mum,' he says, grinning at me as he hands back the door keys, 'I remembered to thank him for the Pokémon cards.'

And so it is. I feel all wobbly all of a sudden. Can't be the Pimm's. I only had the one.

'How's your arm?' I say lightly. 'Still in one piece?'

'Most peculiar,' he says. 'All sort of pale and wan and shrivelled. It looks quite bizarre, in fact. All the muscles have disappeared. It's half the size of the other one. Anyway, where've you been? I've been trying you for ages.'

Which makes the hairs on the back of my neck prickle. 'At my sister's,' I tell him. 'We stayed there to eat. Why? What's up?'

'Nothing's *up*, Lu. I just wondered if you'd managed to sort things for Thursday OK. Have you?'

Which is the point at which I could insert the word 'no'. The point at which I could put a stop to the dreadful yammering that has started up in my chest.

'Yes, Joe,' I tell him. 'I've sorted things for Thursday. Thursday will be fine.'

'Excellent!' He sounds relieved. Del is right. If it's an important meeting, it would have been mean to refuse. 'Right,' he says. 'Listen. I'm not going to need a lift in tomorrow because I'm costing a job in Newport, so can I leave you to get on with the contract amendments for me? I might make it back in. Might not.'

'And what time should I book for?'

'Book?'

'The shuttle, of course.'

'Oh, right! Of course. No, no. Don't worry about that,' he says. 'All sorted already. See you sometime on Wednesday afternoon.'

When I put down the phone it occurs to me that

346

there are worse ways to live your life than the one Del's analysis suggests I've chosen. I feel hot and cold and anxious and exposed. Like my little seed pod has been already broached. Do I need this stuff? Really?

24

Thursday 21 June

So we were off to France again.

I dropped Leo off at Del's at six thirty, with a hug and a kiss and a pre-breakfast Penguin and with instructions not to take his new cards into school. And with his Pokémon wish list tucked safely in my pocket. French cards, he had told me, would be so way cool. Then I purred off down the road accompanied by a small family of druids and faerie folk, who were stringing up bunting for the solstice somewhere in my gut. For it was Midsummer Eve. The first day of the rest of my life, in fact, and, oh dear, I wasn't quite ready for it.

The morning was fine and hazy – the sort of morning that promised much in the way of sunshine. Even now dew was rising, like pale swirls of netting, over grass that had already shaken off its wet coat. But there was no sign of life at Joe's whatsoever, except the bulbs that burned in the twin carriage lamps that stood guard on the gateposts. For a moment I wondered if I'd misheard the timings. I rang the bell, and it was a good couple of minutes before I detected a response. The carriage lights went out and the hall light came on and there he was in the hallway, barefoot on the carpet and buttoning a pale denim shirt. He was right. His left hand did look peculiar. As if it had been shrunk in a sci-fi machine. 'God, sorry,' he said. 'Come in for a minute. I've only been up half an hour.'

His case was standing ready by the front door, and beside it was a suit-carrier. I tried not to look at the whorls of dark hair on his chest. 'No panic,' I said. 'I'll go and put these in the car.'

'Oh, don't be daft, Lu. Come in. I can do that.'

'I thought you said you weren't supposed to be using your arm for a week?'

He raised his right one. 'Look, Mummy,' he chortled, 'got two of them. Remember?'

Courage. That's all it takes.

And, oh dear. I'm so utterly fixated on what it is I *could* say to him, what it is I *should* say to him, what it is I *would* say to him if I could only find the right sort of moment to do so that I can't seem to manage any ordinary conversation. I can't think of a single thing to say to him right *now*. Thus we soon dispense with all the work-related matters (he, I have noticed, has forgotten his laptop. I, he has noticed, have forgotten the map), and by the time we reach Swindon we have lapsed into the sort of bland, sporadic, rather halting conversation that self-conscious strangers on an aeroplane might have.

'Nice day for it, anyway,' he suggests.

'Absolutely.'

'Anyway,' he goes on, 'how was your class?'

'My art class?'

'Yes, of course your art class. Or have you signed up for nuclear physics as well? It was your last one on Tuesday night, wasn't it?'

'Oh. Oh, that. Yes.' It seems like for ever ago.

'And did you give him what-for?'

349

'Who?'

'That tutor of yours. About splashing you all over the broadsheets last week.'

'Oh. You saw it, then?'

He laughs. 'Took a peek.'

'No, as it happens. I didn't. What's the point? As you said yourself, it's done now, isn't it? No use fretting about it. Though I draw the line at having a bit part in his cheesy documentary. No. I've decided to draw a line under all of it, in fact. I've decided I'm not going to go to college after all.'

'No?' He sounds unsurprised.

'No.'

'So what will you do instead? A different sort of course?'

'I'm not sure yet. I'm going to look at some prospectuses. Something, at any rate, but not full time. I don't think I'm really cut out for it, to be honest. Don't have the right complement of body piercings.'

'Uh-huh,' he says, nodding. 'Well, I can't say I don't think that's a sensible idea. You never really struck me as bohemian enough. And, besides, seems to me there's a world of difference between appreciating art – which you obviously do – and elevating it into some sort of quasi-religion. You like a painting. You don't like a painting. You don't need three years of flakes and pompous bores spouting at you to tell you that. Do you?'

He is speaking my very thoughts. It's unsettling. 'No.'

'And if you want to paint yourself – well, get on and paint. Nothing to stop you – oh, I don't know – joining a class to improve your technique.'

And I don't want to talk about painting this morning. 'No.'

'Or doing one of those painting holidays. I think Liz

350

has been on one, now I come to think of it. Tuscany, I think it was.'

Or holidays. 'Mmm.'

'What sort of paintings do you do, anyway? You've never said.'

I want to talk about *us*. 'Watercolours,' I reply. 'Old buildings, mainly.'

'There we are, then. Have a commission. You can come and paint my house.'

He reaches into his pocket and pulls out some gum. He chews for a minute or so, gazing out of the side window. 'I know,' he says at last. 'Shall we play I-Spy?'

'What?' *What?*

'I-Spy,' he repeats. 'You know, I spy with my little eye, something beginning with . . .'

'Why?'

'Because it'll be fun, Lu. Something to do. You know. Pass the *time*?'

'Oh,' I say, mystified. 'All right. If you want to. Shall I start?'

'No, no,' he says. 'My idea, so I start. OK? Right. I spy with my little eye, something beginning with . . . let me see now . . . LI . . . no, no . . . LWIIAVSMTMA . . . er, and . . . IWSTMWA. There.'

'What? All *that*?'

'All that.'

'But that's far too many words.'

'There's no rule about how many words you can have.'

'Yes, there is.'

'No, there isn't. Go on. Humour me. Have a stab at it.'

I scan the scene ahead of me. It's obviously a trick one. Lay-bys. No. Lights. *Lights*. 'OK, Lights With . . .'

'Nope.'

There's a lorry ahead of us with a very long name on

the side. I crane to read it. Norbert Dentressangle, or something. So no. I rack my brains. 'Lamp-post—'

'Nope.'

'Long Wheelbase—'

'Nope.'

'Oh, I don't know. I give up.'

'Ah!' he says. 'So do you want a clue?'

'Go on, then. Give me a clue.'

He turns in his seat. 'Right,' he says. 'The L stands for Lu. That help at all?'

'Ah. Yes.' I'm warming to this now. 'Maybe. What were the letters again?'

'LWIIAVSM—'

'OK, stop there. How about Lu With Insects . . . er . . . In . . . A Violin . . . um . . . Sitting Munching . . . What was the rest of it?'

'Wrong,' he says. 'Try again.'

'Bah! OK. How about Lu Wondering If It . . . Oh, I don't know.'

I glance across. He's looking at me strangely. 'Give up, then?'

'Give up.'

'OK, then. The "Lu" you know already. Then it's Who—'

'Who?'

'Who Is.' I can feel him looking at me still. 'Who Is In A Very Strange Mood This Morning And I Wish She'd Tell Me What About. You see? Simple.'

Just like that.

'Oh,' I said. 'Oh. No, I'm not.'

'Yes, you are,' he said. 'So. *Are* you going to tell me?'

'But I'm not, Joe.'

'Liar.'

'I'm *not*. I mean, if I *was*, then—'

'Right! That's enough!' he says suddenly. ' "Reading

Services one mile", it says on that sign. Take me there, woman, and take me there *now*. I want to see the whites of your eyes.'

There's an outside seating area at the front of the services. Half a dozen grey-looking tables with bench seats, and a small children's play area, ringed by a hedge. I head for the nearest and straddle the seat, then pull my arms from the sleeves of my jacket and wait. I feel like I'm in a dentist's waiting room. Except there's no goldfish to look at. No moth-eaten copies of *Top Gear* to flick through. Just a gaggle of policemen and a flimsy-looking stand that says, 'Berkshire Constabulary. Be smart. Be safe. Get your windows etched NOW.'

Joe negotiates these and comes back with a tray. He places it carefully on the table in front of me, then sits down opposite and grins. I notice he's wearing a little woven friendship band on his left wrist. 'So,' he says, prising the lids from the milk pots, 'here we are, then. Sugar?'

'No sugar.'

'No sugar. Right, then.' He smiles at me encouragingly. 'Shoot. I'm all ears.'

I take a pot of milk and begin to do likewise. Only I can't seem to get a grip on the little flap on the foil cover. I bend it and tweak it, but it won't come. And then the whole tab snaps off.

'Here,' he says, holding out his hand to take it. 'Let me do that for you. What a wonderful thing it is to have both hands back in action. Can't tell you. So many little things you take for granted.' He pushes a nail into the pot and milk fountains all over his hand. 'Bugger! Like the fact,' he says, ruefully, brushing at his shirt sleeve, 'that these bloody things always *do* that. Anyway,' he

353

says again, 'here we are, like I said.' He starts stirring his coffee and raises one eyebrow. Oh, God. He's so *bouncy*. I wish he'd seem like he had some sort of idea.

'Oh, dear,' I say. 'I don't know what to say. I'm not in a funny mood, Joe, I'm just – oh, dear, this is so embarrassing.'

'I can tell. You've gone scarlet,' he observes. He looks at me carefully. 'Embarrassing *why*?'

'Embarrassing because . . . well, because I don't know what to say to you, that's all.'

'Say about what, Lu?'

'Say about – say about me. About you. About Birmingham—'

'*Ah.*'

'About what happened. About what *didn't* happen. Joe, it's just that – well, I'm sorry, that's all.'

He has stopped stirring his coffee. I start to stir mine. Energetically. Paying particular attention to the little brown vortex I'm creating. I wish it would suck me in.

He takes a sip from his. 'Sorry?' he says. 'What for exactly?'

'Sorry I didn't, you know, *stay* after all.'

His brows knit a little. 'Ri-ight. Got that bit, I think. And?'

'And – and that's it.' I put my stirrer down. 'Only I think I might have given you the impression that I wasn't – and, well, given you the impression *overall*, so to speak, that I wasn't, you know—'

He grins. 'I'm lost.'

Oh dear. I pick it up again and roll it between my fingers. 'Joe, *interested*. That I haven't been, in general, you know, *interested*. Um. In you.'

There is a tiny but perceptible change in his expression. Then he says, 'Yes. That's true. You have. You most definitely have.'

I look hard at him. 'So you do understand what I'm saying?'

He looks back. Even harder. 'Kind of,' he says. 'Tell you what. Run it by me again, why don't you?'

I pick up my coffee and sip it. It's scalding. Oh, this is too, too excruciating. I don't have to do this now. I could wait till we get to Blois. I could drink an obscene quantity of wine and just let happenstance take over. Let it just happen by itself. It's way too sunny out here. Way too bright and penetrating and difficult. I could just wait and see what happens, couldn't I? I've been waiting all my life. I'm very good at waiting.

But *he* is waiting now, head cocked to one side, smile enquiring.

'Joe, you're not making this very easy for me.'

'I know I'm not.'

'You do?'

'Yep.'

'So you *do* know what I'm saying?'

'Oh, yes. You're saying you wish you'd stayed after all. You just said so.'

'Um. Right. Yes. Right.'

'But you didn't.'

'Right.'

He puts both hands, palms up, on the table. And then exhales. 'So *why* didn't you, Lu?'

'Because, because – well, for lots of reasons. Because – because you didn't – well, when you could have done, when you had the chance to, you – well, you didn't make a move. You didn't *kiss* me, did you?'

He looks slightly offended. Like a schoolboy who's been charged with someone else's crime. Indignant, almost. 'I nearly did,' he responds. 'I most probably *would* have done, if you'd given me half a chance. But you didn't, did you? You shot off.'

This conversation isn't going quite how it ought to. 'I didn't "shoot off", as you put it,' I retort. 'I just changed my mind about staying.'

He looks at me in a way that suggests my mind-changing tendency is getting more than a little unfathomable for him. He folds his arms. 'And?'

'All right,' I say eventually. 'I went because I thought – I mean I wasn't sure if *you*—' Oh, sod it. Might just as well be hung for a sheep as a lamb. 'Joe,' I say finally, 'who is Jeannine?'

25

'Jeannine?' he asked, wide-eyed. 'Jeannine *Carver*? Now I *am* confused. What on earth's *she* got to do with this?'

'That's just it. I don't *know*, Joe.'

He looked faintly uncomfortable. No. Not uncomfortable, exactly. Just slightly disconcerted. Just that. And bemused. Oh, God. This was becoming more difficult by the minute.

'Well, that makes two of us,' he said, raising his eyebrows. 'Because neither do I.'

'It's just that . . .' I took a breath '. . . well, you're seeing her, aren't you? And if you're *seeing* her, well . . .'

I stopped. I couldn't even *begin* to elucidate. So much for all my gung-ho resolutions. I could feel my confidence draining away like yesterday's dishwater. There was only so much humiliation a girl could stomach. He put down his coffee and studied me carefully. And the look of bemusement that had been playing on his face was replaced by one of enlightenment. Then a smile. A wide smile, getting wider by the moment.

'Oh, *seeing* her,' he repeated slowly. 'I *see*. And funnily enough, Lu, you're right. I am.'

He pushed his hand into the back pocket of his trousers and pulled out his wallet, then flipped it open in front of him. I continued to sip my coffee, cringing. An early wasp footled among the sugar sticks and milk pots. A woman walked past us. A child swung on the swing.

And then he shook his head, chuckled, and said, 'Of course,' to himself.

He started riffling through the various pockets in his wallet. To the left there was a photo of Angharad. To the right, a black American Express card. Behind which, more plastic. A wodge of receipts. And some business cards, one of which he eventually extracted, which he then wordlessly handed to me.

It was a simple white card. No logo. Plain typeface. An address in the corner. Cedar Folly, obviously. And some more words. Jeannine. And then, of course, Carver. Then some letters; PhD, DHP, MNRHP.

And then another word. Heavily embossed. In italics. I read it. Looked back at Joe. Read it again.

'Good Lord,' I exclaimed. 'She's a *hypnotherapist*?'

He nodded. 'Yes, she's a hypnotherapist,' he said wryly. 'And as you rightly said, I am seeing her, Lu. But professionally. *Professionally*.' He leant back. 'Have been, on and off now, for a while.' He grinned at me and did a little smoking mime with his fingers. 'Over nine weeks without a single cigarette now. Almost three months this time. My best effort so far.'

I looked at the card again. My mind was now teeming, not with questions, but answers. All dashing around like headless chickens. Falling over each other and jockeying for position and fitting themselves, shrieking and whooping and cheering, into the boxes of questions I'd stockpiled for so long. Oh, my. Oh, *my*!

'Oh, Joe,' I said, 'why didn't you *say*?'

He narrowed his eyes and looked at me through his lashes. 'It's not something I'm generally given to talking about, Lu.'

'But why ever not?'

His answering smile was so sweet and childlike that I wanted to scoop him up and kiss him all over. 'Oh, come *on*,' he answered ruefully. 'Would you?'

Oh, *happy* day. I passed him the card back. 'But all sorts of people get help with things like that these days. It's nothing to be embarrassed about.'

'Hmm,' he said. 'So Jeannine always tells me. But even so, I am.' He slipped the card back into his wallet, and the wallet back into his pocket. I thought of Joe and his unreconstructed world of combustion and boilers and ducting and flanges and, well, blokedom, basically. I wondered if hypnotherapy would sit quite so well there.

'Which is not to say that I wouldn't recommend her,' he went on. 'She's very good at what she does, and she's also a very good friend. I've known her for a long time. Her husband's been a mate of mine since school.' He picked up his coffee again and tipped his head back to finish it. 'Anyway, there you have it. My guilty secret is out.'

So many stupid misconceptions. So much time wasted. So much almost lost. 'Oh, God, I feel so stupid, Joe. I thought you and she were – well, what with everything, I just put two and two together. I just assumed—'

'Ah! Busy making assumptions, were you?' He laughed. 'Well, you're very good at that, so it certainly figures. As does,' he added, linking his hands on the table in front of him, 'pretty much everything else all of a sudden. So,' he said briskly. 'where *were* we, Ms Fisher? In my hotel room last Thursday, wasn't it? At the point, let me see now . . . when you, as I recall, were waiting for me to do something. Ah, yes. That's it. You were waiting for me to kiss you. That was it, wasn't it?' He raised a finger and grinned at me. 'Hang on a tick.'

He stretched out his hand and scooped up all the debris; the coffee cups, stirrers, our four little milk pots, the sugar, the tray, a stray remnant of foil. He put them on the tray and pushed the tray to one side. The wasp buzzed away. The sun winked off his watch strap.

'There,' he said. 'Come on, then. Lean a little closer.'

'Closer?'

'Of course, Lu. Let's get this thing done.'

'Get what done?'

His eyes glittered. 'That kiss, of course, stupid.'

'What, here? What, *now*?'

'Of course now,' he said.

Oh, happy, *happy* day. 'Oh, Joe,' I said, finally. 'I'm so stupid. So monumentally stupid. You must think I'm such an idiot.'

He shook his head and traced the back of his hand gently over the side of my face. 'I think nothing of the sort. I think you're lovely. Just lovely. But much as I'd like to sit here and gaze at you, we'd better get going. It's almost ten.'

I had quite forgotten the time. I had quite forgotten the day.

'Oh, gosh, you're right,' I said, flustered, reaching for my bag. 'Or we'll be late. If the traffic on the M25 is anything like it was last time it'll be way past eleven before we reach the M20. And if they've still got all those roadworks going on outside Folkestone . . .'

He stood up. 'Oh, don't worry about those,' he said, standing up. 'We're not going to Folkestone.'

'We're not?'

He took my hand and we started heading back to the car. 'No.'

'But why ever not? What about your meeting?'

He beamed. 'I lied. There's no meeting, Lu.'

I gaped. 'No meeting?'

'No meeting. I'm taking you to lunch.'

'*Lunch?* Lunch where?'

'Er, Paris, as it happens.'

I stopped dead in my tracks. '*Paris?*'

He pulled at my hand. 'So we'd better get a move on, hadn't we? On second thoughts, give me the keys. I'll take over.'

We had reached the Jag by now. 'What? But I thought you couldn't drive.'

'Oops!' he said, holding his hand out to take them. 'Naughty old me. Lied again, I'm afraid.'

I handed him the keys and followed him round to the passenger door, which he held open while I, speechless now, clambered in. It was strange to be sitting on that side of the car. Strange and exciting and absolutely perfect. He slipped into the driver's side and manoeuvred the seat back into its regular position.

'You're kidding,' I told him, as the car shuddered gently into life. 'You mean we're driving all the way to Paris *for lunch*? But it'll take *hours*.'

'No, it won't,' he said happily. 'Because we're flying.'

'Flying?'

He nodded. 'From Heathrow.'

'*Flying?* We're *flying* to Paris for lunch?'

Under his control the car seemed to float, almost, back on to the motorway. Or perhaps it was just me. I was up with the cirrus. 'We are indeed,' he said. 'People do, you know. But you're right. It is an awfully long way to go just for a bite to eat, isn't it?' He paused to switch lanes, then turned round to glance at me. 'So we're stopping on for dinner as well.'

'*Dinner?*'

Once in the outside lane, the car, now in its natural habitat, was gliding effortlessly along. I could feel the pull of the acceleration in my chest. 'Oh,' he said. 'And breakfast, of course.'

'*Breakfast?* You mean we're spending the night in Paris? Oh, Joe, I don't know what to say. You mean you planned all this? You just fixed this whole thing up on your own without my knowing?'

'Well, not *just*, exactly. In actual fact, I had already decided I wanted to take you somewhere – do something nice. As a thank-you for all the slog you've had to put up with for the past couple of months. And I'd kind of *half* decided to take you somewhere special – he glanced at me again '– somewhere *romantic*. But then I got the impression – *can't* think why, can you? – that I was going to be a bit of a non-starter where you were concerned. That bloody Stefan, for one thing. And then there was all that nonsense with the flowers, and then I thought maybe it wouldn't be such a good idea after all. And then –' he was smiling to himself '– *then* I thought, No. Sod her. And I decided – if I'm going to be completely honest about this – that the only reason Lu Fisher had such a downer on chivalry and flowers and romantic gestures *per se* was that she had some pretty stupid half-baked notions about men generally. And that I could either take note of her prejudices and act accordingly, or prove to her that, in this case, she was wrong.'

He drew a hand across his jaw then glanced at me again.

'So?' I said.

'So I decided I would just have to prove you wrong.' He smiled at me wryly. 'Thing is, Lu, I'm no better at this than you are. I know you take a dim view of some of the stuff I do—'

'Oh, I don't, Joe. I don't.'

'OK, *took*, then. But that's *me*, Lu. I don't know any

other way to be. I'm not even sure I *want* to. In fact, no. I *know* I don't want to. So, though I knew how I felt about you, I didn't have the first clue how to deal with you. But I don't give up easily. So, like I said, I thought, Sod her. I'll take her to Paris, I'll wine her and dine her, I'll stroll along the Seine with her. I'll drag her up the Eiffel Tower. I'll do all that wet, soppy, romantic stuff that she finds so hard to swallow and, well, here we are.' He lifted his hand. 'And my fingers are very much crossed.'

Junction five came and went. Signs for Gatwick flashed by. Heathrow, straight on. And Paris next stop. Paris! 'Oh, Joe, I'm *so* excited, I can't tell you. I've never been up the Eiffel Tower.'

'No?'

'I've never walked along the Seine, either.'

'No?'

'Joe, you don't realize. I've never *been* to Paris!'

'Is that right?'

'I haven't! We never went abroad as children – my mother was an anglophile with a fixation with Cornwall – and, well, I must have fixed up a billion school French trips, but *I* never went. I had Leo, didn't I? Oh, I've *always* wanted to see Paris, Joe. The galleries, Montmartre . . . Oh, this is so exciting! But, God, Joe! I nearly didn't come! What if I'd refused to come? After all, I've given you every reason to think that I—'

'Tell me about it! But don't worry. I don't work on odds that long, Lu. I did have an accomplice.'

'An accomplice?'

He indicated left and we moved across the motorway to the exit lane. 'Your sister.'

'*Del?* You mean Del *knows* about this?'

'Well, I had to tell her, didn't I? I couldn't fix all this

up *without* telling her. You might have had something else on. *She* might have had something else on. So I called her. And she told me two things. One, you'd always wanted to go to Paris and, two, that despite all the evidence to the contrary, she had a small hunch,' he looked embarrassed, 'well, that you *did* like me, Lu.'

My sister. My sister had known all about it. My sister had known I was going to Paris. My sister had *known* how Joe felt about me. But my sister, in her wisdom, had decided not to tell me. Had decided, oh, bless her, that I should find out for myself. I recalled our conversation. All that big-sister ranting. The rat. The adorable, *wonderful* rat. We pulled up at the lights at the roundabout for Heathrow. They had just turned to red.

I leaned over, wound my arms round his neck, and I kissed him. Kissed him like I really should have kissed him all those weeks back. Like I meant it. No accident. Because mean it I did.

'Boy, Lu!' he said. 'She was right about that, then.'

'Del's right about most things,' I purred. 'But not that one.'

I kissed him again. I could kiss him for ever.

'Like you, indeed!' I shook my head firmly. 'No, no. She's wrong. You can uncross your fingers. *Je n'est pas* like – *je t'adore*, Joe Delaney!' I pointed ahead. 'The light has gone green, by the way.'

THE END

VIRTUAL STRANGERS
by Lynne Barrett-Lee

Fed up, frustrated and fast approaching forty, Charlie Simpson hasn't had many high points in her life just lately. The only peak on the horizon is her ambition to climb Everest, if she could only get organized and save up the cash.

Unfortunately, though, she has more pressing things to deal with; her eldest son moving out, her father moving in, and her best friend moving two hundred miles away. She finds solace, however, via her newly acquired modem, when she stumbles upon a stranger who's a like-minded soul. Like-minded, perhaps, but no fantasy dream date. Though virtual, he's of the real-life variety – he may be a hero, but he has a wife.

Charlie hasn't a husband, but she certainly has principles, and they're about to be hauled up a mountain themselves. And, of course, her mum's always said she shouldn't talk to strangers. The question is, is now the time to start breaking the rules?

'Charming . . . An original and optimistic novel about modern love'
Hello!

A Bantam Paperback

0 553 81305 6

JULIA GETS A LIFE
by Lynne Barrett-Lee

Forget all that stuff about finding the inner child; it's sexual healing Julia Potter is after when husband Richard strays from the marital bed. The one he's been playing in belongs to Rhiannon (North Cardiff single mum, siren and witch). He's sorry, or so reads his Post-it apology, but, as he says, 'It's so hard being a man . . .'

But Julia's not ready to forgive or take up handicrafts quite yet. Re-styled, re-vamped and re-acquainted with hair gel, her new mission statement is 'Up'. Unfortunate, then, that where sex is concerned, the only 'up' she can manage is up the wrong tree.

But at least Julia's photographic career is back in focus. And it isn't long before she's swapping her Teletubbies and tripod at Cardiff's Time of Your Life Photo Studio for the slinkier lines of a low-slung black Pentax – the better to zoom in on the more mature torsos of Kite, Britain's megastar number one band. But while Julia's finding out who put the 'Mmm . . .' into mega, has her marriage to Richard gone into freefall?

'A fantastic book that gets you hooked from the first page'
New Woman

'I absolutely loved it – hurray for Julia! This is funny, original, well-written and unguessable – I had no idea how it would end. It also has the very best closing paragraph I've read in years. Completely wonderful, dazzlingly entertaining, unputdownable'
Jill Mansell

A Bantam Paperback

0 553 81304 8

A SELECTED LIST OF FINE WRITING
AVAILABLE FROM BLACK SWAN AND BANTAM BOOKS

THE PRICES SHOWN BELOW WERE CORRECT AT THE TIME OF GOING TO PRESS. HOWEVER TRANSWORLD PUBLISHERS RESERVE THE RIGHT TO SHOW NEW RETAIL PRICES ON COVERS WHICH MAY DIFFER FROM THOSE PREVIOUSLY ADVERTISED IN THE TEXT OR ELSEWHERE.

77083	3	I'M A BELIEVER	Jessica Adams	£6.99
99933	4	OUT OF LOVE	Diana Appleyard	£6.99
81305	6	VIRTUAL STRANGERS	Lynne Barrett-Lee	£5.99
81304	8	JULIA GETS A LIFE	Lynne Barrett-Lee	£5.99
99950	4	UNCHAINED MELANIE	Judy Astley	£6.99
77097	3	I LIKE IT LIKE THAT	Claire Calman	£6.99
81256	4	THE MAGDALEN	Marita Conlon-McKenna	£5.99
81331	5	PROMISED LAND	Marita Conlon-McKenna	£5.99
99840	0	TIGER FITZGERALD	Elizabeth Falconer	£6.99
81333	1	FAR FROM THE TREE	Deberry Grant	£5.99
50556	4	TRYIN' TO SLEEP IN THE BED YOU MADE		
			Deberry Grant	£5.99
99887	7	THE SECRET DREAMWORLD OF A		
		SHOPAHOLIC	Sophie Kinsella	£6.99
81337	4	THE ICE CHILD	Elizabeth McGregor	£5.99
99938	5	PERFECT DAY	Imogen Parker	£6.99
99909	1	LA CUCINA	Lily Prior	£6.99
81291	2	CITY LIVES	Patricia Scanlan	£5.99
81292	0	FRANCESCA'S PARTY	Patricia Scanlan	£5.99
99952	0	LIFE ISN'T ALL HA HA HEE HEE	Meera Syal	£6.99
81299	8	GOING DOWN	Kate Thompson	£5.99
81298	X	THE BLUE HOUR	Kate Thompson	£5.99
99819	2	WHISTLING FOR THE ELEPHANTS	Sandi Toksvig	£6.99
99872	9	MARRYING THE MISTRESS	Joanna Trollope	£6.99
99902	4	TO BE SOMEONE	Louise Voss	£6.99
81372	2	RAISING THE ROOF	Jane Wenham-Jones	£6.99
99723	4	PART OF THE FURNITURE	Mary Wesley	£6.99
99835	4	SLEEPING ARRANGEMENTS	Madeleine Wickham	£6.99
99651	3	AFTER THE UNICORN	Joyce Windsor	£6.99

All Transworld titles are available by post from:
Bookpost, PO Box 29, Douglas, Isle of Man IM99 1BQ
Credit cards accepted. Please telephone 01624 836000,
fax 01624 837033, Internet http://www.bookpost.co.uk or
e-mail: bookshop@enterprise.net for details.
Free postage and packing in the UK.
Overseas customers allow £1 per book.